PENGUIN  CLASSICS

## MEDIEVAL ENGLISH LYRICS

THOMAS GIBSON DUNCAN was educated at Ardrossan Academy, Glasgow University, and Pembroke College, Oxford. He tutored at Oxford and was Assistant Lecturer in English Language at Manchester University. He returned to Scotland to lecture in English Language and Medieval Literature at St Andrews University, where he is now a Senior Lecturer. His main research interests are Medieval English sermons and lyrics, and he has published in both fields in books and learned journals. His other major interest is music. At Glasgow University he was a Choral Scholar in the Chapel Choir. Since then he has given organ recitals throughout Europe and America and has conducted many choral and orchestral concerts.

# MEDIEVAL ENGLISH LYRICS
## 1200—1400

*Edited with an introduction and notes by*
THOMAS G. DUNCAN

PENGUIN BOOKS

PENGUIN BOOKS

Published by the Penguin Group
Penguin Books Ltd, 27 Wrights Lane, London w8 5tz, England
Penguin Books USA Inc., 375 Hudson Street, New York, New York 10014, USA
Penguin Books Australia Ltd, Ringwood, Victoria, Australia
Penguin Books Canada Ltd, 10 Alcorn Avenue, Toronto, Ontario, Canada m4v 3b2
Penguin Books (NZ) Ltd, 182–190 Wairau Road, Auckland 10, New Zealand

Penguin Books Ltd, Registered Offices: Harmondsworth, Middlesex, England

First published 1995
10 9 8 7 6 5 4 3 2 1

Introduction and notes copyright © Thomas G. Duncan, 1995
All rights reserved

The moral right of the editor has been asserted

Set in 9.5/12pt Monophoto Janson
Typeset by Datix International Ltd, Bungay, Suffolk
Printed in England by Clays Ltd, St Ives plc

For I.A.A.

# CONTENTS

## PART II: *Penitential and Moral Lyrics*   47

## PART III: *Devotional Lyrics*    93

## PART IV: *Miscellaneous Lyrics*   147

# PREFACE

This anthology offers a comprehensive selection of thirteenth- and fourteenth-century English lyrics, including all pre-Chaucerian love lyrics (other than a few brief snatches). The Love Lyrics (Part I) and the Devotional Lyrics (Part III) are, as is explained in the Introduction, arranged according to genre and theme; the Penitential and Moral Lyrics (Part II) and the Miscellaneous Lyrics (Part IV) are ordered chronologically. The dating of these lyrics is, at best, approximate; some may considerably pre-date the manuscripts in which they first appear. Thus, *I syng of a mayden* (79) may well have been written much earlier than the fifteenth-century manuscript, MS. B.L. Sloane 5293, in which it is found, as may some of the other Sloane lyrics included here. Inevitably, '*circa* 1200 to *circa* 1400' would more accurately express the time-span of this anthology. The critical appraisal offered in the Introduction seeks to place these lyrics in the context of the development of English literature from Old English to Chaucer, and through them to represent the main currents in literature and culture, sensibility and life, in the Middle English period. Textual, contextual and linguistic information is provided in the Commentary, beginning on page 181.

Every effort has been made to present these Middle English texts in a readily readable form. The language of the lyrics has been normalized in accordance with the grammar and spelling of late fourteenth-century London English. As the language of Chaucer, this is the form of Middle English most familiar to modern readers. Corruptions of sense, metre and rhyme have been removed wherever plausible emendation has seemed possible. Metre, a subject frequently passed over with little attention in editions of Middle English lyrics, is considered at length in the Introduction and in two Appendices, and guidance is given in the texts on the pronunciation of unstressed syllables. Generous glossing is provided to meet the needs of readers who have little or no acquaintance with Middle English. The glosses usually keep as close as possible to the literal sense and word order of the Middle English; they are not meant to serve as a translation but as an aid to the reader in coming to a fuller understanding of the Middle English text itself. Where the sense or grammar of the text requires further explanation, this is provided in the Commentary.

Manuscripts, facsimiles and microfilms have been consulted for most of the lyrics in this anthology, including all the lyrics from the manuscripts mentioned on page xlv. For the remainder, standard scholarly editions have been relied upon. The editorial approach has been eclectic. For lyrics which survive in more than one manuscript, the readings of the base manuscript have usually been followed; but where that manuscript fails in sense or rhyme, or is questionable with regard to metre, superior readings from other manuscripts have been freely adopted.

My most obvious debt, as will be evident from the range of references in the Commentary, is to editors of these lyrics, past and present. Their work I gratefully acknowledge, and not least that of the late Professor E. J. Dobson. My interpretation of the music which survives with English songs before 1400 differs from his, and, accordingly, the texts of the lyrics included here differ from those in *Medieval English Songs*; nevertheless, his zeal for rescuing Middle English lyrics from the deformed state in which the hazards of scribal transmission have so often left them has strengthened my resolve to tackle the task of editing positively. For their help and advice, I wish to thank friends and colleagues, especially Christine Gascoigne (St Andrews University Library), Margaret Connolly (University of Cork), Amanda Corely, Anne Hargreaves, Michael Herbert (University of St Andrews), Julia Prescott, Jane and Nick Roe (University of St Andrews) and Jeremy Smith (University of Glasgow). My path to publication was greatly smoothed by Michael Alexander, Berry Professor of English in the University of St Andrews, and by John Burrow, Winterstoke Professor of English in the University of Bristol. Joan Stansbury kindly read most of this book at various stages of preparation and made many valuable criticisms. Finally, my greatest debt is to Professor Douglas Gray (Oxford); I thank him heartily for all his generous help and encouragement.

# ABBREVIATIONS AND REFERENCES

## Books and Editions

| | |
|---|---|
| AV | The Holy Bible, Authorised King James Version |
| Benson | Benson, L. D., ed., *The Riverside Chaucer*, 3rd edn (Oxford, 1988) |
| Brook | Brook, G. L., ed., *The Harley Lyrics*, 4th edn (Manchester, 1968) |
| Brown XIII | Brown, C., ed., *English Lyrics of the XIIIth Century* (Oxford, 1932) |
| Brown XIV | Brown, C., ed., *English Lyrics of the XIVth Century*, 2nd edn revised by G. V. Smithers (Oxford, 1952) |
| Brown XV | Brown, C., ed., *Religious Lyrics of the XVth Century* (Oxford, 1939) |
| *CT* | *The Canterbury Tales* by Geoffrey Chaucer |
| *EMEVP* | *Early Middle English Verse and Prose*, eds J. A. W. Bennett and G. V. Smithers, with a Glossary by Norman Davis, 2nd edn (Oxford, 1968) |
| *Fasc. Mor.* | *Fasciculus Morum*, with translation, ed. S. Wenzel (Pennsylvania, 1989) |
| Gray, *Selection* | Gray, D., ed., *A Selection of Religious Lyrics* (Oxford, 1975) |
| Greene | Greene, R. L., ed., *The Early English Carols*, 2nd edn (Oxford, 1977) |
| *Index* | *Index of Middle English Verse*, eds C. Brown and R. H. Robbins (New York, 1943) |
| *MED* | *Middle English Dictionary*, eds H. Kurath and S. M. Kuhn (Ann Arbor, 1956– ) |
| *MES* | *Medieval English Songs*, eds E. J. Dobson and F. Ll. Harrison (London, 1979) |
| *MEV* | *The Oxford Book of Medieval English Verse*, eds C. Sisam and K. Sisam (Oxford, 1970) |
| Mustanoja | Mustanoja, T. F., *A Middle English Syntax* (Helsinki, 1960) |

| | |
|---|---|
| *OED* | *Oxford English Dictionary* |
| Robbins, *Hist.* | Robbins, R. H., ed., *Historical Poems of the XIVth and XVth Centuries* (Oxford, 1959) |
| Robbins, *Sec.* | Robbins, R. H., ed., *Secular Lyrics of the XIVth and XVth Centuries*, revised edn (Oxford, 1955) |
| *Suppl.* | *Supplement to Index of Middle English Verse*, eds R. H. Robbins and J. L. Cuter (Lexington, Kentucky, 1965) |
| Whiting, *Proverbs* | Whiting, B. J. and H. W., eds, *Proverbs, Sentences and Proverbial Phrases from English Writings mainly before 1500* (Cambridge, Massachusetts, 1968) |
| Woolf | Woolf, R., *The English Religious Lyric in the Middle Ages* (Oxford, 1968) |

Other editions, books and articles referred to in this volume are to be found in the Select Bibliography, beginning on page 258; they are cited by the author's surname and the date of publication.

## Biblical References

The names of the Books of the Old and New Testaments are given as found in the Authorised Version, abbreviated as follows:

| | |
|---|---|
| Acts | The Acts of the Apostles |
| Eccles. | Ecclesiastes |
| Eph. | Ephesians |
| Gen. | Genesis |
| Lam. | Lamentations |
| Matt. | Matthew |
| NT | New Testament |
| Ps. | Psalms |
| Rev. | Revelation |
| S. of S. | Song of Solomon |
| 2 Tim. | 2 Timothy |

## Other Abbreviations

| | |
|---|---|
| 13c. | thirteenth-century |
| 14c. | fourteenth-century |
| adj. | adjective |
| adv. | adverb |
| B.L. | British Library |
| Bodl. | Bodleian Library |
| *c.* | *circa* |
| cf. | compare |
| Coll. | College |
| conj. | conjunction |
| d. | died |
| lit. | literally |
| ME | Middle English |
| MS. | manuscript |
| MSS | manuscripts |
| n. | noun |
| OE | Old English |
| OF | Old French |
| om. | omitted |
| ON | Old Norse |
| p. | page |
| pl. | plural |
| pp. | pages |
| refl. | reflexive |
| sc. | *scilicet*, 'understand' or 'supply' |
| sg. | singular |
| v. | verb |

# INTRODUCTION

## Medieval English Lyrics

| | |
|---|---|
| With longing I am lad, | *I go* (lit. *am led*) |
| On molde I waxë mad, | *on earth I am going mad,* |
| A maidë marrëth me. | *distresses* |
| | [1, 1–3] |

With words like these Middle English poets expressed their love. This love-longing was something new; it was certainly foreign to Old English literature. Occasionally a cry of love is heard in Old English, as in the following lines from the enigmatic poem *Wulf and Eadwacer*:

Wulf, O my Wulf, my yearning for you
Has made me ill; the rareness of your visits,
My sorrowing spirit, not a lack of food.

Here, however, the speaker is not a man but a woman. In the heroic world of Old English poetry, a man's concern centred on his duty to his lord; his supreme values were those of loyalty and courage in battle. The ideal of love as devotion to a lady was as yet unknown.

The twelfth century was the watershed between the heroic and the romantic worlds of the earlier and later Middle Ages. This period was remarkable not only for pilgrimages and crusades, commercial expansion and social change, ecclesiastical reform and the revitalization of the Church, the flourishing of the cathedral schools and the emergence of the universities; it was also a time of momentous developments in art and architecture, in literature and learning, and, above all, in modes of thought and feeling. It was in the twelfth century in the south of France that there emerged, in the poetry of the Troubadours, a new concept of love, one which has dominated western literature ever since.

The idea that love was noble and ennobling was, of course, nothing new; viewed in one way or another, such a notion would not have surprised Plato, Virgil, St Paul or St Augustine. But the belief that the proper object of love was a woman, and that unqualified devotion to a woman was the true inspiration of refined and noble conduct, would have astonished them. This, however, was the Troubadours' creed. For them, the feudal concept of service to a lord was transformed, in the name of love, to become the service of a lady. Devotion to a lady was the only thing which made life worth living; such love was the ultimate joy. In the words of the twelfth-century Troubadour Bernart de Ventadorn, 'A man is really dead when he does not feel some sweet taste of love in his heart.'[1] It is to this Troubadour ideal of romantic love that western culture owes so much – not only an extensive love literature in all European languages from the later Middle Ages to the present day, but even such current manifestations as the cult of St Valentine's Day and the phenomenon of Hollywood film goddesses.

So important was this new concept of love in the later Middle Ages that it seems appropriate to begin this anthology with its portrayal in Middle English lyrics. Most of the love lyrics before Chaucer survive in one manuscript – MS. Harley 2253 in the British Library. In many of these (1–5 and 17–20 here), urgent and repeated appeals are made to a lady for her 'pity', her 'mercy'.

> Lady, thou rewë me,                    *have pity on me*
>   To routhe thou hast me rad,          *to grief; brought*
>   Be bote of that I bad,               *be the remedy for which I have prayed*
>   My lyf is long on thee.              *my life is dependent on you*
>
> [1, 7–10]

The poet's very life may depend upon her, but the main focus of attention is not primarily on the lady; it is on the lover and his sufferings for *derne love*, 'secret love'.

> Nis no fire so hot in helle
>   Al to mon                            *as a man*
> That lovëth derne and dar not telle   *in secret; dares*
>   What him ys on.                      *what is wrong with him.*
>
> [2, 9–12]

There is, however, little here of the intensity of devotion and the analysis of love characteristic of the Troubadours. Nor are these personal lyrics of private, intimate love. On the contrary, they are public poems

---

[1] Goldin (1973), p. 127.

operating within and through well-recognized conventions. The lover
sighs, lies awake, feels condemned to death, and pleads for mercy; the
lady shines, her hair is golden, her neck long, her waist slender, and, not
infrequently, she is described as prudent and wise. There is even a
common currency in the vocabulary of these lyrics, not least in the
frequent use of alliterative tags; the lady is a 'byrde in a bour', 'brightest
under bis', 'geynest under gore' and 'beste among the bolde' – all
phrases used as much as anything for their alliteration.

Literary convention here, however, does not make for lifeless verse.
Quite the reverse. What a reader may sense is the relish with which
these poets make play with a range of conventions. Thus, the *reverdie*,
the description of spring-time with which several of the lyrics begin (e.g.
17–19), can be more than a conventional opening. In *Lenten ys come with
love to toune* (20), an entire poem is devoted to the *wynnë wele*, the 'wealth
of joys', of spring. A profusion of blossoms and flowers, with the singing
of nightingales and song thrushes, and with animals of all kinds mating
on hillside and riverside, culminates in an ironic contrast of worms and
women:

> Wormës wowen under cloude,          *worms make love under ground*
> Wommen waxen wonder proude,          *become amazingly haughty*
> So wel it wol hem seme.          *it becomes them*
>
> [20, 31–3]

In spring-time nature rejoices and even worms make love; but women
become difficult and men suffer! With understated brevity, the excellent
little song, *Foulës in the frith* (16), presents the same contrast understood
within the same convention. The rhetorical device known as oxymoron,
so familiar in exclamations like 'I burn, I freeze' in Elizabethan love
poetry, is deftly exploited as a structural principle in *A waylë whyte as
whallës bon* (2) where the poet begins a sequence of opposing stances with:

> Ich unne hire wel, and she me wo,          *I wish her well, she (wishes)*
> Ich am hire frend, and she my fo.          *and she (is) my foe*
>
> [2, 13–14]

Ladies are sometimes described through a series of comparisons – most
frequently with flowers or precious stones. The elaboration of this
convention in *Ichot a byrde in a bour* (5) is nothing less than a *tour de force*.
Again, in *Moste I ryde by Rybbësdale* (25), the detailed description of a lady

from head to foot (as advocated in medieval Latin treatises on poetic style) is skilfully elaborated within the flow of the verse without any sense of artificiality or stiff formality. Allegory is effectively used at the end of *Ichot a byrde in bourë bryght* (3) where the lover appeals to Love against the activities of the lady's knights, Sighing, Sorrowing and Perplexity.

A significant part of the appeal of these lyrics lies in their song-like qualities. These are not poems in which the poet tries to argue his lady into love; nor does he philosophize. These poems celebrate love in motifs and conventions which are pleasing because they are familiar, and in language which finds its music in a harmony of rhyme and alliteration. As the poet laments and pleads in familiar form, there is nothing tough or intellectually challenging to impede the rhythm and flow of the verse. This poetry, as it were, 'sings' of love – with a parade of suffering, indeed, but without personal *angst*. Nowhere, perhaps, do these qualities make for a more effective expression of the joy of love than in:

| | |
|---|---|
| An hendy hap Ichave y-hent, | *good fortune I have received* |
| Ichot from hevene it is me sent, | *I know; sent to me* |
| From allë wommen my love is lent | *has gone* |
| And light on Alysoun. | *and alighted* |
| | [18, 9–12] |

This *hendy hap*, a 'good fortune' no less than heaven-sent, dances in these lines. Yet, in the very mention of all the women in whom the poet's interest ceases with the advent of Alison's love (unusually, the poet's beloved is named here) there is a sense of the world at large and of other relationships which would be alien to the singular devotion and claustrophobic atmosphere of many a Troubadour lyric. The ecstasy of this refrain runs in counterpoint to the content of the stanzas: the lover's love-longing of stanza 1, the description of the beloved and the poet's despair of stanza 2, his nightly anguish of stanza 3, and his final plea of the concluding stanza.

Some of the lyrics reflect a genre typical of the thirteenth-century Trouvère poets of northern France, the *chanson d'aventure*. Characteristically these poems open with lines like:

| | |
|---|---|
| As I me rode this endrë dai | *went riding the other day* |
| On mi playinge. | *for my pleasure* |
| | [21, 1–2] |

In the French *pastourelle* (one form of the *chanson d'aventure*) the poet rides out (riding marks his aristocratic status) to seek pleasure in a pastoral landscape where he comes upon a girl, often a shepherdess under a tree or in a sweet arbour, lamenting lost love. Usually he offers to 'comfort' her, and usually his offer is accepted. However graceful and charming the French poems may be, the protagonist is scarcely more than a high-born seducer; the abject devotion of a Troubadour to his lady is totally reversed. Again, unlike the Troubadour *chansons d'amour*, these are dialogue poems in which the woman's voice is heard. Of a handful of Middle English poems reflecting this genre (21–5), the earliest, *As I me rode this endrë dai* (21), is nearest to the manner and pastoral setting of the French *pastourelles*. As in French poems, the poet indeed 'rides' out for pleasure and meets a maiden singing 'in a sweet arbour'. But here, the bitter and vengeful tone of the girl's words – 'The clot him clinge!' (line 8) and 'If I mai, it shal him rewe' (line 25) – stand in marked contrast to the pastoral setting and the elegance of the verse. There is an Old French poem which closely resembles this lyric.[2] In the French, however, the maiden's tone, though distressed, is not harsh. The French poem also has an extra stanza in which the maiden accepts the poet's love. One may wonder if, perhaps, an equivalent final stanza of the English poem has been lost, or if the girl's tone precluded further overtures on the part of the English poet.

Even further from the style and tone of French *pastourelles* is *In a fryth as I gan farë fremëde* (22). It opens with the poet walking (not riding) as a stranger in a wood (rather than in a familiar pastoral setting) and finding not a shepherdess but a *fair fengë* – a 'fair prize'! This poet proves to be a man of guile, but the girl is a match for him in the cut-and-thrust of sexual politics. The alliterative verse of this poem matches the weightier moral debate which ensues, in the course of which various poetic genres (the 'complaint of the betrayed maiden', the *chanson de mal mariée*[3] and the *chanson des transformations*[4]) are skilfully exploited.[5] Different again is *As I stod on a day* (23): the maiden here is of quite another stamp, well dressed and sophisticated. After a rather arch response to the poet's flattering greeting, she wittily dismisses his subsequent advances.

---

[2] See Bartsch (1870), No. II. 7.
[3] See Commentary, 22, 36 n.
[4] See Commentary, 22, 45 n.
[5] See Commentary, 22, and Woolf (1969), pp. 56–8.

Rather in the manner of the lover of the *chanson d'amour* he begs to become 'her man', only to be accused in her reply of raving, humbug and folly:

> 'Wher gospellëth                                    *what is the message of*
>         al thy speche?                               *(pious) talk*
> Thou findëst her noght here                          *her not here*
>         the sot that thou seche.'                    *idiot; seek*
>
> [23, 20–21]

The poet's further protestations are met with irony ('there must be some other girl who might choose you as chaste!', lines 27–8) and an ignominious dismissal. Here, indeed, is a fourteenth-century feminist, and one with poise and panache. The 'clerk' of *My deth I love, my lyf Ich hatë* (24) suffers in a typically love-lorn manner, and makes his appeal to his *swete lemman*, her response is, to say the least, curt: 'Do wey, thou clerk, thou art a fol.' The contrast of this brusque girl and the plaintive lover is comical to the point of farce. Yet three stanzas later, with a sudden *volte-face*, and echoing the clerk's first pathetic rejoinder – 'Welawei, why seist thou so?') – she succumbs to his entreaties. Can this extraordinary poem be anything other than a burlesque by a Middle English poet merrily exploiting the ludicrous extremes of different traditions of love poetry?

Love is also the theme of a scattering of short Middle English lyrics in a more popular vein (7–15, 26). The shortest are by turn intriguingly suggestive (10 and 12), plaintive (11), and rueful (13), and, in the case of a couplet found in the same manuscript as 12 and 13 –

> Ne shaltou never, levedi,
>         Twynklen wyth thin eyen

– sinister. In 14 appears the splendid image of a lover so patient in his cold vigil outside his beloved's house that his foot has frozen to the gate-post. Both 7 and 8 bear witness to the heart-ache of lost love. The poet of 7 may have lost his beloved to some local lord (lines 5–7); and perhaps there may be detected in 8 a whiff of class or even nationalistic antagonism on the part of a jilted lover who would have avenged hurt to his erstwhile beloved from any quarter – even from the son of the king of Normandy! These verses invite endless speculation: they survive without local habitation, name or context.

The Chaucerian love lyrics (32–5 probably, but not certainly, by Chaucer) are of an entirely different order. In the earlier lyrics, castle and hall, bower and tower were mentioned, but hardly realized. With Chaucer, in 'at a revel whan I see you daunce' (29, line 6), the courtly ambience is immediate. In style and manner the earlier lyrics seem at many removes from the poetry of the Troubadours; Chaucer's poems stand directly in the tradition of the French verse of the courtly milieu in which he was educated. He was probably the first poet to write ballades and roundels in English, poetic forms favoured by his French contemporaries Machaut, Deschamps and Froissart. His fluency and skill in the roundel form – a short lyric in which the opening line or lines recur in the middle and at the end – are immediately evident in the lively flowing lines of *Now welcome, somer* (28). From the short poems which survive, it would appear that the ballade was Chaucer's preferred form. Except that it lacks a concluding envoy, *To Rosëmounde* (29) is in classical ballade form – three eight-line stanzas, each ending with the same line as a refrain, and each following the same rhyme scheme, *a b a b b c b c*. In other ballades (including the moral ballades *Truth* (63) and *Gentilesse* (64), and 120, his *Complaint* to his purse) Chaucer uses rhyme royal (a seven-line stanza rhyming *a b a b b c c*), a form already used in ballades by Machaut and Deschamps. *Fortune* (62) is a triple ballade, that is, three consecutive ballades in eight-line form concluding with an envoy. Whereas continental influences in the earlier lyrics are French, the cultural context within which Chaucer wrote was both French and Italian. Among Chaucer's lyrics an especially noteworthy instance of Italian influence is found in the *Canticus Troili* (31), where a Petrarchan sonnet, eloquently rendered in rhyme royal, makes its first appearance in English.[6]

In his treatise on the art of poetry, *L'art de dictier et de fere chançons, balades, virelais et rondeaux*, Chaucer's friend Deschamps distinguished between the song lyric (which was sung) and the literary lyric (which was recited rather than sung). Chaucer's ballades are of the latter type, a poetry of complexity and sophistication unsuited to singing. This fundamental contrast with many of the earlier Middle English lyrics is immediately apparent in the involved syntax of Chaucer's speculations about love and his attempts to persuade or excuse by argument. His poetry is also more intimate: Rosemounde, whoever she was, is addressed directly: 'Madame, ye ben of al beauté shryne'. Unlike the earlier nameless poets, with Chaucer we find not only a name but a personality. The humorous exaggeration of weeping a barrel full of tears (29, line 9)

[6] See Gray (1983), pp. 97–8.

or the witty image of the poet in love like a pike steeped in galantine
sauce (**29**, lines 17–18) are typically Chaucerian, as are the opening lines
of the third part of *Merciles Beauté*:

> Sin I fro Love escapëd am so fat,
> I never thenk to ben in his prison lene.        *lean*
>
>                                      [**34**, 27–8]

Elsewhere Chaucer alludes to his portly figure (e.g. in the *Envoy a
Scogan*, line 31, and *The House of Fame*, line 574); here, echoing the line
'Puiz qu' à Amours suis si gras eschappé', from a ballade by his
contemporary, the Duc de Berry, he jokingly asserts that as a fat man –
pining lovers are supposed to be lean! – his escape from the prison of
love is guaranteed.

Unlike the love lyrics, the Middle English penitential and moral
lyrics stand in a tradition of themes already well represented in Old
English, both in homiletic prose and in poetry. In an age of faith when
life expectancy was often short, it is not surprising that such themes as
the Day of Judgement, the terrors of hell, death and the transience of
this world's joys should have figured so prominently. Man's soul was
constantly threatened by three powerful enemies – the world, the flesh
and the devil; salvation was to be attained only by sincere and thorough
repentance. A considerable proportion of Middle English literature
dwells on such concerns; and it was evidently considered a valid and
important function of poetry to stimulate moral reflection and penitential
contrition. This may seem alien to present-day taste; yet, at their best,
lyrics reflecting such characteristically medieval preoccupations can
readily engage the imagination of the modern reader with their urgency
and sense of conviction.

Middle English moral verse tended to be more popular in style
than Old English 'gnomic' poetry; it also reflected significant cultural
differences.

> Where is the horse? Where is the young hero? Where is the
>     generous lord?
> Where are the places of banqueting? Where are the joys of the hall?
> Alas the bright cup! Alas the mail-clad warrior!
> Alas the glory of the prince!

In these lines from *The Wanderer*, an Old English poem well known
through modern English translations (including a version by Ezra

Pound), the poet speaks of the inevitable transience of the things of this world, but with a sense of overwhelming regret at the passing of an aristocratic, heroic culture which the horse, the hero, the banqueting halls, the golden cup, the warrior and the prince represent. The same *ubi sunt* topos is used in a very different manner in a Middle English penitential poem. 'Where are those who were before us?', asks the poet of 47. The following description of lords with their hawks and hounds, of ladies with gold in their hair and their splendid robes, of their banqueting, their revelry, their courtly dalliance and their pride, climaxes suddenly with:

> And in a twinkling of an eye
> > Here soulës were forlorn.      *their souls were lost*
> > > [47, 11–12]

They had their paradise here: now they pay for it in hell fire, where:

> Long is 'ay!' and long is 'o!',      *ah! / ever; oh! / always*
> Long is 'wy!' and long is 'wo!'      *alas!; woe!*
> > [47, 22–3]

The tone is unmistakably that of a popular preacher contemptuously revelling in the fate of aristocratic pomp and pleasure.

Typical of the Middle English penitential lyric is the manner in which traditional homiletic exhortations find direct and personal expression. In *Lavedy seynte Marie* (37), the poet speaks in the first person. He dreads the consequences of a misspent youth – his sins in word and deed, in bed and at board; his excessive indulgence in food, wine and sumptuous clothing; his neglect of alms-giving and the needs of the poor – and beseeches Mary to intercede with Christ on his behalf for protection from the pains of hell. Often, as in this poem, urgent though the sense of contrition may be, the penitent is not individualized; he speaks, in effect, not only for himself but for every contrite reader. Likewise, the reluctant penitent of *Lord, thou clepedest me* (49) – a deft but ominous rendering in Middle English verse of famous words of St Augustine[7] – speaks for any sinner. However, in *Hye Loverd, thou here my bone* (51), one of the best of the penitential lyrics, the speaker, again lamenting a misspent life and the miseries of old age, emerges vividly and poignantly. Enduring insults – he is a mere 'floor-filler', a 'good-for-nothing fire-gazer'! – he

[7] See Commentary, 49.

sits forlornly lodged by the fire like a social outcast. The romantic dalliance of youth is now a mere memory barely to be hinted at: 'Nou I may no finger folde' (line 21 and, similarly, line 40). His days of accomplished horsemanship and splendid robes are gone (lines 30–31); now the sight of strong steeds only accentuates his pathetic limping and his despair. Once he cut a dashing figure (he includes himself in the remarkable and ironic simile, 'as haughty is the servant in the house as the head hound in the hall', lines 84–5); now, in words reminiscent of Donne or Hopkins, he can only urge Death not to delay:

> Dredful Deth, why wilt thou dare? *tarry*
> Bring this body that is so bare *take this body*
> And in bale y-bounde. *torment*
>
> [ 51, 86–8]

Other prominent themes find exceptional expression in the form of a lullaby in 50. However tender the tone of the refrain, *Lullay, lullay, litel child, child, lullay, lullow*, the mother's song is far from one of joy and expectation for her child. Here the child's bitter weeping reflects its unhappy lot in this hostile world where it is not even a pilgrim but merely an alien guest! Other creatures may prosper, but not the 'wretched brat of Adam's blood' (lines 19–20). The mother bids the child reflect on the three last things (lines 29–30), the theme of 41 and 42; the child's foot is already on Fortune's wheel (lines 43–6), an omnipresent medieval moral theme (cf. 58 and 59); the bitter pain of death is inescapable (lines 67–8).

A rather different manner of writing, more discursive and philosophical, is encountered with 60 and 61, two of the refrain lyrics found in the Vernon MS., a late fourteenth-century compilation, largely of religious and didactic works. The theme of each poem is anchored in a key-word repeated in the refrain, the final line of each stanza. In 60, the reader is constantly bidden to heed the lessons of 'yesterday' – to recognize the transient nature of existence in the light of past experience. Illustrations are presented and arguments persuasively advanced within the flow of the verse, and sometimes with some imaginative flair, as in the twelfth stanza where the image of children chasing by candle-light shadows which, inevitably, they cannot catch is used to express the futility of human endeavour. *This world fareth as a fantasy* is the refrain of 61, a poem which draws heavily on the Book of Ecclesiastes. After earnest reflection on the mutability of all things and all creatures and on the futility of all theology and philosophy, the poet surprisingly concludes: 'But make we merry and slay care' (line 123). This advice is, indeed, immediately followed by 'And worship God while we are here' (line 124) and a plea for God's mercy, but the devout conclusion comes as something of an afterthought; the inspiration of both Vernon lyrics is wisdom rather than faith.

In Chaucer's moral lyrics there is none of the insistent and sometimes rather wearing didacticism of the Vernon poems. Chaucer's manner is urbane. His Boethian themes – fortune, truth and *gentilesse* 'nobility' – are those central to all medieval literature of any philosophical pretension; in his lyrics they are handled with poise, imagination and control hitherto unequalled in English moral verse. This world is not man's true home, as the mother of *Lullay, lullay, litel child* (50) had recognized; but only in Chaucer's hands could this familiar Boethian theme find expression as:

> Here is non home, here nys but wildernesse:      *no home; is nothing but*
> Forthe, pilgryme, forthe! Forthe, beste, out of thy stal!      *
> Knowe thy contré, loke up, thank God of al;      *look up*
> Holde the heye weye and lat thy gost thee lede,      †
> And trouthe thee shal delyvere it is no drede.

> \* *onward, pilgrim; beast*
> † *keep to the main; let; spirit*
> [63, 17–21]

If the penitential and moral lyrics continue themes and traditions already present in Old English literature, many of the devotional lyrics, like the love lyrics, reflect the thought and feeling of a new age. In the finest of Old English religious poems, *The Dream of the Rood*, Christ is depicted as a young warrior in the heroic tradition. Yet, however exceptional the depth of feeling with which the experience of the crucifixion is related by the personified cross in this poem, it is not an emotion akin to such direct expressions of tenderness as:

> Swetë Jhesu, king of blisse,
> Min hertë love, min hertë lisse,      *heart's love, my heart's joy*
> Thou art swetë mid y-wisse,      *sweet indeed*
> Wo is him that thee shal misse.      *who will lose you*

> [67, 1–4]

It is to the eleventh century rather than to the twelfth that one may look for the sources of this later medieval sensibility. One important new departure emerged in St Anselm's fundamental reappraisal of the Doctrine of the Atonement. Previously the doctrine of salvation had been conceived of in heroic terms. God and the Devil were like two feudal lords. Man had withdrawn his service from God and had given himself into the service of the Devil. But because man had done so of his own free will, the Devil had thereby gained 'rights' over man. In justice, therefore, God could not simply use his omnipotence to defeat the Devil. He had to turn to strategy. The master plan was that in Christ, God should become man. The Devil, not recognizing Christ's divinity, subjected Him to death. But this he did illegally – for he had no rights over Christ – and Christ was then able to defeat the Devil and thus to rescue man. In this version, salvation was a cosmic struggle between God and the Devil with man as a passive pawn and Christ as a rather impersonal hero. For Anselm, the very notion of the Devil having any 'rights' was unacceptable. He presented a new account of salvation. Man by his sin had incurred the penalty of death. Christ, out of love for man, became a man, and by suffering death paid for man that penalty which man alone could not pay. A cosmic view thus changed to a personal vision – a vision of Christ as a man, suffering for his fellow man out of love. This new doctrinal emphasis on Christ's love for man and on love as man's appropriate response to Christ contributed to a fundamental change in later medieval piety already to be seen emerging in forms of monastic devotion in the eleventh century, new modes of meditation dwelling with love and compassion on the humanity of Christ, on his earthly life, and on his agony on the cross, especially characteristic of the Cistercian order and its leading twelfth-century figure, St Bernard of Clairvaux. 'It was the Cistercians,' claims R.W. Southern, 'who were the chief agents in turning the thin stream of compassion and tenderness which comes from the eleventh century into the flood which, in the later centuries of the Middle Ages, obliterated the traces of an older severity and reticence.'[8]

Middle English devotional lyrics reflect this tenderness and compassion. The theme of the first group here (67–73) is love, the mode and language of love characteristic of later medieval devotional poetry

[8] Southern (1959), p. 242.

expressing man's love for Jesus and His love for man. The sweetness of the very name of Jesus, Jesus as a 'sweet lover', Jesus who freely but so dearly 'bought' us with 'woundës sore and peynës strong', with His very heart's blood, Jesus 'my love ... my God ... my kyng ... my lyght ...', Jesus 'al my thought' – such are the characteristically new expressions of love as seen in *Jhesú, swete is the love of thee* (68), a lyric which was inspired by and which echoes the famous Cistercian poem *Jesu, dulcis memoria*.[9] Here is the source of much that is familiar in later English devotional verse as, for example, in the work of the great seventeenth-century poet, George Herbert. In the lyrics concerning Mary, the Annunciation, and the Virgin and child (74–83), the same tenderness prevails. Sometimes it is matched by joy, as in the superb lullaby *Lullay, myn lyking* (80), a Christmas carol still popular today; sometimes it merges with mystery, as in *I syng of a mayden* (79), a simple but unique expression of the paradox of the Virgin birth; and sometimes with sorrow, as at the nativity, pictured here in the later medieval manner with manger, ox and ass:

| | |
|---|---:|
| Jhesu, swetë sonë dere, | *dear* |
| In porful bed thou list now here, | *on a pitiful bed you lie* |
|    And that me grevëth sore; | *grieves me bitterly* |
| For thi cradel is as a bere, | *byre* |
| Ox and assë ben thi fere, | *are your companions* |
|    Wepe may I therfore. | *weep* |
| | [83, 7–12] |

Wholly unlike the Old English *Dream of the Rood*, the crucifixion lyrics (84–95) focus directly on Christ's suffering and humanity, often expressed through the intimate human relationships of mother and child, son and mother. With poignant irony, the Virgin is reluctant to sing 'as do mothers all' at the child's request (81, lines 13–16); the misery of a cold weeping baby prompts her to think of suffering in store:

| | |
|---|---:|
| Lullay, lullay, litel grom, | *lad* |
|    king of allë thinge, | *things* |
| Whan I thenke of thy mischeef, | *misfortune* |
|    me list wel litel singe. | *I have very little wish to sing* |
| | [82, 13–16] |

[9] See Commentary, 68.

Mary, at the foot of the cross, pleads not only with her son (91); with dramatic force she directs her mother's grief at His persecutors:

> Why have ye no routhe on my child?        *no pity*
> Have routhe on me ful of mourning;
> Tak doun o rode my derworth child,    *from the cross my precious child*
> Or prik me o rode with my derling!    *or nail me; darling*
>
>                         [92, 1–4]

Yet, though the emphasis of the crucifixion lyrics is on Christ's suffering, Middle English lyrics do not characteristically make this theme an occasion for excessive detail and lurid description. It is their restraint in this regard which makes for the finest poetry. The power of the burden of 93 (possibly inspired by a painting or a crucifix) derives from its restricted focus, the evocation of Christ's suffering in terms of a single tear:

> *Lovely ter of lovely eye,*         *tear*
>   *Why dost thou me so wo?*     *do you cause me such grief*
> *Sorful ter of sorful eye,*       *sorrowful*
>   *Thou brekst myn herte a-two.*   *you are breaking; in two*
>
>                         [93, 1–4]

This concentration in the burden on Christ's tear, at once lovely and sorrowful, controls the poem as the stanzas widen to embrace first Christ as man of sorrows and mighty redeemer, then the pride of the sinner ('I proud and kene / Thou meke and clene'), then the sorrowing mother, and finally the paradox of the cross – Christ crucified as Christ victorious:

> Thin herte is rent,
> Thi body is bent,
>   Upon the rodë tre;
> The weder is went,         *storm is past*
> The devel is shent,         *destroyed*
>   Crist, thurgh the might of Thee.
>
>                         [93, 23–8]

Similarly, images generic and particular (the setting sun and the grief-darkened face of Mary), images of immediate effect and deeper Biblical and liturgical resonance,[10] can combine with an absolute simplicity of language to create evocative strength in a mere quatrain:

> Now goth sonnë under wode,            *goes the sun under the wood*
> Me reweth, Marie, thi fairë rode.     *I grieve, Mary, for your fair face*
> Now goth sonnë under tre,                          *the tree*
> Me reweth, Marie, thi sone and thee.                  *son*
>
> [84]

This simplicity is not, however, that of unlettered poets. Rather, it reflects an awareness that in devotional poetry the appropriate level of style was what was known as the *sermo humilis*, the 'humble style'. Nor do these poems lack literary skill. In *Love me broughte* (70), for instance, the diction could not be more simple. However, the use of anaphora (the rhetorical device of beginning successive lines or sequences of lines with the same words) and the handling of rhythmic effect are masterly. The sequence *Love / And love / Man* (A) and *Love / And love / And love* (B) of the initial words of the two three-line groups of stanza 1 is almost mirrored in reverse by *Love / And love / And love* (B) and *Love / For love / Man* (A) of stanza 2. The rhythmic pattern is, of course, exactly maintained. The repeated pronoun of these stanzas is 'me'. The emphasis and balance of this arrangement – Love / me / man – changes in the final stanza. Without anaphora, the rhetorical emphasis is partly on the pronouns, now of both first and second person – thee / I / thee / me / I. There is also a significant change in rhythm. The initial lines of stanzas 1 and 2 both began with a stressed syllable; the first line of stanza 3 now breaks this pattern by beginning with an unstressed syllable. But the crucial change arrives with the rhetorical and dramatic effect of the initial stress on *Wel* of 'Wel is me' in line 17, the only middle line of any of the three-line groups to have initial stress. The joyous effect here – a joyous conclusion to the perplexing paradox of love[11] – is similar to the sudden and triumphant stress on *Modor* and *Wel* at the beginning of lines 17 and 19 of *I syng of a mayden* (79).

Simplicity of language in these lyrics is matched by the absence of any display of ecstasy or agony. There is nothing to compromise the direct sincerity of the speaking voice, whether it be that of Christ or the sinner.

---

[10] See Commentary, 84.
[11] See Commentary, 70 and 97; see also, Woolf, pp. 166–8.

> Levëdie, Ich thonkë thee,                          *Lady, I thank you*
>   With hertë swithë milde,                            *very humble*
> That god that thou hast i-don me              *for that good which*
>   With thine swetë childe.
>
>                                                   [74, 1–4]

This is a personal voice, but it is not self-absorbed: it speaks for all, for
every sinner, for 'Everyman'. It is appropriate to a uniquely shared
context, that of Christian devotion. Likewise, the address of Christ to
man is equally direct and personal:

> My folk, now answerë me,
>   And sey what is my gilt;                            *say; guilt*
> What might I mor ha don for thee,                     *have done*
>   That I ne have fulfilt?                              *fulfilled*
>
>                                                   [100, 1–4]

Echoing such familiar texts as '*Popule meus*' or '*O vos omnes*' from the
Easter Liturgy, Christ's voice came to medieval readers with an immediacy and intimacy unknown to those of post-Reformation, non-liturgical
traditions.

  Sometimes the language and conventions of secular love poetry are
used in the devotional lyrics, but to very different effect. *Now I se blosmë
sprynge* (**69**) opens with the conventional *reverdie*; the poet speaks of a
'swetë love-longinge' (line 3) which 'gladëth al my song' (line 7) and
upon which his life and joy depend. The poet's beloved is not, however,
a lady, but Jesus. The situation of the secular lyric is reversed. The true
lover and sufferer of love's anguish is here the beloved, the crucified
Christ. The poet, for all his 'love-longing', fails in his love – 'Of love ne
can I nought!' (line 37) – and in his service of his *lemman softe*, his 'gentle
lover':

> Jhesu, lemman softe,
> Thou yif me strengthe and might,                      *give me*
> Longinge sore and ofte                   *yearning sore and often*
> To servë thee aright.
>
>                                                   [**69**, 41–4]

The lover poet of the devotional lyric is humble and contrite; he has
nothing of the secular lover's self-indulgent anguish. Nor is Christ, his
beloved, at a distance like the typical lady of a secular lyric.

There is also to be found in some of the devotional lyrics a sophistication of style and play of wit. *In the vaile of restles mynd* (73) opens in the manner of a *chanson d'aventure*, with the poet seeking to find true love in the landscape of his troubled mind. On a hill he hears a voice lamenting:

> 'See, dere soule, my sidës blede,                                    *bleed*
> *Quia amore langueo.*'                                 *because I languish for love*
>
>                                                                   [73, 7–8]

– the voice of Christ suffering for love. Images of Christ as king, knight, lover, mother, husband emerge and merge within the poem. In particular, the poet draws on the romantic theme of Christ as the Lover Knight searching for and ready to sacrifice himself in the service of his beloved, man's soul. As king or knight, the lover's care for and generosity towards his beloved brings but ironic recompense:

> My faire love, and my spousë bryght,
>     I saved hyr fro betyng, and she hath me bet;          *beating; beaten*
> I clothed hyr in grace and hevenly lyght,
>     This blody surcote she hath on me set                        *surcoat*
>
>                                                                   [73, 25–8]

– and not only a 'bloody surcoat', but gloves, not white but red and stained, gloves which will not come off (lines 41–5), and nails to buckle his feet (lines 49–52). (Ironic contrast between items of clothing – this time those of a courtly dandy – and Christ's 'garments' is again exploited in 101.) The Song of Songs was one of the most important Biblical sources of allusion and echo both in secular and in devotional lyrics. Here it is the source, not only of the refrain *Quia amore langueo* ('because I languish for love') itself, but also of the evocative associations in lines such as the following:

> My swetë spouse, will we go play?
>     Applës ben rype in my gardine;                        *are ripe; garden*
> I shall clothe thee in new array,
>     Thy mete shall be mylk, honye, and wyne.                    *your food*
>
>                                                                   [73, 81–4]

The miscellaneous lyrics which make up the final part of this volume are in some ways those most readily accessible to the modern reader. Stable-boys and lackeys, bailiffs and haywards, blacksmiths and pedlars, amorous clerics and ubiquitous friars may not be part of the present-day scene, but the concerns of these lyrics – unjust imprisonment, exploitation and impoverishment, bribery and corruption, and even noise pollution – are. Along with poems of moving complaint and biting satire which suggest a world far from the Merry England of popular fancy, this small selection also offers others which in their zest, wit, humour, *double entendre*, roguery and sheer fun bear witness to a lighter side of medieval life.

*Er ne couthe Ich sorwë non* (**109**) dates from the first half of the thirteenth century and is probably the earliest of these lyrics. Though the speaker, a prisoner, gives few details of his plight beyond the fact that he is an innocent victim of the misdeeds of others, his complaint in the form of a prayer is movingly personal. This lyric is in fact a song, written not to be read but to be sung to the tune of a French poem of which it is a translation. Indeed, it can only be properly appreciated as sung, for some of its lines are slightly awkward to read, reflecting, perhaps, some difficulty on the part of the English adapter in matching the verse form of the French. Of a considerable body of Middle English verse of social complaint and satire concerning the sufferings of the rural poor, *Ich herde men upon mold* (**113**) is one of the most telling and specific. The expense of foreign wars from the reign of Edward I (d. 1307) on through the fourteenth century added considerably to the burden of taxation on the English peasantry. Here the plight of the small peasant farmer is vividly depicted: exposed to the tyranny of petty officials – the hayward, the bailiff, the wood-keeper and, most of all, tax-gatherers – he is stripped of his savings, his seed-corn and his farm animals; his land is bare, or crops lie ruined by storms and flooding. The effectiveness of the poem in conveying its harsh picture derives partly from the force of its alliterative lines, partly from its colloquial language ('the green wax' for 'tax' has something of the smack of Cockney slang), partly from the oppressive sense of all-pervading social corruption as Will and Falsehood personified stalk the land, and partly from the use of direct speech to recreate the callous, overbearing arrogance with which tax collectors dealt with the peasantry.

Alliterative verse is used in several other poems here, in each to different effect. Its potential for the linking of words in two-beat alliterative phrases is exploited to the full in a forceful and fast-moving tirade of invective directed against idle attendants, lackeys, stable-boys, and menials in general in *Of rybaudz I ryme* (**115**), a poem of personal polemic rather than social satire. The élan of this lyric lies in a relish of sustained abuse, sometimes crude, sometimes ironic, akin to that found in the later Scottish poet Dunbar; and, as in some of Dunbar's poems, the popular, racy, idiomatic style here involves the use of words and phrases the exact sense of which is difficult to determine even if the gist is usually clear enough. Indeed, a straining of sense is by no means uncommon where, in the rhetoric of invective, the choice of words is mainly determined by the demands of alliteration. *Swarte smekëd smithes smatered with smoke* (132) is another poem of invective in alliterative form, this time against blacksmiths, by a poet deprived of sleep on account of their nightly din. This shorter poem is no less forceful, but it is more tightly wrought; the poet's exasperation provokes more than a flood of abuse. Here the zest is as much that of composition, the joy of a wordsmith, expertly fashioning in sustained alliteration a vivid and detailed presentation of blacksmiths at work, both in sight and, with skilful onomatopoeia, in sound:

| | |
|---|---|
| The mayster longëth a litel | *the master smith lengthens a small piece* |
| and lashëth a lesse, | *and hammers out a smaller bit* |
| Twynëth hem twayn | *twists the two together* |
| and touchëth a treble. | *and strikes a treble note* |
| Tik, tak! hic, hac! | |
| tiket, taket! tik, tak! | |
| Lus, bus! lus, das! – | |
| swych lyf they leden! | *such a life they lead* |
| | [132, 17–20] |

All the sounds are here – the plosive 't's and 'k's with different vowels evoking the anvil's response to various kinds of hammer-strokes; the 's' consonants for the splutter and hiss of red-hot iron plunged into water.

It is mainly in song that a lighter side of life finds expression in these lyrics. In the famous Cuckoo Song, *Somer is y-comen in* (110), with cuckoos singing loudly and merrily, meadows and woods blossoming, ewes bleating, cows lowing, bullocks and bucks leaping and cavorting, the vitality of nature is absolute, uncomplicated by the agonizing of pining lovers. Sung with the lively merriment of a round, the joy of this lyric is complete. Though no music survives with any of the other lyrics in this section, it seems virtually certain that *Ich am of Irlande* (117) and *Maiden in the morë lay* (118) were dance songs; *D . . . dronken* (119), also from MS. Rawlinson D. 913, may have been a drinking song, but is more likely to have been a dance song too. Sloane 2593 is a small, pocket-sized manuscript with all the appearance of a minstrel's song book, and although lacking musical notation, many of its lyrics seem eminently singable. Some, like *I have a gentil cok* (122) and *I have a newe garden* (125), excel in subtle sexual innuendo. In a masterpiece of parody and welcome seduction (129), the jolly, twinkling priest Jankin sings merrily and treads suggestively on the girl's foot during the mass – and all to her pleasure – 'And yet me thinketh it dos me good' – even if – 'Deo gratias!' – she ends up pregnant. The variety runs on: poets on their purses (120 and 121), another drinking song (123), a warning against older wives (127), a rogue peddling sex (128), ballad-like poems about Judas (112) and St Stephen (126), and satirical accounts of the doings of friars.

It has to be admitted that of all the lyrics Chaucer's are among the finest – at least if one's taste runs to urbanity, a quality again evident in his humorous complaint to his purse (120). Parodying the relationship of the courtly lover and his mistress, he addresses his purse as his 'lady dear'. To her alone he complains, punning adroitly on the words 'light' and 'heavy'. He will die unless she is 'heavy again' – i.e. 'serious' in affection, 'heavy' with cash! Chaucer's art is witty and sophisticated. Nevertheless, the Sloane lyric, *Whan I have in myn purs y-now* (121), however different, also has its own excellence – the ease, the immediate appeal, the lighter rhythms of the simpler song lyric – qualities characteristic of so many of the best Middle English lyrics. But by no means all the earlier poems are songs. *Man in the moonë stont and strit* (114), a Harley lyric as far removed from the cosmopolitan Chaucer as alliterative is from decasyllabic verse, is a poem of subtle wit, humour and imagination which, in its own manner, is without equal. The reader of Middle English lyrics need never want for variety.

## Lyric Stanza and Metre

How are Middle English lyrics to be read? In the Middle Ages they would have been sung or read aloud. To enjoy these poems to the full, modern readers must, at the very least, be able to read them with a confident sense of the movement of the verse, and this depends on some understanding of the metre in which they were written.

Old English poetry of all kinds was written in the same verse form. This was the alliterative line, so called because its two halves were linked by alliteration. Each half had two stressed and a variable number of unstressed syllables. A development of this line continued into Middle English and is used in several of the lyrics in this volume.

Rhyme and stanza form, modelled on French and Latin verse, first appeared in English in Middle English poetry. The very structure of the stanza declares its origin in song. Thus, the rhyme scheme *a a b; a a b; b a a b* of *With longing I am lad* (1) marks out a stanza structured as two three-line units followed by a four-line unit, corresponding to the melodic structure *A, A, B* – that is, a tune in two parts with the first part sung to the first three lines and repeated for the second three, and the second part sung to the final quatrain of the stanza. However, while originating in song, stanza form continued as a prosodic pattern for so-called 'literary lyrics', that is, lyrics written to be recited rather than sung.

With rhyme schemes as a guide, the stanza forms of the lyrics present few problems. However, the convention of representing units of verse as separate lines is largely a post-medieval practice. The representation of poetic form was often at best a matter of secondary importance for a medieval scribe; his overriding concern was usually with economy, with saving space. Hence, in the manuscripts, these poems were frequently written out as prose or in long lines (i.e. with two or more lines written as one) in order to make the maximum use of every page. The way a poem was copied sometimes depended on how the page on which it was begun had been divided for the previous item. Thus, in MS. Harley 2253, the beginning of *Of rybaudz I ryme* (115) is written out in short lines because the page on which it starts had already been divided into two columns; but when the scribe began a fresh page he changed to copying the rest of the poem (from line 24) in long lines. Similarly, John of Grimestone copied the first stanza of **92** as four short lines, and then, to fill space at the bottom of the page, he copied the second stanza as two long lines. Like many others, the scribe of MS. Sloane 2593 sometimes marked the division of his long lines into units by punctuation marks; he also had the habit of saving space by copying the last line of a stanza in the right-hand margin. The line division and stanza form adopted in this volume are, therefore, for the most part editorial, following the modern convention of representing units of verse by separate lines.

If the stanzaic form of Middle English lyrics is generally clear, the same cannot be said of the metre. Even in non-alliterative verse, lines have usually been described in terms of number of stresses. An obvious disadvantage of this is that it is often unclear what is to count as a 'stressed syllable' – a syllable carrying 'natural' stress, or, perhaps, 'metrical' or 'rhetorical' stress? A more serious disadvantage is that unstressed syllables are left out of account. It has commonly been thought that English poets, accustomed to relative freedom with regard to the number of unstressed syllables in traditional native alliterative verse, were happy with some flexibility in the syllable-count when writing non-alliterative verse. This may be true of some verse, but as a generalization it is much too sweeping and may owe more to a quaint form of nationalistic pride than to any systematic analysis. Middle English verse, it has been claimed, by 'the admission of extra unstressed syllables ... refused to surrender ... [to] mere slavish following of French and Latin forms'.[12] Whatever the truth, a crucial question confronts us in assessing the metre of Middle English lyrics: precisely which unstressed syllables in a line *as written* are to be counted? It is difficult to answer this question for two reasons. First, no contemporary account of the metrical principles and practices of Middle English poets survives, if, indeed, any such treatise was ever written. The second is simply this: whereas it is clear to a present-day reader how many syllables are represented in a modern English text, in a Middle English text this is far from self-evident.

For guidance on this question it is therefore necessary to look, at least in the first instance, to sources of evidence independent of the actual texts. Two such sources immediately suggest themselves: one is the verse tradition from which the lyrics derived, French and Latin songs; the other is the music which survives with some of the Middle English lyrics. A fundamental requirement of a song is that its words should fit the tune, and do so for all stanzas – a requirement which calls for a considerable degree of regularity. Indeed, from a study of Troubadour and Trouvère songs, Professor John Stevens concludes that in the matching of words and music the 'most important single controlling factor is the number of syllables in any given line or stanza'.[13] It may well be, therefore, that in English stanzaic lyrics within this tradition (whether surviving with music or not) the principal poetic constraint continued to be a matter of a syllabic match, line for line and stanza by stanza.

---

[12] Saintsbury (1907), pp. 376–7.
[13] Stevens (1982), p. 2. See also Stevens (1986), *passim*.

Indeed, of the Middle English songs which survive with music, a recent editor, Professor E. J. Dobson, took the view that 'the music ... may require perfect or near-perfect metrical regularity, in syllable-count and in rhythm'.[14] However, while this is broadly speaking true, the evidence of the actual surviving musical notation supports greater flexibility than Dobson allowed, especially with regard to two significant matters: first, the variation – common in Middle English verse – of lines beginning with or without an initial unstressed syllable; and second, the extent of freedom acceptable in metrical rhythm. A fuller account of the evidence of the music is given in Appendix A (pages 251–3).

The syllable-count of a line may conveniently be expressed as its number of metrical (i.e. pronounced) syllables, counting from the first stressed syllable to the rhyme syllable (not counting the second syllable of feminine rhymes). Occasionally, as in some lines beginning with the word 'and', metrical or rhetorical stress will determine the first stressed syllable. An initial unstressed syllable may be regarded as an optional extra syllable. As a common variant in lines of this kind, the initial stress pattern $x/$ may be inverted to give $/x$ and so, for instance, an eight-syllable line in the form $/x\ x/x/x/$. However, regular alternation of stressed and unstressed syllables often depends on imposing a rhythm of 'metrical' stresses. Thus, though the lines of *With longing I am lad* (1) may be described as three-stress lines, such a description makes sense only in terms of 'metrical' stressing, for in natural speech rhythm many of the lines read more convincingly with two stresses: e.g. *With lónging I am lád*, or *For sélden I am sád*, or *That sémly for to sée*. It makes more sense, then, to view lines of non-alliterative verse not as fixed in number of stresses (some merely 'metrical') but rather (at least, in careful verse) as basically constant in number of syllables, with flexibility in the number and rhythm of natural stresses. Such a view accords well with John Stevens' claim that the rhythm of Middle English verse is that of 'very speech itself';[15] and although some lyric verse was meant to be sung rather than read aloud,[16] when it is so read a reader may appropriately follow the natural rhythms of speech.

How, then, does this view square with the surviving lyric texts? Unfortunately, as already stated, it is not self-evident from a Middle

---

[14] *MES*, p. 32.
[15] Stevens (1982), p. 7.
[16] This is especially true of *contrafacta*. See Commentary, 109.

English text *as written* which unstressed syllables are to be pronounced. The most obvious difficulty lies in the interpretation of the word endings '-e', '-est' and '-eth', '-ed' and '-es'. Moreover, other syllables in Middle English *as written* may or may not be pronounced, depending on the operation of linguistic principles such as elision, hiatus, synizesis, syncope and apocope. These are matters fundamental to any appraisal of metre; however, as they are of a technical nature, they are discussed separately in Appendix B (pages 254–7).

Even if Middle English lyrics had survived in autograph copies, an understanding of their metrical form would have been possible only in the light of such considerations. However, none of the surviving lyric texts is demonstrably an author's copy, and most are manifestly the end product of successive scribal transcriptions, and possibly, in some cases, versions made from dictation or from memory. Such copies are notoriously unreliable.[17] Since there was no such thing as a standard form of Middle English – no standard spelling, no standard grammar – scribes wrote in accordance with the pronunciation and usage of their own dialects and the spelling habits which prevailed in the schools or scriptoria where they had learned to write. Furthermore, Middle English scribes tended to alter the language of the texts they copied to conform with the spellings and forms familiar to them, a widespread practice known as 'linguistic revision'. Clearly metre and rhyme were vulnerable to such changes. Chaucer himself was all too aware of this danger, as his famous plea at the close of *Troilus and Criseyde* makes clear:

> And for ther is so gret diversité            *because; diversity*
> In Englissh and in writyng of oure tonge,
> So prey I God that non myswrité the,            *thee*
> Ne the mysmetre for defaute of tonge.            *lack of skill in language*
> [*Troilus*, V, 1793–6]

Typically, a scribe might copy a word such as *sinne* ('sin') as *sunne* or *senne* according to his own dialect, thus spoiling a rhyme. Numerous

---

[17] Readers unfamiliar with the extent of textual corruption in Middle English lyrics – words added or omitted, the order of words, lines and even stanzas altered, stanzas added or omitted – not to mention the effects of scribal linguistic revision (see below), need only compare the different versions of **39, 75, 46, 40, 38** and **91** printed by Carleton Brown [Brown XIII, Nos. 10, 17, 28, 32, 46 and 49] or the texts of **69** from MS. B.L., Royal 2.F.viii [Brown XIII, No. 63] and **94** from MS. Bodl., Digby 2 [Brown XIII, No. 64] with the versions of the same lyrics in MS. B.L., Harley 2253 [Brook, Nos. 18 and 22].

words in Middle English, including prepositions, adverbs, nouns and especially verbs, had the endings '-en' or '-e' as variant forms. Scribes readily copied '-en' instead of '-e' or vice versa. Since '-e' frequently disappeared with elision which was prevented by '-en', it is evident how easily metre could be distorted by such alterations alone. Among other common variants affecting metre were: *havest / hast*; *haveth / hath*; *haveth / haven / have / han*; *haved / had*; *for to / to*; *upon / on*; *unto / to*; *other / or*; *also / so* /as; *muchel / much*; *loverd / lord*; *lavedy / lady*; *heved / hed*; *ne wot / not*; and single *ne*, *nought* and double *ne . . . nought* negatives.[18]

By now it will be evident why Middle English lyric metre is so problematic. Nevertheless, when analysed in the light of the linguistic principles mentioned briefly above – elision, hiatus, syncope, synizesis and apocope – many of the non-alliterative lyrics in this anthology do reveal a marked consistency in syllable-count. When a lyric is characteristically regular in its metre, it is reasonable to assume that an occasional irregularity may well have resulted from the hazards of 'linguistic revision'. Where an alternative form – e.g. *drive* instead of *driven*, or *to* instead of *unto* – readily rectifies the metre, such an alternative is silently introduced into the text. In the same way, alternative forms of the third singular present (*haveth* and *hath*), of the present plural (*haveth*, *have(n)* and *han*), and of the past tense (*haved* and *had*) of the verb 'to have' are silently adopted, and final '-e' is restored, as metrically preferable. However, but for a few exceptions noted in the Commentary, the spellings '-est', '-eth', '-ed' and '-es' stand unaltered. Metrical irregularities occasionally invite emendation, especially where suspect sense or syntax is involved; and even if emendation can never guarantee to restore the original text – for all emendation must remain to a degree speculative – the restoration of metre is a positive editorial gain. In some lyrics the syllable-count in all but a minute proportion of lines would be irregular only if the endings '-est', '-eth', '-ed' or '-es' were always to be counted as full syllables. It is evident, not least from Chaucer's verse, that not infrequently the verb endings '-est' and '-eth', written as full forms, concealed reduced pronunciations; and it is difficult to resist the conclusion that with '-ed', and even '-es', the option of

---

[18] Numerous examples of 'mismetring' and spoilt rhymes caused by variants adopted by scribes other than the forms of the original text are readily to be seen by comparing the texts of lyrics printed from more than one manuscript in Brown XIII. See also Commentary, 75, 14 n.

reduced unstressed endings was already available to poets even as early as the thirteenth century. Clearly, however, readers who are not persuaded of this view are at liberty to read such endings as full where they so choose.

But not all lyrics are metrically regular. One kind of verse frequently used in lyrics – a long line of seven stresses which usually divides into two lines, one of four and one of three stresses – has lines of three plus three stresses as a common variant. This type of scansion developed from the Septenarius, a seven-foot syllabic metre popular in medieval Latin verse; it is the form of verse used in the two dramatic, ballad-like poems about Judas (112) and St Steven (126) and was, indeed, the origin of what is now known as Ballad Metre. Lyrics of a more popular kind, as one might expect, are often freer in their scansion. Occasionally metre defies consistent analysis. *Lavedy seynte Marie* (37), for instance, seems to fluctuate between alliterative and syllabic verse. In some of the later lyrics (in striking contrast with Chaucer) lines with extra weak syllables are common. This is true of the two Vernon lyrics in this anthology (60 and 61). The considerable textual discrepancies between the two manuscripts of *In the vaile of restles mind* (73) make it impossible to tell how authentic the apparently loose metre of this lyric, written *c.* 1400, really was. Again, textual corruption may account for the metrical irregularities found in some of the Sloane lyrics.

Inevitably, the interpretation of lyric metre depends on hypothesis and personal judgement. Lines will sometimes scan in more ways than one. Nevertheless, an editor's duty to attempt an informed analysis and to offer guidance remains despite the uncertainties encountered.

## Guidance on Metrical Reading

In final syllables and in internal unstressed syllables the vowel 'e' is marked as 'ë' where it was probably pronounced, and left unmarked where it may well have been silent.

(1) It is essential that the reader should be aware that many final '-e's were sounded in Middle English which are silent in modern English; but also, that, as a random or conventional spelling, or because of elision, a final '-e' in Middle English was often silent. Thus, final '-e' is pronounced in *waxë* (1, line 2), *maidë* (1, line 3), *rewë* (1, line 7), *allë* (1, line

11), etc., but is silent in *molde* (1, line 2), *grede* (1, line 4), *grone* (1, line 4), *routhe* (1, line 8), etc.

(2) The ending '-eth' of the present tense, third person singular of the verb is sometimes pronounced as a full ending, as in *marrëth* (1, line 3), *revëth* (1, line 33), *lovëth* (2, line 11), etc. Frequently, however, the ending is reduced: thus, *bereth* (1, line 35), *woneth* (1, line 37), *thinketh* (2, line 15), etc., may have been pronounced as 'berth', 'wonth', 'thinkth', etc.

(3) Similarly, the ending '-est' of the present tense, second person singular of the verb was sometimes reduced and sometimes pronounced as a full ending: e.g. *singestou* (21, line 18) as 'singstou', and *spekëst* (24, line 66) as two syllables.

(4) The endings '-ed' of the past tense and the past participle of the verb, and '-es' of the genitive and plural of nouns and of some adverbs, were usually pronounced as full syllables: e.g. *marrëd* (2, line 38), *sewëd* (3, line 69), *listenëd* (3, line 77), etc., and *Godës* (2, line 17), *whallës* (2, line 19), *tounës* (2, line 22), etc. However, these endings may occasionally have been reduced as in modern English: e.g. *y-loved* (13, line 3), *loved* (17, line 16), *lovede* (24, lines 51 and 55), *unwarned* (60, line 170), *deyed* (65, line 18), etc., and *tales* (27, line 37), *whiles* (30, line 7), *tydinges* (41, line 1), *sawes* (51, line 10), *sides* (51, line 78), *mirthes* (51, line 81), etc.

(5) Some words can vary in pronunciation. Thus, in words like *comely*, *dereworthe*, *dereworthliche*, *lasteles*, *levely*, *leveliche*, *stedefast*, etc., the unstressed 'e' within the word could be pronounced or not as metrically required. The very common word *hevene* could be pronounced with two syllables as in modern English, or as *hevenë* (with the final '-e' sounded and the middle 'e' lost by syncope – see Appendix B), or with three syllables as *hevënë* (51, line 107), as required by metre. With syncope, and elision with a following word beginning with a vowel, it could even be reduced to one syllable as in *Hevene I* (1, line 39) and *heven and* (2, line 53). Again, see Appendix B.

In alliterative verse and in rhymes it is especially difficult to tell whether final unstressed syllables are full or reduced, or, in the case of final '-e', silent. Middle English alliterative verse, unlike its Old English ancestor, appeared to enjoy considerable freedom in the number of weak syllables per line. Guidance on pronunciation in alliterative lyrics is, therefore, largely impressionistic. Again, since it is difficult to tell when final

'-e' was sounded in rhymes, it has usually been marked for pronunciation only as required by music or probably needed as a grammatical marker. However, the reader is alerted to the probability that it may have been pronounced much more frequently.

## Middle English: Manuscripts and Language

Most Middle English lyrics have survived only by chance. Some were merely jotted in the margins of manuscripts, some casually copied on fly-leaves, some quoted in sermons. How many manuscripts with lyrics have perished? Who can tell? Of some, only a single damaged leaf remains. Had MS. Harley 2253 perished, half of the love lyrics from before Chaucer's time – and those the best – would have been lost. The majority of lyrics to survive are found in a few important manuscripts. Of the lyrics in this volume, eight appear in MS. Trinity College, Cambridge 323 (c. 1250), six in MS. Digby 86, Bodleian Library, Oxford (c. 1275), four in MS. Arundel 248, British Library, London (c. 1280–1300), a manuscript especially important for its music, seven in MS. Rawlinson D 913, Bodleian Library, Oxford (c. 1325–50), twenty-nine in MS. Harley 2253, British Library, London (c. 1340), fifteen in MS. Advocates 18.7.21, National Library of Scotland, Edinburgh (1372), five in the 'Vernon' manuscript, MS. Engl. poet. a.1, Bodleian Library, Oxford (c. 1380–1400), and fourteen in MS. Sloane 2593, British Library, London (c. 1400–1450). Of these, MS. Rawlinson D 913 is a single leaf of parchment, much faded and partially illegible. The Cambridge and Edinburgh manuscripts are Franciscan compilations of materials for preachers. MS. Sloane 2593 is the only manuscript completely devoted to lyrics: although it has no music, it has, with some justice, been called a minstrel's song book. In the other manuscripts, the lyrics are found as part of wide-ranging anthologies of religious and secular texts, in prose and verse, in Latin, French and English.

These lyrics differ widely in dialect and present the reader with a great diversity of spellings and grammatical forms. The language of the surviving copies is clearly the product of scribal transmission and linguistic revision (see pages xli–xlii); it is seldom if ever demonstrably the actual language of the original poets. Dialect variants are sometimes of literary significance, as in rhyme or in alliteration. In the main, however, the linguistic diversity of the lyrics, while of interest to philologists, only constitutes a needless barrier between the reader and the Middle English poems as poems.

This barrier is not removed simply by replacing special Middle English characters like 'þ' and 'ȝ' with their modern equivalents – 'th' for 'þ', and 'gh' or 'y' for 'ȝ'; for not only is one still left with many different dialect spellings of the same word (e.g. *sunne, senne, zenne, sinne,* etc. – some of many spellings of the word 'sin'), but also with such idiosyncratic spellings as *Nv yh she* 'Now I see', the opening words of 69 in MS. B.L. Royal 2.F.viii. Worse still, if a manuscript form like *necheð* (36, line 3) is merely 'normalized' to *necheth,* or if forms like *ho* and *hende* (47, lines 22 and 60) are left unaltered, a non-specialist reader, who does not know that in *necheth* the spelling 'ch' does not represent the initial sound of modern 'cheese', or that in the other forms the '*h*' is silent, is likely needlessly to be misled.

To avoid such difficulties, the spelling and grammar of the texts in this volume have been 'revised' in accordance with the language of late fourteenth-century London English. In effect, this is just the kind of linguistic revision which a London scribe would have made. This kind of 'normalization' has two considerable advantages. The first is that the language of the texts in this volume remains at all times authentic Middle English and not the medley of half-changed forms produced by some attempts at normalization. The second is that, since late fourteenth-century London English is Chaucer's language, it is the form of Middle English most familiar to modern readers and, moreover, one which most readily allows for the possibility of reading these poems aloud in something like a reasonable approximation of one type of Middle English pronunciation – in the case of lyrics, a matter of some consequence. Occasionally, forms from other dialects are retained as required by rhyme or alliteration. The vocabulary of the lyrics is also preserved; words which were regional or archaic, not current in ordinary late fourteenth-century London, are retained, just as they would have been by a faithful scribe, as an integral part of a poem's texture and diction. An element of dialect mixture of this kind is in no way inauthentic; it was, indeed, typical of most Middle English texts.

The London language itself varied considerably both in spelling and in grammatical forms, as Chaucer manuscripts readily demonstrate. From this diversity the most common forms and the more familiar spellings have generally been adopted. However, the common conventions of Middle English writing have been respected: final '-e', both as a random spelling and as found in such common alternative spellings as *yet / yette, had / hadde, wel / welle,* etc., and the free variation of the spellings *ou* and *ow* (as in *nou / now* 'now' and *soule / sowle* 'soul'), of *o, ou* and *ow* (as in *thoght / thought / thowght* 'thought'), and of *i* and *y* (as in *him / hym* 'him' or *while / whyle* 'while') have been partly, though not systematically, retained. Such characteristics of authentic written Middle English will scarcely disturb a modern reader. However, the use of the letters 'u' and 'v' has been standardized according to modern usage, and, where appropriate, capital 'F' replaces 'ff' of the manuscripts.

## Pronunciation Guide

An approximation to the pronunciation of late fourteenth-century London English, Chaucer's English, may be achieved if the following significant differences from Modern English Received Pronunciation are observed.

(1) The spellings *a, e (ee), i (y), o (oo), ou (ow),* and *u* for long vowels represent the sounds they have in modern French, Spanish and Italian:

| | | |
|---|---|---|
| *a* | as in French *la gare* | – e.g. ME *name, tale, maken,* 'make' |
| *e (ee)* | as in French *le café* | – e.g. ME *swete* 'sweet', *meten* 'meet', *see* 'see' |
| *e (ee)* | as in French *la mère* | – e.g. ME *techen* 'teach', *speken* 'speak', *see* 'sea' |
| *i (y)* | as in French *le livre* | – e.g. ME *tyme / time* 'time', *while* 'while', *ryden* 'ride' |
| *o (oo)* | as in French *le mot* | – e.g. ME *gode / good* 'good', *mone* 'moon', *don* 'do' |
| *o (oo)* | as in French *l'homme* | – e.g. ME *gon* 'go', *hom* 'home', *stone* 'stone' |
| *ou (ow)* | as in French *Toulouse* | – e.g. ME *house* 'house', *now* 'now' |
| *u* | as in French *la lune* | – e.g. ME *vertú* 'virtue', *natúre* 'nature' |

Modern English spelling and pronunciation can often help in distinguishing the appropriate pronunciation of Middle English *e (ee)* and *o (oo),* as follows: Middle English *e (ee)* is pronounced as French *é* in words where the modern spelling is *ee,* and as French *è* where the modern spelling is *ea;* Middle English *o (oo)* is pronounced like *o* in French *mot* in words which now have the vowel sound of present-day *moon,* and like *o* in

French *homme* in words which now have the vowel sound of present-day *stone*.

(2) Where in Modern English the spellings *u* or *o* are pronounced as in *but / hut / love / son*, the Middle English pronunciation was as in Modern English *put / full* – e.g. ME *but, muchel* 'much', *sunne* 'sun', and *love, comen* 'come', *sone* 'son'.

(3) The diphthongs spelt as *ai* (*ay*) or *ei* (*ey*) were probably pronounced like *y* in Modern English *my* – e.g. ME *saide / seyde* as Modern English *side*. The diphthong spelt *au* (*aw*) had the sound of *ow* in Modern English *now* – e.g. ME *cause, lawe, drawen* 'draw'.

(4) At the end of a word the letter 'e', when pronounced, had the rather neutral sound of *e* in Modern English *enough*, or *a* in Modern English *above* – e.g. *swetë, sunnë, lovë*, etc. Where a final '-e' is marked with an acute accent – e.g. ME *beauté* 'beauty', *leauté* 'loyalty', *pité* 'pity' – the pronunciation is as in French *café*. The suffix *-io(u)n*, as in ME *confusion, nacioun* 'nation', *transmutacioun*, etc., was pronounced '-i-o(u)n', that is, as two syllables.

(5) Consonants.

(a) The spelling *gh* was pronounced as *ch* in Scottish *loch* after back vowels – e.g. *noght, boughte, foughte, caughte* – and as *ch* in German *ich* after front vowels – e.g. *night, light, fighten* 'fight'.

(b) Initial *g, k*, and *w* were still sounded in words like *gnawen* 'gnaw', *knowen* 'know' and *writen* 'write', as was *l* before consonants, as in *half* and *folk*. The consonant *r*, often silent in Modern English, was always pronounced, and probably trilled, as in present-day Scottish speech.

(c) The pronunciation of *ng* was as in Modern English *hunger*. Thus in Middle English *singer* would rhyme with *finger*.

(6) The accentuation of some words derived from French varied. Thus in *vertú, natúre, miróur, manére, servíce, savóur*, etc., the accent could fall on the second syllable as in French; but sometimes such words occur with initial accentuation as in English – e.g. *mírror, máner*, etc. Sometimes accentuation could fall on a suffix, as in the rhymes on *-aunce, -esse* and *-nesse* in **30**. Likewise, in the earlier lyrics, rhymes sometimes involve the suffix *-ing / -yng*.

# PREFACE TO TEXTS

The language of the lyrics in this volume (except for 95, 102 and 116) has been normalized in accordance with the spelling and grammar of late fourteenth-century London English. Occasional non-London forms are retained for the sake of rhyme or alliteration. Capitalization, punctuation, word-division and metrical arrangement are editorial. The letter 'e' in unstressed syllables is marked with the diacritic "'" where it is pronounced. In the case of common Middle English variants such as *hath/haveth*, *to/unto*, *to/for to*, etc. (forms which vary without distinction of meaning from manuscript to manuscript in the course of scribal transmission – see pages xli–xlii), a different form from that of the base manuscript has sometimes been silently adopted where metrically preferable. All substantive emendations, with the readings of the base manuscripts and selected variants from other manuscripts, are recorded in the Commentary. Variants from versions which appear to be re-workings, that is, essentially different poems rather than copies, are ignored unless they offer significant information.

# PART I: *Love Lyrics*

# 1. With longing I am lad

With longing I am lad, — *I go* (lit. *am led*)
On molde I waxë mad, — *on earth I am going mad*
   A maidë marrëth me. — *distresses*
I grede, I grone, unglad, — *cry out; groan; anguished*
5  For selden I am sad — *seldom; tired*
   That semly for to see. — *that fair one; of seeing* (lit. *to see*)
Lady, thou rewë me, — *have pity on me*
To routhe thou hast me rad, — *to grief; brought*
Be bote of that I bad, — *be the remedy for which I have prayed*
10 My lyf is long on thee. — *my life is dependent*

Lady of allë londë, — *all lands*
Les me out of bondë, — *release me; bonds*
   Brought Ich am in wo. — *I am*
Have resting on hondë, — *bring about respite*
15 And send thou me thy sondë — *response*
   Sone, er thou me slo; — *soon, before you slay me*
My reste is with the ro. — *peace of mind; roe*
Though men to me han ondë, — *towards me have enmity*
To love nil I nought wondë, — *I will not hesitate*
20 Ne lete for non of tho. — *nor desist for any* (lit. *none*) *of them*

Lady, with al my might
My love is on thee light — *settled* (lit. *alighted*)
   To menskë when I may. — *to honour* ( *you*)
Thou rew and red me ryght, — *pity and guide me aright*
25 To dethe thou hast me dight, — *condemned*
   I deye longe er my day. — *before*

Thou leve upon my lay,                              *believe in my song*
Trouth Ich have thee plight,                        *fidelity; pledged*
To don that Ich have hight                          *to do what I have promised*
30 While mi lif lastë may.

Lylie-whyte she is,
Hire rode so rose on rys,                           *her complexion as; on a stem*
    That revëth me my rest.                         *who robs me of*
Womman war and wys,                                 *prudent and wise*
35 Of pride she bereth the pris,                    *in excellence she takes the prize*
    Byrde one of the best.                          *a lady*
This womman woneth by west,                         *dwells in the west*
Brightest under bys;                                *fairest in fine linen*
Hevene I tolde al his                               *I would consider entirely his*
40 That o night were hire gest.                     *who for one night might be her guest*

## 2. A waylë whyte as whallës bon

. . . . . . . . . . . . . . . . . .
. . . . . . . . . . . . . . . . . .
. . . . . . . . . . . . . . . . . .

Ne half so fre;                                     *nor half so noble*
5 Whoso wole of love be trewe                       *will; true*
    Do listnë me.                                   *listen to*

Herknëth me, I you telle,
In such wondryng for wo I welle,                    *perplexity for woe I seethe*
Nis no fire so hot in helle
10    Al to mon                                     *as a man*
That lovëth derne and dar not telle                 *in secret; dares*
    What him ys on.                                 *what is wrong with him*

Ich unne hire wel, and she me wo,                   *I wish her well; she (wishes)*
Ich am hire frend, and she my fo,                   *she (is) my foe*
15 Me thinketh min herte wol breke atwo             *it seems to me; in two*

For sorwe and syke;                              *sighing*
In Godës greting moote she go,        *in God's grace may she be* (lit. *go*)
    That waylë whyte.                       *beauty; white* (i.e. *radiant*)

A waylë whyte as whallës bon,                    *a beauty; whale's bone*
20  A greyn in golde that goodly shon,    *a jewel; which shines beautifully*
A turtel that min herte is on                    *a turtle-dove; is* (*set*) *on*
    In tounës trewe;                             *among men; true*
Hire gladshipe nis never gon           *her grace will never go* (*unsung*)
    While I may glewe.                                        *sing*

25  While I may glewe, when she is glad,              *she is gracious*
Of al this world namore I bad                           *would ask*
Than be with hire myn one bistad                     *alone; settled*
    Withouten strif;                                       *dispute*
The care that Ich am in y-brad          *sorrow that I am burnt alive in*
30      I wite a wyf.                                *I blame on a woman*

A wyf nis non so worthly wrought!    *there is no woman as excellently made*
When she is blythe to bedde y-brought,                 *is joyously*
Wel were him that wiste hire thought,         *who enjoyed her favour*
    That thriven and thro;                *that beautiful and excellent* (*one*)
35  Wel I wot she nil me nought,                *know she does not want me*
    Myn herte is wo.                     *woeful* (lit. *woe is to my heart*)

How shal myn herte that lefly syng    *that lovely one; celebrate in song*
That thus is marrëd in mournyng?                           *vexed*
She me wol to dethë bryng                                    *will*
40  Longe er my day;                                  *before my time*
Gret hire wel, that swetë thing                            *greet*
    With eyen gray.                                         *eyes*

Hire yen han woundëd me ywisse,              *eyes have; assuredly*
Hire bendë browës bringen blisse,          *arched eyebrows; joy*
45  Hire comely mouth that mightë kisse            *the man who might*
    In much mirth were;                           *great happiness*
I wolde changë myn for his                      *change my* (*mirth*)
    That is hire fere.                          *who is her companion*

Wolde hire ferë be so fre,                              *companion; noble*
50 And worthës were that so myghte be,          *equivalents* (i.e. *for exchanging*)
Al for one I wolde yeve three                                     *give*
        Withouten cheep;                                              *haggling*
From helle to heven and sonne to see                   *sun to sea*
        Nis none so yeep.                                   *there is none as prudent*


55 Ich wolde Ich were a thrustelcok,                        *song thrush*
A bountyng other a laverokke;                       *bunting; skylark*
        Swetë bryd,                                                   *sweet bird*
Bitwen hire kirtel and hire smok              *gown; undergarment*
        I wolde ben hid.


## 3. Ichot a byrde in bourë bryght

*Blow, northerne wind,*
*Send thou me my swetyng;*                               *sweetheart*
*Blow, northerne wind,*
*Blow, blow, blow.*


5 Ichot a byrde in bourë bryght                       *I know a lady; bower*
That selly semly is on syght,               *who wonderfully comely is to see*
Menskful maide of muchel myght,                *a noble; great attraction*
        Fair and fre to fonde;                  *beautiful and gracious to know*
In al this worthlichë won,                              *excellent world*
10 A byrde of blodë and of bon,                        *of blood and bone*
Never yet I nistë non,                            *knew I any* (lit. *none*)
        Lufsomere in londe.                                *lovelier on earth*
            *Blow*, etc.


With lokkës levëliche and longe,                *tresses lovely and long*
15 With frount and facë fair to fonde,              *forehead; to behold*
With mirthës mony mote she monge,    *with merriment many may she inspire*
        That brid so breme in boure;              *maiden so excellent*
With lufsom eyen grete and gode,            *lovely eyes large and good*
With browës blisful under hode,              *eyebrows; under (her) hood*

20 He that reste him on the rode                    *may He who rested on the cross*
      That leflich lyf honoure.                     *that dear creature; honour*
        *Blow*, etc.


   Hirë lerë lemëth light,                          *her complexion shines brightly*
   Asë a launterne anight,                          *as a lantern at night*
25 Hirë ble blikëth so bright,                      *her face gleams so radiantly*
      So fair she is and fyn.                       *exquisite*
   A swetly swire she hath to holde,                *charming neck; to embrace*
   With armës, sholdrës, as man wolde,              *shoulders; as one would wish*
   And fyngrës fairë for to folde,                  *to clasp*
30    God woldë she were myn.                        *would God*
        *Blow*, etc.


   Middel she hath menskful smal,                   *a waist; gracefully slender*
   Hire loveliche cherë as cristal,                 *lovely face (is) as crystal*
   Thighës, leggës, fet and al
35    Y-wroght was of the beste.                     *fashioned*
   A lufsom lady lastëles                           *faultless*
   That sweting is and ever wes,                    *was*
   A better birdë never nes                         *never was (lit. was not)*
      Y-heried with the heste.                      *honoured among the best (lit. highest)*
40      *Blow*, etc.


   She is derëworthe in day,                        *precious*
   Graciousë, stout and gay,                        *poised*
   Gentil, jolif so the jay,                        *merry as the jay*
      Worthliche when she wakëth;                   *splendid; wakens*
45 Maiden, miriest of mouth,
   By est, bi west, by north and south
   There nis fiëlë ne crouth                        *there is not viol nor fiddle*
      That such mirthës makëth.                     *merriment*
        *Blow*, etc.


50 She is coral of godnesse,
   She is rubie of ryghtfulnesse,                   *uprightness*
   She is cristal of clennesse,                     *purity*
      And baner of beuté;                           *banner of beauty*
   She is lilie of largesse,                        *generosity*

55  She is parvenke of prowesse,                *periwinkle of excellence*
    She is solsecle of swetnesse,               *marigold*
        And lady of leauté.                     *loyalty*
        *Blow*, etc.


    To Love, that leflich is in londe,          *who is dear everywhere*
60  I tolde him, as Ich understonde,            *as I*
    How this hende hath hent in honde           *this gracious one has seized*
        An hertë that myn wes;                  *a heart that was mine*
    And hirë knightës me han soght,             *have sought*
    Syking, Sorëwyng and Thoght,                *Sighing, Sorrowing and Perplexity*
65  Tho three me han in balë broght             *those three; grief*
        Ayain the power of Pees.                *against; Peace*
        *Blow*, etc.


    To Love I puttë pleyntës mo,                *I made further complaints*
    How Sykyng me hath sewëd so,                *pursued*
70  And ekë Thoght me thret to slo              *also; threatened to slay me*
        With maistrye if he myghte;             *force*
    And Sorwë swore in balful bende             *grievous bondage*
    That he woldë for this hende                *this gracious one*
    Me ledë to my lyvës ende                    *lead me*
75  Unlawfulliche in lyghte.                    *unlawfully (and) openly*
        *Blow*, etc.


    Love me listenëd ech word
    And begh him to me over bord                *leaned to me across the table*
    And bad me for to hente that hord           *ordered me to seize that treasure*
80      Of myn hertë hele;                      *heart's salvation*
    'And biseche that swete and swote,          *that sweet and gentle creature*
    Er then thou falle as fen of fote,          *before; as mud from the foot*
    That she with thee wol of bote              *will concerning a remedy*
        Derëworthliche dele.'                   *affectionately negotiate*
85      *Blow*, etc.


    For hirë love I carke and care,             *for love of her I grieve and sorrow*
    For hirë love I droupne and dare,           *pine and despair*
    For hirë love my blisse is bare,
        And al Ich waxë wan;                    *grow pale*

90   For hirë love in slep I slake,                       *I lose my sleep*
      For hirë love al night Ich wake,                     *I lie awake*
      For hirë love mournyng I make                      *I grieve*
         More than any man.
            *Blow*, etc.

## 4. Litel wot it any man

Litel wot it any man                           *little does anyone know*
    How dernë love may stonde,                 *secret love may last*
But it were a fre womman                 *unless; noble woman*
    That muche of love had fonde.             *who; had experienced*
5 The love of hire ne lastëth nowight longe;     *her love lasts not long at all*
She hath me plyght and wytëth me wyth wronge.         *
    Ever and oo,                             *ever and always*
For my lef Ich am in gretë thoghte;          *dear one; perplexity*
I thinke on hire that I ne see noght ofte.         *whom I do not see*

10 I wolde nempnë hyre to-day                   *I would name her*
    And I dorste hire minne;            *if I dared; mention her*
She is that fairestë may                      *maiden*
    Of ech ende of hire kinne.     *of any member of her sex* (lit. *kin*)
But she me love of me she havëth sinne.     *unless; she will wrong me*
15   Wo is him                       *woe is his* (lit. *to him*)
That loveth the love that he may ner y-winne.         †
    Ever and oo,
For my lef Ich am in gretë thoghte;
I thinke on hire that I ne see noght ofte.

20 Adoun I fel to hire anon        *down; before her; straight away*
    And crie, 'Lady, thin ore!               *cry; mercy*
Lady, ha mercy of thy mon,          *have mercy on your man*
    Leve thou no false lore:                *believe; tales*
If thou dost, it wol me rewë sore;       *it will grieve me painfully*
25 Love drecchëth me that I may live namore.'      *afflicts; so that I*
                              *promised; blames me wrongly*
                            †*who loves; whom; never win*

Ever and oo,
For my lef Ich am in gretë thoghte;
I thinke on hire that I ne see noght ofte.

Mery it is in hyrë tour                         *in her (castle) tower*
30    Wyth hathele and wyth hewe;               *with knight and with servant*
So it is in hyrë bour                           *in her chamber*
    With gamen and with glewe.        *amorous play; (musical) entertainment*
But she me lovë sore it wol me rewe.
    Wo is him
35  That loveth the love that never nil be trewe.
    Ever and oo,
For my lef Ich am in gretë thoghte;
I thinke on hire that I ne see noght ofte.

Fayrest fodë upon loft,                         *fairest creature alive*
40    My gode lef, I thee grete,               *my beloved; greet*
As felë sythë and as oft                        *as many times*
    As dewës dropës wete,                       *of dew; drops; wet*
As sterres in welkne and grassës sour and swete.        *
Whose loveth untrewe his herte is seldë sete.   *whoever loves an unfaithful*
45    Ever and oo,                              *[ person; seldom at ease*
For my lef Ich am in gretë thoghte;
I thinke on hire that I ne see noght ofte.

                              * *the sky; herbs bitter and sweet*

## 5. Ichot a byrde in a bour

Ichot a byrde in a bour                         *I know a lady in a bower*
    as beryl so bright,                         *as bright as beryl*
As saphyr in silver                             *as a sapphire (set) in silver*
    semly on sight,                             *beautiful to behold*
As jaspe the gentil                             *as the noble jasper*
    that lemëth with light,                     *shines*
As gernet in golde                              *as a garnet (set) in gold*
    and ruby wel right;                         *and (as) a ruby completely virtuous*
5  As onycle she is on                          *as an onyx she is*

| | |
|---|---|
| y-holden on hight, | *highly esteemed* |
| As diamaund the dere | *precious* |
| in day when she is dight. | *by day; dressed* |
| She is coral y-kid | *she is coral famous* |
| with cayser and knight; | *with emperor and knight* |
| As emeraude amorewen | *as an emerald in the morning* |
| this may havëth might: | *this maiden has power* |
| The might of the margarite | *the power of the pearl* |
| haveth this may mere; | *has this excellent maiden* |
| 10  For charbocle Ich hire ches | *as a carbuncle-stone I esteem her* |
| by chin and by chere. | *for (her) chin and (her) face* |
| | |
| Hire rode is as rose | *her colour is like the rose* |
| that red is on rys, | *which is red on the spray* |
| With lilye-white lerës | *lily-white complexion* |
| lufsom she is; | *lovely* |
| The primerole she passëth, | *primrose; surpasses* |
| the pervenke of pris, | *the prized periwinkle* |
| With alisaundre thereto, | *and alexanders likewise* |
| ache and anys. | *parsley and anise* |
| 15  Cointe as columbine – | *pretty as columbine* |
| such hire kinde is – | *such is her nature* |
| Glad under gore | *delightful in attire* |
| in grey and in gris; | *in grey furs* |
| She is blosme upon ble, | *her face is a flower* |
| brightest under bis, | *(that) fairest (one) in fine linen* |
| With celydoyne and sauge | *(she is) like celandine and sage* |
| as thou thyself sis. | *as you yourself see* |
| That seeth upon that semly | *whoever looks upon that lovely creature* |
| to blis he is brought; | |
| 20  She is solsecle | *marigold* |
| to save is forsought. | *(which) for healing is sought out* |
| | |
| She is papejay in pine | *she is a parrot (who) in (my) sorrow* |
| that betëth me my bale; | *eases for me my distress* |
| To trewe turtel in a tour | *to (you) true turtle-dove in a tower* |
| I telle thee my tale; | |
| She is thrustle thriven in thro | *she is a thrush doughty in dispute* |
| that singëth in sale, | *who sings in the hall* |

The wilde laverokke and wolc — *the wild lark and the hawk*
and the wodëwale; — *and the golden oriole*
25   She is faucon in frith, — *she is a falcon in the forest*
dernest in dale, — *hidden in the valley*
And with everich a gomë — *and to every man*
gladest in gale. — *most delightful in song*
From Weye she is wisest — *from the Wye*
into Wyrhale; — *to the Wirral*
Hire name is in a note — *her name is in a note*
of the nightëgale: — 
In annote is hire namë — — *in a note is her name*
nempnëth hit non! — *let no one mention it*
30   Whoso right redëth — *whoever guesses correctly*
roune to Johón. — *(let him) whisper to John*

Muge she is and mandrake — *musk; mandrake*
thurgh might of the mone, — *by the power of the moon*
Trewe triacle y-told, — *as a true remedy; esteemed*
with tongës in trone; — *by reputation enthroned*
Such licoris may leche — *liquorice; cure*
from Lyne to Lone, — *from Lyn to Lune*
Such sucre man sechëth — *sugar is sought after*
that sanëth men sone; — *which heals men quickly*
35   Blithe y-blessed of Crist — *happily blessed by Christ (she is)*
that baithëth me my bone — *who grants me my prayer*
When derne dedës in day — *secret deeds by day*
derne are done. — *are secretly done*
As gromil in greve — *(she is) like gromwell in the grove*
grene is the grone, — *whose seed is green*
As quibibe and comyn — *(she is) like cubeb and cummin*
kid is in crone, — *(which is) famed for its crown*
Kid comyn in court, — *esteemed (as) cummin in the court*
canel in cofre, — *(as) cinnamon in a chest*
40   With gingere and cetewale — *and ginger and setwall*
and the gylofre. — *and the gillyflower*

She is medicine of might, *a powerful remedy*
   mercie of mede *gracious in favours*
Rekene as Regnas *ready as Regnas*
   resoun to rede, *to give advice*
Trewe as Tegeu in tour, *true as Tegeu in the tower*
   as Wyrwein in wede, *as Wyrwein in (her fine) garments*
Bolder than Byrne *bolder than Byrne*
   that oft the bore bede; *who often challenged the boar*
45 As Wylcadoun she is wise,
   doughty of dede, *doughty in deed*
Fayrer than Floyres
   folkës to fede, *to people a pleasure (lit. peoples to please)*
Kid as Cradoc in court *renowned*
   carf the brede, *who carved the roast*
Hender than Hilde, *more gracious than*
   that haveth me to hede. *(the one) who has me to care for*
She haveth me to hede, *she has me to look after*
   this hendy, anon, *this fair one, from now on*
50 Gentil as Jonas, *gracious*
   she joyëth with Jon. *she rejoices with John*


## 6. Love is soft, love is swet

Love is soft, love is swet,
   love is good sware; *a kind response*
Love is muchë tenë, *great suffering*
   love is muchel care. *great sorrow*
Love is blissënë mest, *of joys the most*
   love is bot yare; *a ready remedy*
4 Love is wandred and wo, *misery and woe*
   with for to fare. *to live (lit. travel) with*

Love is hap who it havëth, *good luck whoever has it*
   love is god hele; *good fortune*
Love is lecher and les, *lewdness and lying*
   and lef for to tele; *ready to deceive*

Love is doughty in the world,                           *honourable*
    with for to dele;                           *to deal with*
8 Love makëth in the land
    many unlele.                               *many unfaithful*

Love is stalworthe and strong                   *sturdy and strong*
    to striden on stede;                       *to mount a horse*
Love is loveliche a thing
    to wommanë nede;                       *necessary for women*
Love is hardi and hot                                   *fierce and hot*
    as glowindë glede;                         *as glowing coal*
12 Love makëth mani may                          *many a maiden*
    with terës to wede.               *with tears to be distraught*

Love hath his styward                                       *steward*
    by sti and by strete;                *along paths and highways*
Love makëth mani may                             *many a maiden*
    hire wongës to wete;                  *her cheeks; (to) wet*
Love is hap, who it havëth,                              *good luck*
    on for to hete;   *to be inflamed with (lit. one to inflame)*
16 Love is wis, love is war,                            *wise; prudent*
    and wilful anséte.          *and a strong-willed adversary*

Love is the softestë thing                               *gentlest thing*
    in hertë may slepe;                     *that may sleep*
Love is craft, love is good                                  *strong*
    with carës to kepe;            *for engaging with sorrows*
Love is les, love is lef,                               *false; desirable*
    love is longinge;                             *pining*
20 Love is fol, love is fast,                     *foolish; steadfast*
    love is frovringe;                            *comfort*
Love is sellich an thing,                          *a marvellous thing*
    whosó shal soth singe.                 *tell the truth*

Love is wele, love is wo,                         *happiness; woe*
    love is gladhede,                            *gladness*
Love is lif, love is deth,                               *life; death*
    love mai us fede.                               *feed*

24   Were love also longdrei                           *as long-lasting*
    as he is first kene,                      *eager*
Hit were the wordlokstë thing        *it would be the most precious thing*
    in world were, Ich wene.      *in the world that might be, I suppose*
Hit is y-said in an song,
    soth is y-sene,                           *the truth is evident*
Love comsëth with carë                          *begins*
    and endëth with tene,                   *suffering*
28   Mid lady, mid wivë,                     *with lady, with woman*
    mid maidë, mid quene.       *with queen (or, harlot!)*


## 7. Though I can wittës ful-iwis

Though I can wittës ful-iwis,            *I am able in mind most certainly*
Of worldës blissë n'ave Ich non,                       *none*
For a lady that is pris                  *on account of; the most excellent*
Of allë that in bourë gon.                      *bowers; dwell (lit. go)*
5   Sithen first that she was his,                        *since*
Y-loken in castel wal of ston,                *locked; wall of stone*
Nas Ich hol ne blithe iwis,              *I was not well nor happy indeed*
Ne thrivinge mon.                           *nor a prospering man*
Livëth man non bildëth me         *no man lives who can persuade me*
10   Abide and blithë for to be –               *to be patient and to be happy*
Ned after my deth me longëth.       *of necessity for my death I long*
I may sayen wel by me                     *I may say assuredly for my part*
Hardë that wo hongëth.                      *that grief weighs bitterly*


## 8. Were ther outher in this toun

Were ther outher in this toun                     *were there either*
Ale or wyn,                                                  *wine*
Ich hit woldë bye                              *I was glad to buy it*
To lemman myn.                                   *for my beloved*

5  Welawey was so hardy                     *woe befell (anyone) so rash*
    For to make my lef al blody;          *as to; dear one; bloody*
    Though he were the kyngës son
    Of Normaundy,
    Yet Icholde awrekë be                     *I would be avenged*
10  For lemman myn.

    Welawey was me tho,                    *woe befell me then*
    Wo was me tho;               *woe was mine (lit. to me) then*
    The man that lesëth that he lovëth    *the man who loses the one whom*
    Him is also.                  *(woe) is his (lit. to him) also*

15  So she me lerdë:                     *so (much); taught*
    Ne more I ne can!                 *no more can I do*
    But Christ Ich hire bitechë          *to Christ; commit*
    That was my lemman.                    *who*

## 9. Of every kinnë tre

    Of every kinnë tre,                    *every kind of*
    Of every kinnë tre,
    The hawthorn blowëth swetest,        *blossoms sweetest*
4  Of every kinnë tre.

    My lemman she shal be,                   *lover*
    My lemman she shal be,
    The fairest of every kinnë,
8  My lemman she shal be.

## 10. Al night by the rosë, rosë

    Al night by the rosë, rosë,
    Al night bi the rose I lay,
    Dorst Ich nought the rosë stele,         *dared; steal*
4  And yet I bar the flour away.             *bore the flower*

## 11. Al gold, Janet, is thin her

Al gold, Janet, is thin her,                                    *hair*
Al gold, Janet, is thin her;
Save thin Jankin, lemman dere,                        *sweetheart; dear*
4  Save Jankin, lemman dere,
Save thin onlye dere.                                      *only beloved*


## 12. Dorë, go thou stillë

Dorë, go thou stillë,                                       *door; quietly*
Go thou stillë, stillë;
Yate, Ich havë in the bourë                              *gate; bower*
4  Y-don al myn willë, willë.                        *accomplished; desire*


## 13. Ich have y-don al myn youth

Ich have y-don al myn youth,                       *I have loved* (lit. *done*)
Oftë, ofte, and ofte;
Longe y-loved and yerne y-beden –                    *eagerly desired*
4  Ful dere it is y-bought!                    *very dearly has it cost me*


## 14. So longe Ich havë, lady

So longe Ich havë, lady,
Y-hovëd at thi gate;                                          *lingered*
That mi fot is frore, faire lady,                              *frozen*
4  For thy love faste to the stake.                         *(gate-) post*

## 15. Bryd onë brerë

Bryd onë brerë, brid, brid onë brerë,                *bird on the briar*
Kynd is comë of Lovë, lovë to cravë;               *Nature; from Love; beg*
Blithful biryd, on me thou rewë,                     *joyous bird, have pity on me*
4  Or greith, lef, greith thou me my gravë.        *or prepare, dear (bird); for me*

Ich am so blithe so bright bird onë brerë                *as happy as a*
Whan I see that hendë in hallë;                      *that gracious one in the hall*
She is whit of lime, lovely, trewë,                        *white in limb*
8  She is fair and flour of allë.                           *flower (i.e. best)*

Mightë Ich hirë at willë havë,
Stedfast of lovë, lovëly, trewë,
Of mi sorwë she may me savë,
12  Joy and blissë were me newë.                     *ever; to me; renewed*

## 16. Foulës in the frith

Foulës in the frith,                                    *birds; wood*
The fishës in the flod,                                        *sea*
And I mon waxë wod;                                *and I must go mad*
Much sorwe I walkë with
5  For beste of bon and blod.              *finest (creature) of bone and blood*

## 17. When the nyghtëgalë singeth

When the nyghtëgalë singeth,
   the wodës waxen grene;                            *grow green*
Lef and gras and blosmë springe                            *leaf*
4    in Avëryl, I wene;                                      *I know*

And love is to myn hertë gon                    *has gone to my heart*
  with onë spere so kene,                 *a spear so sharp*
Night and day my blod hit drynketh;             *blood*
8  myn hertë doth me tene.                   *causes me pain*


Ich have lovëd al this yer
  that I may love namore;                   *such that; no more*
Ich have sikëd moni syk,                        *sighed; sigh*
12  lemman, for thin ore.                     *sweetheart; mercy*
Me nis love never the ner,                      *to me is love no nearer*
  and that me rewëth sore;                   *grieves me bitterly*
Swetë lemman, think on me,
16  Ich have loved thee yore.                 *for a long time*


Swetë lemman, I preyë thee
  of lovë onë speche,                        *one word*
Whil I live in world so wyde,
20  other nil I seche.                        *another shall I not seek*
With thy love, my swetë leef,                   *dear*
  mi blis thou mightëst eche;                *happiness; increase*
A swetë cussë of thy mouth                      *kiss from your mouth*
24  mightë be my leche.                       *physician*


Swetë lemman, I preyë thee                      *beg*
  of a lovë-bene;                            *for a love-token*
If thou me lovëst, as men seyth,                *as it is said (lit. as one says)*
28  lemman, as I wene,                        *I believe*
And yif hit thy willë be,                       *wish*
  thou loke that hit be sene.                *make sure that it is apparent*
So mochel I thinke upon thee,
32  that al I waxë grene.                     *I become quite green*


Bitwene Lyncolne and Lyndëseye,                 *Lindsey*
  Nórhamptoun and Lounde,                    *Lound*
Ne wot I non so fair a may                      *I do not know; maiden*
36  as I go for y-bounde.                     *bound (i.e. in bonds of love)*

Swetë lemman, I preyë thee,
   thou lovë me a stounde.       *love me soon*
   Y wol mone my song       *I will sing* (lit. *tell*)
40 On whom that hit ys on y-long.     *of the one whom it depends on*

## 18. Bitwenë March and Avëril

Bitwenë March and Avëril,      *April*
When spray biginneth to springe,    *the twig; sprout*
The litel foul hath hirë wil,     *bird; her desire*
On hyrë lede to synge.      *in her language*
5 Ich live in love-longinge,
  For semeliest of allë thynge,   *the fairest; creatures* (lit. *things*)
  She may me blissë bringe,     *joy*
  Ich am in hire baundoun.     *power*
    An hendy hap Ichave y-hent,  *good fortune I have received*
10    Ichot from hevene it is me sent,  *I know; sent to me*
    From allë wommen my love is lent  *has gone*
    And light on Alysoun.     *and alighted*

On hew hire her is fair ynogh,    *in colour; hair*
Hire browës broune, hire eyen blake,  *brown eyebrows; black eyes*
15 With lufsom chere she on me logh,  *with a lovely expression; smiled*
With middel smal and wel y-make.   *waist; slender; well made*
But she me wol to hirë take    *unless; will; to herself*
  For to ben hire owen make,    *to be; companion*
  Longe to live Ichulle forsake   *I will refuse*
20 And feyë falle adoun.      *doomed* (to death)
    An hendy, etc.

Nightës when I wende and wake –   *at night; toss and lie awake*
Forthy myn wongës waxen won –   *for which cause my cheeks grow pale*
Lady, al for thinë sake,
25 Longinge is y-lent me on.     *yearning has come upon me*
In world nis non so wyter mon    *no man so wise*
That al hire bounté tellë con,   *excellence; can give account of*

Hire swyre is whitter then the swon,          *her neck is whiter than the swan*
And fairest may in toune.                      *and (she is the); maiden alive*
30      An hendy, etc.

Ich am for wowyng al forwake,         *loving; worn out (for lack of sleep)*
Wery so water in wore,                       *weary; a troubled pool*
Lest any revë me my make                    *rob me of my mistress*
Ichave y-yernëd yore.                         *yearned for so long*
35   Beter is tholen whilë sore            *suffer for a time grievously*
Then mournen evermore.                       *than mourn*
Geynest under gore,                 *kindest in the world* (lit. *in clothing*)
Herknë to my roun.                                    *song*
An hendy, etc.

## 19. In May it mirieth when it dawës

In May it mirieth when it dawës,                  *it is pleasant; dawns*
In dounës with thise deerës plawës,   *on hillsides; with these frolicking animals*
    And leef is light on lynde;                    *leaf; (lime) tree*
Blosmës breden on the bowës,                      *flourish; boughs*
5   Al thise wyldë wyghtës wowës,          *these wild creatures make love*
    So wel Ich underfynde.                         *as I well perceive*
I not non so frely flour          *I do not know any; so excellent; flower*
As ladies that ben bright in bour,         *who are radiant in (their) bower*
    With love who mighte hem bynde.              *whoever; them; fetter*
10   So worly wommen are by west,      *such splendid women there are in the west*
    One of hem Ich herie best,             *I praise above all* (lit. *best*)
    From Irlond into Ynde.                                *to India*

Wommen were the bestë thing                         *would be*
That shoop oure heighë hevenë kyng   *which* (obj.); *created; king of heaven*
15      If felë falsë nere;                 *if many (men) were not false*
They ben too rad upon here red   *they (women) are too hasty in their decision*
To love ther me hem lastës bed      *to love where they are tempted to sin*
    When they shulle fongë fere.                  *take a companion*
Lite in londë are to leve,           *few (men) anywhere are to be believed*
20   Though me hem trewë trouthë yeve,   *they (women) are given a true pledge*
    For trecherye to yere;                    *(men are) too ready to deceive*

When trechour hath his trouthe y-plight,                              *
Byswike he hath that swetë wyght            betrayed; that sweet creature
    Though he hire othës swere.                 to her; oaths; should swear


25  Wommen war thee wyth the swyke          guard; against the dissembler
That fair and frely is to fyke,      pleasant and comely; in flattery (lit. to flatter)
    His fare is o to founde.               his conduct is always to be tested
So wide in world is herë won,               so ubiquitous; their dwelling
In ech a toune untrewe is on,               in every town; false; one
30      From Leycëstrë to Lounde.                 Leicester to Lound
Of trouthë nis the trechour noght     fidelity means nothing to the deceiver
But he have his will y-wroght               other than having had his way
    At stevenyng embë stounde.               at a tryst from time to time
Ah, faire ladies, be on war,                    be on (your) guard
35  Too latë comëth the yeynchar                    the turning back
    When love you hath y-bounde.


Wommen ben so fair on hewe                         in appearance
Ne trowe I none that nerë trewe     I do not believe any would not have been true
If trechour hem ne taughte;               if a dissembler; them; had not taught
40  Ah, fairë thingës, frely bore,                  fair creatures, nobly born
When me you woweth, be war bifore   when you are wooed, be aware beforehand
    Which is worldës aughte.                  what (this) world's danger is like
Al to late is lend ayein                      all too late it is to turn back
When the lady lith byleyn                        lies deflowered
45      And liveth by that she laughte.              with what she has got
Ah, woldë lylie-ler in lyn                   would the lily-white one in linen
Y-herë lefly lorës myn,                      listen willingly to my advice
    With selthe we weren saughte.             with joy we would be reconciled


                                    * when the deceiver has plighted his troth


## 20. Lenten ys come with love to toune

Lenten ys come with love to toune,          spring has come; to the world
With blosmës and with briddës roune           blossoms; birds' song
    That al this blissë bringëth.

Dayëseyës in this dalës,                     *daisies in these dales*
5  Notës swete of nyghtëgalës,
   Ech fowel hire song singëth.
The threstelcok him thretëth oo,             *the song thrush chides continuously*
Away is herë wynter wo                       *gone; their winter sorrow*
   When wodërovë springëth                   *the woodruff*
10 This foulës singen ferly fele,            *these birds; wonderfully many*
   And wlyten on here wynnë wele,            *warble in their wealth of joys*
      That al the wodë ringëth.

The rosë raylëth hirë rode,                  *presents her rosy hue*
The levës on the lightë wode                 *leaves in the bright wood*
15    Waxen al with wille.                    *grow*
The monë mandëth hirë ble,                   *moon sends forth her radiance*
The lilie lufsom is to se,                   *lovely*
   The fenyl and the fille.                  *fennel; chervil*
Wowen thisë wildë drakës,                    *make love; these wanton drakes*
20 Milës mirien herë makës                   *animals gladden their mates*
   As strem ther strikëth stille.            *as the stream; flows softly*
Mody menëth, so don mo,                      *the sorrowful man laments; do more*
Ichot Ich am one of tho                      *I know; of them*
   For love that likëth ille.                *because of love which causes distress*

25 The monë mandëth hirë lyght,              *sends forth*
So doth the semly sonnë bryght               *fair sun*
   When briddës singen breme;                *gloriously*
Dewës donken on the dounës,                  *the dew is moist* (lit. pl.); *downs*
Derës with here dernë rounës                 *animals with their secret cries*
30    Domës for to deme;                     *(their) wishes to express*
Wormës wowen under cloude,                   *worms make love under ground*
Wommen waxen wonder proude,                  *amazingly haughty*
   So wel it wol hem seme;                   *it becomes them (ironic!)*
If me shal wantë wille of on,                *if I must do without; the favour of one*
35 This wynnë wele I wil forgon              *wealth of joys; forgo*
   And wight in wode be fleme.               *and straight away; be a fugitive*

## 21. As I me rode this endrë dai

Nou springeth the spray,   *sprouts the twig*
Al for love Ich am so syk   *I am so sick*
That slepen I ne may.

As I me rode this endrë dai   *went riding the other day*
5   On mi playinge,   *for my pleasure*
Seigh I where a litel may   *saw; maiden*
Bigan to singe:
'The clot him clinge!   *clod (i.e. earth); to him; cling*
Wo is him in love-longinge   *woeful is anyone who*
10   Shal liven ay.'   *must live for ever*
  Nou springeth, etc.

Sone Ich herde that merye note,   *as soon as*
Thider I drogh;   *thither I drew*
I found hire in an herber swot,   *her; arbour; sweet*
15   Under a bogh,   *bough*
With joie ynogh.   *joyously (lit. with joy enough)*
Sone I asked: 'Thou merye mai,   *straight away I asked*
Why singestou ay?'   *do you sing; always*
  Nou springeth, etc.

20   Than answerde that maiden swote   *sweet*
Mid wordës fewe:   *with*
'Mi lemmán me hath bihote   *my lover has made me a pledge*
Of lovë trewe:
He changeth anewe.   *again*
25   If I mai, it shal him rewe,   *he will regret it*
By this day.'
  Nou springeth, etc.

## 22. In a fryth as I gan farë fremëde

| | |
|---|---:|
| In a fryth as I | *wood* |
| gan farë fremëde, | *walked as a stranger* |
| I founde a wel fair | *very fair* |
| fengë to fere; | *prize for a companion* |
| She glystnëde as gold | *shone* |
| when hit glemëde, | *gleams* (lit. *gleamed*) |
| Nas ner gome | *never was anyone* |
| so gladly on gere. | *so radiant in clothing* (i.e. *alive*) |
| 5  I wolde wyte in world | *I wished to know* |
| who hire kenëde, | *had given birth to her* |
| This byrdë bright, | *maiden* |
| if hire wil were; | *if she were willing* (*to tell me*) |
| She me bad go my gatës | *bade me go away* (lit. *my ways*) |
| lest hire gremëde; | *lest she should get angry* |
| Ne keptë she | *she did not wish* |
| non henyng here. | *any dishonourable proposal; to hear* |

| | |
|---|---:|
| 'Y-here thou me nou, | *listen to me* |
| hendest in helde, | *most comely in grace* |
| 10  N'ave I thee none | *I do not bring* (lit. *have*) *any* |
| harmës to hethe. | *troubles to mock* (*you*) |
| Caste I wol thee | *I will free you* |
| from carës and kelde, | *from sorrows and cold* |
| Comely I wol | *beautifully I will* |
| thee nou clethe.' | *clothe* |

| | |
|---|---:|
| 'Clothës y have | |
| on for to caste, | *to put on* |
| Such as I may | |
| werë with wynne; | *wear with pleasure* |
| 15  Better is werë | *to wear* |
| thinnë bute laste, | *threadbare* (*robes*) *without taint* |
| Then sydë robës, | *than ample* |
| and synke into synne. | |
| Have ye your wyl | *if you have your way* |
| ye waxen unwraste, | *you will become fickle* |

Afterward
    your thonk be thynne;          *gratitude will be slight*
Better is make
    forewardës faste,             *pledges; firm*
20 Then afterward
    to mene and mynne.'         *moan and regret*

'Of mynning ne mintë      *of regretting do not think*
    thou namore;             *any more*
Of menskë thou were      *of honour you would be*
    worthe by my myght;    *worth all I could offer*
I take on honde            *I undertake*
    to holde, that I hore,   *to abide, until I grow grey*
Of al that I                  *by*
    thee have byhight.        *promised*
25 Why is thee loth   *why are you loath (lit. is it loath to you)*
    to leven on my lore     *to trust in my advice*
Lengere then my love     *(any) longer than*
    were on thee lyght?    *had settled on you*
Another myghtë
    yerne thee so yore   *entreat you (ever) so long*
That nolde thee noght     *who would not*
    redë so ryght.'       *advise (you) so well*

'Such reed me myghtë      *advice I might*
    spaklichë rewe        *soon regret*
30 When al my ro           *peace*
    were me atraght;     *was taken from me*
Sone thou woldëst
    fecchen anewe         *seek afresh*
And take another      *another (lover)*
    withinne nynë naght.    *nine nights*
Thenne might I
    hungren on hewe,    *starve in (my) family*
In ech an hird        *in every household*
    ben hatëd and forhaght,  *be hated and despised*

35 And ben y-cayrëd                                          *separated*
    from alle that I knewe,                    *had known*
And bedë cleven                              *and (be) bidden to cling*
    ther I hade claght.'              *where I had clung* (i.e. *embraced*)

'. . . . . . . . . . . . . . . . . . . '                        [Stanza missing]

'Better is taken
    a comeliche in clothe                *a well-attired person*
In armës to kepen                                              *hold*
    to kisse and to clyppe,                   *embrace*
Then a wrecche                                    *than that a wretch*
    I weddëd so wrothe,        *I should marry; so ill-tempered*
40 Though he me slowe,                           *should beat me*
    ne myght I him aslyppe.                    *escape*
The bestë red                                               *advice*
    that I can to us bothe,              *I know for us both*
That thou me take                       *(is) that you should take me*
    and I thee toward hyppe;         *and I should jump at you*
Though I swore
    by trouthe and othe,                 *pledge; oath*
That God hath shapëd                           *what; decreed*
    may non atlyppe.                      *may no one escape*

45 With shaping ne may                 *by shape-shifting (it) may not*
    hit me ashunchë;                *be evaded* (lit. *one evade it*)
Nas I never                                             *I was never*
    wycchë ne wyle;                 *a witch nor a sorceress*
Ich am a maide,
    that me ofthunchëth;                      *vexes me*
Leef me werë                                    *dear to me would be*
    gomë but gyle.'                  *a man without guile*

## 23. As I stod on a day

As I stod on a day                              *one day*
    me self under a tre:              *by myself*
I met in a morweninge                           *morning*
    a may in a medë,                  *maiden; meadow*
A semlier to min sight                          *lovelier*
    saw I ner non;                    *never any* (lit. *none*)
Of a blak burnet                                *of a dark fine brown cloth*
    al was hir wedë,                  *attire*
5 Purfilëd with pellour                          *trimmed with fur*
    doun to the ton;                  *down; toes*
A red hod on hir heved,                         *hood; head*
    shragëd al of shredës,            *edged; with strips (of cloth)*
With a riche riban,                             *precious ribbon*
    gold-begon.                       *embroidered with gold*
That bird rad on hire boke                      *read upon her book*
    evere as she yedë,                *walked*
Was non with hir                                *no one with her*
    but hir selve al on;              *only herself alone*
10 With a cri
    gan she me se;                    *see*
She wold awrenchen awey                         *would have run away*
    but for I was so ne.              *except that; near*


I sayd to that semly                            *fair one*
    that Christ should hir savë
For the fairest may
    that I ever met.
'Sir, God yeve thee grace                       *give*
    god happës to havë,               *good fortune*
15 And the lyinges of love,'                     *joys*
    thus she me gret.                 *greeted*
That I might become hir man                     *her*
    I began to cravë;
For nothing in hird                             *in public*
    fonden wolde I let.               *to be tried; allow*

She bar me fast on hond         *she speedily accused me*
   that I began to ravë,
And bad me fond ferther         *try elsewhere*
   a fol for to fet;         *fool; find*
20  'Wher gospellëth         *what is the message of*
   al thy speche?         *(pious) talk*
Thou findëst hir noght here         *her not here*
   the sot that thou seche.'         *idiot; seek*

For me thoughtë so fair         *because it seemed to me so attractive*
   hir will wold I tastë,         *her resolve; wished; to test*
And I freynëd hir of love –         *asked her for love*
   therat she lowe.         *laughed*
'A, sire,' she sayd,
   'hurt thou for non hastë;         *tax yourself not for any haste*
25  If it be your wille,         *by your leave*
   ye an sayd ynowe;         *you have said enough*
It is no mister         *there is no point*
   your word for to wastë.         *in wasting your words*
Ther most a bolder byrd         *finer*
   billen on the bow;         *sing; bough*
I wende be your semblant         *would imagine; demeanour*
   she chese you for chastë.         *she might choose you as chaste*
It is non ned         *there is no need*
   to make it so tow.         *to be so pressing*
30  Why rewen ye         *why do you regret*
   what I redë?         *advise*
Wend fort there ye wenen         *move on to where you may expect*
   better for to spedë.'         *better to succeed*

## 24. My deth I love, my lyf Ich hatë

My deth I love, my lyf Ich hatë,
   for a lady shene,         *radiant*
She is bright so dayës light,         *as*
4   that is on me wel sene;         *indeed evident*
Al I falwe so doth the lef         *I fade as does the leaf*

in somer when hit is grene,
If my thoght helpëth me noght,
8     to whom shal I me mene?                    *complain*

Sorwe and syke and drery mod                   *sighing; sad mood*
     bynden me so faste,
That I wene to walkë wod                        *expect to go mad*
12    if hit me lengere laste;                  *longer*
My sorwe, my care, al with a word
     she myghte awey caste;
What helpëth thee, my swete lemman,            *what help is it to you*
16    my lyf thus for to gaste?                 *ruin*

'Do wey, thou clerk, thou art a fol,           *be off; fool*
     with thee bidde I noght chyde;            *wish; argue*
Shalt thou never lyve that day
20    my love that thou shalt byde.            *experience*
If thou in my boure art takë,                  *caught*
     shame thee may bityde;                    *harm; befall*
Thee is better on fotë gon                      *on foot to go*
24    then wycked hors to ryde.'               *than*

'Weylawei, why seist thou so?                   *alas, why do you say so*
     thou rewe on me, thy man;                 *have pity*
Thou art ever in my thoght
28    in londë wher Ich am.                    *wherever*
If I deyë for thi love,                         *die*
     hit is thee michel sham;                  *to you great dishonour*
Thou lete me lyve and be thy leef,             *let; love (lit. dear one)*
32    and thou my swete lemman.'               *lover*

'Be stille thou fol, I calle thee right,       *be quiet you fool*
     canst thou never blinne?                  *can you never leave off*
Thou art waytëd day and nyght                  *watched out for*
36    with fader and al my kynne.              *by father; relations*
Be thou in mi bour y-take                       *if you are; caught*
     lete they for no synne,                   *they will (not) refrain for any sin*
Me to holde and thee to slen –                 *to kill*
40    the deth so thou might wynne.'           *death; so that; meet*

'Swetë lady, thou wend thy mod,      *change your mind*
    sorwë thou wilt me kythe;    *(with) sorrow; you will acquaint me*
Ich am al so sory man      *just as sorrowful a man*
44    so Ich was whylom blythe.    *as; once happy*
In a window ther we stod    *where we stood*
    we kiste us fyfty sithe;    *fifty times*
Fair biheste maketh mony man    *a gracious promise; many a man*
48    al his sorwës mythe.'    *hide*

'Weylawey, why seist thou so?    *alas*
    my sorwe thou makëst newe.    *anew*
I lovede a clerk al par amour,    *quite passionately*
52    of love he was ful trewe.
He nas noght blythë never a day,    *he was not happy*
    but he me sonë seye;    *unless; soon; saw*
I lovede him better then my lyf,
56    what bote is hit to leye?'    *what use is it to lie*

'Whil I was a clerk in scole,    *scholar in school*
    wel moche I couthe of lore,    *I knew about learning (i.e. love!)*
Ich have tholëd for thy love    *suffered*
60    woundës felë sore,    *many; grievous*
Fer from hom and eke from men,    *far from home; also*
    under the wodë-gore;    *(deep) in the forest*
Swetë lady, thou rewe of me,    *have pity on me*
64    nou may I no more.'    *now may I (do)*

'Thou semëst wel to ben a clerk,    *you appear indeed to be*
    for thou spekëst so stille;    *quietly*
Shalt thou never for my love
68    woundës tholë grylle;    *suffer; terrible*
Fader, moder and al my kin
    ne shal me holde so stille,    *keep so subdued*
That I nam thin and thou art myn,    *that I shall not be yours and you (be) mine*
72    to don al thy wille.'    *your pleasure*

## 25. Moste I ryde by Rybbësdale

| | |
|---|---|
| Moste I ryde by Rybbësdale | *if I could; through* |
| Wildë wymmen for to wale, | *vivacious; choose* |
| And weldë which Ich wolde; | *could have whichever I desired* |
| Foundë were the fairest one | *would be* |
| 5   That ever was made of blod and bone, | *blood* |
| In bourë best with bolde. | *bower; in noble company* |
| As sonnëbem hire ble is bright, | *a sunbeam; her face is radiant* |
| In echë londe she lemëth light, | *in every; shines brightly* |
| Thurgh tale as man me tolde. | *by all accounts as I am told* |
| 10   The lylie lufsom is and long, | *lily (i.e. lady); lovely; slender* |
| With richë rose and rode among, | *splendid rose and pink intermingled* |
| A fyldor fax to folde. | *gold thread; (her) hair; to bind* |

| | |
|---|---|
| Hire hed when Ich biholde upon, | *head; gaze upon (it)* |
| The sonnëbem aboutë noon | |
| 15     Me thoughtë that I seye; | *it seemed to me that I saw* |
| Hire yen are grete and gray ynough, | *eyes; large; grey* |
| That lufsom, when she on me lough, | *that lovely one; smiled* |
| Y-bend wax eyther breye. | *arched became either eyebrow* |
| The mone wyth hirë muchel might, | *moon; its (lit. her) great power* |
| 20   Ne lenëth non such light anight, | *does not send forth any; at night* |
| (That is in hevenë heye) | *high* |
| As hirë forhed doth in day, | *her forehead does by day* |
| For whom thus muche I mournë may – | *grieve* |
| For dool to deth I dreye. | *for sorrow to the point of death I suffer* |

| | |
|---|---|
| 25   She hath browës bend on heigh, | *high-arched* |
| Whyte bitwene and noght to neigh, | *white between; close* |
| Lufsom lyf she ledëth; | *a pleasant life she leads* |
| Hire nose is set as it wel semëth – | *in seemly fashion* |
| I deye for deth that she me demëth – | *to which she condemns me* |
| 30   Hire speche as spicës spredëth; | *voice as the (aroma of) spices wafts* |
| Hire lokkës lefly are and longe, | *beautiful* |
| For sone she mighte hire mirthës monge | *readily she could; laughter; mingle* |
| With blissë when it bredëth; | *with merriment; arises (lit. spreads)* |

Hire chin is chosen, and eyther cheke *excellent*
35 Whit ynough and rode on eke *and pink withal*
  As roser when it redëth. *rose-bush; blossoms (lit. reddens)*

She hath a mery mouth to mele, *for speaking (lit. to speak)*
Wyth lefly redë lippës lele *true*
  Romauncës for to rede;
40 Hire teth are white as bone of whal, *whale-bone*
Even set and atlëd al, *evenly set; placed; all*
  As hende mowe taken hede; *gentle knights may observe*
Swannës swyre swythe wel y-sette, *a swan's neck very well set*
A spannë lengere than I mette, *a span longer; have met*
45   That frely is to fede; *excellent; and pleasing (lit. to please)*
Me were lever kepe hire come *I would rather await her coming*
Than ben Pope and ryde in Rome, *be Pope*
  Stythest upon stede. *mightiest upon a steed*

When I byholde upon hire hond, *gaze*
50 The lylie-whitë, lef in lond, *lily-white one, dear in the land*
  Best she mightë be;
Eyther arm, an elnë long, *ell*
Balóygnë mengëth al bymong, *whale-bone white mingles overall*
  As baume ys hirë ble; *(fragrant) as balm; skin*
55 Fingrës she hath fair to folde, *clasp*
Mighte Ich hirë have and holde,
  In world wel werë me. *in (this) world well would I be*
Hyre tyttës are anunder bis *breasts; under fine linen*
As applës two of Paradys,
60   Yourself ye mowen se. *may see*

Hire girdel of beten gold is al, *belt of beaten gold*
Umben hirë middel smal, *about her slender waist*
  That trikëth to the to, *hangs down to the toe*
Al with rubies on a rowe *in a row*
65 Withinnë corven, craft to knowe, *set within, skill to show*
  And emeraudës mo; *and emeralds more*
The bokle is al of whallës bon; *buckle*
There withinnë stont a ston *stands*
  That warnëth men from wo; *protects; woe*

70  The water that it wetëth in,                          *it is dipped in*
    Ywis, hit worthëth al to wyn –                        *indeed, it turns everything to wine*
        That seyen seyden so.                             *those who have seen (it) said so*

    She hath a metë middel smal,                          *neat; waist; slender*
    Body and brest wel made al,
75      As fenix withoute fere;                           *the phoenix; without equal*
    Eyther sidë soft as sylk,
    Whitter than the morwen-milk,                         *morning milk*
        With lefly lit on lere.                           *with lovely colour in (her) cheek*
    Al that Ich you nempnë noght,                         *do not mention*
80  Hit is wonder wel y-wroght,
        And ellës wonder were.                            *otherwise strange it would be*
    He myghtë seyn that Christ hym seye                   *say; had looked after him*
    That myghtë nightës neigh hyre leye:                  *who; by night; near; lie*
        Heven he haddë here.                              *heaven he would have here*


## 26. Alas, hou sholde I sing

    Alas, hou sholde I singe;                             *should*
    Y-loren is my playinge;                               *lost; delight*
    How sholde I with that oldë man
    To live and letë my lemman,                           *abandon my lover*
    Swetest of al thing?


## 27. Weping hath myn wongës wet

    Weping hath myn wongës wet                            *my cheeks*
    For wikked werk and wane of wit;                      *wicked deeds; lack of understanding*
    Unblithe I be til I ha bet                            *unhappy I shall be; have atoned for*
    Brechës broken, as bok bit,                           *offences committed, as the book requires*
5   Of ladys love, that I ha let,                         *concerning the love of ladies; abandoned*
    That lemen al with lefly lyt.                         *who shine; with beautiful hue*
    Oft in song I have hem set                            *in verse; them; put*
    That is unsemly ther hit syt;                         *unseemly where it applies (lit. sits)*

Hit syt and semëth noght   *it applies but (lit. and) is inappropriate*
10 Ther hit is seid in song;   *where*
That I have of hem wroght   *what; written (lit. wrought)*
Ywis hit is al wrong.   *indeed*

Al wrong I wroghtë for a wyf   *wrote on account of a woman (i.e. Eve)*
That made us wo in world ful wyde;   *caused*
15 She rafte us allë richesse ryf   *robbed us all (of) wealth abundant*
That durfte us noght in reynës ryde.   *needed us not; on reins; ride*
A stythie stinte hire sternë stryf   *an excellent person stopped her fierce discord*
That is in hevenë hert in hyde;   *who is in the heart of heaven in hiding*
In hirë lyght, on ledëth lyf,   *born (lit. alighted); one (i.e. Christ) lives*
20 And shon thurgh hirë semly syde.   *shone*
Thurgh hirë side he shon
As sonne doth thurgh the glas;   *glass*
Womman nas wicked non   *(there) was not; any (lit. none)*
Sithe He y-borë was.   *since; born*

25 Wycked nis non that I wot   *is none; I know*
That durste for werk hire wongës wet;   *
Alle they live from last of lot   *(free) from blame as to conduct*
And are al hende as hawk in chete.   *gracious; hall*
Forthy on molde I waxë mot   *therefore on earth I become sorry*
30 That I sawës have seid unsete;   *words; unbecoming*
My fikel flesh, my falsy blod,   *deceitful flesh*
On feld hem fele I falle to fete;   *ground (lit. field); often; at their feet*
To fet I falle hem fele,   *at their feet I fall often*
For falslek fifti-folde,   *for falsehood fifty-fold*
35 Of alle untrewe on tele   *for all (the) false (things) in slander*
With tonge as I er tolde.   *that I hitherto have said*

Though told ben tales untoun in toune –   *evil; among men*
Such tiding may tide, I nil noght teme –   †
Of bridës bryght with browës broune,   *concerning ladies*
40 Your blisse they beye, thise briddës breme.   ‡

* *who needed for (wicked) deeds wet her cheeks*
† *(that) such a thing may happen; vouch*
‡ *joy; purchase; these excellent ladies*

In rudë were roo with hem roune     *in boorish company; peace; to speak*
That hem mighte hente as him were heme.             *\**
Nys kyng, cayser, ne clerk with croune     *there is no king, emperor; tonsure*
Thise semly serve that mene may seme.     *for serving; who; less; would seem*
45     Seme him may on sonde     *it may become him on an errand*
    Thise semly serven so,     *these fair ones thus to serve*
    Both with fet and honde,
    For on us warp from wo.     *for the sake of one (who); rescued*

Nou wo in world is went away     *has gone*
50 And wele is comen as we wolde,     *joy*
Thurgh a mighty, methful mai     *gentle maiden*
That us hath cast from carës colde.     *freed*
Ever wymmen Ich herie ay     *praise always*
And ever in hyrd with hem Ich holde,     *always in public*
55 And ever at nede I nyckenay     *always when in difficulty I deny*
That I ner nemnëde that they nolde.     *I ever mentioned what they did not wish*
    I nolde and nullyt noght     *I would not and do not wish it*
    For nothing nou, a nede;     *for anything* (lit. *nothing); of necessity*
    Soth I of hem ha wroght     *truth; have written*
60     As Richard erst gan rede.     *first said*

Richard, rote of resoun right     *source* (lit. *root) of good sense*
Rekening of rym and ron,     *paragon of verse and poetry*
Of maidnës mekë thou hast might     *over maidens meek; sway*
On molde I holde thee miriest mon.     *on earth I consider you*
65 Kindë comely as a knight     *well-born*
Clerk y-kid that craftës con,     *a scholar; famous; versed in skills*
In ech an hyrd thin athel is hight,     *in every household; excellence; mentioned*
And ech an athel thin hap is on.     *every man; your destiny; is concerned with*
    Hap that hathel hath hent     *good fortune that splendid fellow has obtained*
70     With hendelec in halle;     *with courtesy in the hall*
    Selthë be him sent,     *happiness*
    In londe of ladies alle.

    *who from them might receive what suited him*

## 28. Now welcome, somer, with thy sonnë softe
by Chaucer

Now welcome, somer, with thy sonnë softe,                    *sun*
That hast thes wintrës wedrës overshake,          *these; storms; shaken off*
And driven away the longë nyghtës blake!

Saynt Valentyn, that art ful hy on-lofte,          *very highly exalted above*
5   Thus syngen smalë foulës for thy sake:
Now welcome, somer, with thy sonnë softe,
That hast thes wintrës wedrës overshake.

Wel han they causë for to gladen ofte,          *greatly have they cause; rejoice*
Sith ech of hem recovered hath hys make,          *since each; found again; mate*
10   Ful blissful mowe they syngë when they wake:          *may*
Now welcome, somer, with thy sonnë softe,
That hast thes wintrës wedrës overshake,
And driven away the longë nyghtës blake!

## 29. *To Rosëmounde* by Chaucer

Madame, ye ben of al beauté shryne                    *the shrine*
As fer as cerclëd is the mapamounde,          *circumscribed; map of the world*
For as the cristal glorious ye shyne,
And lyke ruby ben your chekës rounde.
5   Therwith ye ben so mery and so jocounde,                    *cheerful*
That at a revel whan I see you daunce,          *at a festive occasion*
It is an oynëment unto my wounde,                    *an ointment for*
Thogh ye to me ne do no daliaunce.                    *offer no encouragement*

For thogh I wepe of terës ful a tyne,          *weep; tears; a barrel*
10   Yet may that wo myn hertë nat confounde;                    *not overcome*
Your semy voys that ye so smal out twyne   *light voice; so ethereally spin out*
Makëth my thoght in joy and blys habounde.          *in joy and bliss to abound*

So curtaysly I go wyth lovë bounde       *in courtly manner*
That to myself I sey in my penaunce,       *say in my suffering*
15 'Suffysëth me to love you, Rosëmounde,       *it is sufficient for me*
Thogh ye to me ne do no daliaunce.'

Nas never pyk walwëd in galauntyne,    *a pike steeped in galantine* (a sauce)
As I in love am walwëd and y-wounde,       *am steeped*
For whych ful ofte I of myself devyne       *concerning myself suppose*
20 That I am trewë Tristam the secounde.       *Tristan*
My love may not refreydë nor affounde,       *grow cold; grow numb*
I brenne ay in an amorous plesaunce.       *burn ever; delight*
Do what you lyst, I wyl your thral be founde,       *you please; slave*
Thogh ye to me ne do no daliaunce.

## 30. *Womanly Noblesse* by Chaucer

So hath myn hertë caught in remembraunce
Yowre beauté hoole and stidefast governaunce,       *
Yowre vertues al and yowrë hie noblesse,       *exalted honour*
That yow to serve is sette al my plesaunce.       *set; delight*
5 So wel me liketh youre womanly contenaunce,    *pleases me; appearance*
Youre fresshë fetures and youre comlynesse,
That whiles I live myn hert to his maystresse       *while; as its mistress*
Yow hath ful chose in trewe perseveraunce    *utterly chosen; constancy*
Never to chaunge, for no maner distresse.

10 And sith I shal do you this observaunce,       *homage*
Al my life withouten displesaunce       *displeasure*
Yow for to serve with al my besynesse,       *diligence*
Taketh me, lady, in your obeisaunce,       *under your authority*
And have me somwhat in your souvenaunce.       *remembrance*
15 My woful hertë suffrëth grete duresse,       *great hardship*
And loke how humblëly with al symplesse       *simplicity*
My wil I conforme to youre ordynaunce,       *command*
As yow best list, my peynes for to redresse.    *it best pleases you; to alleviate*

\* *your complete beauty; behaviour*

Considryng eke how I hange in balaunce                    *also*
20  In yowre servicë, suche, loo, is my chaunce,           *fortune*
Abidyng grace, whan that yowre gentilnesse               *graciousness*
Of my grete woo list do allegëaunce,          *is pleased to make alleviation*
And with youre pité me som wise avaunce         *in some way to favour*
In ful rebatyng of myn hevynesse;                    *abatement; sadness*
25  And thynketh by resoun that wommanly noblesse      *it seems reasonable*
Shuld nat desire for to do the outrance               *cause harm*
Ther as she fyndëth non unbuxumnesse.               *no disobedience*

*Lenvoye*

Auctor of norture, lady of plesaunce,       *originator of good manners; delight*
Soveraigne of beautée, floure of wommanhede,
30  Take ye non hede unto myn ignoraunce,
But this receyvëth of your goodlihede,
Thynkyng that I have caught in remembraunce,
Your beauté hole, your stidefast governaunce.          *your complete beauty*

## 31. *Canticus Troili* by Chaucer                    *Troilus's song*

If no love is, O God, what fele I so?                         *feel*
And if love is, what thing and which is he?
If love be good, from whennës cometh my woo?
If it be wikke, a wonder thinkëth me,                *wicked; it seems to me*
5   When every torment and adversité
That cometh of hym may to me savory thinke,         *seem pleasant to me*
For ay thurst I, the more that Ich it drynke.                *for always*

And if that at myn owen lust I brenne,            *for my own desire; burn*
From whennës cometh my waillynge and my pleynte?            *lament*
10  If harm agree me, wherto pleyne I thenne?       *is agreeable to me; complain*
I noot, ne whi unwery that I feynte.        *I know not, nor why unweary; faint*
O quikë deth, O swetë harm so queynte,            *O living death; so strange*
How may of the in me swich quantité,   *may (there be) of thee; such a quantity*
But if that I consentë that it be?                        *unless I*

15 And if that I consente, I wrongfully
   Compleyne, iwis. Thus possëd to and fro,                    *indeed; tossed*
   Al sterëlees withinne a boot am I                           *rudderless; boat*
   Amydde the see, bitwixen wyndës two,
   That in contrarie stonden evere mo.
20 Allas, what is this wondrë maladie?                         *amazing*
   For hote of cold, for cold of hote, I dye.


## 32. *Against Women Unconstant* ?by Chaucer

Madáme, that throgh your newëfangelnesse          *(you) who; desire for novelty*
Many a servaunt have put out of grace,                     *expelled from grace*
I take my leve of your unstedfastnesse,                          *inconstancy*
For wel I woot, whyle ye have lyvës space,                  *I know, while you live*
5 Ye can not love ful half yere in a place,               *half a year in one place*
To newë thing your lust is ay so kene;               *for new things; desire; keen*
In stede of blew, thus may ye were al grene.        *instead of blue; wear; green*


Right as a mirour nothing may impresse,                         *imprint upon*
But, lightly as hit cometh, so mote it pace,              *it comes; must it pass*
10 So fareth your love, your werkës bere witnesse.
Ther is noo feyth that may your herte enbrace,           *no loyalty; embrace*
But as a wedercok, that turneth his face                        *weathercock*
With every wind, ye fare, and that is sene;                     *go; evident*
In stede of blew, thus may ye were al grene.


15 Ye might be shrynëd for your brotelnesse   *enshrined (as a saint); fickleness*
Bet than Dalyda, Creseyde or Candace,                        *better; Delilah*
For ever in chaunging stant your sikernesse;              *is your constancy*
That tache may noo wyght from your herte arace.  *that blemish; eradicate*
If ye lese oon, ye can wel tweyn purchace;
20 Alle lyght for somer, ye wote wel what I mene,  *you know well what I mean*
In stede of blew, thus may ye were al grene.

## 33. *Complaynt D'Amours* ?by Chaucer

I, which that am the sorowfullest man
That in this world was ever yit living,
And leste recoverer of himselven can,    *least; a healer; knows (how to be)*
Beginne right thus my deedly compleyning    *grievous complaint*
5  On hir that may to lyf and dethe me bringe,    *about her; life and death*
Whiche hathe on me no mercy ne no reuthe    *who has; pity*
That love hir beste, but sleethe me for my treuthe.    *who; slays; fidelity*

Can I nought doon ne seye that may yow lyke?    *do; what may please you*
Ne, certës, now; allas, allas the whyle!    *not, indeed, now; the time*
10  Youre plesaunce is to laughen whan I sike,    *pleasure; sigh*
And thus ye me from al my blisse exile.
Ye have me caste in thilkë spitous yle    *that inhospitable island*
Ther never man on lyvë might asterte;    *escape*
This have I, for I love yow beste, swete herte.    *because*

15  Soothe is, that wel I woot, by lyklynesse,    *I know, in all probability*
If it were a thinge possible to doo
For to acounte your beautée and goodnesse,    *to estimate*
I have noo wonder though yee do me woo,    *you cause me grief*
Sithe I, th'unworthiest that may ride or goo,    *since; walk*
20  Durste ever thinken in so hie a place:    *dared ever aspire to; high*
What wonder is, though ye do me noo grace?

Allas, thus is my lyf brought to an ende;
My dethe, I see, is my conclusioun.    *my death*
I may wele sing, 'In sorye tyme I spende
25  My lyf.' That song may have confusioun!    *cursed be that song*
For mercy, pitée, and deep affeccioun,
I sey for me, for al my deedly chere,    *for my part; despite; appearance*
Allë this dide, in that, me love yowe dere.    *these made, in this case; dearly*

And in this wyse and in dispayr I lyve    *manner*
30  In love; nay, nay, but in dispayre I dye!
Bút shal I thus yowe my dethe foryive,    *death forgive*
That causëles dothe me this sorow drye?    *makes me suffer this sorrow*

Yee, certës, I! For she of my folye            *oh yes, indeed; with my folly*
Hath nought to done although she do me sterve;   *nothing; cause me to die*
35  Hit is nought with hir wille that I hir serve.      *it is not with her agreement*

Than sithe I am of my sorowe the cause             *since*
And sithe that I have this withoute hir rede,        *encouragement*
Than may I seyne right shortly in a clause,           *may I say*
It is no blame unto hir womanhede
40  Though suche a wrecche as I be for hir dede.        *such; dead*
Yét alwey two thingës doone me dye,                 *cause me to die*
That is to seyne, hir beauté and myn eye;              *eye*

So, algatës, she is the verray roote           *nevertheless; root (i.e. cause)*
Of my diseese and of my dethe also,               *of my suffering*
45  For with oon worde she mightë be my boote,           *cure*
If that she vouchëd sauf for to do so.               *agreed*
Bút than is hir gladnesse at my woo?        *is she glad (lit. is her gladness)*
It is hir wonë plesaunce for to take             *her custom pleasure*
To seen hir servaunts dyen for hir sake!

50  But certës, thanne is al my wondering –        *then; my cause for amazement*
Sithen she is the fayrest crëature,
As to my doom, that ever was livinge,                *in my judgement*
The benignest and beste eke that Nature            *kindest and best also*
Hath wrought or shal, whil that the world may dure –     *last*
55  Why that she leftë Pité so behinde?        *why (was it); she (Nature); Pity*
It was, ywis, a greet defaute in Kinde.        *certainly; failing on Nature's part*

Yit is al this noo lak to hir, pardée,               *fault in her, to be sure*
But God or Nature hem soore wolde I blame.         *them bitterly would I*
For though she shewe no pité unto me,
60  Sithen that she dothe othere men the same,
I n'oughtë to despise my ladyes game;            *ought not; conduct*
It is pleye to laughe when that men sykëth,      *amusement; when one sighs*
And I assente al that hir liste and lykëth!    *assent to; delights and pleases her*

Yet wolde I, as I dare, with sorwful herte

65  Biseche unto your mekly womanhede                          *gentle*
    That I now dorste my sharpë sorwës smerte        *I now dare; painful*
    Shewë by word, and ye wolde onës rede    *express; and (that); once read*
    The compleynte of me, which I full sore drede        *my complaint; fear*
    That I have seid here, through myn unkonnynge,                      *

70  In any word unto yowre displesinge.                      *your displeasure*


    Loothest of anything that ever was loth                  *most hateful*
    Were me, as wisly God my soulë save,            *it would be to me; surely*
    To seyne a thing through which ye might be wroth;          *say; angry*
    And, to that day that I be leyde in grave,          *until; when I am laid*

75  A trewer servaunt shulle ye never have;
    And, though that I have pleyned unto yow here,    *have made my complaint*
    Forgyveth it me, myn owne lady dere.


    Ever have I been, and shal, how-so I wende,            *however I fare*
    Outher to lyve or dye, youre humble trewe.          *either; true (servant)*

80  Yee ben to me my gynnyng and myn ende,    *you are to me my beginning*
    Sonne of the sterre so bright and clere of hewe;                      †
    Alwey in oon to love yow freshly newe,                      *continually*
    By God and by my trouthe, is myn entente;                    *intention*
    To live or dye, I wolle it never repente!                          *I will*


85  This compleynte on Seint Valentinës day,
    Whan every foughel cheesen shall his make,          *bird; choose; mate*
    To hir, whos I am hole and shall alwey,              *wholly; shall always be*
    This woofull songe and this compleynte I make,
    That never yit wolde me to mercy take;

90  And yit wolle I evermore her serve                          *will I*
    And love hir best, although she do me sterve.            *cause me to die*


                      * *lest I have spoken; lack of skill*
                      † *sun (i.e. source of light); star; in appearance*

## 34. *Merciles Beauté?* by Chaucer

### I

Your yën two wol slee me sodenly;                    *eyes; will slay; suddenly*
I may the beautée of hem not sustene,                          *bear*
So woundëth hit thourghout my hertë kene.                      *keenly*

And but your word wol helen hastily                  *unless; heal*
5  My hertës wounde whilë that hit is grene,          *fresh* (lit. *green*)
     Your yën two wol slee me sodenly;
     I may the beautée of hem not sustene.

Upon my trouthe I sey you feithfully
That ye ben of my lyf and deeth the quene,          *queen* (i.e. *ruler*)
10 For with my deeth the trouthë shal be sene.                *evident*
     Your yën two wol slee me sodenly;
     I may the beautée of hem not sustene,
     So woundëth it thourghout my hertë kene.

### II

So hath your beautée fro your hertë chacëd                  *expelled*
15 Pitée, that me n'availëth not to pleyne,      *is of no avail to me to lament*
For Daunger halt your mercy in his cheyne.       *Disdain; holds; chain*

Giltlës my deeth thus han ye me purchacëd;     *brought about* (lit. *bought*)
I sey you sooth, me nedëth not to feyne;      *tell you the truth; dissemble*
     So hath your beautée fro your hertë chacëd
20    Pitée, that me n'availëth not to pleyne.

Allas, that Nature hath in you compassëd                  *encompassed*
So greet beautée, that no man may atteyne                    *attain*
To mercy though he stervë for the peyne.               *die; anguish*
     So hath your beautée fro your hertë chacëd
25    Pitée, that me n'availëth not to pleyne,
     For Daunger halt your mercy in his cheyne.

## III

Sin I fro Love escapëd am so fat,
I never thenk to ben in his prison lene;                    *lean*
Sin I am free, I counte him not a bene.                    *bean*

30  Hé may answere and seye this and that;
I do no fors, I speke right as I mene.        *I pay no heed; mean*
   Sin I fro Love escapëd am so fat,
   I never thenk to ben in his prison lene.

Love hath my name y-strike out of his sclat,        *struck; slate*
35  And he is strike out of my bokës clene                    *clean*
For evermo;  ther is non other mene.            *way (lit. means)*
   Sin I fro Love escapëd am so fat,
   I never thenk to ben in his prison lene;
   Sin I am free, I counte him not a bene.


## 35. *A Balade of Complaynte?* by Chaucer

Compleyne ne koude ne might myn hertë never,            *lament*
My peynës halve, ne what torment I have,               *half (of)*
Thoughe that I shoulde in youre presence ben ever,
Myn hertës lady, as wisly He me save       *as truly may He save me*
5  That Bountée made, and Beautée list to grave              *
In youre persone, and bade hem bothe in-fere          *together*
Ever t'awayte, and ay be wher ye were.                  *remain*

As wisly He gye alle my joyës here              *as truly may He guide*
As I am youres, and to yow sadde and trewe,      *constant and true*
10  And ye my lyf and cause of my gode chere,       *you (are); spirits*
And dethe also, when ye my peynës newe,       *death; pains renew*
My worldës joye, whom I wol serve and sewe,             *follow*
Myn heven hole, and al my suffisaunce       *complete; fulfilment*
Whom for to serve is sette al my plesaunce.       *set all my delight*

* *goodness;  was pleased to engrave*

15  Beseching yow in my moste humble wyse                    *manner*
    T'akcepte in worthe this lytel porë dyte,      *to accept favourably; poor poem*
    And for my trouthe my servyce not despyse,                  *fidelity*
    Myn observaunce eke have not in despyte,           *homage also; scorn*
    Ne yit to longe to suffren in this plyte;          *(have me) to suffer; plight*
20  I yow beseche, myn hertës lady, here,                *hear (my complaint)*
    Sith I yow serve, and so wil yere by yere.           *since; year by year*

PART II: *Penitential and Moral Lyrics*

## 36. Miri it is while sumer i-last

| | |
|---|---|
| Miri it is while sumer i-last | *lasts* |
| With foulës song; | *birds' song* |
| Oc now neghëth windës blast | *but; approaches (draws nigh)* |
| And weder strong. | *weather; rough* |
| 5 Ei, ei, what this night is long, | *how* |
| And Ich with wel michel wrong | *for very great wrong doing* |
| Sorwe and murne and fast. | *sorrow; grieve* |


## 37. Lavedy seynte Marie

| | |
|---|---|
| Lavedy seynte Marie | *Lady saint Mary* |
| moder and medë, | *mother and maiden* |
| Thou wissë me nouthë | *guide me now* |
| for Ich am eredë; | *perplexed* |
| Unnit lif | *a worthless life* |
| to longe Ich ledë, | *too long I have led* |
| 4 Whanne Ich me bethinkë | *take stock of myself* |
| well sore Ich me adredë. | *I am afraid* |

| | |
|---|---|
| Ich am y-bounde sorë | *grievously* |
| mid well felë sennë, | *by very many sins* |
| Mid smale and mid gretë, | *great* |
| mid well felë kennë; | *very many kinds* |
| Day and night Ich fondë | *I seek* |
| to wendende hennë, | *to go hence* |
| 8 Weldë God an heven | *let God in heaven decide* |
| to whichërë wennë. | *to what bliss* |

Slep me hath my lif forstolë                     *sleep* (i.e. *of sin*);  *stolen away*
   right half other morë;                       *or more*
Away! too late Ich was y-war                      *aware*
   now hit me rewëth sorë.                   *now I regret it bitterly*
In slepe ne wende Ich endë nought                *I did not intend to end*
   though Ich slepe evermorë;                *shall sleep*
12 Whoso liveth that wakerer be                    *more vigilant*
   think of minë lorë.                       *advice*

All too longë slepth the man
   that never nile awakë;
Whose understant well his endeday                 *final day*
   well yernë he mot spakë                   *eagerly he must hasten*
To dondë sinne away from him                      *put*
   and fele almessë makë;                    *many acts of charity;  perform*
16 If him ne shal, whanne he forthwent             *goes hence*
   his breechgirdel quakë!                   *let his loins quake with fear*

Slep me hath my lif forstolë
   er Ich me biseyë,                         *myself;  paid heed to*
That Ich well ayittë now                          *perceive*
   by sightë of min eyë;
My brownë heer is whit bicome                     *hair;  white*
   Ich not for which leyë,                   *I do not know;  hair lotion*
20 And my toughë rode y-turned                      *my robust complexion*
   all into othrë deyë.                      *another hue*

Biforn Ich have y-sinnëd                          *previously*
   mid worke and with wordë,                 *deed*
While in mine bedde                               *sometimes*
   and while attë bordë;                     *at the table*
Oftë win y-drunke                                 *wine*
   and selde of the fordë;                   *seldom from the ford* (i.e. *stream*)
24 Muche Ich have y-spendëd
   too lite Ich have on hordë.               *in store*

Hord that Ich telle
    is almessë-dedë,            *charitable deeds*
Yive the hungrie mete           *food*
    and the nakede y-wedë,       *clothing*
Redë the redlesse       *guide the ignorant person*
    that is withoutë redë,       *advice*
28 Luvë God almighty
    and of Him havë dredë.

Inne mete and inne drinke
    Ich have y-ben overdedë,       *excessive*
And inne well-sittinge shoon,    *well-becoming shoes*
    in proudere y-wedë;    *more sumptuous clothing*
Whanne Ich y-herde of Godë spekë
    ne hedd Ich what men sedë;  *I heeded not what was said*
32 Whan Ich hereof rekenë shal,    *take account*
    well sorë me may drede.

Beforn Ich have y-sinnëd
    mid workës and mid mouthë,    *in deeds*
And mid allë minë limës    *with all my limbs*
    sith Ich sinnen couthë,  *since I knew how to sin*
And well felë sinnës y-don  *very many sins committed*
    that me athinkëth nouthë,    *I repent of now*
36 And so me hadde aforn y-don
    if hit me Crist y-youthë.    *had granted*

Moder ful of milce,    *grace*
    I biddë, my mod wendë;  *pray; heart; change*
Lete me stewë my flesh    *curb*
    and mine foo shendë;  *foe (i.e. the Devil); defeat*
Edmodnesse lovë    *humility*
    to mine livës endë;
40 Love to Gode and to man
    Ich biddë that thou me sendë.

Lavedy seynte Marie
    understand now sinnë minë,
Ber min erende well          *bear my petition*
    to derë sonë thinë,        *dear son*
Whos flesh and blod y-halwëd is    *consecrated*
    of bred, of water, of winë,    *from*
44  That us y-shelde He ever       *may protect*
    fram allë hellë-pinë.        *pains of hell*


## 38. Worldës blis ne last no throwë

Worldës blis ne last no throwë,    *Worldly bliss; lasts; time*
It went and wit awey anon;    *comes; passes away soon*
The longer that Ich it y-knowë    *I know it*
The lesse Ich findë pris theron,    *less; value in it*
5  For al it is y-meynd mid carë,    *mingled with*
With sorwës and with evel farë,    *misfortune*
And attë lastë poure and barë    *in the end poor and naked*
It lat man whan it ginth agon.    *leaves; when it departs*
Al the blis this her and tharë    *bliss which is*
10  Biloukth at ëndë wep and mon.    *amounts in the end to weeping and sorrow*

Al the blis of thisë livë    *joy*
Thou shált, man, enden innë wep –    *bring to an end in weeping*
Of hous and hom, of child and wivë.    *(the joy) of*
Sely man, nim therof kep!    *wretched man, take heed of this*
15  Thou shalt al bileven herë    *leave*
Th'aghtë wherof lord thou werë;    *the wealth of which*
Whan thou list upon the berë    *you lie; bier*
And slepst that swithë drery slep,    *very dreadful sleep*
Ne shaltou have with thee no ferë    *companion*
20  But thinë werkës on a hep.    *other than your deeds in a heap*

Al shal gon that man here owëth,    *pass away; possesses*
And al it shal bicome to naught;    *come to nought*
The man that here no god ne sowëth,
Whan othrë repe he worth bi-caught.    *others reap he will be ensnared*

25 Think, man, forthy, whilstou hast mightë,     *

That thou thy giltë here arightë,     *atone for*

And werchë god by day and nightë,     *do good*

Er than thou be of livë laught.     *before; from life; snatched*

Thóu nost whannë Crist our drightë     *you know not when; lord*

30 Thee askëth that He hath bitaught.     *will ask you; has entrusted*


Man, why setstou thought and hertë     *why do you set*

On worldës blis that nought ne last?     *does not last*

Why tholstou that thee s'ofte y-smertë     *do you allow; should so often anguish*

For thing that is unstedëfast?     *transitory*

35 Thou lickëst hony of thorn iwis,     *you lick honey from a thorn indeed*

That setst thy love o worldës blis     *who set; on*

For ful of bitternes it is.

Ful sorë thou might ben agast,     *afraid*

That here despendëst aught amis,     *who here spend wealth wrongly*

40 To ben therthurgh into hellë cast.     *to be thereby*


Think, man, wherto Crist thee wroughtë     *to what end; created*

And do way pride and filth and mood.     *put away pride and lust and anger*

Think how derë He thee boughtë     *dearly*

O rodë mid his swetë blood.     *on the cross with His*

45 Himself he yaf for thee in pris     *gave; in ransom*

To beyn thee blis yif thou be wis.     *buy; if you are wise*

Bithink thee than and up aris     *then; rise up*

Of sinne, and agin werchen good     *from sin, and begin to do good*

Ther whyls timë to werchen is,     *while; to act*

50 For siker ellës thou art wood.     *for certainly otherwise you are mad*


Al day thou might understondë     *every day*

And thy miróur bifor thee sen,

What is to don and what to wondë     *to be done and what to be avoided*

And what to holde and what to flen;     *to be held to and what to be fled*

55 For ál day thou seest with thine eyë

How thís world went and how men deyë.     *goes; die*


\* *therefore; while you have the ability*

That witë wel, that thou shalt dreyë     *know this well, that you will suffer*
As othrë dide and eek ded ben;     *as others have done and also die*
Ne helpëth nought ther non to leyë,     *it helps no one then (lit. there) to lie*
60   Ne may no man be deth ayen.     *nor can any man withstand death*

Shal no good ben unforyoldë     *unrequited*
Ne no qued ne worth unbought;     *any evil; be unpaid for*
Whan thou list, man, under moldë     *when you lie; the earth*
Thou shalt have as thou hast wrought.     *earned*
65   Bithink wel forthy, Ich thee redë,     *consider well therefore; advise*
And clensë thee of ech misdedë,     *cleanse; misdeed*
That Crist thee helpe at thinë nedë,     *so that; may help you in your need*
That so derë hath thee bought,
And to hevenë blissë ledë     *lead (you)*
70   That ever last and faillëth nought.     *lasts*

## 39. Man mai longe him livës wenë

Man mai longe him livës wenë     *for himself; life; expect*
Ac oftë him lyëth the wrench,     *deceives; the quirk of fate*
Fair weder ofte him went to renë     *turns to rain*
And ferlichë makëth his blench.     *suddenly plays its trick*
5   Therfore, man, thou thee bi-thench,     *take heed*
Al shal falëwi thy grenë.     *fade; youthful vigour (lit. greenness)*
Weilaway, nis king ne quenë     *alas; queen*
That ne shal drinke of Dethës drench.     *of Death's draught*
Man, er thou fallë of thy bench,     *off*
10      Thy sinne aquench.     *overcome*

Ne mai strong, ne stark, ne kenë     *may not prevail; nor mighty; bold*
Ayein Dethës wither-clench;     *against Death's hostile grip*
Young and old and bright and shenë,     *beautiful*
Al he rivëth an his strength.     *tears to pieces in his strength*
15   Fox and ferlich is the wrench,     *crafty and sudden is his (lit. the) twist*
Ne may no man thertoyenë,     *no man may prevail thereagainst*
Weylaway, threting ne benë,     *alas, neither threats nor entreaty*

Medë, list, ne lechës drench.　　　　　*bribery, cunning, nor a doctor's potion*
Man, let sinne and lustës stench,　　　*abandon sin and the stench of lust*
20　　Wel do, wel thench!　　　　　　　　　*think*

Do bi Salomonës redë,　　　　　　　　*act according to Solomon's advice*
Man, and so thou shalt wel do;
Do als he thee taught, and hedë　　　*if you do as; take heed*
What thin ending thee bringth to,
25　Né shaltow never misdo –
Sorë thou might thee adredë!　　　　　*sorely you may fear for yourself*
Weylaway, swich wenth wel ledë　　　*Alas, such a man as fully expects to lead*
Long lyf, and blissë underfo,　　　　*a long life and to enjoy happiness*
There Deth lutëth in his sho　　　　　*Death lurks there in his shoe*
30　　To him fordo.　　　　　　　　　　　*to destroy him*

Mán, why niltow thee bi-knowë,　　　*acknowledge your nature*
Mán, why niltow thee bi-se;　　　　　*consider yourself*
Of foulë filth thou art i-sowë,　　　*begotten*
Wormës metë thou shalt be.　　　　　　*food*
35　Her nastou blissë dayës three,　　　*here you do not have; for three days*
Al thy lif thou drist in wowë;　　　　*you endure in sorrow*
Weylaway, Deth thee shal throwë　　　*alas*
Doun ther thou wenst hyë ste;　　　　*when (lit. where) you expect; high; to rise*
In wo shal thi welë te,　　　　　　　　*into misery will your prosperity pass*
40　　In wop thy gle.　　　　　　　　　　*to weeping your merriment*

World and welë thee biswikëth　　　　*prosperity; deceive*
Iwis, they ben thine ifo;　　　　　　*assuredly; foes*
If thy world mid wele thee slikëth　*with prosperity; flatters you*
That is for to do thee wo.　　　　　　*cause you harm*
45　Therfore let lust overgo,　　　　　　*pass*
Man, and eft it wel thee likëth.　　*and afterwards it will please you well*
Weylaway, hou sore him wikëth　　　　*how sorely it serves him*
That in one stundë other two　　　　　*who in an hour*
Werkth him pinë evermo:　　　　　　　　*earns himself; torment*
50　　Ne do, Man, swo!　　　　　　　　　　*Man, do not so*

## 40. On hire is al mi lif y-long

On hire is al mi lif y-long        *her (Mary); dependent*
  Of whom Ich willë singë,
And herien Him ther-among,    *(will) praise Him (Christ) in the process*
  That gan us botë bringë      *who brought us deliverance*
5 Of hellë-pinë that is strong,   *from the torment of hell; severe*
And brought us blisse that is so long     *enduring*
  Al thourugh hire childingë.   *all through her child-bearing*
Ich biddë hirë in mi song,        *I beseech her*
  He yeve us god endingë,   *that He (Christ) may grant us*
10     Though we do wrong.

Al this world hit shal ago        *pass away*
  With sorwë and with sorë,     *sorrow; grief*
And al this blisse Ich mot forgo,     *I must forgo*
  N'ofthinke it me so sorë.   *though it displease me bitterly*
15 This world nis but ourë fo,     *is nothing but our foe*
Therfor Ich wille hennë go       *hence*
  And lernen Goddës lorë;     *teaching*
This worldës blis nis worth a slo.     *sloe*
  Ich biddë, God, thin orë,   *I pray, O God, for Thy mercy*
20     Now and evermo.       *evermore*

To longe Ich havë sot i-be    *too long; a fool; been*
  Ful sore I me adredë;    *right sorely I am afraid*
Y-loved Ich havë gamen and gle    *sport and pleasure*
  And aughte and fayrë wedë.   *and wealth and fair garments*
25 Al that nis nought, ful wel Ich se,     *nothing*
Therfore Ich willë sinnës fle
  And letë my sothedë.     *abandon my folly*
Ich biddë hirë me bi-se,   *I beseech her to look upon me*
  And helpë me and redë,     *advise*
30     That is so fre.     *who is so gracious*

Thou art hele and lif and light    *salvation and life*
  And helpëst al mankennë;     *mankind*
Thou us hast ful wel i-dight,    *for us; provided*
  Thou yaf us wele and wennë.   *you have given us well-being and joy*

35   Thou broughtëst day, and Evë night,
     She brought wo, thou broughtëst right,                      *evil*
        Thou álmesse, and she sennë.                          *charity; sin*
     Thou do us merci, lady bright,                   *have mercy upon us, lady*
        Whan we shullen hennë,                         *when we shall go hence*
40      Ful wel thou might.                                        *can*

     Agilt Ich havë, weilawy,                              *offended; alas*
        Sinful Ich am and wrechë,                                *wretched*
     Thou do me merci, lavëdi,                         *have mercy upon me, lady*
        Er deth me hennë fecchë.               *before death; hence; fetches*
45   Yif me thi love, Ich am redi,                                *give me*
     Let me live and amendi,                                      *reform*
        That fendës me ne drecchë.           *so that fiends; may not afflict*
     For minë sinne Ich am sori,                                 *my sins*
        Of thís lif Ich ne recchë.                      *for; I do not care*
50      Lady, merci!

## 41. Ech day me comëth tydinges thre

     Ech day me comëth tydinges thre,
     For wel swithë sore ben he:                   *very very grievous are they*
     The on is that Ich shal hennë,                    *one; I must go hence*
     That other that Ich not whennë,                    *I do not know when*
5    The thriddë is my mestë carë,                         *greatest grief*
     That Ich not whider Ich shal farë.                    *where I must go*

## 42. Whan I thenkë thingës thre

     Whan I thenkë thingës thre,                                 *ponder*
     Ne may I never blithë be:                                   *happy*
     That on is that I shal away,                 *must depart* (lit. (*go*) *away*)
     That other is I not which day,                           *do not know*
5    The thriddë is my mostë carë,                        *my greatest sorrow*
     I ne wot whider I shal farë.                          *where I must go*

## 43. If man him bithoughtë

| | |
|---|---:|
| If man him bithoughtë | *bethought himself* |
| Inderliche and oftë | *earnestly* |
| How harde is the forë | *journey* |
| Fro beddë te florë, | *from bed to floor* |
| 5 How rewful is the flittë | *lamentable is the passing* |
| Fro florë te pittë, | *to grave* |
| Fro pittë te pinë | *to torment* |
| That never shal finë, | *end* |
| I wenë non sinnë | *think no sins* |
| 10 Should his hertë winnë. | |

## 44. Whan mine eyen mistëth

| | |
|---|---:|
| Whan mine eyen mistëth, | *eyes grow dim* |
| And mine erës sissëth, | *ears buzz* |
| And my nosë coldëth, | |
| And my tongë foldëth, | *speech fails* |
| 5 And my rodë slakëth, | *complexion fades* |
| And mine lippës blakëth, | *grow pale* |
| And my mouth grennëth, | *gapes* |
| And my spotel rennëth, | *spittle runs* |
| And min her risëth, | *hair stands on end* |
| 10 And min hertë grisëth, | *heart quakes* |
| And mine hondës biviëth, | *hands tremble* |
| And mine fet stiviëth – | *feet stiffen* |
| Al to latë, al to latë, | *all too late* |
| Whan the bere is at the gatë. | *bier* |
| 15 Than I shal flit | *must pass* |
| From beddë to florë, | |
| From florë to herë, | *haircloth shroud* |
| From herë to berë, | *bier* |
| From berë to pit, | *grave* |
| 20 And the pit fordit. | *will close* |
| Than lith myn hous uppë myn nesë: | *my house will lie; upon my nose* |
| Of al this world ne give Ich a pesë! | *for; I shall not give a pea* |

## 45. Whan the turuf is thy tour

Whan the turuf is thy tour,      *turf; tower*
And thy pit is thy bour,      *grave; bower*
Thy fel and thy whitë throtë     *skin; throat*
Shullen wormës to notë.   *shall (be) good for worms*
5 What helpëth thee thennë
Al the worildë wennë?      *world's delights*

## 46. Whan Ich thenche on domës-dai

Whan Ich thenche on domës-dai  *when I think on the Day of Judgement*
 ful sore I me adredë;     *I am afraid*
Ther shal after his werek  *according to his deeds (lit. work)*
4 ech man fongen medë.    *receive (his) reward*
Ich havë Christ agilt      *sinned against*
 with thoughtës and with dedë,    *deeds*
Loverd helend, Goddës sone,    *Lord saviour*
8 what shal me to redë?   *what will be my remedy*

That fyr shal comen in this world   *fire; upon this world*
 on one sonnë-nightë,    *on a Saturday night*
Forbrennen al this middelerd  *to burn up all this earth*
12 so Crist hit wolë dightë,  *as Christ; will command*
Bothen water and the lond,     *both*
 the flourës that ben brightë;
Y-heriëd be oure loverd,    *praised; lord*
16 muchel is his mightë.      *great*

Four englës in the dai-red   *four angels at dawn*
 blowen herë bemë,    *will blow their trumpets*
Thennë comëth Ihesus Crist     *when*
20 His domës for to demë,  *judgements; pronounce*
Ne helpëth hit nought thenne
 to wepen ne to remë    *weep; cry out*
To him that litel hath y-don  *for the person who*
24 that Cristë was y-quemë.  *which to Christ; pleasing*

From that Adam was y-wrought *from the time that; created*
    that comëth domësday, *until*
Mony of the richë men
28    that werden fou and gray, *who wore lavish furs*
And riden upon stedës *rode; steeds*
    and upon palëfray; *fine mounts*
They shulle attë domë *at the Judgement*
32    singen weilaway. *alas*

Ne shul they ther nought fighten
    with sheldës ne with sperë,
With helmë ne with brinie *helmet; coat of mail*
36    ne with non other gerë; *any other weapons*
Ne shal ther noman other
    with wisë wordës werë; *attack*
But here almësdedës *only their charitable deeds*
40    her erindës shal berë. *petitions; advance*

They shulle y-sen that maiden
    that Ihesu Crist ofkendë, *gave birth to*
Bitwenen hirë armës
44    Swetëliche him wendë; *enfold*
The whilë that we mighten, *while we could have*
    to litel we hire sendë, *did we send to her*
That makëdë the worsë, *that the Devil caused*
48    so fule he us ablendë. *so completely; blinded*

They shulle y-sen the king
    that al the worild wroughtë, *created*
And upon the swetë rodë *sweet cross*
52    with strongë pinës boughtë; *severe torments; redeemed*
Adam and his ofspring,
    in hellë He hem soughtë –
To bidden thennë milcë *to beg then for mercy*
56    to late they ben bithoughtë. *too late they had considered*

Ther shullen the rightwisë ben                   *righteous*
    on Goddës rightë hondë,
And the sinfullë shullen
60    atelichë stondë                         *in dread*
With herë sinne y-writen,              *sins recorded*
    that is muchel shondë;          *great shame*
Alle they shullen hem y-sen     *all those they shall see*
64    that livëden in londë.          *who lived on earth*

To the rightwisë He spekëth         *will speak*
    wordës swithë swetë:         *very sweet*
'Comëth her mine frends,
68    your sinnës forto letë;         *to abandon*
In mine fader house             *father's*
    you is y-makëd setë,    *for you is made a lasting home*
Ther you shullen englës
72    swetëlichë gretë.'

To the sinfulë He spekëth
    so ye mowe y-herë:          *as you may hear*
'Goëth ye awariedë,            *damned*
76    with fendës y-ferë,    *with devils as companions*
Into brenning fyr;           *burning fire*
    of blissë ye ben skerë    *of bliss you will be bereft*
Forthy that ye your sinnës      *because*
80    out of this worild berë.'       *take*

Biddë we our lavëdy,      *let us pray to our lady*
    swetest alrë thingë,       *of all things*
That she bere our erendë     *take our petition*
84    to the hevenë kingë,
That for his holy name     *that for the sake of*
    and for hir erendingë,     *her advocacy*
That He ourë soulës
88    to hevenrichë bringë.   *to the kingdom of heaven; may bring*

## 47. Where ben they before us were

*Ubi sunt qui ante nos fuerunt*

Where ben they before us were,         *where are they who*
Houndës ladde and hawkës bere,      *who led hounds; carried hawks*
   And haddë feld and wode;           *possessed*
The richë ladies in here bour           *their bower*
5 That werëd gold in here tressour      *wore; head-dress*
   With herë brightë rode?           *complexion*

They ete and dronke and made hem glad,   *made (themselves) merry*
Here life was all with gamen y-lad,   *in pleasure; spent (lit. led)*
   Men knelëd hem biforen;
10 They beren hem wel swithë hye   *bore themselves very proudly*
And in a twinkling of an eye
   Here soulës were forloren.           *lost*

Where is that laughing and that song,
That trailing and that proudë gong,   *those trailing robes; bearing*
15    The hawkës and the houndës;
All that joye is went away,          *has passed away*
That wele is come to weilaway,   *that happiness; lamentation*
   To many hardë stoundës.          *dire times*

Here paradis they nomen here,       *their paradise; took*
20 And now they lye in helle y-fere,       *together*
   The fire hit brennëth ever;          *burns*
Long is 'ay!' and long is 'o!',   *ah!/ever; oh!/always*
Long is 'wy!' and long is 'wo!',      *alas!; woe!*
   Thennës ne come they never.          *thence*

25 Dreye here, man, then if thou wilt       *endure*
A litel pine that man thee bit,   *suffering; that is required of you*
   Withdraw thine esës ofte;         *forgo; comforts*
Though thy pinë be unrede,      *pain; should be severe*
And thou thinkë on thy mede      *if you think; reward*
30    It shall thee thinken softe.         *seem mild*

If that fend, that foulë thing,                                      *fiend*
Thurgh wikkë roun, thurgh fals egging,      *evil counsel; deceitful incitement*
   Nether thee hath y-cast;                              *down*
Up and be good champioun,
35 Stond, ne fal namore adoun
   For a litel blast.

Thou take the rodë to thy staf                              *cross as*
And think on Him that theron yaf                            *gave*
   His lyf that was so leef;                          *so dear*
40 He it yaf for thee, thou yelde hit Him,      *He gave it; repay Him for it*
Agains His fo that staf thou nim                          *against; take*
   And wreke Him of that theef.               *avenge; on that thief*

Of right bileve thou nim that sheld                  *take that shield*
The whilës thou art in that feld,                          *while*
45    Thin hand to strengthen fonde;          *try*
And keep thy fo with stavës ord,          *hold; at the point of the staff*
And do that traitour seye that word,                      *make*
   Biget that mery londe.                    *achieve; happy*

Therin is day withouten night,
50 Withouten endë, strength and might,
   And wreche of everich fo;                    *vengeance on*
With God himselven echë lif                              *eternal*
And pes and rest withouten strif,                          *peace*
   Welë withouten wo.                            *bliss*

55 Maiden, moder, hevenë quen,
Thou might, and canst, and owest to ben                    *ought*
   Our sheld again the fende;          *against the fiend (Devil)*
Help us sinnë for to fleen                                  *flee*
That we mote Thy son y-seen                              *may; see*
60    In joye withouten ende.

## 48. No more ne will I wiked be

No more ne will I wiked be,                          *wicked*
Forsake Ich wille this worldës fe,                   *wealth*
This wildës wedes, this folës gle,       *wanton's dress; fool's delight*
    Ich wol be mild of chere;                 *gentle in manner*
5  Of knottës shal mi girdil be,                      *girdle*
    Become Ich wil frere.                             *a friar*

Frer menour I wil me make,                           *minor*
And lecherie I wil asake;                             *renounce*
To Ihesu Crist Ich wil me take
10    And serve in holi chirche,
    Al in mi hourës for to wake,              *(canonical) hours*
    Goddës wille to wirche.                           *do*

Wirche I wil this workës gode,           *do; these good works*
For Him that bought us in the rode;     *redeemed us on the cross*
15  From his sidë ran the blode,
    So dere He gan us bye;               *dearly; redeemed us*
For sothe, I tel him mor than wode       *truly, I consider him; mad*
    That hauntëth licherie.        *who habitually practises lechery*

## 49. Lord, thou clepedest me

Lord, thou clepedest me,                        *you called me*
An Ich noght n'answerde thee        *and I answered you nothing*
But wordës slow and slepy:                            *sleepy*
'Thole yet, thole a litel.'                     *forbear yet*
5  But 'yet' and 'yet' was endelis,                   *endless*
And 'thole a litel' a long wey is.

## 50. Lullay, lullay, litel child, why wepëstou so sore?

Lullay, lullay, litel child,
   why wepëstou so sore?         *bitterly*
Nedës mostou wepe,         *of necessity must you weep*
4   it was i-yarkëd thee of yore     *ordained for you long ago*
Ever to live in sorwe,
   and sigh and mournen evermore,     *sighing*
As thine eldren did er this,        *forebears*
8   whil they alivës wore.       *alive; were*
Lullay, lullay, litel child,
   child, lullay, lullow,
Into uncouth world        *an unknown world*
12   y-commen so artou.       *are you*

Bestës and tho foulës,       *beasts and the birds*
   the fishës in the flode,       *sea*
And ech shaft alivës,       *creature alive*
16   makëd of bone and blode,      *made*
Whan they commen to the world,
   they don hemself some gode,     *some good*
Allë but the wrecchë brol      *the wretched brat*
20   that is of Adames blode.
Lullay, lullay, litel child,
   to care artou bemette;     *to sorrow you are destined*
Thou nost nought this worldës wild   *you know not (that); power*
24   before thee is y-sette.      *is set against you*

Child, if it betidëth       *happens*
   that thou shalt thrive and thee,    *prosper*
Think thou were y-fostrëd     *remember that*
28   up thy moder kne;     *upon your mother's knee*
Ever have mind in thyn hert     *remember*
   of tho thingës thre,      *those*
Whan thou commëst, what thou art,   *whence*
32   and what shall come of thee.    *become*

Lullay, lullay, litel child,
  child, lullay, lullay,
With sorwe thou com into this world,         *came*
36  with sorwe shalt wend away.         *pass away*

Ne tristou to this world,         *do not trust in*
  it is thy fullë fo;         *declared enemy*
The rich he makëth pouer,         *he* (i.e. *the world*); *poor*
40  the pouer rich also;         *likewise*
It turnëth wo to wel,         *misery to prosperity*
  and ekë wel to wo;         *also*
Ne trist no man to this world         *let no one trust in*
44  while it turnëth so.         *changes*
Lullay, lullay, litel child,
  thy fote is in the whele;         *wheel*
Thou nost whider it wil turne,         *which way*
48  to wo other to wele.         *to misery or to prosperity*

Child, thou art a pilgrim
  in wikkednes y-born;
Thou wandrëst in this falsë world,
52  thou lokë thee beforn!         *look ahead*
Deth shall comen with a blast
  out of a well dim horn,         *very sombre horn*
Adames kin adoun to cast –
56  himself hath don beforn.         (*Adam*) *himself he* (*Death*) *did*
Lullay, lullay, litel child,
  so wo thee worth Adam,         *thus your misfortune; became*
In the lond of paradis,
60  through wikkednes of Satan.

Child, thou n'art a pilgrim
  but an uncouth gest;         *alien guest*
Thy dawës ben y-told,         *days are numbered*
64  thy journeys ben y-cest;         *travels are charted*
Whider thou shalt wend,         *wherever; go*
  by north other by est,
Deth thee shall betide         *befall*
68  with bitter bale in brest.         *pain*

Lullay, lullay, litel child,
   this wo Adam thee wrought, *wrought for you*
Whan he of the appil ete
72   and Eve it him betought. *gave*


## 51. Hye Loverd, thou here my bone

Hye Loverd, thou here my bone, *Lord on high; hear my prayer*
That madëst middelerd and mone, *earth and moon*
   And man of mirthës minne; *and man to think of pleasures*
Trusty king and trewe in trone, *true on your throne*
5 That thou be with me saughtë sone, *reconciled with me soon*
   Assoilë me of sinne. *absolve*
Fol Ich was in folies fayn, *a fool I was delighting in folly*
In lithere lastës I am lain, *in base vices I have lain*
   That maketh myn thriftës thinne; *which makes my lot unhappy*
10 That semly sawes was wont to sain, *one who fair words; wont to utter*
Nou is marrëd al my main, *destroyed; all my authority*
   Away is al my winne. *gone; joy*

Unwin hath myn wongës wet, *unhappiness; cheeks*
   That maketh me routhës rede. *(words of) remorse; utter*
15 Ne seme I nought ther I am set, *I do not suit (the place) where*
Ther me callëth me 'fillë-flet' *I am called 'floor-filler'*
   And 'waynoun waytëglede'. *'good-for-nothing fire-gazer'*

While Ich was in willë wolde, *formerly; in pleasure's mastery*
In ech a bour among the bolde *in every chamber in noble company*
20   Y-holdë with the heste; *counted among the best (lit. highest)*
Nou I may no finger folde, *clasp*
Litel loved and less y-tolde, *less esteemed*
   Y-levëd with the leste. *abandoned with the least*
A goute me hath y-greythëd so *gout; afflicted*
25 And other evelës many mo, 
   I not what bote is beste; *I do not know what remedy*
Ther er was wildë as the ro *where formerly I was wild; roe*
Nou I swyke, I may nought so, *I leave off*
   Hit sewëth me so faste. *it (? gout or old age) pursues*

30  Faste I was on horsë heigh                          *high*
        And werëde worly wede;                *wore splendid garments*
    Nou is faren al my feigh –                      *gone; my wealth*
    With sorwe that Ich hit ever seigh! –                  *saw*
        A staf is nou my stede.                           *steed*

35  When I se stedës stithe in stalle,              *steeds strong*
    And I go halting in the halle,                      *limping*
        Min hertë ginneth to helde.                        *sink*
    That er was wildest inwith walle    *one who formerly was; within walls*
    Nou is under fote y-falle
40      And may no finger felde.                          *clasp*
    Ther Ich was lef Ich am ful loth,    *where; loved; utterly hated*
    And alle my godës me at-goth,                        *desert*
        Myn gamenës waxen gelde;            *pleasures become barren*
    That fairë founde me mete and cloth,  *those who kindly; food and clothes*
45  They wrie away as they were wroth –            *turn; angry*
        Such is evel and elde.                *misfortune and old age*

    Evel and elde and other wo
        Folewen me so faste
    Me thinketh myn hertë breketh atwo;          *will break in two*
50  Swetë God, whi shal hit so,
        How may hit lenger laste?                       *longer*

    Whil mi lif was lither and les:           *formerly; base and false*
    Glotonie mi gleman wes,                            *minstrel*
        With me he wonde a while;                        *dwelt*
55  Pridë was my pleië-fere,                        *playfellow*
    Lecherie my lavendere,                    *laundress (i.e. mistress)*
        With hem is Gabbe and Gile;           *Falsehood and Deceit*
    Coveytise myn keyës bere,                *Covetousness; carried*
    Nithe and Ondë were mi fere,        *Envy and Anger; companions*
60      That ben folkës fyle;                              *vile*
    Lyer was mi latymer,                      *Liar; interpreter*
    Slouthe and Slep mi beddëfere,      *Sloth and Sleep my bedfellows*
        That wenen me umbe while.          *which attract me at times*

Umbë while I am to wene,                                    *at times I am attracted*
65    When I shal mirthës meten;                          *merriment; encounter*
Mannë mest I am to mene,                                   *most of men; to be pitied*
Lord, that hast me lif to lene,                            *life (i.e. eternal life); to grant*
    Such lotës lef me leten.                              *such evils let me abandon*

Such lif Ich havë lad ful yore,                           *led for a long time*
70    Merci, Lord, I nil namore,                          *will not (do so) any more*
    Bowen Ich wille to bete;                             *submit; to atone*
Siker hit sewëth me ful sore,                             *truly they (lit. it) pursue me*
Gabbës les and lither lore –                              *lies untrue and wicked ideas*
    Sinnës ben unsete;                                   *sins (which) are evil*
75    Godës heste ne held I nought,                       *command; I did not keep*
But ever ayein His wille I wrought –                      *against His will I acted*
    Man lerëth me to lete;                               *I am urged to desist*
Such sorwë hath myn sides thurghsought                    *pierced*
That al I welwe away to nought                            *I wither*
80    When I shal mirthës mete.                           *merriment; encounter*

To metë mirthes Ich was wel fous                          *very eager*
    And comely man to calle;                             *and a fine fellow; to be called*
I say by other as by ous:                                 *I speak of others just as of ourselves*
As is hirman halt in hous,                                *servant; haughty; house*
85    As heved hunte in halle.                            *head hound*

Dredful Deth, why wilt thou dare?                         *tarry*
Bring this body that is so bare                           *take*
    And in bale y-bounde;                                *torment*
Careful man y-cast in care                                *a sorrowful man*
90    I falwe as flour y-let forthfare,                   *I wither; left to die*
    I have myn dethës wounde;                            
Mirthës helpen me no more,                                
Help me, Lord, er than Ich hore,                          *before I turn grey*
    And stint my lyf a stounde;                          *and end my life soon*
95    That yokkyn hath y-yernëd yore,                     *the man who; passion; yearned for*
Nou hit sorwëth him ful sore,                             *it pains him most grievously*
    And bringëth him to grounde.

To grounde it havëth him y-brought:
    What is the bestë bote                      *remedy*
100 But herie him that hath us bought,           *praise*
Our Lord that al this world hath wrought,
    And fallen him to fote?                  *at his feet*

Nou Ich am to dethe y-dight,         *for death; prepared*
    Y-don is al my dede.                  *finished*
105 God us lenë of His light                  *grant*
That we of seyntës haven sight           *saints*
    And hevënë to mede!     *heaven as (our) reward*

## 52. Wynter wakenëth al my care

Wynter wakenëth al my care,        *awakens; sorrow*
Nou this levës waxen bare;    *now that these leaves become*
Ofte I sike and mournë sare     *sigh and grieve bitterly*
    When hít comth in my thought
5 Of this worldës joie hou hit goth al to nought.    *how it goes*

Nou hit is and nou hit nys,            *is not*
Also hit ner nere ywys.    *as if it had never been indeed*
That many man saith, soth hit is,      *what; true*
    Al góth but Godës wille,       *passes; except*
10 Allë we shul deyë though us likë ylle.    *shall die; it displeases us*

Al that grein me gravëth grene,    *grain which is planted unripe*
Nou hit falwëth al bydene;          *withers utterly*
Iesu, help that hit be sene,    *this (lit. it) may be made clear*
    And shildë us from helle,         *shield*
15 For I not whider I shal ne hou longe her dwelle.   *know not where I*
                                         *shall (go)*

## 53. Nou shrinkëth rose and lylie-flour

Nou shrinkëth rose and lylie-flour, *withers*
That whilom bar that swete savour *once bore; scent*
   In somer, that swetë tide; *time*
Nis no queene so stark ne stour, *mighty or strong*
5  Ne no lady so bright in bour *so radiant in bower*
   That deth ne shal by-glyde. *whom; steal upon*
Whoso wol flesh-lust forgon *physical desire; forgo*
   And hevenë blis abyde, *wait for*
On Iesu be his thought anon *constantly*
10   That thirlëd was his side. *whose side was pierced*

From Petrësbourgh in o morning, *one morning*
As I me wende o my playing, *took my way for pleasure*
   On my folie I thoughte; *folly*
Menen I gan my mourning *I addressed my lament*
15 To hir that bar the hevenë kyng, *who bore*
   Of merci hire bysoughte. *for mercy; begged*
Lady, preye thi son for ous *entreat*
   That us derë boughte, *dearly*
And shild us from the lothë hous *shield; hateful*
20   That to the fend is wroughte. *for the Devil; made*

Myn herte of dedës was fordred *at deeds; terrified*
Of synne that I have my flesh fed *of sin; fed to*
   And folwëd al my time,
That I not whider I shal be led *so that I do not know whither; taken*
25 When I ligge on dethës bed, *lie*
   In joie or into pyne. *to bliss or to torment*
On o lady myn hopë is, *on one lady*
   Moder and virgyne,
We shulen into hevenë blis *shall go to*
30   Thurgh hirë medicine.

Betere is hire medycyn
Than any mede or any wyn;                              *mead; wine*
    Hire herbës smellen swete;
From Catenas to Dyvelyn.                          *Caithness to Dublin*
35  Nis ther no lechë so fyn                      *physician so excellent*
    Our sorëwës to bete.                                   *to cure*
Man that felëth any sor               *the person who feels any remorse*
    And his folie wol lete                            *will abandon*
Withouten gold other tresór                        *or treasure*
40      He may be sound and sete.                  *healed and at ease*

Of penaunce is hir plaster al,                          *remedy*
And ever serven hire I shal
    Nou and al my lyve;
Nou is fre that er was thral                *who formerly was enslaved*
45  Al thurgh that lady gent and smal,          *graceful and slender*
    Heried be joiës fyve!                       *praised be the five joys*
Wherso any man sek is                       *wherever anyone; sick*
    Thider hyë blyve;           *thither (to her) let him hasten quickly*
Thurgh hirë ben y-brought to blis
50      Bo mayden and wyve.                                *both*

For He that dide his bodi on tre            *in order that He who placed*
Of ourë sinnës have pité,                   *on our sins may have pity*
    That weldëth hevenë bourës,             *(He) who rules heaven's bowers*
Womman with thi jolitée,                                 *gaiety*
55      Thou thénch on Godës shourës;              *think; sufferings*
Though thóu be whyt and bright on ble,   *fair (lit. white) and radiant of face*
    Falwen shule thy flourës.                              *fade*
Iésu, have mercí of me,
    That al this world honourës.                    *whom (i.e. Jesus)*
        Amen.

## 54. Middelerd for man was mad

| | |
|---|---|
| Middelerd for man was mad, | *earth; made* |
| Unmighty are his mostë mede; | *puny; its greatest rewards* |
| This edi hath on hond y-had | *this blessed one; brought it about* |
| That heven hem is heist to hede. | *for them is most important to heed* |
| 5 Ich herde a blissë bedel us bad | *a herald of joy (who) bid us* |
| The drery domësday to drede, | *terrible; dread* |
| Of sinful saughting sone be sad | *of acquiescing in sin; soon to be weary* |
| That dernë don these dernë dede; | *those who secretly; hidden deeds* |
| Though they ben dernë done, | *they are* |
| 10 These wrackful workës under wede, | *wicked deeds under cover* (lit. *clothes*) |
| In soulë sutelen sone. | *(they) become manifest soon* |
| | |
| Sone is sutel as Ich you say, | *(it) is manifest* |
| This sake, although hit semë swete; | *sin; seems sweet* |
| That I telle a pourë play | *that I count a poor sport* |
| 15 That first is fair and sithe unsete: | *afterwards evil* |
| This wildë willë went away | *passionate desire passes* |
| With mone and mourning muche unmete; | *lamentation; grief; excessive* |
| That liveth on liking out of lay, | *he who lives in unlawful pleasure* |
| His hap he doth full harde on hete | *his fate; violently; call out against* |
| 20 Agains he hovëth henne; | *at the time he goes hence* |
| Alle his thrivenë thewës threte | *virtuous qualities rebuke* |
| That thinkëth nought on thenne. | *the person who; on that time* |
| | |
| Againës thenne us threten thre. | *regarding that time; three* (i.e. *foes*) |
| If they ben thriven and thowe in thede, | *thriving and prosperous among men* |
| 25 Our soulës bonë so broerli be | *destroyers as brotherly may be* |
| As bernë best that bale forbede. | *as the best of men who; harm; prevent* |
| That wil withstonden strength of theo, | *the person who; of them* |
| His rest is revëd with the rede. | *peace is robbed like the reed* |
| Fight of other ne thar he floe | *the assault; need he not flee* |
| 30 That fleshës faunyng first foryede, | *who; allure; has withstood* |
| That falsest is of five; | *most insidious; of the five* (i.e. *senses*) |
| If we leven any lede, | *believe any people* |
| Werryng is worst of wyve. | *the onslaught of women is worst* |

Wyvës willë were ded wo       *a woman's lust were deadly peril*
35 If she is wikked for to welde;       *hard to control*
That burst shal betë for hem bo,    *he who; the damage; is to remedy; both*
Shal him berwen though he hire belde.    *he must save himself; shelter*
By body and soule I say also
That some ben founden under felde    *on earth*
40 That have to fere his mostë fo;    *as a wife his worst enemy*
Of gamenës he may gon al gelde,    *pleasures; be (lit. go) utterly deprived*
   And sore ben ferde on folde,    *and (yet) be sore afraid on earth*
Lest he him to harmës held    *himself; submit*
   And happës hente unholde.    *suffer (lit. seize) a disastrous outcome*

45 Hom unholdest her is on    *home; the most disastrous; here*
Withouten helle, as Ich hit holde,    *outside; maintain*
So fele are founden mannës fon.    *so many; foes*
The first of hem biforen I tolde:    *I mentioned*
There afterward this worldës won    *world's riches*
50 With muche unwynne us woren wolde.    *much sorrow; would disturb*
Sonë ben these gamenës gon    *pleasures; gone*
That maken us so brag and bolde    *so lively*
   And bidden us ben blythe;    *merry*
An ende they casten us ful colde    *in the end; destine; without compassion*
55    In sinne and sorwë sithe.    *to sin and a time of sorrows*

In sinne and sorowe I am seint,    *am sunk*
That sewen me so selly sore;    *which pursue; exceedingly painfully*
My mirth is al with mourning meint,    *with grief mingled*
Ne may Ich mythen hit namore.    *conceal it*
60 When we ben with this world forwleynt,    *puffed up*
That we ne listnen lyvës lore,    *so that we do not listen to life's teaching*
The fend in fyght us fint so feint    *fiend; finds; so feeble*
We falle so flour when hit is frore,    *as a flower; withered*
   For folkës fader al fleme;    *because of the father of mankind; all fugitives*
65 Wo him was y-warpë yore    *destined long ago*
   That Crist nil nowight queme.    *will in no way please*

To quemë Crist we were y-core         *to please; chosen*
And kend his craftës forto knowe.         *and taught his power to know*
Leve we nought we ben forlore,         *let us not believe; ruined*
70  In lustës though we lyen lowe;         *in pleasures; lie sunk* (lit. *low*)
We shul arise our fader afore,
Though fon us fallen umbë throwe;         *foes defeat us at times*
To borwe us alle He was y-bore.         *to save us; born*
This bannyng when Him bemës blowe,         *summons; for Him; trumpets*
75     He bit us ben of hyse,         *will command us to be of His company*
And on His right hond hentë rowe         *take (our) position*
    With rightwis men to arise.         *with righteous*


## 55. Erthë tok of erthe erthë wyth wogh

Erthë tok of erthe         *earth*
    erthë wyth wogh;         *sin*
Erthe other erthë
    to the erthë drogh;         *drew*
Erthë leyde erthe         *laid*
    in erthënë throgh;         *an earthen pit*
4  Tho hevëde erthe of erthe         *had*
    erthe ynogh!         *enough*


## 56. Wrechë man, why art thou prowde

Wrechë man, why art thou prowde         *wretched man; proud*
    That art of erthë makëd?         *made*
Hider ne broughtëst thou no shroude,         *hither*
    But poure thou come and naked.         *poor you came*
5  When thy soule is faren out,         *has gone forth*
    Thy body with erthe y-rakëd,         *raked over*
That body that was ranke and loude         *haughty and bold*
    Of allë men is hatëd.

## 57. Was ther never caren so lothe

Was ther never caren so lothe        *corpse so hateful*
As man when he to pittë goth        *to the grave goes*
  And deth hath layde so lowe.        *laid (him)*
For when deth drawëth man from other,        *a man from another*
5  The sister nil not se the brother,        *see her* (lit. *the*) *brother*
  Ne fader the sone y-knowe.        *recognize his* (lit. *the*) *son*

## 58. The Lavëdi Fortunë is bothe frend and fo

The Lavëdi Fortunë        *Lady Fortune*
  is bothe frend and fo,
Of poure she makëth riche
  of richë poure also,
She turnëth wo al into wele        *misery into prosperity*
  and wele al into wo,
4  Ne tristë noman to this wele        *let no man trust to this prosperity*
  the wheel it turnëth so.        *wheel (i.e. of Fortune)*

## 59. Kynge I syt and loke aboute

[Primus:]
  Kynge I syt and loke aboute,
  Tomorwen I may ben withoute.        *may be*

Secundus:
  Wo is me, a kynge I was,
4  This worlde I loved but that I las.        *lost*

Tercius:
  Nought longë gon I was ful ryche,
  But now is riche and poure ylyche.        *alike*

Quartus:

    I shal be kyng, that men shul se,
8    When the wrechë ded shal be.                    *wretch is dead*


## 60. Whan men ben meriest at her mele

    Whan men ben meriest at her mele                    *at their meal*
    With mete and drink to make hem glade,              *food; themselves*
    With worship and with worldlich wele               *honour; worldly prosperity*
    They ben so set they conne not sade.    *so concerned they cannot have too much*
5   They have no deynté for to dele                    *no inclination to have to do*
    With thinges that ben devoutli made,               *which are works of devotion*
    They weene her honour and here hele                *imagine; their health*
    Shal ever last and never diffade.                  *fade*
    But in her hertes I wolde they hade                *I wish they considered (lit. had)*
10  Whan they gon richest on aray,                     *go about in greatest splendour*
    Hou sone that God hem may degrade,                 *may humble them*
        And sum tyme think on yesterday.               *sometimes*


    This day as leef we may be light                   *we may gladly be cheerful*
    With al the mirthes that men may vise,             *merriment; may devise*
15  To revel with this birdës bright,                  *to make merry; these ladies*
    Ech man gayest on his gyse.                        *merriest in his own manner*
    At the last hit draweth to night
    That Slep most maken his maistryse;        *when Sleep must assert his authority*
    Whan that he hath y-kid his might,                 *he (Sleep) has shown his power*
20  The Morwe he buskëth up to rise,                   *the Dawn; prepares*
    Then al drawe hem to fantasyse;                    *(they) all become an illusion*
    Wher they bicome can no man say,                   *what became of them*
    (And yif they wiste they were ful wise!)           *knew they would be very wise*
        For al is tornd to yesterday.                  *changed*


25  Whose wolde thinken upon this                      *whoever*
    Mighte fynde a good enchesoun why                  *good reason*
    To preve this world alwey, ywis,                   *to prove; always, to be sure*
    Hit nis but fantome and fairy;               *is nothing but illusion and fantasy*

This erthly joye, this worldly blis,
30  Is but a fikel fantasy,
For nou hit is and nou hit nis,                        *is not*
Ther may no man therin affy;                           *trust*
Hit chaungeth so ofte and sodenly,
Today is her, tomorwe away;                    *(it) is here, tomorrow gone*
35  A siker ground who wol him gy,          *on sure ground; will make his way*
    I rede he thinke on yesterday.           *I advise (that) he should think*

For ther nis non so strong in stour,                   *in battle*
Fro tyme that he ful waxen be,                 *from the time; full grown*
From that day forth, everich an hour,          *(who) from; every hour*
40  Of strengthe ne lest a quantité;                  *does not lose*
Ne no birde so bright in bour,                       *nor any lady*
Of thritty winter, I ensure thee,         *of thirty years (lit. winters); assure*
That she ne shal fade as a flour,
Lite and lite lese hire beauté;                   *little by little lose*
45  The soth ye may yourself y-se                     *truth; observe*
Be your eldrës, in good fay.              *from your ancestors, truth to tell*
Whan ye ben gretest in your degré,                    *reputation*
    I rede ye thinke on yesterday.                     *advise*

Nis non so fresh on fote to fare,                       *to go*
50  Ne non so fayr on fold to fynde           *on earth; to be found*
Ne shal a bere be brought ful bare –       *on a bier be borne full naked*
This wrecched world nis but a wynde;      *is nothing but a puff of wind*
Ne non so stif to stynte ne stare,        *so resolute (as) to stand or stare*
Ne non so bold berës to bynde,              *so bold as to chain up bears*
55  That he nath warnynges to be ware,           *who has not; to be wary*
For God is so curtéis and kinde.                      *so gracious*
Bihold, the lame, bedrede, the blynde                 *bedridden*
Bid you be war whil that ye may,                      *be cautious*
They make a mirour to your mynde                   *for your mind*
60      To se the shap of yesterday.                   *shape*

The lyf that any man shal lede                         *lead*
Ben certein dayës attë last;              *numbered days in the end*
Than moste our termë shortë nede,     *then must our span shorten necessarily*
Be o day come another is past.                *if one day has come*

65  Herof and we wolde take good hede,                    *if we would take good heed*
    And in our hertes acountës cast,                     *tallies; make*
    Day bi day, withouten drede,                         *without doubt*
    Toward our ende we drawe ful fast.
    Than shal our bodies in erthe be thrast,             *into the earth be thrust*
70  Our careyns couchëd under clay;                       *our corpses lodged*
    Herof we oughte ben sore agast                        *sorely aghast*
        And we wolde thinke on yesterday.                 *if we*

    Salamon saide in his poesy
    He halt wel beter with an hounde                     *has much greater preference for*
75  That is lyking and joly                              *pleasing and frisky*
    And of seknesse hol and sounde,                      *free and healthy*
    Then be a leon though he lye                         *than for a lion if*
    Cold and ded upon the grounde;
    Wherof servëth his victory
80  That was so stif in eche a stounde?                  *so valiant on every occasion*
    The mostë fool, I herde respounde,                   *I have heard it said*
    Is wiser whil he lyvë may                            *is alive*
    Than he that hadde a thousand pounde                 *he (who)*
        And was buried yesterday.

85  Socrates seith a word ful wys:                       *speaks*
    Hit were wel beter for to se
    A man that nou partëth and dys                       *departs and dies*
    Then a feste of realté.                              *a feast of royal splendour*
    The feste wol make his flesh to rise
90  And drawe his herte to vanité;
    The body that on the berë lys                        *bier lies*
    Shewëth the same that we shal be.                    *what* (lit. *the same*); *become* (lit. *be*)
    That ferful fit may no man fle                       *fearful seizure*
    Ne with no wiles win hit away,                       *put it*
95  Therfore among al jolité
        Sum tyme think on yesterday.

    But yit me merveilëth over al                        *I marvel above all*
    That God let many man croke and elde     *allows; to become bent and grow old*
    Whan might and strengthe is from 'hem fal          *(to the point) when*
100 That they may not hemself a-welde;           *so that; control themselves*

And now this beggers most principal        *these beggars; in particular*
That good ne profyt may non yelde.        *yield*
To this purpos answere I shal        *to this point*
Why God sent swich men boote and belde:        *

105 Crist that made both flour and felde        *flower and field*
Let swich men live, forsothe to say,        *allows*
Whan a yong man on hem bihelde        *(so that) when; looked*
    Sholde se the shap of yesterday.        *(he) should see*


Another skile ther is for whi        *reason*
110 That God let swich men live so longe;
For they ben treacle and remedi        *a salve*
For synful men that han do wronge;
In hem the seven dedes of merci        *works of mercy*
A man may fulfille among;
115 And so this proude men may therbi        *thus these proud; therein*
A feir mirour underfonge.        *a fair mirror; find*
For ther nis non so stif ne stronge,        *bold; valiant*
Ne no lady stout ne gay –        *stately*
Bihold what over her hed can honge,        *hangs over their heads*
120     And sum tyme think on yesterday.


I have wist sin I cuthe men        *known since I could remember*
That children han bi candel light        *have by*
Her shadewe on the wal i-sen        *their shadow; seen*
And runne therafter al the night.
125 Bisie aboutë they han ben
To cacchen hit with al her might,
And whan they cacche hit best wolde wene,        *to catch it; most expect*
Sannest hit shet out of her sight;        *immediately it shoots*
The shadewe cacchen they ne might
130 For no lynes that they couthe lay.        *snares which they could lay*
This shadewe I may likne aright        *liken exactly*
    To this world and yesterday.


* *sends such men relief and comfort*

Into this world whan we ben brought
We shul be tempt to cuvetise;                    *tempted to avarice*
135  And al thi wit shal be thurghsought            *mind; intent*
To more good then thou may suffyse.             *on more possessions; need*
Whan thou thinkest best in thi thought
On richesse for to regne and rise,              *wealth; succeed and rise*
Al thi travaile turneth to nought               *effort; nothing*
140  For sodeynly on deth thou dyse,                *you die*
Thi lyf thou hast y-lad with lyes               *spent in lies*
So this world gan thee bitray.                  *betrayed you*
Therfore I rede thou this dispyse          *I advise (that) you despise this*
And sum tyme think on yesterday.

145  Man, yif thi neighbor thee manas              *threatens*
Other to kille other to bete,                   *either . . . or; beat*
I knowe me siker in the cas                     *sure in that event*
That thou wolt drede thi neighbores threte,
And never a day thy dore to pas                 *leave*
150  Withoute siker defense and grete,            *secure*
And ben purveyed in eche a plas        *arrangements being made; place*
Of sikernes and help to gete;                   *for safety*
Thin enemy woltou not foryete                   *forget*
But ay be aferd of his affray.          *(you will) be afraid; assault*
155  Ensaumple herof I wol you trete   *an instance of this; elaborate for you*
To make you think of yesterday.

Wel thou wost withouten fayle                    *know*
That Deth hath manast thee to dye,  *threatened you with death* (lit. *to die*)
But whan that he wol thee asayle
160  That wost thou not ne never may spye.         *find out*
Yif thou wolt don be my counsayle,              *act on my advice*
With siker defence be ay redye;                 *ever ready*
For siker defence in this batayle
Is clenë lyf, parfyt and trye;        *a pure life, perfect and exemplary*
165  Put thi trust in Godes mercye,
Hit is the best at al assay,                    *in every trial*
And ever among thou thee ennie     *and again and again show distaste*
Into this world and yesterday.                  *towards*

Sum men seyn that Deth is a thef,
170  And al unwarned wol on hem stele,          *without warning will on them steal*
And I sey nay, and make a pref              *say no, and give as proof*
That Deth is stedefast, trewe and lele,                          *loyal*
And warnëth ech man of his gref,           *warns; of the (lit. his) sorrow*
That he wol o day with him dele.     *he (Death); will one day allot to him*
175  The lyf that is to you so lef,                                *so dear*
He wol you reve and eke your hele;   *take from you and also your health*
Thise poyntes may no man him repele,  *these intentions; turn him from*
He cometh so boldely to pyke his pray.            *to select his prey*
Whan men ben meriest at her mele,
180      I rede ye think on yesterday.                        *advise you*


## 61. I woldë wite of sum wys wight

I woldë wite of sum wys wight          *would like to know; wise person*
Witterly what this world were;     *truly what the nature of; might be*
Hit farëth as a foulës flight,                         *goes; bird's*
Now is hit henne, now is hit here,                         *far off*
5   Ne be we never so muche of might,          *so great in strength*
Now be we on benche, now be we on bere;                      *
And be we never so war and wight,          *vigilant and strong*
Now be we sek, now be we fere;                  *sick; healthy*
Now is on proud withouten pere,               *one proud; equal*
10  Now is the selve y-set not by;       *the same person thought nothing of*
And whos wol alle thing hertly here,    *whoever; earnestly heed (lit. hear)*
This world fareth as a fantasy.                   *an illusion*

The sonnës cours we may wel kenne,                    *perceive*
Arisëth est and goth doun west;
15  The ryvers into the see they renne,                   *sea; run*
And hit is never the more almest;       *it (the sea); hardly*
Wyndës roshen her and henne,             *hither and thither*
In snow and rain is non arest;                      *ceasing*
Whan this wol stinte, who wot, or whenne,      *stop; or by what cause*
20  But only God on groundë grest?        *(who is) on earth the greatest*

* *one moment we are; the next; on a bier*

The erthe in on is ever prest,                    *in the same (condition) is always ready*
Now bedroppëd, now al drye;                       *bedewed; dry*
But eche gome glit forth as a gest,               *each man glides away like a guest*
    This world fareth as a fantasye.

25  Kinredes come and kinredes gon                 *generations*
    As joynen generacions;                      *join*
    But alle they passen everichon               *they all pass away*
    For al her preparacions;
    Sum are foryetë clene as bon                 *forgotten clean as bone*
30  Among alle maner nacions;                      *all kinds of peoples*
    So shul men thenke us nothing on             *have no thought of us*
    That nou han th'ocupacions;                  *have the control of affairs*
    And alle these disputacions                  *disputations*
    Ideliche all us occupye,                     *in vain*
35  For Crist maketh the creacions,                *makes created things*
    And this world fareth as a fantasye.

Which is man, who wot, and what,                  *of what nature is man, who knows*
Whether that he be ought or nought?               *anything or nothing*
Of erthe and eir groweth up a gnat,               *air*
40  And so doth man whan al is sought;             *examined*
    Though man be waxen gret and fat,            *should grow*
    Man melteth away so doth a mought.           *a moth*
    Mannës might nis worth a mat                 *is not worth a mat (i.e. is worthless)*
    But noyeth himself and turneth to nought.    *
45  Who wot, save He that al hath wrought,         *created*
    Wher man bicometh whan he shal dye?          *where man goes to*
    Who knoweth bi deth ought but bi thought?    *about death anything except*
    For this world fareth as a fantasye.         *[by speculation*

By ensaumple men may se,                          *example; see*
50  A gret tre groweth out of the grounde;
    Nothing abatëd th'erthe wol be               *reduced*
    Though hit be hugë, gret and rounde.

    * *but only vexes and destroys him(self)*

Right ther will rote the selvë tre,                          *rot the same tree*
Whan elde hath made his kinde aswounde;                      *
55  Though ther were rotë suchë thre,                        *to rot three such (trees)*
The erthe wol not encrece a pounde.                          *increase*
Thus waxe and wane man, hors and hounde,                     *wax and wane*
From nought to nought thus henne we hye;                     *hence we hasten*
And her we stinten but a stounde,                            *we remain only for a moment*
60      For this world is but a fantasye.

Dyëth man, and bestës dye,
And al is on occasioun;                                      *one occurrence*
And al o deth bos bothë drye                                 *and (all) one death must both suffer*
And han on incarnacioun;                                     *have one birth*
65  Save that men ben morë slye,                             *intelligent*
Al is o comparisoun.                                         *all is alike (lit. one comparison)*
Who wot yif mannës soulë stye,                               *ascends*
And bestës soulës synken doun?
Who knowëth bestes entencioun,                               *what animals mean*
70  On her creatour how they crie,                           *their creator*
Save only God that knoweth her soun?                         *understands their utterance*
    For this world fareth as a fantasye.

Ech secte hopëth to be save,                                 *sect; saved*
Boldëly bi her bileve;                                       *confidently according to their belief*
75  And echon upon God they crave –
Why sholde God with hem Him greve?                           *trouble Himself*
Echon troweth that other rave,                               *believes; are mad*
But alle they chesen God for cheve,                          *as (their) lord (lit. chief)*
    And hope in God echon they have,
80  And bi her wit her worching preve.                       *their (own) practice; justify*
Thus mony maters men don meve,                               *raise (lit. move, i.e. for discussion)*
Sechen her wittës how and why;                               *rack their brains*
But Godës merci is al biheve,                                *is necessary for all*
    For this world fareth as a fantasye.


* age; its natural strength; enfeebled

For thus men stumble and sere her wit                  *blight their intelligence*
85  And meven maters many and fele;                      *and raise; numerous*
Sum leveth on him, sum leveth on hit,                   *one believes; it*
As children lernen for to spele.                        *learn to speak*
But non seth non that abit,                             *anyone who survives*
90  Whan stilly deth wol on him stele.                   *silently; steal*
For He that hest in hevenë sit,                         *highest; sits*
He is the help and hope of hele;                        *of salvation*
For wo is ende of worldës wele –                        *woe is the end of the world's bliss*
Eche lif loke wher that I lye –                         *let each person judge whether I lie*
95  This world is fals, fikel and frele,                *frail*
        And fareth but as a fantasye.


Wharto wilne we for to knowe                            *to what end do we wish*
The poyntes of Godës priveté?                           *the particulars; secret purposes*
More than Him list us for to showe                      *it pleases Him*
100  We sholde not knowe in no degré;                   *no way*
An idel bost is for to blowe                            *boast (it) is to brag*
A mayster of divinité.                                  *(that one is) a Master of Divinity*
Thenk we lyve in erthe her lowe,
And God on hye in magesté;                              *on high*
105  Of material mortualité                             *of material mortal matters*
Medle we, and of no more maistrie.              *let us concern ourselves; knowledge*
The more we trace the Trinité,
        The more we falle in fantasye.


But leve we our disputisoun,                            *let us give up our debate*
110  And leve on Him that al hath wrought;              *trust*
We mowe not preve bi no resoun                  *may not explain by any argument*
How He was born that al us bought;
But hol in oure entencioun,                             *undivided*
Worshipe we Him in herte and thought,                   *let us worship*
115  For He may turne kindes upsodoun,       *turn the natural order upside down*
That allë kindës made of nought.                        *created things; from nothing*
Whan al our bokës ben forth brought,
And al our craft of clergye,                            *skill in learning*
And al our wittes ben thurghout sought             *thoroughly investigated*
120      Yit we fare as a fantasye.

Of fantasye is al our fare, *activity*
Olde and yonge and alle y-fere; *all together*
But make we merye and sle care, *slay*
And worshipe we God whil we ben here;
125 Spende our god and litel spare, *substance; save*
And ech man cherice otheres chere. *encourage others' good spirits*
Thinke how we comen hider al bare, *naked*
Our wey-wendyng is in a were; *our departure; state of uncertainty*
Prey we the prince that hath no pere, *equal*
130 Tak us hol to His merci *in entirety*
And kepe our conciencë clere –
    For this world is but fantasy.

## 62. *Fortune* by Chaucer

*Balades de Visage sanz Peinture*

I *Le Pleintif countre Fortune*          *The Plaintiff against Fortune*

This wrecched worldës transmutacioun, *mutability*
As wele or wo, now povre and now honour, *joy or sorrow; poverty*
Withouten ordre or wis discrecioun *wise judgement*
4 Governëd is by Fortunës errour. *fickleness*
But natheles, the lakke of hyr favour *lack; her*
Ne may nat don me syngen, though I dye, *make me sing*
*Jay tout perdu mon temps et mon labour;* *I have lost all my time and effort*
8 For fynally, Fortune, I thee defye. *for in the end; defy*

Yit is me left the lyght of my resoun
To knowen frend fro foo in thi mirour; *friend from foe; your mirror*
So muche hath yit thy whirlinge up and doun
12 Y-taught me for to knowen in an hour.
But trewëly, no force of thi reddour *it does not matter about your severity*
To hym that over hymself hath the maystrye; *control*
My suffysauncë shal be my socour, *self-sufficiency; succour*
16 For fynally, Fortune, I thee defye.

O Socrates, thou stidfast champyoun,
She never myghtë be thi tormentour;
Thou never dreddëst hyr oppressyoun,
20 Ne in hyr cherë founde thou no savour.          *countenance; pleasure*
Thou knewe wel the deceit of hyr colour,                   *her pretence*
And that hir mostë worshipe is to lye.          *her greatest reputation*
I knowe hir ek a fals dissimulour,          *her also (as) a false deceiver*
24 For fynally, Fortune, I thee defye!

II  *La respounse de Fortune au Pleintif*          *The reply of Fortune to the Plaintiff*

No man ys wrecched but hymself yt wene,          *unless; believes it (to be so)*
And he that hath hymself hath suffisaunce.                     *sufficiency*
Whi seystow thanne I am to thee so kene,          *why say you then; so cruel*
28 That hast thyself out of my governaunce?          *(you) who possess; free from*
Sey thus: 'Graunt mercy of thyn haboundaunce          *
That thou hast lent or this.' Why wolt thou stryve?          *before this; argue*
What woost thow yit how I thee wol avaunce?                          †
32 And ek thou hast thy bestë frende alyve.                     *moreover*

I have thee taught divisyoun bytwene          *the difference between*
Frend of effect and frend of countenaunce;                          ‡
Thee nedëth nat the galle of no hyene,          *bile; hyena*
36 That curëth eyen derkëd for penaunce;          *dimmed on account of affliction*
Now seestow cleer that were in ignoraunce.          *you see clearly*
Yit halt thyn ancre and yit thou mayst aryve          *hold fast your anchor; arrive*
Ther bounté berth the keye of my substaunce,          *bears the key; wealth*
40 And ek thou hast thy bestë frend alyve.

How many have I refusëd to sustene
Sin I thee fostred have in thy plesaunce.          *well-being*
Woltow than make a statute on thy quene          *law applying to; queen*
44 That I shal been ay at thyn ordinaunce?          *command*

*say; thank you for; abundance
† what do you yet know of; will advance
‡ friend in actuality; in appearance

Thou born art in my regne of varyaunce,                    *realm of mutability*
Aboute the wheel with other most thou dryve.                              *
My loore is bet than wikke is thi grevaunce,     *teaching is better; harmful;*
48  And ek thou hast thy bestë frende alyve.                        [*affliction*


III  *La respounse du Pleintif countre Fortune*   *The Plaintiff's response to Fortune*


Thy loore I dampne, it is adversité.
My frend maystow nat reven, blinde goddesse;                     *take away*
That I thy frendës knowe, I thanke it thee –
52  Tak hem agayn, lat hem go lye on presse.              *back; in a closet*
The negardye in keping hyr rychesse              *miserliness; their wealth*
Prenostik is thou wolt hir tour assayle;         *is a sign that; their tower*
Wikke appetyt comth ay before syknesse.                 *excessive appetite*
56  In general, this reulë may nat fayle.


*La respounse de Fortune countre le Pleintif*                              †


Thou pynchëst at my mutabylytée                        *findest fault with*
For I thee lente a drope of my rychesse                           *because*
And now me lykëth to withdrawë me.
60  Why sholdëstow my realté opresse?           *sovereign power suppress*
The see may ebbe and flowen more or lesse;
The welkne hath myght to shynë, reyne, or hayle;                      *sky*
Ryght so mot I kythen my brotelnesse.                  *manifest my fickleness*
64  In general this reulë may nat fayle.


Lo, th'execucion of the majestée              *performance; majesty* (i.e. God)
That al purveyëth of his ryghtwysnesse,          *foresees in his righteousness*
That samë thinge 'Fortunë' clepen ye,                               *call*
68  Ye blindë beestës ful of lewëdnesse.                          *ignorance*
The hevene hath propreté of sykernesse,       *the characteristic of stability*
This world hath ever restëles travayle;                *ceaseless suffering*
Thy lastë day is ende of myn intresse.                      *last day; concern*
72  In general, this reulë may nat fayle.

                                    * *around; others; go* (lit. *drive*)
                                    † *The response of Fortune to the Plaintiff*

*Lenvoy de Fortune*                                    *The conclusion of Fortune*

Princes, I prey you of your gentilesse                              *nobility*
Lat nat this man on me thus crye and pleyne,        *cry out and complain*
And I shal quytë you your bysynesse                *reward you for your effort*
76  At my requeste, as three of you or tweyne;                          *two*
And but you list releve him of hys peyne,  *unless you wish* (lit. *it pleases you*)
Preyëth hys bestë frend of his noblesse
That to som beter estat he may attayne.

*Explicit*


## 63. *Truth* by Chaucer

*Balade de Bon Conseyl*                                *Ballade of good counsel*

Flee fro the prees and dwelle with sothefastnesse;           *crowd; truth*
Suffyse unto thy thing though it be smal,        *be content with what you have*
For hord hath hate and clymbyng tykelnesse,                              *
Prees hathe envye and wele blent overal.                *wealth blinds everywhere*
5  Savour no more thanne thee byhovë shal,              *relish; than is your due*
Reule wel thiself that other folk canst rede,      *control; (you) who; advise*
And trouthe thee shal delyvere it is no drede.         *set free there is no doubt*

Tempest thee nought al croked to redresse  *excite; crooked (things); set right*
In trust of hir that turnëth as a bal;              *in reliance on her; ball*
10  Gret restë stant in litel besynesse.      *peace of mind resides; endeavour*
Be war therfore to spurne ayeyns an al,            *of kicking against an awl*
Stryve not, as doth the crokkë with the wal.              *struggle not; crock*
Daunte thyself, that dauntëst otheres dede,    *subdue; (you) who rule; deeds*
And trouthe thee shal delyvere it is no drede.

15  That thee is sent, receyve in buxumnesse;            *what; submissively*
The wrastlyng for the worlde axëth a fal.              *wrestling; invites*
Here is non home, here nys but wyldernesse:        *no home; is nothing but*

\* *avarice; hatred; ambition; instability*

Forthe, pylgryme, forthe! Forthe, beste, out of thy stal!          *
Knowe thy contré, loke up, thank God of al;                    *look up*
20  Holde the heye wey and lat thy gost thee lede,       *keep to the main; let*
And trouthe thee shal delyvere it is no drede.              [*your spirit*

### Envoy

Therfore, thou Vache, leve thine olde wrecchednesse;          †
Unto the world levë now to be thral.                    *cease; enslaved*
Crye Hym mercy, that of His hie goodnesse                *exalted goodness*
25  Made thee of nought, and in especial                       *above all*
Drawe unto hym, and pray in general                    *beg in general terms*
For thee, and eke for other, hevenlich mede;        *yourself; also for others;*
And trouthe thee shal delyvere it is no drede.              [*reward*

*Explicit Le bon counseill de G. Chaucer.*

# 64. *Gentilesse* by Chaucer

*Moral Balade of Chaucier*

The firstë stocke, fader of gentilesse –                 *ancestor; nobility*
What man desirëth gentil for to be              *any man who desires; noble*
Must folowe his trace, and alle his wittës dresse               ‡
Vertue to love and vicës for to fle.                           *flee*
5  For unto vertue longëth dignité                       *honour belongs*
And nought the reverse, saufly dar I deme,          *opposite, safely dare I say*
Al were he mytrë, croune, or dyademe.        *although he (a man) should wear*

This firstë stok was fulle of rightwisenesse,         *full of righteousness*
Trewe of his worde, sobrë, pitous and fre,  *sober, compassionate and generous*
10  Clene of his gost, and lovëd besynesse              *pure in his spirit; activity*
Ayeinst the vyce of slouthe, in honestée;          *against the vice of sloth; honour*

* *onwards, pilgrim; beast*
† *Sir Philip de la Vache*
‡ *his (ancestor's) footsteps; direct*

And, but his heir love vertue as did he                             *unless*
He is nought gentil, though he richë seme,                   *wealthy; appear*
Al were he mytrë, croune, or dyademe.

15   Vice may welle be heire to olde richesse,          *well be heir to ancestral wealth*
But there may no man, as men may welle se,               *may well see*
Bequethe his heire his vertuous noblesse                    *leave to*
(That is appropred unto no degré              *is the property of no social rank*
But to the firstë fader in magestée,                    *but of*
20   That makëth hem his heirës that hym queme),              *who please him*
Alle were he mytrë, croune, or diademe.


## 65. Every day thou myghtëst lere

*Gay, gay, gay, gay,*                                                *Gay*
*Think on dredful domësday.*

Every day thou myghtëst lere                                      *learn*
To helpe thiself whil thou art here;
5   Whan thou art ded and leyd on bere,                     *bier*
    Cryst help thi soule, for thou ne may.

Thynk, man, on thi wyttës fyve;                              *senses*
Do sum good whil thou art on lyve;                          *alive*
Go to cherche and do thee shryve,               *make your confession*
10      And bryng thi soule in good aray.             *into a good state*

Thynk, man, on thi synnës seven;
Think how meri it is in heven;
Prey to God with myldë steven                           *gentle voice*
    He be thin help on domësday.                      *that He may be*

15   Lokë that thou non thing stere       *see that you offer incense to nothing*
Ne non fals wytnessë bere;
Thynk how Cryst was stunge with spere                      *pierced*
    Whan he deyed on Good Fryday.

Lok that thou ne sle non man
20 Ne do non foly with non womman;            *nor commit adultery*
Thynk, the blod fro Ihesu ran
    Whan he deyed, withouten nay.

## 66. If thou serve a lord of prys

    *Bewar, sqwyer, yeman and page,*            *servant*
    *For servyse is non heritage.*            *inheritance*

If thou serve a lord of prys,            *worth*
Be not to boystous in thin servys;            *too zealous*
5 Damne not thin sowlë in non wys,            *way*
    For servyse is non heritage.

Winteres wether and wommanes thought
And lordës lovë chaungëth oft;
This is the sothe if it be sought,            *truth*
10     For servyse is non heritage.

Now thou art gret, tomorwen shal I,            *I shall be*
As lordës chaungen her baly;            *their bailiff*
In thin welthe werk sikerly,            *for your (own) prosperity work steadily*
    For servyse is non heritage.

15 Than serve we God in allë wyse,
He shal us quiten our servyse            *repay*
And yeve us yiftës most of pryse,            *worth*
    Hevene to be our heritage.

# PART III: *Devotional Lyrics*

## 67. Swetë Jhesu, king of blisse

Swetë Jhesu, king of blisse,  
Min hertë love, min hertë lisse,      *heart's love, my heart's joy*  
Thou art swetë mid y-wisse,      *sweet indeed*  
4  Wo is him that thee shal misse.      *who will lose you*

Swete Jhesú, min hertë light,      *heart's*  
Thou art dai withouten night,  
Thou yeve me strengthe and ekë might      *give me; and also*  
8  For to loven thee al right.      *aright*

Swete Jhesú, my soulë bote,      *soul's salvation*  
In min herte thou sette a rote      *may you plant a root*  
Of thy love that is so swote,      *so sweet*  
12  And wite hit that hit springë mote.      *guard it so that it may grow*

## 68. Jhesú, swete is the love of thee

Jhesú, swete is the love of thee,      *sweet is*  
Noon other thing so swete may be;  
No thing that men may heere and see  
4  Hath no swetnesse ayeyns thee.      *compared with thee*

Jhesú, no song may be swettér,  
No thing in hertë blisfullér,      *in heart more blissful*  
Nought may be feelëd lightsomér,      *be felt more joyous*  
8  Than thou, so swete a lovyér.      *lover*

Jhesú, thi love was us so fre                    *to us so generous*
That it fro hevenë broughtë thee;
For love thou derë boughtëst me,                         *dearly*
12  For love thou heng on roodë tre.        *hung on the rood tree (cross)*


Jhesú, for love thou tholëdest wrong,                  *suffered*
Woundës sore, and peynës strong;              *torments severe*
Thine peynës reuthful were and long,                    *pitiful*
16  No man may hem telle, ne song.              *them tell; nor song*


Jhesú, for love thou bood so wo               *experienced such woe*
That blody stremës ronne thee fro;              *ran from you*
Thi whytë sides woxe blew and blo,            *became black and blue*
20  Oure synnes it made so, weylawo!                     *alas!*


Jhesú, for love thou stigh on roode,        *ascended upon the cross*
For love thou yaf thin hertë bloode;         *gave your heart's blood*
Love thee made my soulës foode,                    *Love made you*
24  Thi love us boughtë til al goode.            *for all that is good*


Jhesú my love, thou were so fre;                  *so generous*
Al that thou didest for love of me;
What shal I for that yeldë thee?                    *render you*
28  Thou askëst nought but love of me.    *you ask nothing but love from me*


Jhesú my God, Jhesú my kyng,
Thou askëst me noon other thing,                  *ask of me no*
But trewë love and hert-yernyng,           *heartfelt yearning*
32  And lovë-teeres with swete mournyng.     *tears of love; longing*


Jhesú my love, Jhesú my lyght,
I wol thee love and that is right;                      *I will*
Do me love thee with al my myght,                  *make me*
36  And for thee mourne bothe day and nyght.          *yearn*


Jhesú, do me so yernë thee          *make me so to desire thee*
That my thought ever upon thee be;
With thin eyë loke to me,
40  And myldëly my nedë se.          *gently; need; look upon*

Jhesú, thi love be al my thought,
Of other thing ne recche me nought;                    *I care nothing*
Thanne have I thi wille al wrought,
44 That havëst me ful derë bought.                          *dearly*


## 69. Now I se blosmë sprynge

Now I se blosmë sprynge,                          *blossom flourish*
Ich herde a foulës song,                          *I heard a bird's song*
A swetë love-longinge
Myn hertë thurghout sprong,              *throughout; has sprung up*
5 That is of lovë newe,                              *about a new love*
That is so swete and trewe,                          *so sweet and true*
Hit gladëth al my song;                                    *it gladdens*
Ich wot al mid y-wisse                          *know with certainty*
My lyf and eke my blysse                                  *and also*
10 Is al theron y-long.                                   *dependent*

Of Jhesu Crist I synge,
That is so fayr and fre,                                    *noble*
Swetest of allë thynge,                              *of all beings*
His owne Ich owe wel be;            *His own I ought indeed to be*
15 Fúl fer He me soughte,                                      *far*
Míd hard He me boughte                            *with suffering*
With woundës two and thre;
Wel sóre He was y-swonge,              *very painfully; scourged*
For me mid spere y-stonge,                    *with a spear; pierced*
20 Y-nailëd to the tree.

Whan Ich myselvë stond                                    *stand*
And mid herte y-see,                          *with (my) heart; see*
Y-thirlëd fet and honde                  *pierced; the feet and hands*
With gretë nailës three –
25 Blody was His heved,                                      *head*
Of Him nas nought by-levëd                        *was no part left*

That of pyne was fre –                    *from pain was free*
Wel oughtë myn herte,
Al for His lovë smerte,                    *smart*
30  Syk and sory be.                       *sigh and be sorry*

A way! that I ne can                       *alas!*
To Him turne al my thought,
And make Him my lemman                     *lover*
That thus me hath y-bought                 *redeemed*
35  With pine and sorwë longe,             *pain*
With woundës depe and stronge –
Of love ne can I nought!                   *I am incapable*
His blod that fel to groundë
Out of His swetë woundë,                   *wounds*
40  Of pine us hath y-brought.             *out of torment*

Jhesu, lemman softe,                       *gentle lover*
Thou yif me strengthe and might,          *give me*
Longinge sore and ofte                     *yearning sore and often*
To servë thee aright;
45  And leve me pinë drye,                 *let me suffer pain*
For thee, swetë Marie,
That art so fayr and bryght.
Mayde and moder milde,
For love of thinë childe,
50  Ernde us hevenë light.                 *obtain for us the light of heaven*

Jhesu, lemman swete,
I sendë thee this songe,
And wel ofte I thee grete                  *greet*
And biddë thee among;                      *pray to you constantly*
55  Yif me sonë lete,                      *grant me soon to forsake*
And minë sinnës bete,                      *atone for*
That I have do thee wrong.                 *whereby; have done*
At mine lyvës ende,                        *life's end*
Whan I shal hennë wende,                   *hence depart*
60  Jhesú, me underfonge!  Amen.           *receive*

## 70. Love me broughte

Love me broughte,
And love me wroughtë, *created*
   Man, to be thi ferë; *companion*
4 Love me fedde,
And love me ledde,
   And love me lettëd herë. *kept me here*

Love me slow, *slew*
8 And love me drow, *drew*
   And love me leyde on berë; *laid on a bier*
Love is my pes, *peace*
For love I ches *chose*
12    Man to byen derë. *buy (i.e. redeem) at a cost*

Ne dred thee nought,
I have thee sought
   Bothen day and night; *both*
16 To haven thee,
Wel is me,
   I have thee wonne in fight. *won*

## 71. Alas! alas! wel evel I sped!

Alas! alas! wel evel I sped! *very ill have I fared*
For sinne Jesú fro me ys fled,
   That levely fere. *dear companion*
4 At my dore He stant alone *at my door He stands*
And calleth 'Undo!' with rewful mone, *with pitiful lament*
   On this manere:

'Undo, my leef, my dowvë dere!                          *my beloved, my dear dove*
8   Undo! Why stond I steken out here?                   *stand I shut out*
Ich am thi make!                                        *your spouse*
Lo, mi lokkes and ek myn heved                          *my locks and also my head*
Are al wyth blody dropes bywevëd                         *covered*
12      For thinë sake.'

## 72. I am Jhesú, that com to fight

I am Jhesú, that com to fight                           *who came*
Withouten sheld and spere,                          *shield and spear*
Ellës were thi deth y-dight,                         *otherwise; destined*
4   Yif mi fighting ne were.                          *if it had not been for*
Sithe I am come and have thee brought                   *since I have come*
A blisful bote of bale,                              *salvation from torment*
Undo thin herte, tel me thi thought,
8   Thi sinnës grete and smale.

## 73. In the vaile of restles mynd

In the vaile of restles mynd                             *vale*
I sought in mounteyn and in mede,                    *meadow*
Trustyng a trewe love for to fynd.
4   Upon an hyll than toke I hede,                     *took I heed*
A voice I herd (and neer I yede)                     *nearer I went*
In gret dolour complaynyng tho,                      *grief; then*
'See, dere soule, my sidës blede,                    *bleed*
8   *Quia amore langueo.*                             *because I languish for love*

Upon thys mount I found a tree,
Under thys tree a man sittyng;
From hede to fote woundëd was he,
12      Hys hertë-blode I saw bledyng;

A semely man to be a kyng,                                          *comely man*
A graciouse face to loke unto.                                      *look upon*
I asked hym how he had paynyng:                                *why he suffered*
16  He said, '*Quia amore langueo.*


'I am trew love that fals was never.
My sister, mannes soule, I loved hir thus;
Bicause I wold on no wyse dissever                          *be separated*
20  I left my kyngdome glorious;
I purveyd hyr a paleis precious;                          *provided; palace*
She flytt, I folowed; I loved her so                                *fled*
That I suffred thes paynës piteous,                             *pitiable*
24  *Quia amore langueo.*


'My faire love, and my spousë bryght,
I saved hyr fro betyng, and she hath me bet;         *beating; beaten*
I clothed hyr in grace and hevenly lyght,
28  This blody surcote she hath on me set.                    *surcoat*
For longyng love I will not let;         *because of love-longing; give up*
Swetë strokës be thes, lo!
I have loved ever as I het,                                     *promised*
32  *Quia amore langueo.*


'I crouned hyr with blis, and she me with thorne,
I led hyr to chambre, and she me to dye;
I brought hyr to worship, and she me to scorne,               *honour*
36  I dyd hyr reverence, and she me vilanye.                    *shame*
To love that lovëth is no maystrye,        *to love one who loves; great skill*
Hyr hate made never my love hyr foo;             *hatred; enemy*
Ask then no moo questions why,                               *no more*
40  *Quia amore langueo.*


'Loke unto myn handës, man!
Thes gloves were given me whan I hyr sought;
They be nat white, but rede and wan,                        *discoloured*
44  Embroudrëd with blode (my spouse them bought!);         *embroidered*

They wyll not off – I leve them nought!    *come off; discard them not*

I wowe hyr with them where ever she go.    *woo her; goes*

Thes handes full frendly for hyr fought,    *so lovingly*

48   *Quia amore langueo.*


'Marvell not, man, though I sitt styll;

My love hath shod me wonder strayte.    *shod me wondrously tight*

She boklëd my fete, as was hyr wyll,    *buckled*

52    With sharpë nailes (well thou mayst waite!).    *may see*

In my love was never dissaite,    *deceit*

For all my membrës I have opend hyr to;    *limbs*

My body I made hyr hertës baite,    *bait for her heart*

56   *Quia amore langueo.*


'In my syde I have made hyr nest;

Loke in, how wide a wound is here!    *inside*

This is hyr chambre, here shall she rest,

60    That she and I may slepe in fere.    *together*

Here may she wasshe, if any filth were;

Here is socour for all hyr wo;

Come if she will, she shall have chere,    *be welcome*

64   *Quia amore langueo.*


'I will abide till she be redy,

I will to hir send or she say nay;    *to her send messages until*

If she be recheless, I will be redy,    *heedless; attentive*

68    If she be dangerous, I will hyr pray.    *disdainful; beseech*

If she do wepe, than byd I nay,    *then shall I beg her not to*

Myn armes ben spred to clypp hyr to.    *to embrace her*

Crye ones, "I come" – now, soule, assay!    *once; try*

72   *Quia amore langueo.*


'I sitt on an hille for to se fer,    *further*

I loke to the vayle, my spouse I se;    *look to the vale*

Now renne she away-ward, now come she ner,    *should she run; nearer*

76    Yet fro myn eye-sight she may nat be.

Some waite their pray, to make hyr flee;   *lie in wait for their prey*
I renne tofore to chastise hyr fo.    *ahead; to subdue*
Recover, my soule, agayne to me,    *return*
80 *Quia amore langueo.*

'My swetë spouse, will we go play?
 Applës ben rype in my gardine;    *are ripe; garden*
I shall clothe thee in new array,
84  Thy mete shall be mylk, honye, and wyne.  *your food*
 Now, dere soule, lat us go dyne;    *let us*
Thy sustenaunce is in my scrippë – lo!   *bag*
 Tary not now, fayre spousë myne,
88 *Quia amore langueo.*

'If thou be foule, I shall make thee clene,
 If thou be sike, I shall thee hele,    *sick*
If thou ought mourne, I shall thee mene – *for anything; comfort*
92  Spouse, why wilt thou nought with me dele?  *
 Thou foundëst never love so lele;    *faithful*
What wilt thou, soule, that I shall do?
 I may of unkindnes thee appele,   *of ingratitude; accuse*
96 *Quia amore langueo.*

'What shall I do now with my spouse?
 Abyde I will hyr gentilnisse.    *await; graciousness*
Wold she loke ones out of hyr house  *if she would look once*
100  Of fleshly affecciouns and unclennisse,  *carnal desires*
 Hyr bed is made, hyr bolster is blysse,  *pillow*
Hyr chamber is chosen – such ar no mo! *choice – there are no more such*
 Loke out at the wyndows of kyndnisse,  *affection*
104 *Quia amore langueo.*

'My spouse is in chamber, hold your pees,  *in (her) chamber*
 Make no noyse, but lat hyr slepe.    *let*
My babe shall suffrë no disese,    *distress*
108  I may not here my dere childe wepe,

        * *have anything to do with me*

For with my pappe I shall hyr kepe.    *for close to my breast I shall*
No wonder though I tend hyr to –    *attend*
   Thys hoole in my side had never ben so depe
112 But *quia amore langueo.*

'Long and love thou never so hye,    *though you yearn and love ever so intensely*
   Yit is my love more than thyn may be;
Thou gladdest, thou wepest – I sitt thee by;    *you rejoice; weep; I will sit*
116    Yit myght thou, spouse, loke ones at me!    *yet if you could; once*
Spouse, shold I alway fedë thee    *feed*
With childës mete? Nay, love, nat so –    *food*
   I preve thy love with adversité,    *test*
120 *Quia amore langueo.*

'Wax not wery, myn owne dere wyfe!    *grow*
   What mede is aye to live in comfort?    *what reward is there always*
For in tribulacioun I renne more rife,    *I run (to help) more readily*
124    Ofter tymes than in disport –    *happiness*
In welth, in wo, ever I support.    *prosperity; misery*
Than, dere soule, go never me fro!    *then*
   Thy mede is marked, whan thou art mort,    *reward is assigned; dead*
128 *Quia amore langueo.*'

## 74. Levëdie, Ich thonkë thee

Levëdie, Ich thonkë thee,    *Lady, I thank you*
   With hertë swithë milde,    *very humble*
That god that thou hast i-don me    *for that good which*
4    With thine swetë childe.

Thou art god and swete and bright
   Of alle other y-coren;    *chosen above all others*
Of thee was that swetë wight    *person*
8    That was Jesús y-boren.    *born*

Maidë mildë, bidde I thee                                   *pray*
  With thine swetë childe,
That thou erendië me                            *intercede for me*
12    To haven Godës milde.                           *God's mercy*


Moder, lokë thou on me
  With thine swetë eye;
Reste and blissë yif thou me,                              *give*
16    My lady, then Ich deye.                         *when I die*


## 75. Of on that is so fayr and bright

Of on that is so fayr and bright,                       *of one*
  *Velud maris stella,*                    *as the star of the sea*
Brighter than the dayës light,
  *Parens et puella;*                          *mother and maiden*
5 Ich crie to thee, thou se to me,                  *look upon me*
Lady, preye thi sone for me,
  *Tam pia,*                                          *so devoted*
That Ich motë come to thee,                               *may*
  *Maria.*


10 Lady, flour of allë thing,
  *Rosa sine spina,*                            *rose without thorn*
Thou berë Jhesu, hevenë-king,                 *bore; king of heaven*
  *Gratia divina.*                                *by divine grace*
Of allë thou berëst the pris,                   *you bear the prize*
15 Lady, quene of Paradys                                *Paradise*
  *Electa,*                                              *chosen*
Maydë mildë, moder ek                                     *also*
  *Effecta.*                                             *proven*


Of carë conseil thou art best,          *in sorrow; counsellor*
20    *Felix fecundata;*                        *happy fruitful one*
Of allë wery thou art rest,
  *Mater honorata.*                              *revered mother*

Bisek thou Him with mildë mod         *beseech; gentle heart*
That for us allë shad His blod         *shed*
25    *In cruce,*         *on the cross*
That we moten come til Him         *we may come to Him*
   *In luce.*         *in light*

Al this world it was forlore         *lost*
   *Eva peccatrice,*         *through Eve the sinner*
30 Til our Loverd was y-bore         *lord; born*
   *De te genitrice;*         *from you, mother*
With '*Ave*' it went away         *'Hail'; it (dark night)*
Thuster night, and com the day         *dark night; came*
   *Salutis;*         *of salvation*
35 The wellë springëth out of thee         *well*
   *Virtutis.*         *of virtue*

Wel He wot He is thi sone         *knows*
   *Ventre quem portasti;*         *whom you carried in the womb*
He wil nought wernë thee thy bone         *deny you your request*
40    *Parvum quem lactasti.*         *little one to whom you gave suck*
So hendë and so god He is,         *gracious*
He hath brought us into blis         
   *Superni,*         *of heaven*
That hath y-dit the foulë pit         *who hath shut*
45    *Inferni.*         *of hell*

## 76. Edi be thou, hevenë quenë

Edi be thou, hevenë quenë,         *blessed; queen of heaven*
Folkës frovre and englës blis,         *comfort; angels'*
Moder unwemmëd and maiden clenë,         *unspotted; pure*
4 Swich in world non other nis.         *such; no other is*
On thee hit is wel eth-senë         *very evident*
Of allë wommen thou havest the pris.         *you are supreme*
My swetë Levedy, her my benë,         *lady, hear my prayer*
8 And rew of me yif thi wille is.         *have pity on me if*

Thou asteye so the day-rewë          *arose like the dawn*
That delëth from the derkë night;          *which parts;  dark night*
Of thee sprang a lemë newë          *from you;  light*
12   That al this world havëth y-light.          *has lit*
Nis non maide of thinë hewë,          *complexion*
So fair, so shene, so rudy, so bright;          *so fair, so beautiful, so rosy*
Swetë Lady of me thou rewë          *have pity on me*
16   And have merci of thin knight.

Sprongë blosme of onë rotë,          *blossom sprung from a single root*
The Holy Gost thee reste upon;          *rested*
That was for mankinnës botë          *salvation*
20   And here soule t'alesen for on.          *their souls to free in exchange for one*
Ladi mildë, softe and swotë,          *gentle and sweet*
Ich crie thee merci, Ich am thy mon,          *your servant*
Bothe to hondë and to fotë,          *both hand and foot*
24   On allë wisë that Ich con.          *in every way that I know*

Thou art erthe to godë sedë,          *earth for good seed*
On thee lightë th'evenë-dew;          *alighted the heavenly dew*
Of thee sprang the edi bledë,          *from you;  blessed fruit*
28   The Holy Gost hire on thee sew.          *sowed it in thee*
Thou bring us out of care, of dredë
That Evë bitterliche us brew;          *brewed for us*
Thou shalt us into hevenë ledë –          *lead*
32   Wel swetë is the ilkë dew.          *that same dew*

Moder ful of thewës hendë,          *gracious virtues*
Maidë dreye and wel y-taught,          *patient*
Ich am in thine lovë-bendë,          *love-bonds*
36   And to thee is al my draught.          *my inclination*
Thou me shild, ye, from the fendë,          *shield me, indeed, from the Devil*
As thou art fre and wilt and maught,          *are generous and willing and can*
Help me to my livës endë,
40   And make me with thin sone y-saught.          *with your son;  reconciled*

## 77. Gabriel, from hevenë king

Gabriel, from hevenë king        *from the king of heaven*
  Sent to the maidë swetë,
Broughtë hire blisful tiding               *tidings*
And faire he gan hire gretë:     *courteously he greeted her*
5 'Hail be thou, ful of grace aright,        *indeed*
For Goddës sone, this hevenë light,    *light of heaven*
  For mannës love
  Wil man bicome,
    And takë
10   Flesh of thee, maiden bright,
  Mankin fre for to makë          *mankind free*
  Of sinne and devlës might.'

Mildëliche him gan answere           *gently*
  The mildë maiden thannë:          *then*
15 'Whichëwisë sholde Ich bere    *in what way; bear*
  Child withouten mannë?'     *without a husband*
Th'angel saidë: 'Ne dred thee nought,
Thurgh th'Holi Gost shal ben y-wrought,  *through; shall be done*
  This ilkë thing         *this very thing*
20   Wherof tiding
    Ich bringë;
  Al mankin worth y-bought   *mankind shall be redeemed*
  Thurgh thy swetë childingë,     *child-bearing*
  And out of pine y-brought.'       *torment*

25 Whan the maiden understod
  And th'anglës wordës herdë,
Mildëliche with mildë mod    *gently with gentle heart*
  To th'angel she answerdë:
'Our lordës thew-maiden i-wis    *handmaiden indeed*
30 Ich am, that her-aboven is.      *who is above*
  Anentës me           *concerning me*
  Fulforthëd be          *be fulfilled*

Thy sawë; *your word*
That Ich, sithe His wil is, *since it is His will*
35 Maiden, withouten lawë, *against the law of nature*
Of moder have the blis. *of a mother; should have*

Th'angel wente away mid than, *at that*
Al out of hirë sightë;
Hirë wombe arisë gan
40 Thurgh th'Holi Gostës mightë.
In hire was Crist biloke anon, *enclosed forthwith*
Soth God, soth man in flesh and bon, *true; bone*
And of hir fles *flesh*
Y-borë wes *was born*
45 At timë. *at the due time*
Wherthrough us cam god won; *whereby; good hope*
He bought us out of pinë, *redeemed; torment*
And let Him for us slon. *allowed himself to be slain for us*

Maiden-moder makëles, *virgin-mother peerless*
50 Of milcë ful y-boundë, *with mercy fully endowed*
Bid for us Him that thee ches, *pray for us to Him who chose you*
At whom thou gracë fundë, *from whom; found*
That He foryive us sinne and wrake, *that He may forgive; injury*
And clene of evry gilt us make, *free from all guilt; make us*
55 And hevnë blis, *and the bliss of heaven*
Whan our time is *when it is our time*
To stervë, *to die*
Us yive, for thinë sake, *give us, (and grant us)*
Him so her for to servë, *here*
60 That He us to Him take. *may take us to Himself*

## 78. Now this foulës singëth

Now this foulës singëth *these birds sing*
and makëth herë blis,
And that gres up thringëth *grass pushes up*
4 ánd levëth the ris; *the branch sprouts leaves*

Of on Ich willë singen                                    *one*
   that is makëles,                       *peerless*
The king of allë kingës
8   to moder He hire ches.              *as mother; chose*

She is withouten sinne
   ánd withouten hore,                   *stain*
Y-come of kingës kinne                               *from a lineage of kings*
12   ánd of Jessës more;               *stock*
The loverd of mankinne                               *lord of mankind*
   of hire was y-boren
To bringe us out of sinne,
16   ellës we were forloren.          *otherwise we had been lost*

Gabriel hire grette                                  *greeted*
   and saidë hire, 'Ave,                *hail*
Marie ful of grace,
20   our loverd be with thee,
The fruyt of thinë wombe
   y-blessëd mot it be.                 *may it be*
Thou shalt go with childe,
24   for sothe Ich seye it thee.'     *in truth; say*

And tharë gretinge,                                  *and about the greeting*
   that angel had y-brought,
She gan to bithenchen                                *began to think*
28   and meindë hirë thought;         *was perplexed*
She saidë to the angel:
   'How may tiden this?                 *happen*
Of mannës y-monë                                     *of intercourse with a man*
32   not I nought, y-wis.'             *I know nothing, for sure*

Maid she was with childe
   and maiden her-biforen,              *before that*
And maiden er sithen                                 *still after*
36   hire child was y-boren;
Maide and moder nas                                  *was not*
   never non but she,                   *ever any* (lit. *never none*)
Wel mightë she berigge                               *the bearer*
40   of Goddës sonë be.

Y-blessëd be that child
   and the moder ek,                               *also*
And the swetë brestë
44    that hire sonë sek;                              *sucked*
Y-herëd be the time                          *praised be*
   that swich child was y-boren,
That lesëd al of pinë         *delivered everyone from torment*
48    that er was forloren.       *who previously had been lost*


## 79. I syng of a mayden

I syng of a mayden
   that is makëles,                               *peerless*
King of allë kingës
4    to here sone she ches.           *as her son she chose*

He cam also styllë                     *as silently*
   ther his moder was,              *where his mother was*
As dew in Aprylle
8    that fallëth on the gras.

He cam also styllë
   to his moderës bowr,                    *bower*
As dew in Aprille
12    that fallëth on the flour.             *flower*

He cam also stillë
   ther his moder lay,                    *where*
As dew in Aprille
16    that fallëth on the spray.         *leafy branch*

Moder and mayden
   was never non but she –            *was never anyone*
Wel may swych a lady                    *such*
20    Godës moder be!

## 80. I saw a fair maiden

    *Lullay, myn lyking,*                             *beloved*
      *my dere sone, myn sweting,*                 *sweet one*
    *Lullay, my dere herte,*
4      *myn owyn dere derling.*                     *darling*

    I saw a fair maiden
      sitten and singe,
    She lullëd a litel child,
8      a swetë lording.                         *sweet little lord*
      *Lullay,* etc.

    That echë Lord is that              *very Lord is he* (lit. *that*)
      that made allë thing;              *who; all things*
12  Of allë lordës he is Lord,
      of allë kingës King.
      *Lullay,* etc.

    Ther was mikel melody                  *much*
16      at that childës birth;
    Allë tho were in hevenë blis,     *those (who); in the bliss of heaven*
      they madë mikel mirth.
      *Lullay,* etc.

20  Aungelës bright, they sang that night
      and saiden to that child,
    'Blissëd be thou, and so be she          *blessed*
      that is both meek and mild.'       *meek and gentle*
24      *Lullay,* etc.

    Prey we now to that child,
      and to his moder dere,
    Graunt hem his blissing          *to grant them; blessing*
28      that now maken chere.         *now rejoice* (lit. *make joy*)
      *Lullay,* etc.

## 81. As I lay upon a night

> *Lullay, lullay, lay lay, lullay:*
> *Mi derë moder, sing lullay.*                    *dear mother*

As I lay upon a night
  Alone in my longing,                              *yearning*
5  Me thoughte I saw a wonder sight,      *it seemed to me; wondrous*
  A maiden child rokking.
    *Lullay, lullay,* etc.

The maiden wolde withouten song                    *wished*
  Hire child o slepë bringe;        *to put her child to sleep*
10 The child thoughtë she dide him wrong,
  And bad his moder singe.
    *Lullay, lullay,* etc.

'Sing now, moder,' seide that child,
  'What me shal befalle              *what is to happen to me*
15 Here after whan I come to ild,          *come to maturity*
  So don modrës alle.                              *as do*
    *Lullay, lullay,* etc.

'Ech a moder, trewëly,                  *every mother, truly*
  That can hire cradel kepe        *who knows how; to watch over*
20 Is wone to lullen lovëly                *is wont to lull lovingly*
  And singe hire child o slepe.                  *to sleep*
    *Lullay, lullay,* etc.

'Swetë moder, fair and fre,                        *gracious*
  Sithen that it is so,                              *since*
25 I preye thee that thou lullë me                    *lull*
  And sing somwhat therto.'            *something as well*
    *Lullay, lullay,* etc.

'Swetë sonë,' seydë she,
　'Wherof sholde I singe?                    *of what*
30 Wist I never yet more of thee                    *knew I*
　But Gabrieles gretinge.            *than Gabriel's greeting*
　　*Lullay, lullay,* etc.


'He grette me godli on his kne            *greeted me graciously*
　And seydë, "Hail, Marie
35 Ful of grace, God is with thee;
　Beren thou shalt Messye."                *bear; the Messiah*
　　*Lullay, lullay,* etc.


'I wondrëd mychel in my thought,            *greatly; mind*
　For man wold I right none.            *a husband; did I wish*
40 "Marie," he seydë, "drede thee nought:            *fear not*
　Let God of hevene alone.                    *leave it to*
　　*Lullay, lullay,* etc.


'"The Holi Gost shal don al this,"                *will do*
　He seyde withouten wone,                *without delay*
45 That I sholde beren mannës blis,            *man's bliss*
　Thee, my swetë sone.
　　*Lullay, lullay,* etc.


'He seidë, "Thou shalt bere a king                *bear*
　In King Davidës see;"                    *kingdom*
50 In al Jacobs wonying,                *the house of Jacob*
　Ther king sholde he be.
　　*Lullay, lullay,* etc.


'He seydë that Elizabeth,
　That baraine was before,                    *barren*
55 "A knavë child conceyvëd hath,            *male; conceived*
　To me leve thou the more."        *believe in me the more (for that)*
　　*Lullay, lullay,* etc.

'I answerëd blythëly,                                    *gladly*
  Fór his word me payde,                                 *pleased me*
60 "Lo, Godës servant her am I;
  Be it as thou me sayde."
    *Lullay, lullay,* etc.

'Ther, as he seidë, I thee bare                          *bore*
  On midwinter night,
65 On maydenhed, withouten care,                         *in virginity, without pain*
  Be grace of God almight.                               *by the grace; almighty*
    *Lullay, lullay,* etc.

'The herdes that wakëd in the wolde                      *shepherds that kept watch on the hill*
  Herde a wonder mirthe                                  *wondrous rejoicing*
70 Of aungëlës ther as they tolde,                       *angels; sang*
  In timë of thi birthe.                                 *at the time of*
    *Lullay, lullay,* etc.

'Swetë sonë, sikerly,                                    *truly*
  No more can I say;
75 And if I coudë, fayn wold I                            *glad would I be*
  To don al at thy pay.'                                 *all to your liking*
    *Lullay, lullay,* etc.

. . . . . . .

Certeynly this sight I say,                              *saw*
  This song I herdë singe,
80 As I lay this Yolës day                                *Christmas Day*
  Alone in my longinge.                                  *yearning*
    *Lullay, lullay,* etc.

## 82. Lullay, lullay, litel child

Lullay, lullay, litel child,
  child réstë thee a throwe,                             *rest you for a while*
Fro heighë hider art thou sent                           *from on high hither*
4   with us to wonë lowe;                                *to dwell below*

Poure and litel art thou mad,                    *poor; made*
    uncouth and unknowe,                          *strange and unknown*
Pine and wo to suffren her                        *torment and misery; here*
8       for thing that was thin owe.              *for a creature who was your own*
    Lullay, lullay, litel child,
        sorwë might thou make;                    *well might you cry*
    Thou art sent into this world,
12          as thou were forsake.                 *as if you were abandoned*

Lullay, lullay, litel grom,                       *lad*
    king of allë thinge,                          *things*
Whan I thenke of thy mischeef,                    *misfortune*
16      me list wel litel singe;                  *I have very little wish to sing*
But caren I may for sorwë,                        *but grieve I may*
    yif love wer in myn herte,
For swichë peynes as thou shalt drye             *such torments; endure*
20      were never non so smerte.                 *any so painful*
    Lullay, lullay, litel child,
        ful wel might thou crie,
    For than thi body is bleik and blak           *for when; pale and wan*
24          sone after shal ben drie.             *soon after it will be shrivelled*

Child, it is a weping dale                        *vale of tears*
    that thou art comen inne,
Thy pourë cloutes it proven wel,                  *poor rags prove it well*
28      thy bed mad in the binne;                 *made; manger*
Cold and hunger thou must thole                   *suffer*
    as thou were gete in sinne,                   *as if you had been begotten*
And after deyen on the tre                        *die*
32      for love of al mankinne.                  *mankind*
    Lullay, lullay, litel child,
        no wonder though thou care,               *lament*
    Thou art come amongës hem                     *among those*
36          that thi deth shullen yare.           *who; will prepare*

Lullay, lullay, litel child,
    for sorwë might thou grete,                   *weep*
The anguissh that thou suffren shalt
40      shal don thee blod to swete;              *will make you sweat blood*

Naked, bounden shalt thou ben,
 and sithen sorë bete,     *afterwards sorely beaten*
No thing fre upon thy body       *free*
44  of pinë shal be lete.      *of torment; left*
 Lullay, lullay, litel child,
  it is al for thy fo,    *because of thine enemy (the Devil)*
 The hardë bond of love-longing   *the cruel fetter of love-longing*
48   that thee hath bounden so.


Lullay, lullay, litel child,
 litel child thin ore!      *have mercy*
It is al for our owen gilt
52  that thou art peynëd sore;    *punished severely*
But woldë we yet kindë be,   *if we would yet be obedient*
 and live after thy lore,    *according to thy teaching*
And leten sinnë for thy love,     *renounce*
56  ne keptëst thou no more.   *you would wish for nothing more*
 Lullay, lullay, litel child,
  softë slep and faste,    *gently sleep and soundly*
 In sorwë endëth every love
60   but thin at the laste.     *except thine*


## 83. Ler to love as I love thee

Ler to love as I love thee,      *learn*
On al my limes thou might y-se    *limbs; see*
 How sore they quake for colde;   *painfully they shiver*
For thee I suffrë mychel wo,    *suffer great anguish*
5 Love me, swetë, an no mo,    *sweet one, and no other*
 To thee I take and holde.


Jhesu, swetë sonë dere,       *dear*
In porful bed thou list now here,   *on a pitiful bed you lie*
 And that me grevëth sore;    *grieves me bitterly*
10 For thi cradel is as a bere,     *byre*
Ox and assë ben thi fere,    *are your companions*
 Wepe may I therfore.       *weep*

Jhesu, swetë, be nought wroth,                          *angry*
I have nother clout ne cloth                            *neither rag nor cloth*
15    Thee inne for to folde;                        *wrap*
I n'ave but a clout of lappe,                           *I have nothing but a piece of sleeve*
Therefore lay thi feet to my pappe                      *breast*
    And kep thee fro the colde.                       *keep yourself from*

Cold thee taketh, I may wel se –                         *cold seizes you*
20 For love of man it motë be,                          *must be*
    Thee to suffren wo;
For bet it is thou suffrë this                           *for better it is that*
Than man forberë hevenë blis –                          *than that man should forgo*
    Thou most him bye therto.                         *must; redeem*

25 Sithe it most nedes that thou be ded                 *since it must needs be; dead*
To saven mankin from the qued,                          *mankind; Devil*
    Thy swetë wil be do.                              *will be done*
But let me nought dwelle her to longe,                   *too*
After thy deth me underfonge                             *take*
30    To ben for evermo.                           *to be (with you) for evermore*


## 84. Now goth sonnë under wode

Now goth sonnë under wode,                               *goes the sun under the wood*
Me reweth, Marie, thi fairë rode.                        *I grieve, Mary, for your fair face*
Now goth sonnë under tre,                                *the tree*
Me reweth, Marie, thi sone and thee.                     *son*


## 85. Whyt was hys naked brest

Whyt was hys naked brest                                 *white*
    and red of blod hys syde,                     *red with blood*
Bleyk was His fair andléd,                               *pale; fair face*
4    his woundës dep and wide,                    *deep*

And hys armes y-streight,                          *stretched*
    hey upon the rode;                          *high upon the cross*
On fif stedes on His body                          *five places*
8    the stremës ran o blode.                   *the streams of blood ran*

## 86. Whyt is thi naked brest

Whyt is thi naked brest
    and blodi is thi side,
Starkë are thine armes                             *rigid*
4    that strecchëde are so wyde.
Falwe is thi fairë ler                             *pale; fair cheek*
    and dimmyëth thi sighte,                   *grows dim*
Drie is thin hendë body                            *lifeless; gracious body*
8    on rodë so y-tighte.                        *stretched*
Thine thighës hongen colde                         *hang*
    al so the marble-ston,                     *as marble*
Thinë thirlëde fet                                 *pierced*
12    the redë blod by-ron.                     *drenched*

## 87. Whan Ich se on rode

Whan Ich se on rode                                *on the cross*
Jhesu mi lemman,                                   *my beloved*
And beside Him stonde                              *stand*
4 Marie an Johan,                                  *and*
And His rig y-swongen,                             *back scourged*
And His side y-stongen,                            *pierced*
For the love of man,
8 Wel ow Ich to wepen                              *ought I to weep*
And sinnës forleten,                              *and forsake sins*
Yif Ich of lovë can,                               *if I am capable of love*
Yif Ich of lovë can,
12 Yif Ich of lovë can.

## 88. Worldës blissë, have god day!

| | |
|---|---|
| Worldës blissë, have god day! | *worldly bliss, good day (to you)!* |
| Now from myn hertë wend away; | *go away* |
| Him for to loven min hert is went | *heart has turned* |
| That thurgh His sidë sperë rent. | *through whose side the spear tore* |
| 5 His hertë blod shadde He for me, | *shed He* |
| Naylëd to the hardë tre; | *hard* |
| That swetë bodi was y-tent, | *stretched* |
|    Prenëd with naylës three. | *pierced* |

| | |
|---|---|
| Ha Jesú! thin holi heved | *holy head* |
| 10 With sharpë thornës was by-wevëd, | *encircled* |
| Thi fairë neb was al bi-spet, | *fair face; spat upon* |
| With spot and blod meynd al by-wet; | *spittle; mingled; drenched* |
| Fro the crounë to the to | *from the crown to the toe* |
| Thi body was ful of pine and wo, | *pain and woe* |
| 15    And wan and red. | *wan and red* |

| | |
|---|---|
| Há Jesú! thi smartë ded | *Ah Jesu! your painful death* |
| Be my sheld, and minë red | *may it be; help* |
|    From develes lorë. | *from the Devil's promptings* |
|    Ha, swéte Jesú, thin órë! | *have mercy* |
| 20 For thinë pinës sorë, | |
| Tech min herte right lovë thee | *to love you properly* |
| Whos hertë blod was shad for me. | *heart's blood was shed* |

## 89. The mildë Lamb, y-sprad o rodë

| | |
|---|---|
| The mildë Lamb, y-sprad o rodë, | *gentle; spread on the cross* |
| Heng bi-ronnen al o blodë, | *hung drenched all in blood* |
| For oure giltë, for oure godë, | *for our guilt, for our benefit* |
|    For He ne giltë nevrë nought. | *He sinned never at all* |
| 5 Fewe of Hise Him were bi-levëd, | *few of His (followers) were left to Him* |
| Dred hem hadde Him al bi-revëd | *fear had deprived Him of them all* |
| Whan they sawen herë heved | *saw their head (i.e. leader)* |
|    To so shanful deth y-brought. | *so shameful a death* |

His moder, ther Him stod bisidë,
10   Ne let no ter other abidë,                           and let no tear await another
His moder, ther Him stod bisidë,
Whan she saw hire child bitidë                               befall her child
    Swich pine and deyen giltëles.                      such pain and die guiltless
Saint Johan, that was Him derë,                               who was dear to Him
On other halve Him stod eek ferë,         on the other side; also as His companion
15   And biheld with mournë cherë                      with sorrowful countenance
    His maister that him loved and ches.               who loved and chose him


Sore and harde He was y-swungen,                               beaten
Fet and hondës thurgh y-stungen,                            pierced through
Ac most of alle His other wunden                      above all his other wounds
20       Him dide His modrës sorwë wo.          His mother's grief caused Him woe
In al His pine, in al His wrakë,                              pain; suffering
That He dreigh for mannës sakë,                               endured
He saw His moder sorwë makë –                               lamenting
    Wel rewfuliche He spak hire to.                   most compassionately


25   He seydë, 'Woman, lo! me herë,                            hear me
Thi child that thou to mannë berë;              whom you in human form bore
Withouten sor and wep thou werë                       pain and weeping
    Tho Ich was of thee y-born.                               when
Ac now thou most thi pinë dreyen,                  but now you must; endure
30   Whan thou seest me with thin eyen                            eyes
Pinë thole o rode and deyen                         suffer torment; die
    To helen man that was forlorn.'          heal (i.e. redeem); who was lost


Saint Johan th'evangelistë
Hir understod thurgh hese of Cristë;               supported her; command
35   Fair he kept hire and biwistë                      kept and looked after her
And servëd hire from hond to fot.
Rewful is the minëgingë                            pitiable is the remembrance
Of this deth and this départingë;                               parting
Therin is blis meind with wepingë,               joy mingled with weeping
40       For ther-thurgh us cam allë bot.       thereby to us came all salvation


He that starf in ourë kendë,                             died in our nature
Leve us so ben ther-of mendë,                       grant us; mindful
That He yeve us atten endë                           may give us at the end
    That He hath us to y-bought.                    what He has bought for us

45  Milsful moder, maiden clenë,                    *merciful; pure*
    Mak thi milce upon us senë,           *make your mercy evident in us*
    And bring us thurgh thi swetë benë        *through thy sweet intercession*
        To the blis that faillëth nought.                    *fails not*


## 90. Jesu Cristës mildë moder

    Jesu Cristës mildë moder                      *gentle mother*
    Stod, biheld hire sone o rodë                 *on the cross*
        That he was y-pinëd on;                        *tortured*
    The sonë heng, the moder stod          *son hung; stood*
5   And biheld hire childës blod,                       *blood*
        How it of hise woundës ron.           *from his wounds ran*

    Tho He starf that king is of lif,            *when He died who*
    Drerier nas never no wif           *sadder was never any woman*
        Than thou werë, lady, tho;                  *lady, then*
10  The brightë day went into night                *turned into*
    Tho Jesu Crist, thin hertë light,       *when; your heart's light*
        Was y-queynt with pine and wo.      *was quenched with pain*

    Thy lif dreigh ful hardë stoundës   *your person suffered very severe pangs*
    Tho thou saw hise blodi woundës,                      *when*
15      And his bodi o rodë don.                       *placed*
    Hisë woundës sore and smertë              *sore and painful*
    Stongen thurgh and thurgh thi hertë,       *pierced through*
        As thee bihightë Simeon.                    *promised*

    Now his hed with blod bispronken,            *besprinkled*
20  Now his side with spere y-stongen,             *pierced*
        Thou biheldë, lady fre.                  *gracious lady*
    Now his hondës sprad o rodë,         *hands spread on the cross*
    Now hise fet washen with blodë                     *washed*
        And y-naillëd to the tre.

25 Now His bodi with scoúrgës beten,                    *beaten*
   And His blod so wide out-leten                       *so widely diffused*
     Maden thee thin hertë sor.                         *made your heart sore within you*
   Wharso thou castest thin eyen                        *wheresoever you cast*
   Pinë strong thou saw Him dreyen –                    *torment; endure*
30   Ne mightë no man tholë more.                       *suffer more*

   Now is timë that thou yeldë                          *that you should pay*
   Kindë that thou him with-heldë                       *Nature what you from him*
     Tho thi child was of thee born.                    *when*
   Now he askëth with goulingë                          *with (your) anguished cries*
35 That thou him in thi childingë                        *for what you from him; child-bearing*
     Al with-heldë ther biforn.                         *completely withheld before*

   Now thou fondest, moder mildë,                       *you experience*
   What woman dreith with hir childë,                   *what a woman suffers*
     Though thou clenë maiden be;                       *you are a pure virgin*
40 Now thee's yolden harde and derë                      *to you is given hard and dire*
   The pinë wherof thou werë                            *the pain of which*
     In thy childing quite and fre.                     *child-bearing quit and free*

   Sone after the night of sorwë,
   Sprang the light of edi morwë                        *blessed morning*
45   In thin hertë, swetë may;                          *maiden*
   Thi sorwës wenden al to blissë,                      *turned*
   Tho thi sone al mid y-wissë                          *when; with complete certainty*
     Aros upon the thriddë day.

   Weila, what thou werë blithë,                        *Lo! how happy you were*
50 Tho H'aros from deth to livë,                         *when He rose*
     Thurgh the holë ston He glod;                      *through the intact stone He glided*
   Also He was of thee boren –                          *in like manner He*
   Bothen after and biforen
     Hol bilof thy maidenhod.                           *intact remained*

55   Newë blissë He us broughtë
    That mankin so derë boughtë       *who mankind so dearly redeemed*
      And for us yaf His derë lif.         *precious life*
    Glade and blithë thou us makë      *glad and happy; make us*
    For thi swetë sonës sakë,
60      Edi maiden, blisful wif.        *blessed maiden, blissful woman*


    Quen of hevenë, for thi blissë,      *for the sake of your bliss*
    Lighte al ourë sorinissë,        *lighten all our sorrow*
      And wend our evel al into god.      *and turn*
    Bring us, moder, to thi sonë,
65   Mak us ever with Him wonë,        *with Him to dwell*
      That us boughtë with His blod.     *who redeemed us*


## 91. Stond wel, moder, under rodë

    'Stond wel, moder, under rodë,     *stand well, mother, under the cross*
    Bihold thi child wyth gladë modë,     *gladsome heart*
      Blythë moder might thou be.'     *a happy mother you may be*
    'Sone, how may I blithë stonden?     *be* (lit. *stand*) *happy*
5   I se thin feet, I se thin honden,      *hands*
      Naylëd to the hardë tre.'

    'Moder, do wey thi wepingë;       *mother, put away*
    I thole this deth for mannës thingë,     *I endure; for man's sake*
    For owen giltë thole I non.'       *for my own guilt*
10   'Sone, I fele the dethë-stoundë,      *pangs of death*
    The swerd is at min hertë-groundë,     *the bottom of my heart*
      That me by-hightë Symeon.'     *which Simeon promised me*

    'Moder, rew upon thy beren!       *have pity upon your child*
    Thow washe awey tho blodi teren,     *wash away those bloody tears*
15   It don me wersë than mi det.'    *they affect me worse than my death*
    'Sone, how might I terës wernen?      *restrain*
    I se tho blodi flodës ernen      *those streams of blood run*
      Out of thin hertë to min fet.'

'Moder, now I may thee seyë,     *I may tell you*
20 Better is that Ich onë deyë     *it is better that I alone die*
  Than al mankin to hellë go.'     *mankind; should go*
'Sone, I se thi bodi swongen,     *body beaten*
Thi brest, thin hond, thi fot thurgh-stongen     *pierced through*
  No selly nis though me be wo.'     *it is no wonder*

25 'Moder, if I dar thee tellë,     *I dare*
Yif I ne dye thou gost to hellë;     *if I do not die you go to hell*
  I thole this deth for thinë sakë.'     *endure*
'Sonë, thou beest me so mindë,     *you are so thoughtful for me*
Ne wit me nought; it is my kindë     *blame me not, it is my nature*
30   That I for thee this sorwë makë.'

'Moder, merci! let me deyen,     *die*
For Adam owt of hellë beyen,     *in order; to buy (i.e. redeem)*
  And al mankin that is forloren.'     *mankind; lost*
'Sonë, what shal me to redë?     *Son, what am I to do?*
35 Thi pinë pinëth me to dedë,     *your agony tortures me to death*
  Let me deyen thee biforen.'     *die*

'Moder, now tarst thou might leren     *now for the first time; learn*
What pinë thole that children beren,     *pain (they) suffer who; bear*
  What sorwë have that child forgon.'     *(they) have who lose a child*
40 'Sone, I wot, I can thee tellë,     *Son, I know*
Bute it be the pine of hellë     *unless; torment*
  Morë sorwë ne wot I non.'     *greater sorrow know I none*

'Moder, rew of moder carë!     *have pity on a mother's sorrow*
Now thou wost of moder farë,     *know about a mother's lot*
45   Though thou be clenë mayden-man.'     *a pure virgin*
'Sonë, help at allë nedë     *in every necessity*
Allë tho that to me gredë,     *all those who; cry*
  Maiden, wif, and fool womman.'     *foolish*

'Moder, I may no lenger dwellë,      *stay*
50  The time is come I fare to hellë,      *to go to hell*
    The thriddë day I rise upon.'      *shall rise*
'Sone, I willë with thee founden,      *go with you*
I deye, y-wis, of thinë wounden,      *I die, truly; wounds*
    So rewful deth was never non.'      *so pitiable a death*

55  When He ros tho fel thi sorwë,      *then your sorrow vanished*
Thy blissë sprong the thriddë morwë,      *on the third morning*
    Wel blithë moder wer thou tho.      *a most happy mother; then*
Moder, for that ilkë blissë,      *for that very bliss*
Bisech oure God oure sinnës lissë,      *beseech; to remit*
60    Thou be oure sheld ayayn oure fo.      *be thou our shield against our foe*

Blissed be thou quen of hevenë,
Bring us out of hellë levenë      *hell's flames*
    Thurgh thi derë sonës might.
Moder, for that heighë blodë      *noble blood*
65  That He shadde upon the rodë,      *shed*
    Led us into hevene light. Amen.      *heaven's light*

## 92. Why have ye no routhe on my child?

Why have ye no routhe on my child?      *no pity*
Have routhe on me ful of mourning;
Tak doun o rode my derworth child,      *from the cross my precious child*
4  Or prik me o rode with my derling!      *or nail me; darling*

More pine ne may me ben y-don      *more hurt may not be done to me*
Than lete me live in sorwe and shame;      *than to let*
As love me bindëth to my sone,
8  So let us deyen bothe y-same.      *die both together*

## 93. *Lovely ter of lovely eye*

Lovely ter of lovely eye,     *tear*
  Why dost thou me so wo?     *do you cause me such grief*
Sorful ter of sorful eye,     *sorrowful*
4     Thou brekst myn herte a-two.     *you are breaking; in two*

Thou sikëst sore,     *you sigh sorely*
Thi sorwe is more
  Than mannës mouth may telle;
8 Thou singest of sorwe,
Mankin to borwe     *mankind to redeem*
  Out of the pit of helle.
  *Lovely*, etc.

I proud and kene,     *bold*
12 Thou meke and clene,     *meek and pure*
  Withouten wo or wile;     *evil or guile*
Th'art ded for me     *you are dead*
I live thurgh thee,     *through you*
16   So blissëd be that while.     *time*
  *Lovely*, etc.

Thi moder seeth     *sees*
How wo thee beeth     *what woe yours is*
  And therfore yerne she yerte;     *earnestly she cried out*
20 To hire Thou speke,     *spoke*
Hire sorwe to sleke –     *alleviate*
  Swet suitë wan thin herte.     *sweet entreaty won*
  *Lovely*, etc.

Thin herte is rent,
24 Thi body is bent,
  Upon the rodë tre;
The weder is went,     *storm is past*
The devel is shent,     *destroyed*
28   Crist, thurgh the might of Thee.
  *Lovely*, etc.

## 94. I sike al when I singe

| | |
|---|---|
| I sike al when I singe, | *I sigh whenever* |
| For sorwë that I se, | *for the sorrow that I see* |
| When Ich with wepinge, | *when I* |
| 4   Biholde upon the tre. | *look upon* |
| I se Jhesu mi swete, | |
| His hertë blode forlete | *shed* |
| For the love of me. | |
| 8   His woundës waxen wete – | *grow moist* |
| Marie, milde and swete, | |
| Thou have mercy of me! | *on me* |

| | |
|---|---|
| Hye upon a doune, | *high upon a hill* |
| 12   As al folke hit se may, | |
| A mile withoute the toune, | *outside* |
| Aboutë the mid-day, | |
| The rode was up arerde; | *raised* |
| 16   His frendes were al aferde, | *afraid* |
| They clungen so the clay. | *shrank like clay* |
| The rod stondëth in ston. | *stands rooted in stone* |
| Mari hirselfe alon, | *by herself, alone* |
| 20   Hir songe was 'waylaway'. | *alas, alas!* |

| | |
|---|---|
| Whan Ich Him biholde | |
| With eye and hertë bo, | *both* |
| I se his bodi colde, | *grow cold* |
| 24   His ble waxëth al blo, | *complexion becomes all livid* |
| He hongëth al of blode | *hangs all bleeding* |
| So hey upon the rode | *high* |
| Bitwixen thevës two – | |
| 28   How sholde I singë mor? | |
| Mari, thou wepë sor, | *wept bitterly* |
| Thou wist of al His wo. | *knew* |

Wel oftë when I sike,                                            *sigh*
32   I makië mi mon;                                          *utter my lament*
Evel hit may me like –                              *ill (indeed) it may please me*
And wonder nis it non –                                *and it is no wonder*
Whan I se hongë hey                                         *hang on high*
36   And bitter peynës drey                                        *suffer*
Jhesu, mi lemmon;                                             *beloved*
His woundës sorë smerte,                                       *smart*
The sper is at his herte,
40   And thurgh His sidë gon.                                  *has passed*


The nailes ben al to stronge,
The smith is al to sleye,                                      *skilful*
Thou bledëst al to longe,
44   The tre is al to heye.                                       *high*
The stonës waxen wete –                                   *grow moist*
Allas! Jhesu mi swete,
Few frendës haddëst neye,                               *had (you) near*
48   But Seint Jon mourning,
And Mari weping,
That al thi sorwë seye.                                     *who; saw*


Wel oftë whan I slepe
52   With sorwe Ich am thurgh-sought;                       *pierced through*
Whan I wake and wepe,                                          *weep*
I thenkë in mi thought:
Allas that men ben wode! –                                      *mad*
56   Biholden on the rode                              *(they) look upon the cross*
And sellen (Ich ly nought)                          *and sell (I am not lying)*
Her soulës into sin                                     *their souls into sin*
For any worldës win,                               *for any worldly pleasure*
60   That were so der y-bought.           *(souls) which were so dearly bought*

## 95. My trewest tresowre

My trewest tresowre                               *truest treasure*
    sa trayturly was taken,                *treacherously*
Sa bytterly bondyn                                *bound*
    wyth bytand bandes,                    *biting bonds*
How sone of thi servandes                         *how soon by your servants*
    was thou forsaken,
4  And lathly for my lufe                      *hatefully for love of me*
    hurld with thair handes.               *buffeted by*

My well of my wele                                *my fountain of my joy*
    sa wrangwysly wryed,                   *so unjustly accused*
Sa pulled owt of preson                           *prison*
    to Pilate at prime;                    *prime (the first hour)*
Thaire dulles and thaire dyntes                   *blows; buffets*
    ful drerely thou dreed                 *right sorrowfully you suffered*
8  Whan thai schot in thi syght                *spat; eyes*
    bath slaver and slyme.                 *both spittle and filth*

My hope of my hele                                *salvation*
    sa hyed to be hanged,                  *thus driven*
Sa charged with thi crosce                        *so burdened; cross*
    and corond with thorne,                *crowned*
Ful sare to thi hert                              *right painfully to your heart*
    thi steppes tha stanged,               *your steps then pierced*
12  Me thynk thi bak burd breke,              *your back ought to break*
    it bendes forborne.                    *weighed down*

My salve of my sare                               *salve of my pain*
    sa saryful in syght,                   *so sorrowful to see*
Sa naked and nayled
    thi ryg on the rode,                   *your back on the cross*
Ful hydusly hyngand,                              *right hideously suspended*
    thay heved thee on hyght,              *they raised you on high*
16  Thai lete thee stab in the stane          *let you be jolted into the rock*
    all stekked that thar stode.           *which stood there all fixed in place*

My dere-worthly derlyng,                                          *my precious darling*
   sa dolefully dyght,                                    *so shamefully treated*
Sa straytly upryght                                                   *tautly*
   streyned on the rode;                                   *stretched*
For thi mykel mekenes,                                           *great meekness*
   thi mercy, thi myght,
20 Thow bete al my bales                                          *cured all my ills*
   with bote of thi blode.                                 *with the remedy*

My fender of my fose,                                             *my defender from my foes*
   sa fonden in the felde,                       *so tested in the field (of battle)*
Sa lufly lyghtand                                           *so graciously descending*
   at the evensang tyde;                                   *evensong time*
Thi moder and hir menyhe                                      *her companions*
   unlaced thi scheld,                                *unfastened your shield*
24 All weped that thar were,                               *all wept who were there*
   thi woundes was sa wyde.

My pereles prynce                                                    *peerless*
   als pure I thee pray,                             *so utterly I you beseech*
The mynde of this myrour                        *the remembrance of this example*
   thou lat me noght mysse;                          *let me not be without*
Bot wynd up my wylle                                           *increase my desire*
   to won wyth thee ay,                              *to dwell with you for ever*
28 That thou be beryd in my brest                      *so that you may be buried*
   and bryng me to blysse.

## 96. Gold and al this worldës wyn

Gold and al this worldës wyn                                    *world's joy*
   Is nought but Cristës rode;               *nothing without Christ's cross*
I wolde be clad in Cristës skyn,
4    That ran so longe on blode,
And gon t'is herte and take myn in,          *go to His heart and take my lodging*
   Ther is a fulsum fode.                       *where there is abundant food*
Than yeve I litel of kith or kyn,                  *then would I give little for*
8    For ther is allë gode.                        *there (i.e. with Christ)*

## 97. Crist maketh to man a fair present

Crist maketh to man a fair present,
His blody body with lovë brent;       *on fire with love*
That blisful body his lyf hath lent,       *has given*
4  For love of man that synne hath blent.    *whom sin has blinded*

  O lovë, love, what hast thou ment?       *intended*
  Me thinketh that love to wrathe is went.   *has turned to anger*

Thi loveliche hondes love hath to-rent,    *lovely; torn to pieces*
8  And thi lithe armes wel streit y-tent;  *gentle arms so tightly stretched*
Thi brest is bare, thi body is bent,
For wrong hath wonne and right is schent.   *won; is destroyed*

Thi myldë bones love hath to-drawe,   *gentle bones; pulled apart*
12  The nayles thi feet han al to-gnawe;  *have quite gnawed to pieces*
The lord of love love hath now slawe,    *slain*
Whane love is strong it hath no lawe.    *law (i.e. limit)*

  His herte is rent,
16  His body is bent
    Upon the rodë tre;
  Wrong is went,       *is overthrown*
  The devel is schent,      *is destroyed*
20    Crist, thurgh the might of thee.   *through*

For thee that herte is leyd to wedde;   *is given as a pledge*
Swych was the love that herte us kedde,   *such; showed*
That hertë barst, that hertë bledde,    *burst*
24  That hertë blood oure soulës fedde.  *heart's blood; fed*

That hertë clefte for treuthe of love,  *broke for constancy of love*
Therfore in Him oon is trewe love;    *in Him alone*
For love of thee that herte is yove,    *is given*
28  Kepe thou that herte and thou art above.  *victorious*

Lovë, love, where schalt thou wone?                    *dwell*
Thi wonyng-stede is thee bi-nome,         *dwelling-place is taken from you*
For Cristës herte, that was thin home –
32   He is deed, now hast thou none.                          *dead*


Lovë, love, whi doest thou so?
Love, thou brekest myn herte a-two.                    *in two*


Love hath schewëd his greet myght,
36   For love hath maad of day the nyght;
Love hath slawe the kyng of ryght,                      *slain*
And love hath endëd the strong fight.


So inliche love was never noon;                    *such deep love*
40   That witen wel Marie and Jon,                        *know well*
And also wite thei everychon,                    *know they each one*
That love with Him hath maad at oon.   *whom love with Him has made at one*


Love makëth, Crist, thin hertë myn,
44   So makëth love myn hertë thin;
Thanne scholdë myn be trewe al tym,         *be true at all times*
And love in love schal make it fyn.               *make it perfect*


## 98. A sory beverage it is

A sory beverage it is                              *sorrowful drink*
   and sore it is abought,                    *grievously it is paid for*
Now in this sharpë time                       *to this bitter moment*
4      this brewing hath me brought.         *this brew has brought me*
Fader, if it mowe ben don                          *may be done*
   as I have besought                              *implored*
Do awey this beverage                             *put away*
8      that I ne drink it nought.


And if it mowe no better ben                   *if it may no better be*
   for allë mannës gilt,                  *because of all man's guilt*
That it ne mustë nedë                    *(than) that it must needs be*
12      that my blod be spilt,                        *should be*

Swetë Father, I am Thy sone
   Thi wil be fulfilt,                    *fulfilled*
I am her, thin owen child,              *here*
16     I wil don as thou wilt.              *do*

## 99. Ye that pasen be the wey

Ye that pasen be the wey,
   abide a litel stounde;          *pause a little while*
Beholdëth, al mi felawes,            *my fellows*
4     yif ani me lik is founde.       *if anyone like me*
To the tre with nailës thre
   wel fast I hangë bounde,      *very fast;  hang*
With a spere al thurgh mi side        *through*
8     to min herte is made a wounde.   *to my heart*

## 100. My folk, now answerë me

My folk, now answerë me,
   And sey what is my gilt;          *say;  guilt*
What might I mor ha don for thee,    *have done*
4     That I ne have fulfilt?        *fulfilled*

Out of Egipte I broughtë thee,
   Ther thou wer in thi wo;       *where;  woe*
And wikkedliche thou nomë me,   *wickedly;  took me*
8     As I hadde ben thi fo.       *as if;  foe*

Over al I leddë thee          *everywhere I led thee*
   And aforn thee I yede;    *and before you I went*
And no frendschipe fond I in thee    *found I*
12     Whan that I haddë nede.     *need*

Fourti winter I sentë thee                          *for forty years*
  Angeles mete fro hevene;                      *angel's food from heaven*
And thou heng me on rodë tre,                        *hung me on a cross*
16  And greddëst with loud stevene.            *reviled (me) with loud outcry*

Heilsom water I sentë thee                           *wholesome*
  Out of the hardë ston;
And eisel and galle thou sentëst me,                 *vinegar and gall*
20  Other yaf thou me non.                     *gave*

The see I parted asonder for thee,                   *sea; asunder*
  And ledde thee thurgh wel wide;              *through with ample space*
And the hertë blod to sen of me,                     *heart's blood to see*
24  Thou smottest me thurgh the side.          *through*

Alle thi fon I slow for thee,                        *all your foes I slew*
  And made thee couth of name;                 *renowned in name*
And thou heng me on rodë tre,                        *hung me*
28  And didest me mychel shame.                *great shame*

A kingës yerde I bitook thee                         *king's sceptre I granted you*
  Til thou wer al beforn;                      *until; above all (others)*
And thou heng me on rodë tre,
32  And crounëdest me with thorn.              *crowned*

I made thin enemies and thee
  For to ben knowen asonder;                   *known apart*
And on an hey hil thou henge me,                     *high hill you hung me*
36  Al the world on me to wonder.              *for all; to wonder at me*

## 101. Jhesus doth him bymene

Jhesus doth him bymene,                              *Jesus complains*
And speketh to synful mon:                           *man*
'Thy garland is of grene,                            *green*
4 Of flourës many on;                                *flowers many a one*
Myn of sharpë thornes,
Myn hewe it makëth won.                              *complexion; pale*

'Thyn hondës streitë glovëd,                          *your hands are tightly gloved*
8  White and clenë kept;                                          *clean*
   Myne with nailës thorlëd                                     *pierced*
   On rode, and eke my feet.                          *on the cross; also*

   'Acros thou berest thyn armes,                            *crossed*
12 Whan thou dauncëst narwe,                   *you dance close together*
   To me hastou non awe                  *for me have you no reverence*
   But to worldës glorie;                          *but only for worldly glory*
   Myne for thee on rode,                                    *my (arms)*
16 With the Jewës wode,                             *by the mad Jews*
   With gretë ropes to-draw.                             *pulled apart*

   'Open thou hast thi syde,
   Spaiers longe and wide,                                  *(with) slits*
20 For veyn glorie and pride,
   And thi longe knif astrout –                            *sticking out*
   Thou art of the gai route;                                *company*
   Myn with sperë sherpe                       *my (side); a sharp spear*
24 Y-stongen to the herte,                                     *pierced*
   My body with scourgës smerte                              *painful*
   Bi-swongen al aboute.                              *beaten all over*

   'Al that I tholede on rode for thee,            *suffered on the cross*
28     To me was shame and sorwë;
   Wel litel thou lovëst me,                                *very little*
   And lassë thou thenkëst on me,                              *less*
       An evene and eke amorwë.                     *night and morning*

32 'Swetë brother, wel might thou se,
   Thes peynës stronge on rodë tre
   Have I tholed for love of thee;                          *suffered*
   They that havë wrought it me                          *done it to me*
36     Mai syngë weylawo.                                     *alas*
   Be thou kinde par charité,                          *for love's sake*
   Let thy synne and love thou me,                           *leave*
   Hevenë blisse I shal yeve thee,                           *give*
40     That lastëth ay and oo.'                      *for ever and ever*

## 102. Lo! lemman swete, now may thou se

| | |
|---|---|
| Lo! lemman swete, now may thou se | *beloved; may you see* |
| That I have lost my lyf for thee – | *my life* |
| What myght I do thee mare? | *do for you; more* |
| 4 Forthi I pray thee speciali | *therefore; especially* |
| That thow forsake ill company | |
| That woundës me so sare; | *sorely* |

| | |
|---|---|
| And take myne armës pryvëly | *my arms* (i.e. *armour*) *secretly* |
| 8 And do tham in thi tresory, | *and put them in your treasury* |
| In what stede sa thow dwellës, | *in whatever place you dwell* |
| And, swete lemman, forget thow noght | *not* |
| That I thi lufe sa dere have boght, | *your love so dearly have bought* |
| 12 And I aske thee noght ellës. | *I shall ask thee nothing else* |

## 103. Stedfast crosse, among alle other

| | |
|---|---|
| Stedfast crosse, among alle other | *among all others* |
| Thou art a tre michel of pris, | *of great price* |
| In braunche and flourë swych another | *branch and blossom such another* |
| 4 I ne wot non in wode ne rys. | *I know none in wood nor thicket* |
| Swete the nailes, and swete the tre, | *sweet* |
| And swetter the burden that hangeth on thee! | *sweeter* |

## 104. What is he, this lordling  by William Herbert

| | |
|---|---|
| 'What is he, this lordling | *young lord* |
| that comëth from the fight | |
| With blod-rede wedë | *blood-red garments* |
| so grisliche y-dight, | *terribly arrayed* |
| So faire y-cointisëd, | *beautifully apparelled* |
| so semlich in syght, | *fair to see* |

4  So stiflichë gangëth,    *who so bravely advances*
      so doughty a knight?'    *valiant*
'Ich hit am, Ich hit am,    *it is I*
      that ne spekë bute right,
Champioun to helen    *save*
      mankinde in fyght.'

'Why thenne is thy shroud red,    *thy clothing red*
      with blod al y-meind,    *all mingled*
8  As tredderes in wringe    *like treaders in the wine-press*
      with must al bispreynd?'    *with must all spattered*

'The wringe Ich have y-treddëd    *wine-press; trod*
      al myself on,    *myself all alone*
And of al mankinde    *for all mankind*
      ne was non other won.    *no other hope*
Ich hem have y-treddëd    *them*
      in wrathe and in grame,    *in wrath and in anger*
12  And al my wede is bispreynd    *my clothing is spattered*
      with here blod y-same,    *with their blood together*
And al my robe y-foulëd    *garment defiled*
      to here gretë shame.    *to their great disgrace*
The day of thilke wreche    *of that vengeance*
      liveth in my thought,
The yer of medës yelding    *year of reward-giving*
      ne foryet Ich nought.    *forget I not*
16  Ich lokëd al aboute    *looked all about*
      som helpynge mon;    *for someone to help (me)*
Ich soughte al the route    *searched all the crowd*
      bote help nas ther non.    *was there none*
Hit was myn owne strengthe
      that this bote wroughte,    *salvation wrought*
Myn owne doughtynesse    *own courage*
      that help ther me broughte.
20  Ich have y-treddëd the folk
      in wrathe and in grame,    *in wrath and in anger*
Adreynt al with shennesse,    *drowned; ignominy*
      y-drawe doun wyth shame.'    *dragged down*

'On Godës milsfulnesse                                          *mercifulness*
    Ich wole bi-thenche me,                              *I will bethink me*
And herien Him in alle thing                             *and praise; everything*
    that He yeldëth me.'                                    *grants*


## 105. As I me rod this ender day

As I me rod this ender day                        *as I rode out the other day*
By grenë wode to sechë play,                *by the green wood to seek pleasure*
Mid herte I thoughte al on a may,       *in my heart; entirely on a maiden*
4    Swetest of allë thinge;                          *of all creatures*
Lithe, and Ich you tellë may                           *listen*
    Al of that swetë thinge.


This maide is swete and fre of blod,                  *noble of blood*
8 Bright and fair, of mildë mod,                  *of gentle disposition*
Allë she mai don us god                                      *do*
    Thurgh hirë bisechinge;                       *her intercession*
Of hirë He tok flesh and blod,                            *from her*
12    Jesus, hevenë kynge.                            *king of heaven*


With al my lif I love that may,                        *that maiden*
She is my solas night and day,                            *comfort*
My joie and eke my bestë play,            *and also my greatest pleasure*
16    And eke my love-longynge;               *and also my love's desire*
Al the bet me is that day                              *the better to me*
    That Ich of hirë synge.                            *of her may sing*


Of allë thinge I love hire mest,                            *most*
20 My dayës blis, my nightës rest,
She counseillëth and helpëth best
    Bothen olde and yinge;                        *both old and young*
Now I may yif that me lest                          *now I may if I wish*
24    The fivë joiës mynge.                           *call to mind*


The firstë joie of that woman
When Gabriel from hevenë cam                          *came*
And seide God sholde bicomen man                     *should*

28 And of hire be bore, *of her be born*
And bringen up of hellë pyn *from the torment of hell*
   Mankyn that was forlore. *mankind which had been lost*

That other joië of that may *second joy; maiden*
32 Was o Cristës-massë day, *was on*
Whan God was bore on thorogh lay, *was born in perfect light*
   And broughtë us lightnesse; *and brought us light*
The ster was seyn biforë day, *(that) the star was seen*
36    This herdës bere wytnesse. *these shepherds bear witness*

The thriddë joie of that lady,
That men clepe th' Epyphany, *which men call the Epiphany*
When the kingës come wery *came weary*
40    To presente hyre sone *to present her son*
With myrrë, gold, and encens hy, *holy incense*
   That was man bicome. *who had become man*

The fourthë joie we tellë mawen, *we may tell*
44 On Ester-morwe when hit gan dawen, *Easter morning when it dawned*
Hyrë sonë, that was slawen, *who was slain*
   Aros in flesh and bon; *bone*
Morë joie men have ne mawen, *may not have*
48    Wyf ne mayden non. *woman nor any maiden*

The fiftë joie of that woman,
When hire body to hevene cam,
The soulë to the body nam *went*
52    As hit was wont to bene. *as (i.e. where) it was wont to be*
Crist leve us alle with that woman *Christ grant us*
   That joie al for to sene. *to see*

Preye we alle to oure lady, *pray*
56 And to the seintes that wone hire by, *dwell beside her*
That they of us haven merci, *may have mercy*
   And that we ne misse *we may not fail*
In this world to ben holy *be*
60    And wynnë hevenë blysse. *win the bliss of heaven*

## 106. Somer is come and winter gon

| | |
|---|---|
| Somer is come and winter gon, | *has come; gone* |
| this day bigineth to longë, | *lengthen* |
| And this foulës everichon | *these birds every one* |
| joyen hem with songë; | *rejoice in singing* |
| 5    So strongë | *such intense* |
| care me bint, | *sorrow binds me* |
| al with joyë that me fint | *despite the joy that is found* |
| in londë, | *everywhere* |
| Al for a child | |
| 10    that is so milde | *gracious* |
| of hondë. | *in manner (lit. with hand)* |

| | |
|---|---|
| That child that is so milde and wlanc | *gentle and noble* |
| and eke of gretë moundë, | *also of great power* |
| Bothe in boskës and in bank | *in woods and on hill-side* |
| 15    y-sought me hath a stoundë; | *has sought me for a while* |
| Y-founde | *found* |
| he havëd me, | *he had (found) me* |
| for an appel of a tre, | *on account of an apple from a tree* |
| y-boundë; | *bound* |
| 20    He brak the bond, | *broke* |
| that was so strong, | |
| with woundë. | *through (His) wounds* |

| | |
|---|---|
| That child that was so wilde and bold | *defiant and daring* |
| to me aloutë lowë; | *bowed low* |
| 25  Fram me to Jewës he was sold, | *by me to the Jews* |
| ne couthe they him nought knowë. | *they could not recognize him* |
| 'Do we', | *Let us* |
| saiden he, | *said they* |
| 'naile we him upon a tre | *let us nail him* |
| 30    a lowë, | *on a hill* |
| Ac erst we shullen | *but first we must* |
| shamen him | *make mock of him* |
| a throwë.' | *for a while* |

Jhesu is the childës namë,
35  king of allë londë;                              *lands*
Of the king they maden game                         *made sport*
  and smiten him with hondë;               *smote him with (their) hands*
    To fonde                                            *to test*
  him on a tre
40 They yeve him woundës two and thre                     *gave*
    mid hondë;                                          *by hand*
  Of bitter drink
    they senden him                                   *sent him*
    a sondë.                                             *a gift*

45 Deth he nam o rodë-tre,                    *accepted on the cross*
    that lif is of us allë;             *he who is life of us all*
  Ne mightë hit nought other be                    *be otherwise*
    but we sholden fallë;                  *unless we were to fall*
      And walle                                      *and to boil*
50    in hellë dep                                        *deep*
  nerë neverë so swet                               *were never*
      with allë;
    Ne mighte us socour                   *nothing could help us*
    castel, tour                               *castle, tower*
55    ne hallë.                                         *nor hall*

Mayde and moder ther astod,                      *remained there*
  Marie ful of gracë,
She let the terës al of blod            *she let her tears, all bloody*
  fallen in the placë;                          *in that place*
60      The trace                                         *trail*
  ran of her blode,
changëd herë flesh and rode                       *complexion*
  and facë;
    He was todrawe,                               *rent apart*
65    so deer y-slawe,                          *like a deer slain*
    in chacë.                                     *in the chase*

Deth he nam, the swetë man,                     *death he accepted*
  wel heigh upon the rodë;                *so high upon the cross*
He wessh our sinnës everichan         *washed away; every one*
70    mid his swetë blodë.                                *with*

Mid flode                                               *with a torrent*
he loute adoun                                          *he bent down*
and brac the yates of that prisoun                      *broke the gates*
    that stode,                                         *which stood (against him)*
75  And ches herë                                       *and from (lit. out of) them chose*
    out that there                                      *those who there*
    were godë.                                          *good*

He ros him ene the thriddë day                          *He rose by His own power*
    and set him on his trone;                           *seated Himself on His throne*
80 He wol come a domës-day                              *will come on Doomsday*
    to dem us everich one.                              *to judge us every one*
        Grone                                           *let (the man) groan*
        and wepë ay,                                    *and ever weep*
    the man that deyth withouten lay,                   *(who) dies without faith*
85          alone;                                      *alone*
        Grant us, Christ,
        with thin uprist                                *resurrection*
        to gon.                                         *go*


## 107. Lullay, lullay, litel child

*Lullay, lullay, litel child,*
*Why wepëst thou so sore?*                              *bitterly*

Lullay, lullay, litel child,
4  Thou that were so sterne and wild,
Now art becomë meke and mild
    To save that was forlore.                           *what was lost*
        *Lullay,* etc.

8  But for my sinne I wot it is                         *only; I know*
That Goddës sonë suffrëth this,
Merci lord, I have do mis,                              *done wrong*
    Y-wis I wile no more.                               *certainly*
12      *Lullay,* etc.

Ayeyns my fadrës wille I ches         *against; chose*
An appel with a rewful res,         *on a lamentable impulse*
Wherfore myn heritage I les,         *lost*
16     And now thou wepest therfore.
       *Lullay*, etc.

An appel I tok of a tre,         *from a tree*
God it hadde forboden me;         *forbidden*
20 Wherfore I sholde dampnëd be,         *damned*
    Yif thy weping ne wore.         *were*
       *Lullay*, etc.

Lullay for wo, thou litel thing,
24 Thou litel barun, thou litel king,         *lord / child*
Mankinde is cause of thy mourning,
    That thou hast loved so yore.         *so long since*
       *Lullay*, etc.

28 For man that thou hast ay loved so         *always*
Yet shaltou suffren peynës mo,         *more pains*
In hed, in feet, in hondës two,
    And yet wepen wel more.         *and still weep much more*
32       *Lullay*, etc.

That peyne us make of sinnë fre,         *may that pain make us free from sin*
That peyne us bringe Jhesú to thee,
That peyne us helpë ay to fle
36     The wikked fendës lore.         *fiend's promptings*
       *Lullay*, etc.

## 108. Adam lay y-bownden

Adam lay y-bownden,         *bound*
    bownden in a bond,
Fower thousand wynter,         *years*
4     thought he not to long.         *too long*

And al was for an appil,
   an appil that he took,
As clerkës fynden writen,                    *scholars find written*
8   writen in here book.                       *their*

Ne hadde the appil takë,                     *had the apple not taken*
   the appil takë ben,                      *(not) been taken*
Ne haddë never our lady                      *our lady would never*
12   have ben hevenë quen.                    *have been queen of heaven*

Blessëd be the tymë
   that appil takë was,
Therfore we mown singen,                     *may sing*
16   'Deo gratias!'                           *thanks be to God!*

PART IV: *Miscellaneous Lyrics*

## 109. Er ne couthe Ich sorwë non

Er ne couthe Ich sorwë non,     *formerly knew I no sorrow*
Nou Ich mot menen min mon;     *must utter my lament*
  Carful, wel sore Ich sichë.     *full of care, most bitterly I sigh*
Giltles Ich tholë muchel shamë;     *guiltless I suffer*
5 Help, God, for thin swetë namë,
  King of hevënë richë.     *King of the kingdom of heaven*

Jesu Crist, soth God, soth man,     *true*
Loverd, thou rew upon me!     *Lord, take pity*
  Of prison ther Ich in am     *from the prison which I am in*
10 Bring me out and makë fre.     *make (me) free*
Ich and minë ferës somë     *some of my companions*
(God wot Ich ne lyë nought)     *God knows I do not lie*
  For othrë han misnomë,     *because others have done wrong*
Ben in thys prison y-brought.     *are in*

15 Almighty,
That wel lightly     *who so readily*
Of bale is hele and botë,     *of torment is salvation and remedy*
Hevenë king,     *King of heaven*
Of this woning     *from this misery*
20 Out us bringë motë.     *may you bring us out*
Foryif hem,     *forgive them*
The wykkë men,     *wicked*
God, yif it is thy willë,
For whos gilt     *whose guilt*
25 We ben y-pilt     *we have been thrust*
In this prison illë.     *into this evil prison*

Ne hopë non to this livë —                    *Let no man trust in this life*
Her ne may he bilivë;                              *remain*
Heighë though he styë,                         *high; ascend*
30  Deth him fellëth to groundë.            *Death fells him*
Nou hath man wele and blissë,          *prosperity and joy*
Rathe he shal ther-of missë;              *soon; lose*
Worldës welë, mid y-wissë,             *worldly prosperity, assuredly*
Ne lastëth bute an stoundë.            *lasts but a moment*


35  Maiden that bare the heven-king,        *bore the King of heaven*
Besech thin sone, that swetë thing,        *beseech*
That he have of us rewsing                        *pity*
And bring us of this woning                  *from this misery*
For his muchëlë milsë.                          *great mercy*
40  He bring us out of this wo                 *may He bring*
And us techë werchen so                        *so to act*
In this life, go how s'it go,                   *go however it may*
That we moten ay and o                *that we may for ever and ever*
Haven the echë blissë.                         *have eternal bliss*


## 110. Somer is y-comen in

*Sing, cuckóu, nou! Sing, cuckóu!*                *Sing, cuckoo, now*
*Sing, cuckóu! Sing, cuckóu, nou!*

Somer is y-comen in,                                     *has come in*
  loudë sing, cuckóu!                            *sing loudly, cuckoo*
5  Growëth sed and blowëth med      *seed grows; the meadow blossoms*
  and springth the wodë nou.            *the wood comes into leaf now*
Sing, cuckóu!

Ewë bletëth after lamb,                           *the ewe bleats for*
  lowth áfter cálvë cóu;                  *the cow lows for the calf*
10  Bullok stertëth, bukkë vertëth,        *leaps; the buck cavorts*
  merye sing, cuckóu!                                 *sing merrily*

Cúckou, cúckou,
Wél singést thou, cúckou,
Ne swik thou never nou!                          *do not stop ever*

## 111. Say me, wight in the brom

'Say me, wight in the brom,                    *tell me, creature in the broom*
Teche me hou I shal don                                      *what I must do*
That min housëbondë                                    *so that my husband*
Me lovien woldë.'                                          *should love me*

5   'Hold thine tongë stillë
And have al thine willë.'

## 112. Hit was upon a Shere Thorsday

Hit was upon a Shere Thorsday                       *Maundy Thursday*
    that oure Loverd aros,                               *our Lord arose*
Ful mildë were the wordës
4      Hé spac to Judäs:                                          *spoke*

'Judás thou most to Jursëlem,                   *must (go); Jerusalem*
    oure metë for to bigge;                            *our food; to buy*
Thritty platës of selver                                 *coins of silver*
8      thou bere upon thy rigge;                    *you are to carry on your back*
Thou comest fer i the brodë strete,     *you will go far along the highway*
    fer i the brodë strete;
Some of thinë kinnësmen                                      *kinsmen*
12      ther thou mayst y-mete.'                                *may meet*

He mettë with his suster                             *he met; sister*
    the swikëlë wommon:                                    *treacherous*
'Judas, thou were worthe                                *you deserve*
16      me stondë thee with ston,                        *to be stoned*

Judas, thou were worthe
  me stondë thee with ston,
For the falsë prophete
20    that thou bilevest upon.'

'Be stillë, levë suster,           *be quiet, dear sister*
  thin hertë thee tobreke!     *may your very heart break*
Wiste min Loverd Crist,       *if my Lord Christ knew*
24    ful wel He wolde be wreke.'   *right thoroughly; avenged*

'Judas, go thou on the rok,     *go on to the cliff*
  heighe upon the ston,       *high upon the crag*
Lay thin heved i my barm,     *head in my lap*
28    slep thou thee anon.'      *go straight to sleep*

Sonë so Judás              *as soon as Judas*
  of slepë was awake,        *from sleep*
Thritty platës of selver
32    from him were y-take.     *had been taken*

He drow hymselvë by the top    *he tore his hair*
  that al it lavede ablode;    *it all streamed with blood*
The Jewës out of Jursëlem
36    awenden he were wode.    *thought he was mad*

Forth hym com the richë Jew    *forward came*
  that hightë Pilatús:       *who was called*
'Wilt thou selle thy Loverd     *Lord*
40    that hightë Jesús?'       *who is called Jesus*

'I nil selle my Loverd        *I will not*
  for nonës kinnës aughte,    *for money of any kind*
But it be for thritty platës    *unless it is for the thirty coins*
44    that He me bitaughte.'    *which he entrusted to me*

'Wilt thou selle thy Loverd Crist
  for enës kinnës golde?'     *gold of any kind*
'Nay, but hit be for the platës' –   *no, unless it is*
48    that he haven wolde.     *that he wished to have*

| | |
|---|---|
| In him com our Lord gon as | *our Lord Christ came walking in* |
| His postlës satte at mete: | *apostles sat at their meal* |
| 'Hów sittë ye, postlës, | *why are you sitting* |
| 52    and why nillë ye ete? | *will you not eat* |
| Hów sittë ye, postlës, | |
| and why nillë ye ete? | |
| Ich am abought and y-sold | *I have been bought and sold* |
| 56    today for ourë mete.' | *food* |

| | |
|---|---|
| Up stod him Judás, | *Judas stood up* |
| 'Lord am I that frec? | *that man* |
| I nas never on the stede | *was never in the place* |
| 60    ther me thee evel spec.' | *where evil was spoken of you* |

| | |
|---|---|
| Up him stod Peter | |
| and spak with al his mightë: | |
| 'Though Pilatus him comë | *though Pilate should come* |
| 64    with ten hundred knightë, | *knights* |
| Though Pilatus him comë, | |
| with ten hundred knightë, | |
| Yet Ich woldë, Loverd, | *would* |
| 68    for Thy lovë fightë.' | *for the love of you* |

| | |
|---|---|
| 'Stillë thou be, Peter, | *be quiet* |
| wel I thee y-cnowe; | *know* |
| Thou wilt forsake me thryës | *thrice* |
| 72    er the cok him crowe.' | *before the cock crows* |

## 113. Ich herde men upon mold

| | |
|---|---|
| Ich herde men upon mold | *I heard men on earth* |
| makë muche mon, | *utter great lamentation* |
| Hou he ben y-tened | *how they are harassed* |
| of herë tilyinge: | *in their farming* |
| Gode yerës and corn | *good years and corn-crops* |
| bothe ben a-gon; | *both have gone* |

Ne kepen here no sawe                    *they care to hear no tales*
  ne no song singe.                        *nor sing any song*
5 Now we mote werche,                     *now we must labour*
  nis ther non other won,                  *there is no other option*
May Ich no lengere                         *I can no longer*
  live with my lesinge;                    *my losses*
Yet ther is a bitterer                     *more bitter*
  bit to the bon,                          *cut to the bone*
For ever the ferthe peni                   *for always every fourth penny*
  mot to the kinge.                        *must go*

Thus we carpen for the king,               *complain because of the king*
  and caren ful colde,                     *and are vexed most bitterly*
10 And wenen for to kevere,                *and hope to recover*
  and ever ben a-cast;                     *and always are cast down*
Whoso hath any god,                        *if anyone has anything of value*
  hopëth he nought to holde,               *he doesn't expect to keep it*
But ever the levest                        *always the dearest possessions*
  we lesen a-last.                         *we lose in the end*

Lither is to lesen                         *wicked it is to lose*
  ther as litel is,                        *where there is little*
And haven many hynen                       *and we have many labourers*
  that hopen therto;                       *who look for their share*
15 The hayward hetëth us harm              *the hayward threatens us trouble*
  to haven of his;                         *to get his bit*
The bailif becknëth us bale                *the bailiff hints at trouble for us*
  and wenëth wel do;                       *and expects to do well*
The wodeward waytëth us wo                 *the wood-keeper treats us badly*
  that loken under rys;                    *who forage under trees*
Ne may us rise no rest,                    *for us there can be no rest*
  richës ne ro.                            *prosperity nor peace*
Thus me pilëth the poure                   *thus the poor man is robbed*
  that is of litë pris:                    *who is of little account*
20 Nede in swete and in swink              *inevitably in sweat and in toil*
  swindë mot so.                           *so must he perish*

Nede he mot swyndë    *he needs must perish*
  (though he hade swore)    *though he had vowed (not to)*
That nath nought an hood    *he who has not a hood*
  his hed for to hide!    *to cover his head*
Thus Wil walkëth in lond,    *so Will walks the land*
  and lawe is forlore,    *abandoned*
And al is pikëd of the poure    *and stolen from the poor is all*
  the prikërës pride.    *the rider's array*

25   Thus me pilëth the poure    *thus the poor are robbed*
  and pikëth ful clene,    *and stripped quite clean*
The riche men reimen    *the powerful plunder*
  withouten any right; 
Her londes and her ledës    *their lands and their property*
  lyen ful lene    *lie completely barren*
Thurgh bidding of bailifs,    *through the demands of bailiffs*
  such harm hem han hight.    *have they threatened them*
Men of religioun,    *men in religious orders*
  me halt hem ful hene,    *are held in utter contempt*
30   Baroun and bonde,    *by baron and peasant*
  the clerk and the knight.    *the cleric and the knight*
Thus Wil walkëth in lond,    *thus Will walks the land*
  and wandred is wene    *poverty is expected*
Falsshipe fattëth    *Falsehood grows fat*
  and marrëth with might.    *and brings ruin by his might*

Stont stille in the stede    *he stands there unmoved*
  and halt him ful sturne    *and behaves most sternly*
That makëth beggeres go    *he who causes beggars to go*
  with burdoun and baggës.    *with staff and bags*
35   Thus we ben hunted    *are hunted*
  from halë to hurne;    *from corner to corner*
That er werëde robës,    *we who formerly wore robes*
  nou weren raggës.    *now wear rags*

Yet comen bideles    *furthermore tax-collectors come*
  with ful muchë bost:    *with such great arrogance*
'Greythë me silver    *pay me silver*
  to the grenë wax;    *for the green wax*

Thou art writen i my writ,   *entered in my schedule*
  that thou well wost!' –   *well know*
40 Mo than ten sithës   *more than ten times*
  told I my tax.   *I have paid my tax*
'Thenne mot Ich have   *then I must have*
  hennës arost,   *roast hens*
Fair on fish-day   *fine; on fish-day*
  laumprey and lax;   *lamprey and salmon*
Forth to the chepinge!' –   *be off to the market*
  gaynëth no chost,   *nothing's to be gained by arguing*
Though I selle my bil   *even though I have to sell my hoe*
  and my borst-ax.   *and my logging axe*

45 Ich mot layë my wed   *I must put down my deposit*
  wel, yif I wille,   *in full, if I am willing*
Other sellë my corn  
  on gras that is grene.   *still green on the blade*
Yet I shal be 'foul cherl',   *yet I shall be (called) 'foul peasant'*
  though they han the fille;   *even though they get the full amount*
That Ich allë yer spare,   *what I all the year save*
  thenne I mot spene.   *then I must spend*

Nede I mot spene   *of necessity I have to spend*
  that I sparëd yore;   *what I previously saved*
50 Ayein this cachereles comen   *against the time these catch-polls come*
  thus I mot care;   *thus I have to worry*
Comëth the maister bidel,   *the chief tax-collector*
  brist as a bore,   *bristling like a boar*
Saith he wille my bigging   *my home*
  bringë ful bare.   *strip completely bare*
Mede I mot minten,   *a bribe; I must think of*
  a mark other more,   *a mark or more*
Though Ich at the set day   *even though I on the set day*
  sellë my mare.   *have to sell my mare*
55 Thus the grenë wax   *so taxation*
  us grevëth under gore –   *grieves us deeply*
That me us huntëth   *that we should be hunted*
  as hound doth the hare.   *as a hound does the hare*

They us hunten as hound
    hare doth on hille;            *on the hill*
Sithe I tok to the lond      *since I took to (tilling) the land*
    such tene me was taught.    *such trouble have I been taught*
N'aven ner bideles        *never have tax-collectors*
    bodëd her fille,      *declared their full takings*
60 For they may scape        *for they can escape*
    and we aren ever caught.    *and we are always caught*

Thus I kippe and cacche      *so I get and come by*
    carës ful colde,      *sorrows most bitter*
Sithe I countë and cot    *since I accounts and a smallholding*
    hadë to kepe.        *had to keep*
To seche silver to the king    *to find silver for the king*
    I my seed solde,
Forthy my lond leye lith,    *for which reason my land lies fallow*
    and lernëth to slepe.    *and learns to sleep*
65 Sithe they my faire fee    *after that; my fine livestock*
    fette y my folde.      *took away from my fold*
When I think o my wele,    *on my (former) prosperity*
    wel nigh I wepe.
Thus breden manye        *so are bred many*
    beggërës bolde,      *bold beggars*
And oure reye is roted     *and our rye is rotten*
    and ruls er we repe.    *and useless before we reap it*

Ruls is oure reye         *useless is our rye*
    and roted in the stree,    *and rotten on the stalk*
70 For wickëde wederes     *because of severe storms*
    by brokes and by brynke.    *by streams and by bank*
Thus wakenëth in the world    *so there awakes in the world*
    wandred and wee –    *distress and woe*
As god is swinden anon    *it is as well to perish forthwith*
    as so for to swinke!    *as so to toil*

## 114. Man in the moonë stont and strit

Man in the moonë
    stont and strit, *the man in the moon*
    *stands still and strides out*
On his bot-forke *on his hay fork*
    his burthen he berëth; *he carries his bundle*
Hit is muchë wonder *it is a great wonder*
    that he n'adoun slit, *that he does not fall down*
For doute leste he falle, *for fear lest he fall*
    he shoddrëth and sherëth. *he trembles and swerves*
5 When the frost fresëth *when the frost freezes*
    muche chele he bit; *great chill he endures*
The thornës beth kene *the thorns are sharp*
    his hattren to-terëth. *which tear his clothes to pieces*
Nis no wight in the world *there is nobody in the world*
    that wot when he sit, *who knows when he sits down*
Ne, bute hit be the hegge, *nor, unless it be the hedge*
    what wedës he werëth. *what garments he wears*

Whider trowëth this man *where does this man think*
    ha the way take? *he is going*
10 He hath set his o fot *he has set one foot*
    his other to-foren. *in front of the other*
For non highte that he hath *whatever haste that he may be in*
    ne seeth me him ner shake, *one never sees him stir*
He is the sloweste man
    that ever was y-boren!
Wher he were o the feld *wherever he might be in the field*
    pichinge stake, *planting cuttings*
For hope of his thornës *hoping with his thorns*
    to ditten his doren, *to stop up his gaps*
15 He mot mid his twi-bil *he must with his two-edged axe*
    other trous make *make another bundle (of thorns)*
Other al his dayës werk *or else all his day's work*
    ther were y-loren. *there would be lost*

This ilkë man upon heigh      *this same man up there*
    when er he were,      *whatever his origin*
Wher he were i the moone      *whether he was in the moon*
    boren and y-fed,      *born and nurtured*
He lenëth on his forke      *he leans on his fork*
    as a grey frere.      *like a grey friar*
20 This crokëdë kaynard      *this hunched idler*
    sore he is adred.      *he is sore afraid*
Hit is mony day go      *it is many a day gone*
    that he was here;      *since he was here*
Ichot of his ernde      *I reckon that in his errand*
    he nath nought y-sped:      *he has not succeeded*
He hath hewe somwher      *he has cut somewhere*
    a burthen of brere,      *a bundle of briars*
Therefore sum hayward      *for this some hedge-keeper*
    hath taken his wed.      *has taken his pledge*

25 'If thy wed is y-take,      *if your pledge has been taken*
    bring hom the trous,      *bring home the bundle*
Sete forth thyn other fot,      *put forward your other foot*
    strid over sty.      *stride along the way*
We shule praye the hayward      *we shall invite the hedge-keeper*
    hom to our hous      *home to our house*
And maken him at eise      *and make him at ease*
    for the maistry;      *as much as possible*
Drinke to him deerly      *drink to him warmly*
    of ful good bous,      *with right good liquor*
30 And our dame douse      *sweet wife*
    shal sitten him by. 
When that he is drunke
    as a dreynt mous,      *as a drowned mouse*
Thenne we shule borwe      *then we shall redeem*
    the wed attë baily!'      *the pledge from the bailiff*

This man herëth me nought      *hears me not*
    though Ich to him crye;      *shout to him*
Ichot the cherl is def,      *I reckon the churl is deaf*
    the del him to-drawe!      *the Devil take him*

35  Though Ich yeiye upon heighe                *I shout at the top of my voice*
        nil he nought hye,                            *he will not hurry*
    The lustlesse ladde                               *the lazy fellow*
        can nought o lawe.                           *cannot get down*
    Hippe forth, Hubert,                                  *get up, Hubert*
        hosede pye!                              *(you) stockinged magpie*
    Ichot th'art amarsclëd                     *I reckon you are bemused*
        into the mawe.                              *to your very vitals*
    Though me tene with him          *though I am (so) furious with him*
        that my teeth mye,                          *that my teeth grind*
40  The cherl nil nought adoun           *the fellow will not come down*
        er the day dawe.                            *before the day dawns*


# 115. Of rybaudz I ryme

Of rybaudz I ryme                               *of menials I rhyme*
    and rede o my rolle,                       *and tell in my roll*
Of gadelinges, gromës,                      *of lackeys, servants*
    of Colyn and of Colle,
Harlotes, hors-knavës,                   *attendants, stableboys*
    by pate and by polle,                            *one by one*
4  To devel Ich hem to-livre            *to the Devil I consign them*
    and take to tolle!                       *and give as payment*

The gadelinges were gadered              *the lackeys were gathered*
    of Gonnylde gnoste;                     *out of Gunnild's spark*
Palfreyours and pagës                        *grooms and pages*
    and boyës with boste,                   *and arrogant boys*
Alle were y-haught                              *all were hatched*
    of an horsë thost;                       *from a horse turd*
8  The devel hem afrete,                    *the Devil devour them*
    raw other aroste!                            *raw or roasted*

The shapere that hem shoop,            *the creator who made them*
    to shame he hem shadde         *for shame he singled them out*
To flees and to flye,                        *for fleas and for flies*
    to tyke and to tadde;                 *for mongrels and for toads*

So saith romaunz,                    *as books say*
　　whoso right radde:              *whoever reads aright*
12 Flee com of flour,                *flea came from flour*
　　and lous com of ladde.          *and louse came from lad*

The harlotes ben horelinges          *the attendants are fornicators*
　　and haunten the plawe;          *and practise copulation*
The gadelinges ben glotouns          *the lackeys are gluttons*
　　and drinken er hit dawe;        *and drink until dawn*
Sathanas here syre                   *Satan their sire*
　　saide on his sawe:              *said in his old saying*
16 Gobelyn made his garner           *Goblin made his granary*
　　of gromënë mawe.                *of a groom's belly*

The knave crammëth his crop          *the knave crams his crop*
　　er the cok crawe;               *before the cock crows*
He momelëth and mocchëth             *he mumbles and munches*
　　and marrëth his mawe;           *and ruins his stomach*
When he is al for-laped              *when he is completely sozzled*
　　and lad over lawe,              *and filled beyond measure*
20 A dozeyne of doggës               *a dozen dogs*
　　ne mightë hyre drawe.           *could not drag payment (out of him)*

The rybaud arisëth                   *the rascal gets up*
　　er the day rewe,                *before the day dawns*
He scrapëth on his scabbës           *he picks at his scabs*
　　and drawëth hem to dewe;        *and makes them ooze*
Sene is on his browe                 *it is evident from his forehead*
　　and on his eye-brewe,           *and from his eyebrow*
24 That he lousëth a losynger         *that he would free a flatterer*
　　and shooëth a shrewe.           *and shoe a shrew*

Nou ben capel-claweres               *now are stableboys*
　　with shamë to-shride;           *shamefully clothed*
They busken hem with botouns         *they adorn themselves with buttons*
　　as hit were a bride,            *like girls*
With lowe-lacëde shoon               *with low-laced shoes*
　　of an heifer-hide;              *of heifer's hide*
28 They piken of here provendre       *they filch from their fodder*
　　al herë pride.                  *all their finery*

Whoso rekenëth with knavës     *whoever settles with lackeys*
   herë costage –     *their wages*
The lithernesse of the ladde,     *the evil of the varlet*
   the pride of the page! –     *the arrogance of the fellow*
Though he yeve hem cattës dryt     *though he gave them cat's shit*
   to here companage,     *for their relish*
32 Yet hem sholde arewen     *yet they would complain*
   of the arrerage!     *about the balance due*

While God was on erthe
   and wandrëdë wide,     *and travelled far and wide*
What was the resoun     *reason*
   why He noldë ride?     *did not wish to ride*
For He noldë no grom     *because he wanted no groom*
   to go by His side,
36 Ne grucchyng of no gadeling     *nor the grumbling of any lackey*
   to chaule ne to chide.     *jabbering or quarrelling*

Spedëth you to spewen,     *you are as quick to vomit*
   as me doth to spelle;     *as I am to speak*
The fend you afrete     *the fiend devour you*
   with flesh and with felle!     *flesh and skin*
Herknëth hiderward, horsmen,     *listen here, stablemen*
   a tidyng Ich you telle,     *a message I have to give you*
40 That ye shulen hangen     *that you will hang*
   and herberewen in helle.     *and lodge in hell*

## 116. Skottes out of Berwik by Laurence Minot

Skottes out of Berwik     *Berwick*
   and of Abirdene,     *Aberdeen*
At the Bannok burn     *Bannock burn / stream*
   war ye to kene;     *you were too bold*
Thare slogh ye many sakles,     *there you slew many an innocent*
   als it was sene,     *as was manifest*
And now has King Edward
   wroken it, I wene.     *avenged it, I reckon*

5 It es wrokin, I wene,        *it is*
   wele wurth the while;     *blest be the hour*
  War yit with the Skottës,   *beware still of the Scots*
   for thai er ful of gile!   *for they are full of guile*

  Whare er ye Skottës      *where are you Scots*
   of Saint Johnës toune?     *of St John's town*
  The boste of yowre baner   *the pride of your banner*
   es betin all doune;      *is beaten*
  When ye bosting will bede,   *taunts; offer*
   Sir Edward es boune     *ready*
10 For to kindel yow care    *to cause you misery*
   and crak yowre crowne.   *crown* (i.e. *top of head*)
  He has crakkëd yowre croune,
   wele worth the while;
  Shame bityde the Skottës,   *befall*
   for thai er full of gile!

  Skottës of Striflin       *Stirling*
   war steren and stout,    *were fierce and bold*
  Of God ne of gude men    *good*
   had thai no dout;      *fear*
15 Now have thai, the pelers,   *the raiders*
   prikëd obout,       *galloped round about*
  Bot at the last Sir Edward   *but in the end*
   rifild thaire rout.      *stripped the lot of them*
  He has rifild thaire rout,
   wele wurth the while,
  Bot ever er thai under    *but ever are they underneath*
   bot gaudës and gile.    (*nothing*) *but tricks and deceit*

  Rugh-fute riveling,      *rough-footed rawhide boot*
   now kindels thi care;    *now kindels your woe*
20 Berebag with thy boste,   *bag-carrier with your boasting*
   thi biging es bare;     *dwelling*
  Fals wretche and forsworn,  *perjured*
   whider wiltou fare?    *where will you go*
  Busk thee unto Brig     *haste you to Bruges*
   and abide thare.

Thare, wretche, shaltou won                     *remain*
 and wery the while;                            *and curse the time*
Thi dwelling in Donde                           *your stay in Dundee*
 es done for thi gile.                          *is over because of your guile*

25 The Skotte gase in Burghës                    *goes to Bruges*
 and betës the stretës,                         *and pounds the streets*
All thise Inglis men                            *(to) all these English*
 harmës he hetës;                               *he threatens harm*
Fast makes he his mone                          *earnestly;  complaint*
 to men that he metës,
Bot fone frendës he findës                      *but few*
 that his bale betës.                           *who ease his misery*
Fune betës his bale,                            *few*
 wele wurth the while,
30 He usës all threting                          *every threat*
 with gaudës and gile.                          *with tricks and guile*

Bot many man thretës                            *makes threats*
 and spekës ful ill
That sum tyme war better                        *who sometimes would be better*
 to be stane-still.                             *to be silent as a stone*
The Skot in his wordës
 has wind for to spill,                         *waste*
For at the last Edward
 sall have al his will.                         *shall have*
35 He had his will at Berwik,
 wele wurth the while!
Skottës broght him the kayës,                   *brought him the keys*
 but get for thaire gile.                       *but look out for their guile*

## 117. *Ich am of Irlande*

Ich am of Irlande                              *from Ireland*
And of the holy lande
  Of Irlande.

Gode sire, pray Ich thee,
5 For of saynte charité                         *for holy charity*
Come and daunce with me
  In Irlande.

## 118. Maiden in the morë lay

Maiden in the morë lay,                     *dwelt in the moor*
  In the morë lay,
Sevenightë fullë –
Sevenightë fullë –                    *for a full seven nights*
5 Maiden in the morë lay,
  In the morë lay,
Sevenightë fullë –
Sevenightë fullë –
  Fullë and a day.

10 Well was hirë mete,                   *excellent was her food*
  What was hirë mete?
The primerole and the –
The primerole and the –
Well was hirë mete,
15   What was hirë mete?
The primerole and the –             *primrose*
The primerole and the –
  And the violet.

Well was hirë dring,                                          *drink*
20      What was hirë dring?
The coldë water of the –
The coldë water of the –
Well was hirë dring,
      What was hirë dring?
25   The coldë water of the –
The coldë water of the –
      Of the wellë-spring.                                   *of the spring*


Well was hirë bour,                                          *her dwelling*
      What was hirë bour?
30   The redë rose and the –
The redë rose and the –
Well was hirë bour,
      What was hirë bour?
The redë rose and the –
35   The redë rose and the –
      And the lilie flour.


## 119. D . . . dronken

D . . . dronken –
dronken, dronken, y-dronken,
. . . dronken is Tabart attë wyne.              *drunk is Tabart with (lit. at the) wine*
Hay . . . suster, Walter, Peter,                              *sister*
5   Ye dronke al depe,                                   *you all drink deeply*
And Ichulle eke.                                       *and I shall too*

Stondëth allë stillë –                               *stand everyone still*
Stillë, stillë, stillë –
Stondëth allë stillë –
10   Stille as any ston:                                     *stone*
Trippe a litel with thy fot,
And let thy body gon.                                       *go*

## 120. *The Complaint of Chaucer to his Purse*

To yow, my purse, and to noon other wight            *to no other person*
Complayne I, for ye be my lady dere.                      *you are; dear*
I am so sory, now that ye been lyght;           *light (in weight) / fickle*
For certës, but ye make me hevy chere,       *unless you take me seriously*
5  Me were as leef be layd upon my bere;          *I would as readily; bier*
For whiche unto your mercy thus I crye                    *for which reason*
Beth hevy ayeyne, or ellës mote I dye.                               *

Now vouchëth sauf this day or hyt be nyght    *now grant; before it is night*
That I of yow the blisful soune may here                    *sound; hear*
10  Or see your colour lyke the sonnë bryght
That of yelownesse hadde never pere.                           *equal*
Ye be my lyfe, ye be myn hertës stere.                   *heart's rudder*
Quene of comfort and of good companye
Beth hevy ayeyne, or ellës moote I dye.

15  Now purse that ben to me my lyvës lyght    *(you) who are; light of my life*
And savëour as doune in this worlde here,                        *down*
Out of this tounë helpe me thurgh your myght,               *town*
Syn that ye wole nat ben my tresorere;     *since you will not be my treasurer*
For I am shave as nye as is a frere.               *shaven as close; friar*
20  But yet I pray unto your curtesye,
Bethe hevy ayen, or ellës moote I dye.

*Lenvoy de Chaucer*

O conquerour of Brutës Albyon,                         *Brutus's Albion*
Which that by lygne and free eleccion                 *who by lineage*
Been verray kynge, this song to yow I sende,           *are true king*
25  And ye, that mowen alle oure harmes amende,    *who are able; to remedy*
Have mynde upon my supplicacion.

                    * *be heavy / serious again; or else I must die*

## 121. Whan I have in myn purs y-now

*Syng we alle and say we thus:*
*'Gramercy, myn owen purs!'*                        *thank you, my own purse*

Whan I have in myn purs y-now,                        *enough*
I may have bothë hors and plow,                        *plough*
5    And also frendës y-now,                        *friends in plenty*
    Through the vertu of myn purs.                        *power/excellence*

Whan my purs gynnëth to slak,
And ther is nought in my pak,
They wil sayn: 'Go, farewel, Jak!
10        Thou shalt no more drynke with us.'

Thus is al myn good y-lorn,                        *all my money lost*
And my purs is al totorn,                        *is all torn to pieces*
I may play me with an horn                        *I may amuse myself*
    In the stede al of myn purs.                        *instead of*

15    Farewel hors and farewel cow,
Farewel cart and farewel plow;
As I played me with a bow,
    I said: 'God, what is al this?'

## 122. I have a gentil cok

I have a gentil cok,                        *noble cock*
    crowëth me the day;                        *who crows for me at day-break*
He doth me risen erly,                        *makes*
4        my matins for to say.

I have a gentil cok,
    comen he is of gret;                        *of great lineage*
His comb is of red corel,
8        his tayil is of jet.

I have a gentil cok,
    comen he is of kinde;                         *of noble birth*
His comb is of red corel,
12    his tayil is of inde.                          *indigo*

His leggës ben of asur,                            *lapis lazuli*
    so gentil and so smale;                        *so graceful and so slender*
His spurës arn of sylver white                     *spurs are of bright silver*
16    into the wortëwale.                           *down to the root*

His eyen arn of cristal,                           *eyes*
    loken al in aumber;                            *set; amber*
And every night he perchëth him
20    in myn ladies chaumber.


## 123. *Omnes gentes plaudite!*

Omnes gentes plaudite!                             *O clap your hands all ye people*
I saw many briddës sitte on a tre,
They token here flight and flowen away             *flew away*
4 With *Ego dixi* – have good day!                  *I said*

Many white federes hath the pye –                  *magpie*
I may noon more singen, my lippes arn so drye;     *no more*
Many white federes hath the swan –
8 The more that I drinke, the lesse good I can.     *the less sense I have*

Lay stikkes on the fire, wel mot it brenne,        *well may it burn*
Yeve us onës drinken er we gon henne.              *give us one more drink; hence*

## 124. I have a yong suster

I have a yong suster                              *sister*
    fer beyond the se,                         *far; sea*
Many be the drueries                       *are the keepsakes*
4    that she sentë me.

She sentë me the cherye                          *cherry*
    withouten any stone,
And so she did the dove
8    withouten any bone.

She sentë me the brere                           *briar*
    withouten any rinde,                       *any bark*
She bad me love my lemman                     *sweetheart*
12    withoutë longing.

How sholde any cherye
    be withoutë stone?
And how sholde any dove
16    ben withoutë bone?

How sholde any brere
    ben withoutë rinde?
How sholde I love myn lemman
20    withoutë longing?

When the cherye was a flour,
    than hadde it non stone;
When the dovë was an ey,                        *was an egg*
24    than hadde it non bone.

When the brerë was onbred                  *had not yet sprouted*
    than hadde it non rinde;
When the mayde hath that she loveth        *has what she loves*
28    she is without longing.

## 125. I have a newe garden

I have a newe garden,
    and newe is begunne;             *and it is newly begun*
Swych another garden                        *such*
4    know I not under sunne.

In the middës of my garden            *in the midst*
    is a perer set,                    *pear-tree*
And it wil non pere bern          *it will bear no pear*
8    but a pere-jonet.     *other than an early pear*

The fairest mayde of this toun
    prayëd me
For to griffen her a gryf       *to plant her a graft*
12    of myn pery-tre.       *from my pear-tree*

When I hadde hem griffëd          *planted*
    alle at herë wille,     *all according to her wishes*
The wyn and the alë         *the wine and the ale*
16    she dide in fille.        *she poured out*

And I griffëd here
    right up in here home,     *deep inside her*
And be that day twenty wekes     *weeks*
20    it was quik in here womb.

That day twelvë month         *months*
    that mayde I met,
She said it was a pere Robert     *a 'Robert' pear*
24    but non pere Jonet.    *but not a 'John' pear*

## 126. Seynt Stevene was a clerk

Seynt Stevene was a clerk    *attendant*
 in Kyng Herówdës halle,
And servëd him of bred and cloth, *with food at table*
4 as every kyng befalle. *as would befit every king*

Steven out of kichen cam *came from the kitchen*
 with borës hed on honde, *with a boar's head in his hands*
He saw a sterre was fayr and bright *a star which was*
8 over Bedlem stonde. *Bethlehem*

He cast adoun the borës hed,
 and went into the halle:
'I forsak thee, Kyng Herówdës
12 and thy werkës alle.

'I forsak thee, Kyng Herówdës,
 and thy werkës alle,
Ther is a chyld in Bedlem born
16 is better than we alle.'

'What aileth thee, Stevene?
 what is thee befalle? *what has happened to you*
Lakketh thee either mete or drynk *do you lack either food or drink*
20 in Kyng Herówdës halle?'

'Lakketh me neither mete ne drynk *I lack neither*
 in Kyng Herówdës halle;
Ther is a chyld in Bedlem born
24 is beter than we alle.'

'What aileth thee, Steven, art thou wod, *are you mad*
 or thou gynnest to brede? *or are you beginning to rave*
Lakketh thee either gold or fee *gold or payment*
28 or any rychë wede?' *fine clothing*

'Lakketh me neither gold ne fee,
 ne non rychë wede;
Ther is a chyld in Bedlem born,
32 shal help us at our nede.'     *in our necessity*

'That is also soth, Steven,    *that is just as true*
 also soth y-wis,     *just as true, indeed*
As this capoun crowë shal     *capon*
36 that lyth here in myn dish.'    *lies*

That word was not so sonë said,   *was no sooner said*
 that word in that halle,
The capoun crew *Christus natus est*   *Christ is born*
40 among the lordës alle.

'Risëth up, myn turmentoures,
 by two and al by on,    *i.e. one and all*
And ledëth Steven out of this town,
44 and stonëth him with ston.'

Token they Stevene      *they took*
 and stoned hym in the way;
And therfore is his even     *his eve*
48 on Cristës owen day.

## 127. Yong men, I warne you everychon

*How, hey! It is non les:*     *it is no lie*
*I dar not sayn whan she saith 'Pes!'* *I dare not speak; peace / be quiet*

Yong men, I warne you everychon,  *young; every one*
Oldë wivës tak ye non,
5 For I myself at hom have on –
 I dare not sayn whan she saith 'Pes !'

Whan I come fro the plow at non,    *from the plough at noon*
In a riven dish my mete is don,   *in a cracked dish my food is put*
I dar not aske our dame a spon –     *spoon*
10  I dar not sayn whan she saith 'Pes!'

If I aske our damë bred,
She taketh a staf and breketh myn hed,    *head*
And doth me renne under the led –  *and makes me run; cauldron*
  I dar not sayn whan she saith 'Pes!'

15 If I aske our damë flesh,       *meat*
She brekëth myn hed with a dish:
'Boy, thou art not worth a rish!' –     *rush*
  I dar not sayn whan she saith 'Pes!'

If I aske our damë chese,       *cheese*
20 'Boy,' she sayth, al at ese,    *quite unmoved*
'Thou art not worth half a pese!' –    *half a pea*
  I dar not say whan she saith 'Pes!'

## 128. We bern aboute no cattës skinnes

*We ben chapmen light of fote,*   *pedlars light of foot*
*The foulë weyës for to fle.*      *flee*

We bern aboute no cattës skinnes,   *carry about*
4 Pursës, perlës, sylver pynnes,     *pearls*
Smale wimpeles for ladies chinnes;  *fine head-dresses*
  Damsele, bye sum ware of me.  *buy some wares from me*

I have a poket for the nones,    *for the purpose*
8 Therin ben tweyne precious stones;    *two*
Damsele, hadde ye assayed hem ones,  *if you once tried them*
  Ye sholde the rather gon with me. *you would the sooner go with me*

I have a jelyf of Godës sonde,                    *jelly by God's grace*
12  Withouten feet it can stonde,                   *stand*
It can smite and hath non honde;                    *no hand*
  Red yourself what it may be.                      *guess*


I have a powder for to selle,
16  What it is can I not telle,
It makëth maydenes wombes to swelle;
  Therof I have a quantité.


## 129. As I went on Yol Day

'Kyrië', so 'kyrië',
Jankin singëth mirïë,                               *merrily*
With 'alëyson'.


As I went on Yol Day                                *Yule (Christmas) Day*
5    in our prosessyon,
Knew I jolly Jankin
  by his mery ton.                                  *tone / voice*
  Kyriëlëyson.


Jankin began the offis                              *office (i.e. of the Mass)*
10   on the Yolë Day
And yet me thinketh it dos me good,                 *does*
  so merie gan he say                               *so merrily did he say*
  Kyriëlëyson.


Jankin red the pistil                               *read the Epistle*
15   ful fair and ful wel,
And yet me thinketh it dos me good,
  as ever have I sel.                               *as ever I may have bliss*
  Kyriëlëyson.

Jankin at the *Sanctus*
20    crakëth a merie note,              *divides*
And yet me thinketh it dos me good –
    I payëd for his cote.             *coat*
      *Kyriëlëyson.*

Jankin crakëth notës             *divides his notes*
25    an hundred on a knot,        *a hundred in a phrase*
And yet he hakketh hem smaller    *splits them smaller*
    than wortës to the pot.      *than herbs for the pot*
      *Kyriëlëyson.*

Jankin at the *Angnus*            *Agnus Dei*
30    berëth the pax-brede,            *pax*
He twinkelëd, but said nought,       *winked*
    and on myn foot he trede.       *trod*
      *Kyriëlëyson.*

*Benedicamus Domino,*         *Let us bless the Lord*
35    Crist fro shame me shilde;  *may Christ shield me from shame*
*Deo gratias* therto –       *Thanks be to God, as well*
    alas, I go with childe!
      *Kyriëlëyson.*

## 130. Thou that sellest the worde of God

Thou that sellest the worde of God,
Be thou barfot, be thou shod,       *bare-foot*
    Com thou never here!
*In principio erat verbum*    *in the beginning was the word*
5  Is the word of God, alle and sum    *all in all*
    That thóu sellest, lewed frere.    *ignorant friar*

Hit is cursëd symonie          *simony*
Eyther to sellen or to bye         *buy*
    Any gostly thinge.         *spiritual*

10 Therfore, frere, go as thou come,                                  *came*
    And hold thee in thy hous at home
        Til we thee almës brynge.

    Goddës lawe ye reversén,                                          *pervert*
    And mennës housës ye persén                                       *penetrate*
15      As Paul berëth witnes.
    As midday develes goinge aboute                                   *midday devils*
    For money lowëly ye loute,                                        *low you bow*
        Flatteringe both more and less.                              *great and humble*


# 131. Allas! what shul we frerës do

    Allas! what shul we frerës do                                     *shall we friars*
    Now lewëd men con holy writ?                                      *lay men know*
    All aboutë where I go
4   They aposen me of it.                                            *they confront me with it*

    Then wondrëth me that it is so                                    *it amazes me*
    How lewëd men con allë wite;                                    *can understand everything*
    Certeinly we ben undo                                             *we shall be ruined*
8   But if we mo amenden it.                                         *unless we can rectify it*

    I trow the devel brought it about                                *I believe*
    To write the gospel in English,
    For lewëd men ben nowe so stout                                  *are now so defiant*
12  They yeve us neither flesh ne fish.                              *meat nor fish*

    When I come into a shoppe
    For to say 'in principio',
    They bidden me 'Go forth, lewd poppe!                            *foolish fop*
16  And werche', and win my silver so.                               *work*

    If I say hit longëth not                                         *it is not fitting*
    For prestes to werchen where they go,                            *wherever*
    They leggen for hem holi writ                                   *claim in their support*
20  And sayen that Seint Paul did so.

Than they loke on myn habíte                        *habit*
And sayn, 'Forsothe, withouten othes,        *truly, without doubt*
Whether it be russet, black, or white,              *whether; brown*
24   It is worthe alle our wering-clothes!'                   *clothing*

I say, 'I biddë not for me,                     *I do not beg for myself*
But for them that haven none.'
They sayn, 'Thou havëst two or three;
28   Yeve hem that neden therof one.'                    *give them*

Thus our deceitës ben aspide                  *deceits are found out*
In this maner and many mo;                              *more*
Few men bedden us abide                       *ask us to tarry*
32   But hyë fast that we were go.         *but to hurry up and be gone*

If it go forth in this maner,                            *if it goes on*
It wol done us muchë gile;                               *harm*
Men shul fynde unnethe a frere          *scarcely a friar*
36   In Englande within a while.

## 132. Swarte smekëd smithes

Swarte smekëd smithes                  *black smoke-begrimed smiths*
   smatered with smoke,                      *smutty with smoke*
Drive me to deth
   with din of here dyntes!                      *din of their blows*
Swich noys on nyghtes                        *such noise at night*
   ne herd men never:
What knavënë cry                        *what a shouting of rascals*
   and clatering of knockes!        *and clattering of hammer-blows*
5   The cammëdë conjouns                  *the snub-nosed rogues*
   crien after 'col, col!'                      *shout for 'coal, coal!'*
And blowen here bellowes
   that al here brain brestes.            *until their very brains burst*
'Huf, puf!' saith that one,                         *the one*
   'haf, paf!' that other.                               *the other*

They spytten and sprawlen                    *they spit and stretch*
   and spellen many spelles;        *tell many a tale*
They gnawen and gnachen,                     *grind and gnash (their teeth)*
   they gronen togider,                 *they grunt together*
10 And holden hem hote                       *and keep themselves hot*
   with here hard hamers.               *with their strenuous hammering*
Of a bolë hyde                               *of bull's hide*
   ben here barm-felles;                *are their leather aprons*
Here shankes ben shakeled                    *their legs are protected*
   for the fire-flunderes;              *against sparks from the fire*
Hevy hameres they han                        *have*
   that hard ben handled,               *which are difficult to wield*
Stark strokes they stryken                   *stout blows they strike*
   on a stelëd stokke:                  *on a steel anvil*
15 Lus, bus! las, das!
   rowten by rowe,                      *they strike in turn*
Swich dolful a dreme                         *such a dreadful noise*
   the devyl it to-dryve!               *the Devil take it*
The mayster longëth a litel                  *the master smith lengthens a small piece*
   and lashëth a lesse,                 *and hammers out a smaller bit*
Twynëth hem twayn                            *twists the two together*
   and touchëth a treble.               *and strikes a treble note*
Tik, tak! hic, hac!
   tiket, taket! tik, tak!
20 Lus, bus! lus, das! –
   swych lyf they leden!                *such a life they lead*
Allë clothemeres –                           *all blacksmiths*
   Crist hem gyve sorwe!
May no man for bren-wateres                  *water-sizzlers*
   on night han his rest.               *for a single night have his rest*

# COMMENTARY

The readings of the base manuscript along with selected variants are given where substantive emendations have been made. Details such as manuscript forms with confused spellings (e.g. of þ and h, þ and y, þ and ȝ, w (as wynn) and þ or ȝ. w and wh, th and ht, etc.), erasures, deletions, marginal and interlinear additions, transposition marks, etc., are usually disregarded. Scribal abbreviations are silently expanded.

## 1. With longing I am lad [*Index* 4194]

MS. London, B.L., Harley 2253

17.  The roe deer occurs in ME as a symbol of wildness, swiftness and agility [see *MED.* **ro** n. (1) (c)] and is commonly associated with restlessness, as in the alliterative phrase *rooles ase þe ro*. A play on words is involved since in ME the word *ro* also means 'peace, rest' as seen in *rooles* 'restless'.

18.  *ondë* Perhaps the enmity of malicious gossips (cf. **4**, 23 n) is meant.

36.  It is tempting to think that the *of* in this line may have been introduced by scribal error, for *one the best*, meaning 'the very best' (in such phrases in Middle English *one* has an intensifying function), would seem more appropriate than 'one of the best' for a lady of such excellence as the poet's beloved. However, the shift of focus from submissive adoration of the lady herself to a more detached stance, that of regarding her as one among others, is in keeping with the change in tone at the end of this and other lyrics where the poet indulges in surprisingly frank sexual comment or speculation concerning the lady – cf. **2**, 55–9 and **25**, 82–4.

38.  *under hys:* lit. 'in fine linen'. This is one of several conventional tags used for convenience of alliteration in describing a lady. Cf. *under bis* (**5**, 17), *under gore* (**5**, 16), *in lyn* (**19**, 46), *on gere* (**22**, 4 and n), etc.

## 2. A waylë whyte as whallës bon [*Index* 105]

MS. London, B.L., Harley 2253

Text: 25 while I may glewe] *added*; 37 myn herte] *added*; 44 bringen] þat bringeþ MS.; 46 were] he were MS.

The title is the well-known first line of this poem as it is found in the manuscript, line 19 of the present text. For the ordering of the stanzas and the emendations adopted here, see Duncan (1992), pp. 111–20.

20.   *shon* – past tense form for sake of rhyme.

22.   The word *toune* appears in the Harley lyrics in the general sense of 'where men live' in such phrases as *in tounës*, here, and *to toune* in 20, 1, which may be translated as 'among men', 'in the world', or the like. The adjective *trewe* is commonly associated with the turtle-dove.

30.   The verb *wite* ('to lay blame for') has the person blamed in the dative: see *OED* **Wite**,v¹, 1. The sense is therefore: 'I blame on a woman'. Beneath the immediate reference here to the poet's beloved, there may also lurk an implicit reference to that archetypal cause of woe, Eve, referred to in 27, 13–16, another Harley love lyric.

47.   The object of *changë* is understood (ironically) from *mirth* in the previous line.

57.   *Swetë bryd* The poet wittily exploits the ambiguity of *swetë bryd* here. Following on lines 55–6, it would first seem that the skylark is meant, and Brook punctuates accordingly. However with lines 58–9 *swetë bryd* may more appropriately be taken as referring to the lady than to any one of the three birds previously mentioned, with *bryd* as 'bird', a term of endearment (see *MED* **brid** n.3b.(a)), or as 'lady' (by association with *bride* from OE *brȳd* – see *EMEVP*, Glossary, under **burde** n.). Cf. *brid* (3, 17), *bridës* (27, 39) and *briddës* (27, 40).


## 3. Ichot a byrde in bourë bryght [*Index* 1395]

MS. London, B.L., Harley 2253

Text: 7 muchel] *added*; 18 eyen] eye MS.; 63 soght] so soht MS.; 77 love] hire loue MS.; 79 for to] *added*; 81 biseche] bisecheþ MS. The burden is indicated in the MS. only after stanzas 1 and 2; *Blow*, etc. is added after the other stanzas in the text here.

This lyric is 'among the earliest preserved secular carols' [Greene, p. 483].

5.   *bourë*: 'bower'. In ME lyrics this word usually means a lady's chamber and not a flowery arbour, the sense more familiar to present-day readers.

7.   *muchel myght* The MS. reading of this line is two syllables short. For the addition of *muchel* here, cf. *muchel might*, 25, 19.

10.   *of blodë and of bon:* 'of blood and bone' – a common tag, equivalent to modern English 'flesh and blood'. Cf. 16, 5 and 25, 5.

12.   *in londe* – another common tag with the general sense of 'anywhere', 'everywhere', 'on earth'. Cf. line 59 and 19, 19.

16.   For the sense of this line see *EMEVP*, p. 328, note to VIII K, line 15.

43.   *jolif so the jay* A common comparison aided by the alliteration. For this, and the association of *jolif* with other birds, see *MED* **joli** adj. 1.(a).

47.   Both *fiëlë* and *crouth* were kinds of medieval stringed instruments. See Panum (1941), pp. 239–45. The word *fiele* may be taken as a form of OF *viele*. However, the viol as such makes its appearance much later, see *OED* **Viol** *sb.*¹

72. *swore* For MS. *sore* as a form of *swore* (with loss of *w* before a lip-rounded vowel), see *EMEVP*, p.329, note to VIII K, line 65.

75. *in lyghte:* lit. 'in the light'.

77. For the removal of MS. *hire*, see Brook, p.82, note to No. 14, line 71. Brandl and Zippel (1917), p.128, removed *hire* in their text and also altered MS. *bisecheþ* to *biseche* in line 81.

## 4. Litel wot it any man [*Index* 1921]

MS. London, B.L., Harley 2253

Text: 16 may] ne may MS.; 25 may] ne may MS.; 30 hathele] haþeles MS.; hewe] heowes MS.; 32 gamen] gomenes MS.; glewe] gleowes MS.; 41 as (2)] *added;* 42 wete] beþ weete MS.; 43 in] beþ in MS. Lines 17–19, 26–8, 36–8 and 45–7 are abbreviated in the MS. to *Euer ant oo etc.*

This poem is preceded in the manuscript by a religious lyric opening with the same words and in the same form as stanzas 1, 3 and 5 of this poem. Carleton Brown took the religious poem to be an adaptation of the secular. [Brown XIII, pp.235–6]

3. *fre* If the *fre womman* is the same as *hire* in line 5, the sense 'noble' for *fre* is ironic since the poet's lady (it is implied) has more experience of love than is compatible with the aristocratic ideal of true love (*derne love*), and apparently feels *fre* (in the sense of 'free to do as she pleases') to ignore her pledge of love, possibly influenced by malicious gossip, as suggested in line 23. However, perhaps a contrast is meant between a *fre womman*, a 'generous woman', and the poet's lady, *hire* of line 5.

9. Lit. 'whom I do not often see'. This is an instance of the rhetorical use of understatement for ironic emphasis known as 'litotes': the meaning is, in effect, 'whom I never see'. See also line 44, where 'seldom at ease' really means 'never at ease'.

11. By the conventions of *dernë love*, the poet dared not mention his beloved's name.

21. *crie* – the historical present, i.e. the use of the present tense to lend immediacy to an action or emotional situation which actually occurred in the past.

23. In medieval love poetry the courtly lover frequently laments the harm caused by malicious gossips.

30. Since *hewe* (30) and *glewe* (32) rhyme with *rewe* (33) and *trewe* (35), the plurals in the manuscript readings in lines 30 and 32 (and presumably those within the line as well as those in the rhymes) are probably to be viewed as scribal corruptions.

39. *upon loft:* lit. 'in the air', but one of several conventional phrases simply meaning 'alive'.

44. For the pronunciation of *whose* as a monosyllable, cf. 61, 11 and n.

## 5. Ichot a byrde in a bour [*Index* 1394]

MS. London, B.L., Harley 2253

Text: 31 thurgh] þouh MS.; 35 baitheth] bayeþ MS.; 36 dedes in day] dede is in dayne MS.; 41 medicine] medierne MS.; 44 oft] of MS.

It was not unusual in medieval literature to sing the praises of a lady by evoking lists of comparisons (precious stones, flowers, birds, etc.; cf. 3, 50–57), but seldom in a manner as sustained as in this lyric. A rather loose form of the alliterative line is used: most half lines have two stresses, but some lines (e.g. 23 and 43) seem to have three in the first half. The only other Harley love lyric in alliterative form is 22.

9. *haveth* – perhaps to be read as *hath* here and in lines 48 and 49.

10. In conventional medieval descriptions of a beautiful lady, the parts of the body which are itemized as features of particular excellence include chin and face. Cf. 25, 34–6.

16. The alliterating pair *grei and gris* (both words mean 'grey', the former of English, the latter of French derivation) was commonly used in Middle English of fine garments of grey fur.

28–30. Courtly convention prevented a poet from naming his beloved – cf. 4, 10–11. Here, however, this poet (presumably John of line 30) plays with the convention by introducing the lady's name by means of a pun on *a note* (meaning 'a note' but implying the name Annot) in line 28 and again as *annote* in line 29, with the spelling *nn* confirming the pun.

34. *man secheth:* lit. 'one seeks'.

37–40. The comparisons must still be with the lady, but the mode of expression in these lines is highly elliptical.

38. *crone:* 'crown, head', here of a plant. 'The cummin is an umbelliferous plant and so has a conspicuous flower' [Brook, p. 76, note to line 38].

41. *of might* – a descriptive genitive, see Mustonoja, pp. 80–81. For *mercie* as an adjective, see *MED* **merci** n.(1), 11.

42ff. The proper names in this stanza (some of them heroes and heroines of romance) have been traced in Germanic, Celtic and Romance sources. See Brown XIII, pp. 226–8. Doubtless the poet expected his audience to be familiar with those named and with their deeds and reputations. Thus *Cradoc* (line 47) was famous because he, alone among King Arthur's knights, succeeded in carving a boar's head, thereby proving the fidelity of his wife.

## 6. Love is soft, love is swet [*Index* 2009]

MS. Oxford, Bodl., Digby 86

Text: 13 hath] had MS.; 16 ansete] an wede MS.; 22 gladhede] geddede MS.

24. *longdrei* – cf. *MED* **dri(e** adj.(2) 1.(b): 'lasting'.

## 7. Though I can wittës ful-iwis [*Index* 3512]

MS. London, B.L., Royal 8. D.xiii

This poem is found jotted in pencil as prose in the margin at the top of folio 25 *recto*. The text here is based on the transcription by Carleton Brown, who observes that 'in places the text is so nearly illegible that it can be deciphered only with difficulty, and the reading of a few letters is not certain' [Brown XIII, p. xii]. I cannot make out anything before *I can* in line 1, and cannot be sure of many other readings, especially from line 8 on, as the manuscript copy is now so faint.

Text: 1 Though] [þe]h þet [Brown XIII, p. xii]; 2 non] nout MS.; 5 that] þe MS.; 8 thrivinge] þriminde [Brown].

## 8. Were ther outher in this toun [*Index* 3898]

MS. Oxford, Bodl., Rawlinson D.913

Text: 15–16 *are based on the text as read by* Dronke (1961), p. 245.

## 9. Of every kinnë tre [*Index* 2622]

MS. Oxford, Bodl., Rawlinson D.913

Text: 3 swetest] suotes MS.; 7 every kinne] euer[y k]inne MS., *so* Dronke (1961), p. 245.

## 10. Al night by the rosë, rosë [*Index* 194]

MS. Oxford, Bodl., Rawlinson D.913

Text: 3 Dorst] darst MS., *so* Dronke (1961), p. 246.

The *rose* here is presumably a girl, the *flour* (line 4) her maidenhood.

## 11. Al gold, Janet, is thin her [*Index* 179]

MS. Oxford, Bodl., Rawlinson D.913

## 12. Dorë, go thou stillë [*Index* 2288]

MS. Worcester, Cathedral Library Q.50

Text: 3 Yate] þat *or* yat MS. – *the initial letter may be* þ *or* y.

The *Index* reference is to ten lines of verse (written as prose by a certain *Robertus seynte Mary Clericus*) which are now taken to be 'three unrelated scraps of song' [Sisam (1965), p.245]. The first 'scrap' consists of the intriguing words:

> Ne shaltou never, levedi,
> Twynklen wyth thin eyen.                          [Wilson (1970), p.167]

*Dorë, go thou stillë* is the third, and 13 (below) the second 'scrap'.

3.    Different interpretations of this poem arise from the alternative readings of the first word in line 3. Either the poet addresses first the chamber door and then the outside gate as he leaves after a fulfilling tryst, or, with the reading *that* 'until', the poet, on entering the chamber, bids the door be silent until his love-encounter is completed.

## 13. Ich have y-don al myn youth [*Index* 2288]

MS. Worcester, Cathedral Library Q.50

## 14. So longe Ich havë, lady [*Suppl.* 3167.3]

MS. Tübingen, University Library Deposit: Berlin, Preussische Staatsbibliothek, Lat. theol. fol.249

From the Latin words *Deum ad cor intrare volentem excludunt* ['God wishing to enter the heart they exclude'] which precede this little poem in the manuscript, it would seem that it was a devotional lyric on the theme of Christ the lover-knight seeking entry to Man's soul (see 71, and Commentary 71); but it may originally have been a secular love lyric adapted to this devotional purpose. See Gray, *Selection*, p.124.

## 15. Bryd onë brerë [*Index* 521]

MS. Cambridge, King's Coll., Muniment Roll 2 W.32, with music. A facsimile is given in Saltmarsh (1935), opposite p.3.

Text: 12 were] were were MS.

This song is irregular. Words, music or both may have been incorrectly copied.

A second part in the music may be missing, to judge from a blank second stave above the first line of words; and it seems likely that in the second stave with music the scribe has written his clef sign on the wrong line. [See 'The Music of *Bryd One Brere*' by F. McD. C. Turner, M.A. in Saltmarsh (1935), pp. 19–20.] However, attempts to regularize this lyric by the Sisams [*MEV*, p.163] and especially by Dobson [*MES*, p.183] are speculative and unconvincing. The manuscript text is followed here except in line 12 where the repetition of *were* has been omitted as it is by Robbins [*Sec.*, p.147]. Final '-e' as marked for pronunciation in the first stanza as required by the musical notation; and with final '-e' as marked in stanzas 2 and 3, the words can easily be fitted to the tune if one assumes, here and there, a slight alteration of the grouping of notes to syllables in these stanzas. Since this presents a modern performer with no difficulty, it is hard to believe that a medieval singer would have been any less capable of such modest flexibility.

1. Another instance of a poet addressing a *bryd one brere* is found in a scrap of ME verse:

> Bryd on brere y tell yt to
> none othur y ne dar.
> [Greene, p.491]

2. The poet, responding to *Kynd*, the law of nature within him, seeks love from Love, personified as is often the case in medieval literature. Perhaps the bird, possibly by association with the nightingale (a frequent representative of love in Middle English poetry as elsewhere) is here thought of as Love's representative and as a confidant of lovers. Thus, in the rest of the stanza, the poet appeals to the bird for compassion.

3. *Blithful biryd* – taken by some to be the poet's lady; but so abrupt a switch in address from the bird in line 1 is unconvincing, and the ambiguous spelling *biryd* of the manuscript cannot be taken to confirm the sense 'lady' (ME *birde*) rather than 'bird' (ME *brid*). Whatever the underlying senses that may be felt in this suggestive lyric, the immediate and overt sense here is that the poet continues his address to the *bryd onë brerë*.

## 16. Foulës in the frith [*Index* 864]

MS. Oxford, Bodl., Douce 139, with music. A facsimile is found in Wooldridge (1897), plate 7.

1. *Foulës* The manuscript spelling is *foweles*. Since, however, the music for this word has two ligatured groups of notes in each part in this two-part song, the pronunciation *foulës*, with two syllables, is evidently required.

3. The sense (with *mon* as 'man') may also be: 'And I, a man, go mad', making the usual contrast in medieval lyrics between the springtime happiness of animals in matters of love and the miseries suffered by men. Cf. **20**, **32** and n.

## 17. When the nyghtëgalë singeth [*Index* 4037]

MS. London, B.L., Harley 2253

24. *leche:* 'physician'. It is a common convention of medieval love literature that only the lady can heal the wounds of love, wounds so graphically described here in lines 5–8.

32. *waxe grene:* lit. 'grow green' – i.e. become ill, in contrast with the flourishing woods of line 2.

33–4. Lincoln, Lindsey, Northampton and Lound are all located in the East Midlands.

38. *a stounde:* 'soon'. For *a stounde* with this sense, see *MED* **stound(e** n. **1b**.(a), where **51** (another Harley lyric), 94 is quoted.

39–40. In the MS. this lyric is written in long lines. In this line, the division into two parts is indicated not only by rhyme (*song* and *y-long*) but also by a large *punctus elevatus* after *song*. This final stanza is thereby marked not only by a departure from the rhyme scheme of the other stanzas but also by a change in rhythm. All the other long lines (as written in the MS.) divide into two short lines of four stresses followed by three; here the rhythmic order is reversed to three stresses followed by four, thus emphasizing the finality of the concluding cadence.

## 18. Bitwenë March and Avëril [*Index* 515]

MS. London, B.L., Harley 2253

Text: 14 browes] browe MS., eyen] eye MS.

The stanza form varies in this lyric: stanzas 2 and 3 are alike; stanzas 1 and 4 are similar, but differ in their fifth and sixth lines.

14. The plurals *browës* and *eyen* give more natural sense. With the instability of final '-n' in ME, it is easy to see how the singulars *browe* and *eye* could mistakenly have replaced the plural forms *browen* and *eyen*.

29. *in toune* A conventional tag meaning 'anywhere' or, simply, 'alive'. Cf. **2**, 22 n, **3**, 12 n, and **4**, 39 n.

35–6. The sense is that it is better to suffer the pangs of love for a time in the hope of ultimate success than never to endure the trials of love and, therefore, never to have any hope of attaining that one state, love, which, in Troubadour thinking, made life worthwhile.

## 19. In May it mirieth when it dawës [*Index* 1504]

MS. London, B.L., Harley 2253

Text: 43 lend] send MS.

1 & 5. The Northern or North-Midland endings '-es' of the 3 sg. present in *dawës* and 3 pl. present in *wowës* are kept for the rhymes with the plural nouns *plawës* and *bowës*.

2.   *thise deerës plawës:* lit. 'the frolickings of these animals'.

15.   *if felë falsë nere* Not, as at first sight, 'if many women were not false', but, 'if many men were not false', as the following lines show. Throughout this stanza a certain initial ambiguity confronts the reader as to the identity of the subject. This was presumably the poet's intention; he may have been seeking to play upon the reactions of his audience, and perhaps especially of the ladies present. The basic argument, that women are less than perfect because men are false – ironically reversing the usual notion of women (through Eve) as the source of deception – is ostensibly the poet's way of excusing his beloved for whatever the problem may be (her susceptibility to the charms of other men?) which has come between them and which requires reconciliation (line 48). In terms of this argument the conclusion of the poem is itself ironic with the poet advising his beloved to trust him, a man!

17.   Lit. 'where one (*me*) has tempted (*bed*) them to sinful conduct (*lastës*)'. The dialect form *bed* (equivalent to London English *bad*), past tense of *bidden*, 'to bid, request', meaning here 'to tempt, entice', is preserved for the rhyme.

19.   *in londë* – cf. 3, 12 n.

20.   Lit. 'though one (*me*) should give them (*hem*, i.e. women) a true pledge' – cf. line 22.

31.   Lit. 'concerning fidelity it is nothing to the deceiver'.

43.   *lend* This emendation is suggested under *MED* **lenden** v. 2.(b), though the sense is rather that of 2.(a), 'go back'. Alliteration and excellent sense support *lend*; the common confusion of the letters 'l' and long 's' would readily explain *send* as a scribal error.

45.   'And live with what she has got' – i.e. either, in a general sense, the situation she has got herself into or, perhaps, the child she has got from an illicit union. Cf. 22, 33–6, and note.


## 20. Lenten ys come with love to toune [*Index* 1861]

MS. London, B.L., Harley 2253

Text: 6 hire] *added;* 11 wynne] wynter MS.; 17 lufsom is] is lossom MS.; 21 ther] þat MS.; 22 don] doh MS.; 28 on] *added.*

1.   *to toune* – cf. 2, 22 n.

11.   *wynnë:* 'of joys' – here and in line 35 this is a genitive pl. form with the ending '-e' from the OE genitive pl. ending '-a'.

17.   For the emended word-order, cf. *lufsom is, 25,* line 10.

20.   *Milës* (? from Welsh *mil* 'animal') occurs only here in ME. However, as Brook notes, *wolc* and *croup* are other possible examples of Welsh loan-words in the lyrics of MS. Harley 2253. See Brook, p.80, note to No.11, line 20.

21.   The emendation *ther* assumes scribal corruption of *þer* to *þat*, possibly through the misinterpretation of a 'þ', with or without an abbreviation mark. Cf. *25,* line

17, where þ in the MS. stands for *þat*. 'Animals gladden their mates as the stream flows softly there' is preferable to 'Animals gladden their mates as a stream that flows softly', a comparison which makes little if any sense.

29.    *dernë rounës*: 'secret cries'. Along with the usual association of *derne* 'secret' with love, there is also here the notion of animal language as 'secret' in the sense of unintelligible to man. Cf. **61**, 69–72.

32.    Love, so easy and natural for animals (even worms!) in springtime, is, by bitter contrast, difficult and painful for man precisely because women become *wonder proude*! This conventional view of the disparity between the happy lot of animals and the misery endured by man is briefly and poignantly expressed in **16**.

34.    Lit. 'If the favour of one will be lacking to me'; *wantë* is an impersonal verb.


## 21. As I me rode this endrë dai [*Index* 360]

MS. London, Lincoln's Inn, Hale 135

Text: 4 As I me rode this endre dai] þis endre dai als i me rode MS.; 8 clinge] clingges MS.; 27 springeth etc.] sprink MS. This poem is written as prose on folio 137 *verso*, the left-hand top corner of which is badly faded. The readings for *Nou springeth* (line 1), *playinge* (line 5) and *in* (line 14) are illegible, and for *seigh* (line 6), *him* (line 9), *longinge* (line 9), and *singestou* (line 18), partly illegible.

'This graceful *chanson d'aventure* is one of the very earliest preserved in the carol-form.' [Greene, p. 487]

1.    'Now the twig is sprouting' – i.e. now spring is here.
8.    'May the clod (earth, i.e. of the grave!) cling to him.'
9.    *Wo is him:* lit. 'woe is to him (who)'.
25.    *it shal him rewe* – an impersonal construction.


## 22. In a fryth as I gan farë fremëde [*Index* 1449]

MS. London, B.L., Harley 2253

Text: 31 thou] þo MS.; 33 hungren] hengren MS.; 38 to kepen] *added;* 47 ofthuncheth] ofþunche MS.

3.    *glemëde* – the past tense form for the sake of rhyme, but the sense is simply 'gleams'.
4.    'Never was a living person so radiant'. Here, as with various other alliterating tags found in the Harley lyrics, *on gere*, literally 'in clothing', simply means 'alive'.
7.    *hire gremëde* – an impersonal verb.
22.    *by my myght:* lit. 'according to my power'.
33–6.    The heartbreak, the social ostracism and the predicament of bearing a fatherless child are, as Rosemary Woolf points out, 'strikingly reminiscent of the lyric genre of the complaint of the betrayed maiden'. [Woolf (1969), p. 56]

36. The fact that the girl now speaks in two successive stanzas, and that verbal linking of stanzas, found elsewhere in this poem, is lacking between lines 36 and 37, suggests the loss, at this point, of a stanza in which the male speaker may have warned against the miserable lot of the *mal mariée* (cf. 26), the girl married to a bad husband, the *wrecche so wroth* referred to in line 39. See Anderson (1980), p. 258.

39. 'Than that I should marry so ill-tempered a wretch'. See *EMEVP*, p. 325, note to VIII F, line 39.

45. Since, as the girl regretfully observes, she is neither a witch nor a sorceress, she cannot escape her fate by shape-shifting, a reference, according to Miss Woolf, to the *chanson des transformations*, a genre 'in which the maiden posits various shapes that she will assume in order to elude her suitor, and the suitor outwits her by inventing shapes for himself that will capture hers'. In illustration, Miss Woolf quotes the ballad of 'The Twa Magicians':

> Then she became a turtle dow,
>   To fly up in the air,
> And he became another dow,
>   And they flew pair by pair.
>
> She turned hersell into an eel,
>   To swim into yon burn,
> And he became a speckled trout,
>   To gie the eel a turn.
>                                      [Woolf (1969), p. 58]

45 / 47. *ashunchë* / *ofthunchëth* For rhymes involving words with unidentical unstressed endings such as '-e' with '-eth', '-es', etc., see *EMEVP*, p. 279, note to lines 83–4.

48. This line may be subtly ambiguous. The surface meaning is: 'Welcome (*leef* 'dear') to me would be a man without guile' – a rueful comment on the artful suitor of this poem. However, following upon the girl's regrets at being a girl (line 47), the underlying sense of 'Gladly would I be a man, without question' (with the verb 'to be' understood) may be hinted at.


## 23. As I stod on a day [*Index* 371]

MS. London, College of Arms 27

Text: 2 mede] medwe MS.; 8 rad] bad MS.; 10 se]sey MS.; 19 fet] feche MS.; 28 she] a MS.; 30 Why rewen] W . . . ri wet MS.

1. The first line neither forms part of the first stanza nor does it alliterate. It may have been a later addition prompted by the popular 'As I etc.' opening of the *chanson d'aventure* tradition.

2. The alternative ME forms *mede* and *medwe* (derived from the oblique stem *mædw-* of OE *mæd*) are synonyms. Clearly *medë* is required by the rhyme rather than MS. *medwe*.

6. *shredës* For the rhymes here involving the unstressed endings '-es' and '-e', see 22, 45 / 47 n.

8.   *rad on* At best, any conceivable sense which might be made of the manuscript reading, such as 'she prayed on her book', would not only be strained but unparalleled; *MED* records no such use of *bidden* with the preposition *on*. Alliteration in this line could easily have prompted a scribe to write *bad* instead of *rad*, obviously the correct reading.

10–11.  The sense is clearly: 'with a cry she spotted me; she would have run off if I had not been so near', and not, as with the manuscript reading *sey*, 'say': 'with a cry she said to me (that) she would have run off, etc.' The girl does not speak at this point; the poet simply observes her startled reaction on seeing him. If *gan* (line 10) is rejected as a scribal addition, the rhymes may have been *sei(gh)*, past singular, 'saw', and *nei(gh)*; a short half-line *she me seigh* for 10b would parallel *al thy speche* and *what I redë* in stanzas 2 and 3. Alternatively, since OE *nē(a)h(e)* gives rise to a variety of forms in ME, the rhyme here may have been of *se* 'see' and *ne* 'near', as adopted in the text.

15.  *lyinges* See *MED* **liinge** ger.(1) 1.(d) 'act of sexual intercourse'. Is there meant to be a saucy subtext in the girl's greeting?

17.  The poet, assuming an air of gallantry and the manner of a courtly lover, proposes, as *hir man* (line 16), that version of refined love (*fin amor*) which is characteristically *derne*, that is, 'secret'.

19.  *fet* – as the rhyme requires. The corrupt MS. reading *feche* has arisen from association with the rhyme which follows.

20.  *gospellëth* This word is not recorded as a verb in *MED*.

27.  *billen* 'sing'? 'Peck' and 'blow' (a horn) are the senses given for this late ME verb under *MED* **bilen** v.(1). *OED* quotes 'bill' as in 'bill and coo' first from Shakespeare.

28.  'She might choose you as chaste' – a wry joke! The MS. form *a* is taken here as a weakened form of the feminine personal pronoun.


## 24. My deth I love, my lyf Ich hatë [*Index* 2236]

MS. London, B.L., Harley 2253

Text: 61 hom] *added*.

17.  *clerk* This word had a wide range of meanings in Middle English: an ecclesiastic, a parish priest, an ecclesiastic lower in rank than a priest, a person in minor orders, a scholar, a student, etc. The 'hende Nicholas' and 'Absolon, that jolif was and gay' of *The Miller's Tale* (*CT*, I, 3199 and 3339), not to mention 'jolly Jankin' (**129**, 6), were all 'clerks' and ardent lovers.

38.  *for no synne:* 'for any sin', i.e. no matter how wicked it would be.

47–8.  The sense is not immediately clear. Perhaps the *fair biheste* refers to an exchange of vows on a previous occasion, the time when the *clerk* was happy (line 44) when the lovers kissed fifty times (line 46). The poet observes that such a *fair biheste*, a gracious promise, makes many a man hide his sorrow, i.e. his initial pangs of love-longing before the lady commits herself. But, alternatively, this may simply be a hint to the lady that a *fair biheste* from her now would 'hide', that is, dispel his present sorrows. Whether moved by such a hint, or rather, as the next stanza suggests, by the memory of their previous love, the girl, now, suddenly and dramatically, changes her attitude from scorn to affection.

## 25. Moste I ryde by Rybbësdale [*Index* 2207]

MS. London, B.L., Harley 2253

Text: 29 she] *added.*

7ff. From this point there follows a detailed description of the lady from head to toe exactly in the manner advocated by medieval writers on the art of poetry in their accounts of how the description of a beautiful woman should be handled. An excellent example of this descriptive convention is found in the *Poetria Nova*, a treatise on poetics written in the early thirteenth century by the Englishman, Geoffrey of Vinsauf. His model description begins with the head and, in order, details the following features: hair (golden), forehead (lily-white), eyebrows (dark and snow-white between), nose, eyes (shining), face (bright and rosy), mouth (gleaming), lips (red and warm), teeth (even), breath (fragrance like scent), chin (polished), neck (a milk-white column), throat (radiant as crystal), shoulders (even), arms (long and slender), fingers (long, straight, white), breasts (jewels side by side), waist (slender), leg (long and slender), foot (small and dainty). Following the account of the waist Geoffrey remarks: *Taceo de partibus infra:/Aptius hic loquitur animus quam lingua* [I am silent concerning the parts below; more aptly does the imagination speak at this point than the tongue]. See Faral (1962), pp.214–15, lines 562–99, translated in Murphy (1971), pp.54–5. See also Brewer (1955). This lyric follows and exploits this medieval literary convention brilliantly; without the slightest sense of stiffness or cataloguing, the sustained description flows easily within the verse form.

11. This line refers to the lady's complexion.

29. The addition of *she* (linking with *hire* in the previous and following lines) improves metre and sense. By common convention in medieval love poetry, it is the lady who condemns the poet to death, not Death (personified) – cf. 1, 25 and 2, 39.

49–51. 'When I gaze upon her hand, the lily-white one, dear in the land, the best (sc. of ladies) she might be'. The very perfection of her hands evokes the poet's ecstatic response to his lady, 'the lily-white one'.

75. The immediate sense is: 'like the Phoenix she is without equal'. Perhaps there is also the suggestion here that, like the Phoenix, she is 'without a companion'.

79–80. See Geoffrey of Vinsauf, *Taceo de partibus infra*, etc., note to line 7ff. above.

## 26. Alas, hou sholde I sing [*Index* 1265]

MS. Kilkenny, Red Book of Ossory

## 27. Weping hath myn wongës wet [*Index* 3874]

MS. London, B.L., Harley 2253

Text: 16 durfte] durþe MS.; 48 on] on þat MS.; 59 Soth] soþ is þat MS.

4.  *bok* – the Bible?

7.  *in song . . . hem set* – i.e. written about them in poems.

16.  'who had no need to ride us on reins (to show her mastery over us)' – so Brook, p. 77, note to No. 6, line 16. This is an allusion to a legend, popular in the Middle Ages, in which Aristotle was humiliated by being bridled, saddled, and ridden like a horse by an Indian girl with whom he had fallen in love.

17–18.  The *stythie* is the Virgin, often referred to as Queen of Heaven.

21–2.  An image commonly found in medieval literature to express the great mystery of Christ being born of a Virgin: she remained as untouched by the natural concomitants of conception and childbirth as glass by the sun's rays. Thus the lines:

> As sunne shineth thrugh the glas,
> So Iesu in his moder was.

28.  *chete*: 'hall'. Some editors adopt this gloss as what is required by the context: *Pearl*, line 184, *I stod as hende as hawk in hall*, is quoted in support of this view. However, *chete* is an uncommon word in ME, and elsewhere means 'cabin, cottage' – see *MED* **chete** n.(1). For a wholly different interpretation of *hende as hawk in chete* as 'courteous as a hawk in a hutch', see Ransom (1985), pp. 15–16, who takes this as one of many instances in this poem of ironic undercutting of the status of women.

32.  *hem . . . to fete:* 'at their feet', lit. 'to them . . . at the feet'; *hem* is a dative of possession.

41.  Brook [p. 78, note to No. 6, line 41] renders this line: 'Among the violent it would be peace to speak with them'.

43–4.  'There is no king, emperor, or tonsured clerk who would seem to be humiliated by serving these seemly ones (i.e. women)' – so Brook, p. 78, note to No. 6, lines 43f.

58–60.  As they stand in the manuscript, and as punctuated by Brook, these lines may be construed as: 'For nothing now, of necessity, is true which I have written of them'. But this reading contradicts the preceding lines, lines 55–7, in which the poet strongly denies (albeit 'when in difficulty'!) that he has ever maligned women, and adds: 'I would not and will not do so', line 57. It is noteworthy, however, that as it is found in the manuscript, line 59 is metrically suspect, having eight instead of six syllables. In a poem as deliberately and skilfully crafted as this, a metrical inconsistency of this order is questionable. I assume that in the MS. reading of line 59, *is þat* after *soþ* has been added in error. If the line is read as: *Soth I of hem ha wroght*, the sudden, emphatic and rather surprising denial of lines 55–8, with lines 57–8 as 'I would not and will not do so for anything' (albeit again undercut by the ambiguous *nou, a nede,* 'now, of necessity'), reaches its logical climax in the claim, 'I have written the truth about them' (line 59). But why the qualification 'now, of necessity'? Is it because (however ironically) now (under pressure?) the poet dare not say anything against women, or because women are now self-evidently beyond reproach after the advent of the Blessed Virgin? Again, it is noteworthy that the claim, 'I have written the truth about them' (line 59), is corroborated by none other than Richard, the paragon of the final stanza. This Richard, however, is perhaps a dubious witness, as one whose success with ladies owes no little to charm (lines 69–70). This blatant and ironic volte-face in the last two stanzas constitutes the brilliant final twist of a highly oblique and ironic poem.

66.   *that craftës con:* lit. 'who has mastery of skills'.


## 28. Now welcome, somer, with thy sonnë softe

MSS: Cambridge, University Library, Gg. 4. 27 (C); Oxford, Bodl., Digby 181 (D); Oxford, St John's Coll., LVII (J). For further details, see Benson, p. 1150, note on lines 680–92. Text based on C.

Text: 1 thy] *om.* C; 3 longe] large C; 10 synge] D, ben C.

This roundel is sung by the birds at the end of Chaucer's *Parlement of Foules* (lines 680–92) as they depart with their mates.


## 29. *To Rosëmounde*

MS. Oxford, Bodl., Rawlinson Poet. 163. Facsimile in Skeat (1892), Plate XII.

Text: 6 whan] whan that MS.; 11 small] synall MS.

2.   Sense: 'throughout the whole world'. The medieval *mapa mundi* presented the world as roughly circular in shape, surrounded at its circumference by ocean.
20.   Tristan was the idealized lover of Isolde in medieval romance.


## 30. *Womanly Noblesse*

MS. London, B.L., Additional 34360

Text: 10 you] *added by* Skeat; 13 *as conjectured by* Furnivall *to supply the line missing at this point in the manuscript*; 16 loke how humblely] how humbly MS., loke how humblely *as emended by* Skeat.

5.   *womanly* For the two syllables required by the metre, Skeat suggested emending to *wyfly.* Perhaps, however, the first two syllables of *womanly* may, in a slurred pronunciation, be reduced to one to accommodate the metre here and at line 25, and similarly in *wommen my* in 18, 11.
7.   *myn hert* is subject: 'my heart has chosen you as its mistress'.

### 31. *Canticus Troili*

For manuscript and printed authorities, see Benson, pp. 1161–2. Text follows Benson, pp. 478–9.

These lines (*Troilus and Criseyde*, Bk I, 400–420), which Troilus sings after falling in love with Criseyde, are a fairly close adaptation of Petrarch's 'S'amor non è', Sonnet 88 (in Vita), No. 132 in the Canzoniere. The fourteen lines of the Italian sonnet are rendered in three seven-line rhyme royal stanzas to accord with the scansion of Chaucer's poem. However, the form of the sonnet is respected in that Chaucer gives two stanzas to the octave, and one stanza to the sestet of Petrarch's poem. With Chaucer, the Petrarchan sonnet is first found in English literature; it was not to appear in English again until the sixteenth century. See Gray (1983), p. 97.

### 32. *Against Women Unconstant*

MSS: Oxford, Bodl., Fairfax 16 (F); London, B.L., Cotton Cleopatra D. VII (C); London, B.L., Harley 7578 (H); and Stowe's edition, 1561 (St). Text is based on F.

Text: 2 grace] your grace FCHSt; 7 & 14 thus may ye ] thus may ye CHSt, *and line 21 in* F, ye may wel F; 8 as] CHSt, as in F; 12 his] CHSt, ay his F; 16 Bet] Better FCHSt; 17 stant] stondeth FCHSt.

7. Blue is the colour of fidelity; green, that of infidelity.

11. The subject in this line may be either *feyth* or *herte*.

16. Delilah, who betrayed Samson; Criseyde, Troilus' unfaithful lover; and Candace, a queen of India who tricked Alexander to get him into her power.

17. There is an implied comparison here with Lady Fortune, whose one constant attribute is her changeability, a point commonly made in medieval literature from Boethius on.

20. *Alle lyght for somer* The sense of this phrase may be that the lady is as changeable as the seasons – *light* ('bright', 'friendly', even 'wanton'?) in summer, but, by implication, also 'dark, hostile, cold' in winter – though the rest of the line hints at some further, more personal significance.

### 33. *Complaynt D'Amours*

MSS: London, B.L., Harley 7333 (H); Oxford, Bodl., Fairfax 16 (F); Oxford, Bodl., Bodley 638 (B). Text is based on H.

Text: 8 doon] *om.* H; 12 thilke] that H; 16 a] *om.* H; 24 sing] FB, say H; 29 in] *om.* H; 48 plesaunce] to plesaunce H; 54 that] *om.* H; 55 lefte] lefe H; 66 sorwes] FB, shoures H; 68 which] þe which H; 69 unkonnynge] FB, unknowynge H; 70 unto] to HFB; 75 shulle] ne shulle H; 77 lady dere] hert dere FB, lady so dere H; 82 Alwey in oon] FB, And I ay oon H.

12.   *thilkë spitous yle* Perhaps Naxos, where Ariadne was deserted by Theseus.

26.   *pitée and* Pronounced as two syllables: 'pi-tyand'.

70.   *unto* – for metre.

76.   The H reading could be kept either with the change of *unto* to *to* (cf. line 70) or by assuming a reduced pronunciation for the '-ed' of *pleyned*.

81.   The star, so clear and bright in appearance, is Venus, the star of lovers.


## 34. *Merciles Beauté*

MS. Cambridge, Magdalene Coll., Pepys 2006

Text: 1 Your yen two] Yowre two yen MS., *but* Youre yen two., *when repeated in lines 6 and 11;* 36 ther] this MS. All repeated lines (i.e. lines 6–7, 11–13, 19–20, 24–6, 32–3 and 37–9) are abbreviated in the MS.

16.   *Daunger* An allegorical figure in the *Romaunt de la Rose* representing an attitude of disdainful rejection on the part of a lady towards her lover.


## 35. *A Balade of Complaynte*

MS. London, B.L., Additional 16165


## 36. Miri it is while sumer i-last [*Index* 2163]

MS. Oxford, Bodl., Rawlinson G. 22, with music

Text: 1 Miri] M *not completed* MS.; 4 weder] e *lost* MS.; 5 is] *lost* MS.; 7 fast] *supplied,* MS. *damaged.*

On music and versification, see Duncan (1994).

2.   *foulës* – MS. *fugheles.* For the disyllabic form here, see Duncan (1994).

6.   This line might alternatively be taken to mean: 'and I with very great injustice'.


## 37. Lavedy seynte Marie [*Index* 1839]

MS. London, B.L., Additional 27909

Text: 23 selde] seldô *corrected from* sele MS.

At some point in the transmission of this poem stanza 8 (lines 29–32) was accidentally omitted and then copied at the end of the poem where it appears as the last stanza in the surviving copy. It is here restored to its correct place in the text. See Duncan (1992). This poem frequently echoes the *Poema Morale*, a poem which perhaps best characterizes the themes of the penitential tradition in early Middle English literature. Specific parallels are found in lines 3–4, 9, 10, 17, 18, 21, 24 and 25. See Patterson (1911), pp.165–6. The metrical form of this lyric is inconsistent: there seems to be some fluctuation between alliterative lines and long lines of seven or six stresses. Suggestions for the pronunciation of unstressed syllables are at best tentative.

7–8.   *to wendende hennë* The poet seeks to escape from his many sins by 'going hence' from this life to 'what joy', the joy of heaven or (ironically) of purgatory or hell, God should decide.

8.   *whichere* The MS. form is *hwuechere*. Here *-ere* may be a survival of the OE dative sg. feminine inflexion or a reduced form of 'ever'. However, *OED* first records 'whichever' from Wyclif (1388) – see *OED* **Whichever**.

9.   *Slep* The equating of sleep and the state of sin is a commonplace in penitential writings.

11.   The sense is that the poet intended to repent before it was too late – before, that is, the eternal sleep of death (cf. **38**, 18), an idea continued in the next stanza.

16.   'If he does not do so, when he goes hence let his loins quake with fear' – i.e. at the prospect of eternal punishment. A vivid, if unpleasant, interpretation of the image here may well be appropriate – see *MED* **quaken** v. **1b**.(c) 'of one's bowels or loins: to be stirred by fear, etc.'

36.   *if hit me Crist y-youthë:* 'if Christ had granted it to me (to do so)'.

## 38. Worldës blis ne last no throwë [*Index* 4223]

MSS: London, B.L., Arundel 248 (A), with music; Oxford, Bodl., Rawlinson G.18 (R), with music; Oxford, Bodl., Digby 86 (D). Text based on A; lines 51–60 from R. Variant readings for English songs from before 1400 surviving in more than one manuscript are listed (with some inaccuracies) in *MES*.

Text: 23 The man] þe mon RD, þe A; 28 Er] ar RD, þar A; 37 *from* RD, *om. in* A; 51–60 *om. in* A, *text from* R; 53 and what] an R, wat is D; 54 and what (2)] and R, and wat D; 58 As ... ben] ase þe dede and eke ded ben D, det al so an oþer det R; 65 Ich thee] I þe D, us ics A, hic R; 66 thee] þe RD, *om.* A.

This poem also echoes the twelfth-century *Poema Morale*. See Brown, XIII, p. 201.

2.   *It went:* lit. 'it goes'.

5.   *mid* The form *mid* is kept here and elsewhere although by the late fourteenth century it had largely been displaced by *with*. This displacement is already found in D and R which have *wiþ* instead of *mid*. Likewise, in line 14, instead of *nim* D and R read *tak*, the Scandinavian borrowing which came in ME to replace the native verb.

9.   *this* The spelling *þis* (for *þe is*) in A and R represents the elision required by the metre. D has *þat is*.

33.   *s'ofte* Again, in A, the spelling *softe* represents the required elision. R has *so ofte*.

35.   A proverbial saying – cf. 'Dere is boht þe hony þat is licked of þe þorne', in the *Proverbs of Hendyng*.

40.   *into hellë* The second syllable of *into* is lost by elision; this is more obvious in the manuscript spelling *into elle*.

42. *pride and filth and mood* – 'pride', 'lust' and 'anger', three of the Seven Deadly Sins.
52. Cf. **60**, 116 n.
58. For this line as emended, see *MES*, pp. 141–2.


## 39. Man mai longe him livës wenë [*Index* 2070]

MSS: Maidstone Museum, A.13 (M), with music; Oxford, Bodl., Laud Misc. 471 (L); London, B.L., Cotton Caligula A.ix (C); Oxford, Jesus Coll. 29 (J). Text based on M. Quotations from this song appear in other works – see *MES*, p. 123. Variants for lines 43–50 have been accidentally omitted in *MES* (see p. 125). A transcription of the music by Bukofzer is given in Reese (1941), p. 243.

Text: 10 Thy] L, þine CJ, þu M; 12 Ayein] þat may agein L, þat may ago CJ, a 3lye *altered from* a slye M; 13 and shene] and schene CJ, a siene M, ne sene L; 17 threting] þreting CJ, *originally* ne þrat3ing M, weping L; 23 hede] sede ML, seide CJ; 29 sho] scho CJ, soo L, swo M; 31 bi-knowe] bicnowe CJ, bicnowen L, biþenchen M; 33 foule filth] fole fulþe CJ, felþe ML; 37–8 throwe / Doun] þrowen dun M, dun þr . . . L, adun þrowe CJ; 39 te] enden M, endi CJ, *lacuna in* L; 41 biswiketh] biswikeþ JCL, bipecheth M; 46 eft it wel] eft it sal M, eft hit JL, eft-zones hit C; 48 that] þat CJ, þanne L, þar M; 49 werkth] wurh M, wurcheþ CJ, a winnet L.

1. *livës wenë* Here, as in Old English, the verb *wene* takes the genitive: 'a man may often expect a long life for himself'. Lines 1–2 echo *The Proverbs of Alfred*, lines 108–9:

     Monymon weneþ þat he wene ne þarf,
     longes lyues, ac him lyeþ þe wrench.

2. 'But the quirk (of fate) often deceives him'. The subject, *wrench*, comes at the end of the line.
15. *fox:* 'crafty' – see *MED* **fox** n. 3. As with *wither-clench* (line 12), the metaphor here probably derives from wrestling.
23. *do:* 'if you do', the conditional imperative – see Mustanoja, p. 477. For the emendation *hede*, see *MES*, p. 128.
35. The reduced forms *nastou* here and *wenst* in line 38 are adopted for the metre; the manuscripts have the full forms.
39. *te* Dobson's emendation, see *MES*, p. 129.
46. *wel* For this emendation, see *MES*, pp. 129–30. Dobson also notes that lines 45–6 are a quotation of a popular Middle English proverb found in the *Poema Morale*, *The Proverbs of Hendyng* and *The Ancrene Riwle*.
47. *wikëth:* 'serves'. The sense is: 'what a grievous service he does himself' – see *MES*, p. 130.

### 40. On hire iʃ al mi lif y-long [*Index* 2687]

MSS: Cambridge, Trinity Coll. 323 (T); London, B.L., Cotton Caligula A.ix (C); Oxford, Jesus Coll. 29 (J); London, B.L., Royal 2F.viii (R). Text based mainly on T.

Text: 8 Ich bidde] CJR, we biddit T; mi] CJR, ure T; 20 evermo] euer mo J, eueremo C, heuer more T, hevre more R; 24 And aughte and] heyte and R, and heuir T, and prude and C, *lacking in* J; 26 Ich wille] yg wlle R, ich þenche C, we sulin T, *lacking in* J; sinnes] sunne C, ur sunnis T, henne R, *lacking in* J; 27 lete] R, alle C, *om.* T, *lacking in* J; my] R, mine C, ure T, *lacking in* J; 28 Ich bidde] C R, we biddit T, *lacking in* J; me bi-se] to me biseo C, us to seo T, þet ys so free R, *lacking in* J; 29 And helpe me] C, helpen hus R, þad con wissin T, *lacking in* J; 31 Thou art] þu art CJR, heo is T; 32 helpest] CJ, helpe ... R, helpit T; 33 Thou] þu CJR, ho T; hast] hauest CJR, hauet T; 34 Thou] þu CJR, ho T; 35 broughtest] brohtest CJR, brutis us T; 42 and] R, an C, a T, *lacking in* J; 43 lavedi] leuedi C, suete leuedy R, lauedi brit T, *lacking in* J; 44 fecche] C, veʒge (*or* vezge) R, wecche T, *lacking in* J; 47 drecche] C R, letten T, *lacking in* J; 48 For] C R, of T, *lacking in* J; 49 this lif] þis world C, my lif T, lyues R, *lacking in* J.

3. *Him* The T reading *him* (CJR *hire*), not listed in *MES* (see p.132), may be right. The poet 'sings' of Mary but celebrates *ther-among* Jesus who saved us from hell. Accordingly, in line 9, the reading *he* of T is 'He' and not 'she' as required if *hire* of the other manuscripts at line 3 is accepted. Thus, it is Christ (not Mary) who gives a good ending; Mary's role is to intercede for such. Cf. 37, 41–4 and 46, 81–8. Although such a theologically correct interpretation may be appropriate in what is essentially a penitential lyric, this poem opens as if it were a Marian devotional lyric and it is easy to see how a change of *him* to *hire* in line 3, making Mary the focus of the whole stanza, could easily have taken place; and it would not, perhaps, have seemed out of place to beseech her, the Queen of Heaven, to grant us a good ending.

8. It seems preferable to continue here in the first person singular as in CJR.

18. *nis worth a slo* This is a Middle English equivalent to the modern English idiom 'not worth a bean'.

20. *evermo* The rhyme requires *-mo* as the final syllable. Perhaps the reduced form *ermo* (cf. *ermor* in Robbins, *Sec.*, No. 60, line 2) is to be understood, as four syllables are required in this line.

23. This line should perhaps be read with the *-ed* of *y-loved Ich* and the *-en* of *gamen and* reduced by syncope.

26–8. Again, the first person singular forms of the other manuscripts are adopted.

35. *Thou* In T, *Thou* comes as an abrupt change after the third person singular forms of lines 31–4. In the other manuscripts (followed here) the Virgin is addressed from the beginning of the stanza.

48. *sinne* – pl. 'sins'. The variant ME plural endings '-e', '-es' and '-en' are all represented in the manuscripts: *svnne* R, *sunnes* C and *sunnin* T. The final *-e* of R allows for the desired elision here and is therefore adopted in the text. Cf. 46, 61 n.

### 41. Ech day me cometh tydinges thre [*Index* 695]

MS. Oxford, Jesus Coll. 29. There are many other versions.

Brown gives an account of various other versions of this text (one of which is given here as 42) and quotes the following Latin version from MS. Oxford, Bodl., Ashmole 1393:

> Sunt tria que vere faciunt me sepe dolere.
> Est primum durum quia scio me moriturum:
> Secundum timeo, quia tempus nescio quando:
> Unde magis flebo, quia nescio quo remanebo.

He considers the Latin 'to be a translation of the corresponding English verses, rather than their source'. [Brown, XIII, pp. 171–3]

2. *he* This non-London form of the plural pronoun 'they' is retained here for the rhyme.

### 42. Whan I thenkë thingës thre [*Index* 3969]

MS. London, B.L., Arundel 292. There are many other versions.

6. *ne wot* Metrically the line may read as / x x / x / x / x / x, or, with syncope of *whider I*, as / x / x / x / x. However, it may well be that *ne wot* should be *not* – cf. *not* in line 4.

### 43. If man him bithoughtë [*Index* 1422]

MS. London, B.L., Arundel 292. There are many other versions and variants.

According to Carleton Brown, this poem 'seems to be the original from which a variety of others developed'. [Brown, XIII, p. 173] A closely related version is used as the concluding lines of the following poem (44) on the signs of death. Like 44 and 45, this is one of several short poems the scansion of which is described by Rosemary Woolf as 'quick-moving, metrically free, two-stressed couplets'. [Woolf, p. 78]

3–4. A reference to the custom of removing the body at death from the bed to lie on the floor before burial.

### 44. Whan mine eyen mistëth [*Index* 3998]

MS. Cambridge, Trinity Coll. 43. There are other versions.

Metrical lists of the signs of death are found in Latin as well as in Middle English. The English tradition may well derive from the Old English period; such a list is found in the 'Address of the Soul to the Body' (? 11th century) recorded in the twelfth-century *Worcester Fragments*.

5–6.  The rhyme with the third singular *slakëth* shows that the manuscript form *blaken* (line 6) is a corruption of the alternative plural form *blakëth*. The southern -eth plural ending, a minority late 14c. London form, has been restored in lines 1, 2, 6, 11 and 12; the sustained -*ëth* endings of the rhyme words lend added force and cohesion to this rhetorical catalogue of the signs of death.

16.  See **43,** n 3–4, above.


### 45. Whan the turuf is thy tour [*Index* 4044]

MS. Cambridge, Trinity Coll. 323

This brief lyric is preceded in the MS. by the Latin text of which it is a translation.


### 46. Whan Ich thenche on domës-dai [*Index* 3967]

MSS: Cambridge, Trinity Coll. 323 (T); London, B.L., Cotton Caligula A. ix (C); Oxford, Jesus Coll. 29 (J); Oxford, Bodl., Digby 86 (D). Text based mainly on T.

Text: 6 thoughtes] þo3tes CJ, þonc T, worde D; 13 the] þe DJ, þat C, þed T; 21 nought] noht CDJ, noþinc T; 29 And riden] JC, Riden DT; 36 non other] non oþer CJ, none DT; 37 ther] þer CJ, *om.* DT; 40 her] heore CDJ, þat hore T; 41–56 *Stanza order as in* CJ; *in* DT *stanzas 6 and 7 are in reverse order;* 42 ofkende] CJ, kende D, inne kennede T; 44 him] hine T, he CDJ; 61 sinne] sunnen CDJ, sunnes T; 71 Ther you] þer ow CDJ, þer inne T.

8.  *what shal me to redë:* lit. 'what shall (be) to me as a remedy?' – i.e. what shall I do?

18.  *bemë* The ME plural form with final '-e' (*beme* CJ, *bemen* T) is kept as required for the rhyme.

28.  *fou and gray* A kind of particoloured fur associated with lavish display – see *MED* **fou** adj.2.

30.  *palëfray* A fine riding horse as opposed to a war horse – see *MED* **palefrei** n.(a).

39–40.  The sense is: 'only their good deeds will act as advocates for them' – see *MED* **beren** v.(1) 1.(e).

46.  *to litel we hire sendë* The sense is: 'too little did we send (petitions, prayers) to her (for help)'.

56.  With *heo* (the form of the plural pronoun in T) the final '-e' of *late* (here) and of *Alle* (in line 63) would, of course, have elided.

57ff.  The Judgement scene as described in this and the following stanzas would have been familiar to the medieval reader from the vivid depictions to be found in stained glass, in paintings, and especially in the tympanum over the west door of many a cathedral or church.

61.  *sinne* Again a plural form with '-e', which elides with the following *y-writen*, is preferable to the endings of *sunnes* (T) and *sunnen* (CJ). Cf. **40**, 48 n.

67.  *frends* The T reading *frents* suggests that a reduction of the ending '-es' following a monosyllabic stem was already possible in the thirteenth century C, D and J have the endingless plural form *freond*.

75.  *Goëth* Probably pronounced as two syllables – cf. *gooid* T.

82.  *alrë* The early ME ending *-re* derives from the OE *-ra* inflexion of the genitive plural of the adjective. In J *alre* has become *alle*. In later ME, forms of *alre* survived only in compounds, as in Chaucer's *alderbeste* 'best of all'.

## 47. Where ben they before us were [*Index* 3310]

MSS: Oxford, Bodl., Digby 86 (D); Oxford, Bodl., Vernon MS., English poet.a.1 (V); London, B.L., Harley 2253 (H); Oxford, Bodl., Laud 108 (L); Edinburgh, N.L.S., Auchinleck MS., Advocates 19. 2. 1 (A). Text based on D.

Text: 7 They] þei VA, huy L, hue H, *om.* D; 33 Nether thee hath] þere neþere þe haueþ D, adoun þe haþ A, adoun haþ þe H, haueȝ þe ene L, V *lacks.*

Originally part of a longer poem known as the 'Sayings of St Bernard', these verses appear in the Digby and Auchinleck MSS as an independent lyric. In Digby, *Vbi sount qui ante nos fuerount* [Where are those who were before us] appears as a title to this poem.

14.  *That trailing* – i.e. trailing of long splendid robes.

22–3.  The words *ay* and *o* are both adverbs meaning 'ever, always', commonly combined in the ME phrase *ai and o*; they are also exclamations of grief. The word *wy* is both a form of the interrogative 'why' and an exclamation meaning 'alas' – see *OED* **Wi**, *int. Obs.* Line 23, reduplicating the punning *ay* and *o* of line 22, is unique to MS. Digby 86. Such exclamations vividly recall the anguished faces and cries of woe of medieval depictions of the tormented in hell.

25.  *then* This marks the turning-point in the poem from the *Ubi sunt* motif to the preaching based on it.

26.  *that man thee bit:* lit. 'that one requires of you'.

37.  By the staff is meant the cross, used as a weapon in this holy war against the devil. This and the following stanza echo Paul's account of the 'whole armour of God' – see Eph. 6, 11ff.

40.  *He it* These words may be elided and pronounced as 'hyit'.

43. Cf. Eph. 6, 16: 'Above all, taking the shield of faith, wherewith ye shall be able to quench all the fiery darts of the wicked'.

47. *that word* – i.e. a word meaning 'surrender', whatever the actual word may have been that the poet had in mind.

## 48. No more ne will I wiked be [*Index* 2293]

MS. Oxford, Bodl., Digby 2

Final '-e' may well have been sounded in the rhyme words in this lyric.

7. *Frer menour* A friar of the Franciscan order.

## 49. Lord, thou clepedest me [*Index* 1978]

MS. Oxford, New Coll. 88

On scansion, see Duncan (1994).

In the MS. this lyric is preceded by the following passage from St Augustine's *Confessions* [VIII, v, 12] of which it is a close translation: *Non erat quid responderem tibi . . ., nisi uerba lenta & sompnolenta: 'modo, ecce modo, sine paululum.' Sed 'modo & modo' non habebant modum & 'sine paululum' in longum ibat.*

1. *clepedest* This is the MS. spelling; perhaps a reduced pronunciation such as 'cleptest' or 'cleped'st' was to be understood in reading the line.

3. It is tempting to wonder whether the manuscript spellings *scloe* and *sclepie* (with initial 'sc') here may possibly have been intended to suggest the pronunciation 'sh' of slurred speech on the part of a drowsy speaker.

## 50. Lullay, lullay, litel child, why wepëstou so sore? [*Index* 2025]

MS. London, B.L., Harley 913

Text: 4 of yore] ȝore MS.; 6 evermore] euer MS.; 8 wore] were MS.; 25 it betideth] betidiþ MS.; 31 what thou] whan þou MS.; 46 thy] þe MS.; 47 it wil turne] turne MS.; 48 to wele] wele MS.; 54 horn] horre MS.; 55 adoun] dun MS.; 66 by north other by est] norþ oþer est MS. In lines 1, 21, 33, 45, 57 and 69 the second *lullay* is abbreviated to '*.l.*' and in line 9, is omitted.

This is the first English lullaby. It is different from other ME lullabies in that the baby addressed here is a human child, not the Christ-child. Miss Woolf quotes lines 13–16 of 81 in support of the view that traditionally 'the subject-matter of a lullaby was often a prophecy of the baby's future (presumably a romantic promise of great and happy achievements)'. [Woolf, p.151] In this melancholy poem, however, the mother offers only grimly moralizing predictions for her child in the light of such common themes as the three last things (cf. **41** and **42**), the legacy of Adam, and the malign operations of Fortune, all familiar in ME moral lyrics. The scribe copied this poem in long lines and marked the division of each line with a point or a *punctus elevatus*. The line division adopted in the text follows these indications. Exceptionally, in the case of lines 3–4 and 5–6, the scribe, following the sense, divides his long line to give a shorter first part. In line 31, an extra point is inserted after *comest* – again following the sense. Though not marked, the final '-e's at the end of some lines may have been sounded.

20. The final *-es* of *Adames* may have been reduced here and in line 55.

37–40. Here 'this world' is responsible for the changes attributed to Lady Fortune in the closely parallel lines of 58.

39. *he* Despite *it* in the previous and following lines, the world seems suddenly to be personified here.

47. *it wil turne* The MS. reading *þou nost whoder turne* of this line means 'Thou knowest not which way to turn'; only by an implausibly oblique ellipsis could it be taken to mean 'Thou knowest not which way it will turn' – the required sense, since the reference is to Fortune's wheel. As emended, lines 47–8 conform to the pattern of 4 plus 3 stresses of the majority of lines.

54. *horn* For this emendation and the alteration of the forms of the rhyme words in lines 50, 52 and 56 from the manuscript readings *ibor*, *bifor* and *befor* – see *MEV*, p. 578. For the notion of Death summoning man with a trumpet blast, see Woolf, p. 354 and fn. 3.

55–6. 'To cast down Adam's kin as he previously did Adam himself.'

58. 'So did Adam become thy misfortune' – lit. 'Thus woe to thee became Adam'.

65–6. With only 9 syllables, the MS. reading of these lines (one long line in the MS.) is metrically anomalous.


## 51. Hye Loverd, thou here my bone [*Index* 1216]

MS. London, B.L., Harley 2253

The stanzaic structure of this poem is varied with its alternation of 12-line and 5-line stanzas, ending with two 5-line stanzas.

10. *wont* – MS. *woned*. Reduced forms were current in the fourteenth century. See *OED* **Wont**, *pa. pple.*

15. The old man is a mere nobody; erstwhile accustomed to move in high places, he is now reduced to enduring insults as, stuck by the fire, he seems useless, a creature who simply takes up space.

27. For 'wild as a roe', cf. **1**, 17 n.

38. *inwith walle* Castle walls are meant. The sense is: 'one who formerly was most lively in the courtly company of the castle'. Now (lines 39–40) he has 'fallen under foot' and may no longer 'clasp any finger', that is, enjoy dalliance with courtly ladies.

54. *wonde* – MS. *wonede*. The reduced form may have been understood as metrically preferable. Cf. line 10, n, above.

63. *wenen* The change to the present tense is continued in the next stanza; temptations are not yet entirely a thing of the past. Here, however, the present tense may also signal an ironic comment by the old man for whom, doubtless, sloth and sleep are indeed now all too frequent companions.

64. *to wene:* '(to be) attracted'. For the passive use of the infinitive in ME, see Mustanoja, pp. 519–21, and cf. *to mene* (66) and *to calle* (82).

66. *Mannë* – the historical form of the genitive plural from OE *manna*.

85. *heved hunte:* 'head hound' or 'chief huntsman' – see Brook, p. 81, note to No. 13, line 85. The comparison of a haughty servant with a status-conscious hound seems much more telling. The sense is: 'as haughty is the servant in the house as the head hound in the hall'.

95. 'One who long has yearned for passion.' The sense of the rare word *yokkyn* (MS. *ʒokkyn*) is uncertain. Brook, in his glossary, gives its meaning as 'desire, craving'.

## 52. Wynter wakenëth al my care [*Index* 4177]

MS. London, B.L., Harley 2253

4. *comth* – MS. *comeþ*. A reduced form is essential for the metre; the fourth line of each stanza is of 6 syllables in this poem.

## 53. Nou shrinkëth rose and lylie-flour [*Index* 2359]

MS. London, B.L., Harley 2253

Text: 1 shrinketh] skrnkeþ MS.; 39 other] oþer eny MS.; 41 hir] his MS.; 46 be] be hir MS.; 47 any man] eny MS.; 58 me] vs MS.

2. *that swete savour* The final '-e' of *swete* is lost by 'apocope' before the unaccented initial syllable of the following word *savóur*. It is, of course, kept in *that swetë tide* in the following line.

13. *folie* In ME this word could mean 'lechery, fornication, adultery' – see *MED* **folie** n. 2. (b).

41. *plaster* In the medical sense a 'compress made from herbs, meal, or other substance, often applied on a cloth to the affected area' – see *MED* **plastre** n. 1. (a). Here it is used figuratively as 'remedy'.

46. The five joys of the Virgin.

47. *any man:* 'any one' – cf. *any man*, 4 (another Harley lyric), 1.

51–9. There may be a line missing in this stanza; it has only 9 lines whereas the other stanzas have 10 lines. However, several Harley lyrics have final stanzas which differ from their other stanzas. Cf. 2 and 17.

55. The point of thinking of Christ's torment on the cross for mankind's salvation is, of course, that such meditation should evoke an appropriate response of penitential gratitude.

## 54. Middelerd for man was mad [*Index* 2166]

MS. London, B.L., Harley 2253

Text: 29 thar] darþ MS.; 37 shal] he shal MS.; 43 him] *added;* 58 meint] meind MS.; 71 afore] byfore MS.

Final '-e' is frequently pronounced within the line and may well have been sounded in rhyme words in this poem. If so, in the rhyme scheme masculine a-rhymes would contrast with feminine b-rhymes in every stanza until the last where all the rhymes would be feminine.

3.     *This edi* Probably Christ, who earned Heaven for us, is meant.

5.     *blissë bedel* Perhaps John the Baptist with his call to repentance or, more generally, any preacher proclaiming the joy of salvation and the terror of Doomsday – a fitting introduction to a poem which is, in effect, a sermon in verse on the theme of temptation, sin and final judgement.

20.    *hovëth:* 'proceed, go' – see *MED* **hoven** v. (1). 3.

23.    The traditional three foes of Man are the World, the Flesh and the Devil. Lust (the Flesh) is the poet's main concern. Only at line 49 does he turn to *this worldës won* (the World), and at line 62, to *the fend* (the Devil).

23ff.  The a-rhymes here depend on the vowel sound required for *theo* (MS. *þeo*], a western variant of the pronoun *þo* 'those', a sound similar to that of the vowel 'ö' in German 'schön'. This was a western dialect pronunciation not found in 14c. London English nor, indeed, in present-day English. The vowel spellings of all four rhyme words have been left as they appear in the manuscript; the 'eo' and 'oe' of *theo* and *floe* will alert the reader to the unfamiliar requirements of these rhymes.

25.    *broerli* A reduced form of *brotherli* – see *MED* **brotherli** adj., and compare the more recent reduction of 'brother' to 'brer' in Brer Rabbit. Brook's emendation to *broþerli*, with its extra syllable, is metrically suspect.

28.    The association of restlessness with the reed is conventional.

29.    'The assault of other (senses) need he not flee.' The manuscript form *darþ* (in form derived from OE *dear* with the addition of an analogical 3 sg. *-þ*) clearly means 'need' and reflects the ME confusion in meaning and form of the reflexes of the OE verbs *þearf* 'need' and *durran* 'dare'. The equivalent in Chaucer's English is *thar*.

54.    *casten ... colde* See *MED* **colde** adv. (b) 'unfeelingly' and **casten** v. 24.(a) 'destine'.

64.    *folkës fader* – i.e. Adam.

74.    'When trumpets blow this summons for him' – i.e. on the Day of Judgement.

## 55. Erthë tok of erthe erthë wyth wogh [*Index* 3939]

MS. London, B.L., Harley 2253

Some forty other manuscripts contain versions (some considerably expanded) of these popular verses.

This version is most plausibly to be read as four-stress lines, each with the first three stresses on the word *erthe*. It is noteworthy that with the historical final '-e' of *erthe* pronounced except when elided, and with the other elisions taken into account (including *the erthë* as 'th'erthë' in line 2), each line has nine syllables. This would suggest that this quatrain may originally have been sung; the fact that the stressed and unstressed syllables are not isorhythmic would not have mattered, especially in an unmeasured melody. This ironic, epigrammatic, riddle-like poem is a punning elaboration of the Biblical text, *Memento homo quod cinis es et in cinerem reverteris* [Remember Man that thou art dust and to dust thou shalt return], used in the Ash Wednesday liturgy. It offers a satirically brief, reductive view of man's existence, of his birth (in sin), marriage (or accumulation of wealth) and death. The abrupt rhythm of the short, three-syllable last half-line *érthe ynógh* (clearly marked off as such in the manuscript by a diagonal line) tellingly underlines the grim irony with which the poem ends.

## 56. Wrechë man, why art thou prowde [*Index* 4239]

MS. Oxford, Bodl., Rawlinson C. 670; also in other (mostly *Fasc. Mor.*) MSS.

## 57. Was ther never caren so lothe

MS. Oxford, Bodl., Rawlinson C. 670; also in other *Fasc. Mor.* MSS.

These verses are preceded in the *Fasciculus Morum* by a Latin quatrain beginning *Vilior est humana caro quam pellis ovina* [Man's flesh is viler than the skin of sheep], along with a comment from St Bernard which (in translation) runs: 'When a man dies, his nose grows cold, his face turns pale, his nerves and veins break, his heart splits in two. Nothing is more abhorrent than his corpse: it is not left in the house lest his family die; it is not thrown into the water lest it become polluted; it is not hung in the air lest it become tainted; but it is thrown in a ditch like deadly poison so that it may not be seen any further, it is surrounded with earth so that its stench may not rise, it is firmly trodden down so that it may not rise again but stay, earth in earth, and the eyes of man shall not behold it any further.' [*Fasc. Mor.*, p. 99] The mention of sister and brother, father and son is reminiscent of the *Poema Morale*.

## 58. The Lavëdi Fortunë is bothe frend and fo [*Index* 3408]

MS. Cambridge, University Library Oo.7.32; also in other (mostly *Fasc. Mor.*) MSS.

These verses also appear in a French translation. Their traditional, proverbial character is confirmed by the words *Unde de illa Fortuna est antiquum proverbium sic canens* [Whence there is an old proverb about Lady Fortune, which goes thus] which introduce the version found in the *Fasciculus Morum*. See *Fasc. Mor*, pp.330, 331. Also, cf. 50, 37–40.

## 59. Kynge I syt and loke aboute [*Index* 1822]

MS. Oxford, Bodl., Rawlinson C. 670; also in other (mostly *Fasc. Mor.*) MSS.

In the *Fasciculus Morum* these verses follow a version of *The Lavëdi Fortunë* (58). The Latin text they render is an expansion of inscriptions often found on representations of Fortune's wheel and, along with some words of introduction, is translated by Siegfried Wenzel as follows:

> Therefore we must not grieve about the loss of temporal goods of fortune, which now are here, now are gone, now abound, now fail, just as various people are depicted as rising and falling on that wheel turned by Lady Fortune. The first of them, sitting on top, says:

> As king I rule; perhaps I lose my realm tomorrow.

The second:
> Alas, I was a king. What use is what I loved?

The third:
> Shortly ago I was rich; now hardly I cover my limbs.

And the fourth:
> I shall be king when you, O wretch, will go to death.

[*Fasc. Mor.* p.333]

## 60. Whan men ben meriest at her mele [*Index* 3996]

MSS: Oxford, Bodl., Vernon MS., English poet.a.1 (V); London, B.L., Additional 22283 (A). Text based on V.

Text: 10 on] men on V, men A; 22 they] he is VA; 33 sodenly] so sodeynly VA; 40 strengthe] his strengþe VA; ne] he VA; 51 Ne] þat þei ne VA; 56 kinde] so kynde VA; 57 bedrede] þe bedrede VA; 58 Bid] þat bit VA; 70 couched] chouched V, chaunged A; 95 among] among A; a mon V; 115 so] also VA; 146 other(2)] oþur A, or V.

This and **61** which follows are two of the well-known collection of moralizing refrain poems known as the 'Vernon lyrics'.

Here, as in other Vernon poems, although the scansion is fairly regular, there is a small but significant minority of lines with one or more extra weak syllables: e.g. 47, 69, 91, 98, 101, 113, 119, 124, 162, 163, 178. Other lines could be read with or without an extra syllable depending on the interpretation of forms such as *thinges* (6), *hertes* (9), *mirthes* (14), *warnynges* (55), *hertes* (66), *wiles* (94), *purveyed* (151), *Godes* (165), *unwarned* (170) and *poyntes* (177); and reduced spellings – e.g. *tornd* 24 (*turned* A) and *tempt* 134 (*tempted* A) – occur sufficiently frequently here and in other texts as to suggest that many such words may be read with reduced endings.

10.   The A reading could reflect an original *richest men a rai* with *a rai* representing *of rai*, 'in clothing' – see *MED* **rai(e** n.(1) (c). However, the text adopted here assumes an original *richest of array* with *men* of the MSS viewed as a superfluous and erroneous addition. The A scribe, having already copied *men*, may have omitted *of* to improve the metre.

12.   One should not be thoughtlessly absorbed in the present but should rather reflect on the past and draw appropriate conclusions. The import is similar to that of the *ubi sunt* topos.

20.   *Morwe* – the dawn personified, cf. *Slep* (line 18) and Death in the final two stanzas. The pronoun *he* is used pleonastically – see Mustanoja, pp. 137–8.

21.   'They all become a figment of the imagination', i.e. as if they had never been. For the reflexive *drawe hem*, see *MED* **drawen** v. 3b. **refl.**

21.   *fantasyse* Brown supplies the ending -*yse* (V -*ye*, A -*ie*) for the sake of rhyme. *MED*, however, records no such form.

22.   In the light of the plural *al drawe hem* in line 21, the reading *he is* (both MSS) must be erroneous. The plurals *heo* and *þei* in line 23 suggest ample scope here for confusion of pronouns. An earlier *heo* or *he* ('they') in this line may have been taken as singular, prompting the reading *he is*.

24.   'For all is changed to yesterday' – i.e. as if it had never been.

25.   *Whose* Perhaps monosyllabic, cf. **61**, 11 and note.

52.   *wynde:* 'puff of wind' – perhaps an ironic reference to the fleeting breath of the man now dead on the bier.

53.   Such common alliterative phrases tend to be semantically vague. The sense here may well be: 'nor anyone so resolute as to stand his ground or stare unflinchingly', i.e. to look the world in the face – see *MED* **stinten** v.3.(a) and **staren** v. 1 .(a).

74.   *halt* – MSS *holdeth*.

77.   *though* For the sense 'if' as required here, see *OED* **Though** adv. and conj. 4.c.

116.  Medieval books of moral instruction were often called 'mirrors'. The understanding was that just as a man may order his appearance in a mirror, so too he can correct his morals in the mirror of a book of instruction or from the mirror of life. Here the latter reflects the example of the good deeds (acts of mercy) of others. Cf. **38**, 51–4.

## 61. I woldë wite of sum wys wight [*Index* 1402]

MSS: Oxford, Bodl., Vernon MS., English poet.a.1 (V); London, B.L., Additional 22283 (A). Text based on V.

Text: 57 wane] wanteþ VA; 63 bos] hos VA; 83 is] vs VA; 85 wit] witte A, wittes V; 99 list us] lust us A, lustnes V.

For the restoration of the fifth stanza (lines 49–60), which comes at the end of the poem in both MSS, to its proper place, see Burrow (1977), p.250. A similar error of scribal transmission occurred in 37. Again in this Vernon lyric (as in 60, above), the scansion is fairly regular, but some lines have extra syllables – e.g. line 6, which, as it stands in both MSS, has at least ten syllables.

In developing the theme of the vanity of human life, this poem draws considerably on Ecclesiastes and on other Biblical sources.

11.    *whos:* 'whoso'. This, the spelling in V (A has *whose*), suggests a monosyllabic pronunciation.

12.    The refrain line varies. It is usually of 9 or 10 syllables, but sometimes it is shorter, the same length as the other lines.

13–17. Cf. Eccles. 1, 5–7: 'The sun also ariseth, and the sun goeth down, and hasteth to his place where he arose. The wind goeth toward the south, and turneth about unto the north; it whirleth about continually, and the wind returneth again according to his circuits. All the rivers run into the sea; yet the sea is not full; unto the place from whence the rivers come, thither they return again.'

21.    Cf. Eccles. 1, 4, quoted below.

25–6. Cf. Eccles. 1, 4: 'One generation passeth away, and another generation cometh: but the world abideth for ever.'

29.    Cf. Eccles. 1, 11; 2, 16 and 9, 5–6.

43.    Mats were commonly made of rushes, straw, or the like, and were readily disposable and relatively worthless.

61–8. Cf. Eccles. 3, 19–21: 'For that which befalleth the sons of men befalleth beasts; even one thing befalleth them: as the one dieth, so dieth the other; yea, they have all one breath; so that a man hath no pre-eminence above a beast: for all is vanity. All go unto one place; all are of dust, and all turn to dust again. Who knoweth the spirit of man that goeth upward, and the spirit of the beast that goeth downward to the earth?'

63.    'And both must endure the same death.' The form *bos* (MSS *hos*) is a northern and north midland 3 sg. present of the verb *bihoven*, 'to be obliged (to do something)' – see *MED* **bihoven** v. 1c. (b). It may well have been unfamiliar to the scribes.

## 62. *Fortune*

See Benson, p. 1188, for the textual authorities, 10 MSS and the editions of Caxton (1477–8) and of Thynne (1532). The text is based on MS. Cambridge, University Library, Ii. 3. 21.

Text: 51 it thee] to thee MS.; 65 th'execution] excussyon MS.; 77 And] That MS., And *most other copies*. After line 64 the MS. reads *Le pleintif*; a similar error is found in all copies.

See Benson, p. 1084 for variant readings and different interpretations of the French subtitle. The ideas of this poem are largely derived from Book 2, proses 1–4 and 8 of *The Consolation of Philosophy* by Boethius. For detailed references to *Boece* (Chaucer's translation), and to *The Romance of the Rose* (also partly translated by Chaucer), see Robinson (1957), p. 860.

7.   This line is quoted as a *newe Frenshe song* in *The Parson's Tale*, X, 248.

10.  That poverty, the result of adverse fortune, shows a man who his true friends are, is a Boethian theme widely echoed in medieval literature.

11.  The reference is to Fortune's wheel.

32.  *beste frend* Possibly a reference to a passage in the famous twelfth-century French allegorical poem, *The Romance of the Rose*, where Friend explains to the Lover that when Poverty had banished his friends,

> . . . Fortune straightway in their stead bestowed
> The open-faced, true love of one real friend.      [Robbins (1962), p. 163, 64–5]

Alternatively, the reference may be to King Richard II, as is probably the case in line 78.

43.  *quene* In Middle English this word means both 'queen' and 'harlot', both applicable to Lady Fortune.

47.  'My teaching benefits you more than your affliction injures you'. [Robinson (1957), p. 860]

52.  *go lye on presse:* 'keep to themselves, stay away (as in a closet)', so Benson, p. 652.

71.  With a man's death Fortune has no more control over, and, therefore, interest in, him. Cf. *Boece*, Book 2, prose 3, 87 ff.

73.  *Princes* Usually taken to be the dukes of Lancaster, York and Gloucester.

76.  Probably a reference to the ordinance of the Privy Council of 1390 which required that no royal gift or grant should be authorized without the consent of at least two of the three dukes.

77–9. A final irony! To attain to *som beter estat* (line 79) would increase rather than relieve pain since material advancement would leave its recipient even more at Fortune's mercy.

## 63. *Truth*

See Benson, p. 1189, for the textual authorities, 21 MSS, two with two copies of the poem, a transcript of a Cotton manuscript, and the editions of Caxton (1477–8) and of Thynne (1532). The text is based on MS. London, B.L., Additional 10340, which alone gives the envoy.

Text: 2 unto thy thing] *some* MSS, þin owen þing MS.; 7, 14, 21 *and* 28 thee] *some* MSS, *om.* MS.; 10 Gret reste] *some* MSS, Muche wele MS. The heading and the *Explicit* do not appear in the base MS.

Miss Kean has pointed out that Chaucer, not least in his shorter moral poems, frequently dwelt on 'the Stoic ideal of the philosophical good man who triumphs, by his inner victory over himself, over fortune and mutability', themes common to Boethius and Seneca. However, she noted in such poems the 'use of a style which is unlike the rather discursive one of Boethius, but which is very reminiscent of the short, pithy, familiarly turned, and at times epigrammatic, sentences of Seneca.' [Kean (1972) I, pp. 38–9]

1. *prees* This probably refers specifically to the ambitious and often envious company which thronged the royal court.

2. This line renders the Latin: *Si res tue tibi non sufficiant, fac ut rebus tuis sufficias* [If your goods don't accommodate you, accommodate yourself to your goods], a sentence thought by Gower (and possibly by Chaucer) to be from Seneca though in fact from the *de Nugis Philosophorum* of Caecilius Balbus. See Kean (1972) I, p. 41.

3. *hord hath hate* Cf. *Boece*, Book 2, prose 5, 15–16: 'For avaryce maketh alwey mokereres [hoarders] to ben hated'.

9. Fortune's symbol was sometimes a wheel, sometimes a revolving sphere.

11. The awl was a sharp tool used by shoemakers for piercing leather. Cf. the Biblical 'kick against the pricks' (Acts 9, 5).

12. A proverbial expression to the effect that an earthenware pot should not (for obvious reasons) strike a wall.

17. This wilderness, the world, is man's place of exile, not his true home. Cf. *Boece*, Book 1, prose 5.

22. *thou Vache* Sir Philip de la Vache (1346–1408) was a country gentleman who, like Chaucer, was out of favour at court during the years 1386–9.

## 64. *Gentilesse*

See Benson, p.1189, for the textual authorities, 10 MSS and the editions of Caxton (1477–8) and of Thynne (1532). The text is based on MS. London, B.L., Cotton Cleopatra D. 7.

Text: 1 gentilesse] *two* MSS, gentilnes(se) MS. *and others;* 7 mytre, croune] coroune miter MS., *but* myter coroune *in lines 14 and 21;* 15 Vice] Vicesse MS.; 20 hem his heires] his heires hem MS., *other* MSS *vary.* The heading is not in the base MS.

1. *firstë stocke* Taken as 'Christ' or 'God' by Henry Scogan (1361?–1407), who, in his *Moral Balade,* quotes the entire text of Chaucer's poem. Compare the words of the old hag in *The Wife of Bath's Tale:*

> Christ wole we clayme of hym oure gentilesse,
> Nat of oure eldres for hire old richesse.          [*CT*, III, 1117–18]

The concept of *gentilesse* in this poem derives mainly from Boethius.

5–6. The sense is that virtue possesses honour but that honour (derived from social status) does not necessarily possess virtue.

## 65. Every day thou myghtëst lere [*Index* 739]

MS. London, B.L., Sloane 2593

1–2. In the MS. the beginning of each stanza is marked in the left-hand margin. The burden, marked in the same way, is copied at the beginning of the poem only, but was doubtless to be repeated after each stanza, though no further indication of this is given.

1. *Gay* At first sight it seems that the repeated word *gay* is to be taken as an adjective used here as a noun in addressing the frivolous, light-hearted, carefree fellow who is to be warned to think of Doomsday. This would also seem to be the immediate sense of the first two lines of another carol in MS. Sloane 2593:

> Yyng men that bern hem so gay,
> They think not on domysday.          [Greene, p.217]

However, Siegfried Wenzel has shown that the medieval reader would have recognized a further sense in the repetitions of *gay* here 'related to a Latin *exemplum* about a false judge or chamberlain named Gayus who, on his deathbed, sees devils dancing around him and singing a carol-like song which includes his name'. [Wenzel (1976), p.85] In MS. Cambridge, Jesus College, 13, the devils sing:

> Gay, Gay, tu morieris.
> Gay, Gay, tu ponderaberis.

> Gay, Gay, tu morieris.
> Gay, Gay, tu iudicaberis.
> Gay, Gay, tu morieris.
> Gay, Gay, tu dampnaberis.

A version of the Latin verses is followed in MS. Worcester Cathedral, F. 126 by a translation into Middle English which begins:

> Gay, Gay, þou ert yhent,
> Gay, þou schalt deyn.
> Gay, Gay, þou ert iblent,
> Gay, þou *etc.*                                        [Wenzel (1976), p. 89]

15.    *stere:* 'to burn or offer incense' – see *MED* **steren** v. (2)(a). The reference is to the Commandment, 'Thou shalt not make unto thee any graven image, etc.' (Exodus 20, 4). Similarly, lines 16, 19 and 20 allude to the Commandments, 'Thou shalt not bear false witness against thy neighbour', 'Thou shalt not kill', and 'Thou shalt not commit adultery' (Exodus 20, verses 16, 13 and 14).

## 66. If thou serve a lord of prys [*Index* 1433]

MS. London, B.L., Sloane 2593

Text: 10 *abbreviated as* for seruyse etc. MS.; 14 *abbreviated as* for etc. MS.

1–2.   Cf. **65**, 1–2 n.
2.      This line 'is one of the commonest and longest-lived of medieval proverbs'. [Greene, p. 445] It is quoted in Act I, Scene iii of *All's Well That Ends Well*.

## 67. Swetë Jhesu, king of blisse [*Index* 3236]

MSS: Oxford, Bodl., Digby 86; London, B.L., Harley 2253 (a longer version of fifteen stanzas); Oxford, Bodl., Vernon MS., English poet.a.1 (as stanzas 2–4 of a longer poem, 'Swete Ihesu, now wol I synge', which also echoes **68**). Text based on MS. Digby 86.

5 & 9.   *Swete Jhesú* Here the accent falls on the second syllable of *Jhesú*, as in **68**. *Swete Jhesú* may be read either in the rhythm / x /, with apocope of the final '-e' of *Swete*, or as *Swetë Jhesú* in the rhythm / x x /.

## 68. Jhesú, swete is the love of thee [*Index* 1747]

MSS: Glasgow, Hunterian Museum, V.8.15 (G); London, B.L., Harley 2253 (H); Oxford, Bodl., Vernon MS., English poet.a.1 (V), an expanded version of the poem; Chicago, Newberry Library, Ry 8 (N). Text based on G.

Text: 7 lightsomer] lightsomere V, lykerusere H, delitfullere G, swettur N;

8 lovyer] louyere V, alumere H, a louere G, staluyere N; 15 reuthful were and] reuþful weore and V, rykene hit were H, weren ful G, N *differs*.

The first two stanzas loosely render those of the popular and much-copied poem *Jesu dulcis memoria*, an expression of piety inspired by devotion to the Holy Name of Jesus [see Woolf, pp.172–9], formerly attributed to St Bernard but probably written by an English Cistercian from Yorkshire at the end of the twelfth century. This poem is still familiar today in J. M. Neale's translation:

> Jesu! the very thought is sweet;
> In that dear Name all heart-joys meet:
> But oh, than honey sweeter far
> The glimpses of His presence are.

Devotion to the Holy Name of Jesus flourished in England from the twelfth century onwards and featured prominently as a theme in the poetry and prose of Richard Rolle and the writings of other fourteenth-century mystics.

7. *lightsomer* The range in sense from 'delightful' to something verging on 'wanton' of the V and H readings is more suggestive in this context, i.e. that of a love song addressed to Christ. These readings are also the *difficiliores lectiones* beside the weaker *delitfullere* of G and *swettur* of N. The V reading is rhythmically preferable.

8. *lovyer* Metrically preferable; with the G reading the seemingly obvious elision in *swete a* would have to be ignored.

15. This line is short in G, and even if altered to *Thinë peynës* etc. would remain weak.

24. *us boughtë til al goode:* 'bought us for all good (i.e. to enjoy all that is good, salvation)'. Cf. **96**, 8. However, *boughte* (*bou3te* G) may be a misreading of *broughte* (as in *brouhte* V and *brohte* H); the word has been omitted in N. These words were frequently confused in such contexts – cf. **69**, 40.

26. *didest* The reduced pronunciation 'did'st' is clearly required.

## 69. Now I se blosmë sprynge [*Index* 3963]

MSS: London, B.L., Royal 2.F.viii (R); London, B.L., Harley 2253 (H). Text based on R. H omits one stanza and orders the others 1, 3, 5, 4 and 6 (by R's numbering).

Text: 3 love-longinge] loue-longynge H, longinge R; 7 song] H, þong R; 8 al] H, *om*. R; 19 For] and for R, *stanza om. in* H; 21 myselve] miselue H, myself R; 27 of pyne was] wes of peynes H, of pine were R; 38 that fel to] þat feol to H, fel to þe R; 40 of] of H, þat of R; hath y-brought] haþ yboht H, hauet hy-brovt R; 41 softe] H, suete R; 45 And leve me pine drye] a[...] lene (*or* leue) pine drye R, pyne to þolie and dre3e H; 46 For] for H, al for R; 48–50 *not in* R, *supplied from* H.

3. The R reading manifestly lacks a syllable.

17.   *woundës two and thre* – the five wounds of Christ. Cf. **106**, 40.

39.   *woundë* The pl. form with final '-e' is retained for the rhyme.

40.   The R reading *þat of pyne hvs hauet hy-brovt* makes the line too long. Again the H reading is metrically correct. The error in R may have arisen from the omission of *þat* in line 38 and its subsequent restoration, mistakenly in line 40, to complete the syntax. Cf. **68**, 24 for confusion of *brought* and *bought* in the manuscript readings.

50.   *ernde:* 'obtain by intercession'.

## 70. Love me broughte [*Index* 2012]

MS. Edinburgh, N.L.S., Advocates 18.7.21

In this lyric Christ himself expresses the paradox of the crucifixion, namely, that when through love He became man's *fere* 'companion' (line 3) to redeem mankind, He was cruelly slain by that very love. Cf. **97**, on the same theme.

## 71. Alas! alas! wel evel I sped! [*Index* 143, L; 3825, A & L]

MSS: London, Lambeth Palace Library, 557 (L); Edinburgh, N.L.S., Advocates 18.7.21 (A). In A the stanza order is reversed and further lines are added. Text from L.

Text: 8 I] i A, *om.* L; 10 mi lokkes and ek myn heved] mi lokkes & ek myn heued A, my heued and myne lockys L; 11 Are al wyth blody dropes byweved] & al my bodi with blod be-weued A, ar al bywevyd wyth blody dropys L.

This poem reflects the medieval allegory in which Christ as a lover-knight dies for his lady (Man's soul) to win her love, and, in particular, the version of the allegory in which the knight comes to the lady's door which she has hard-heartedly barred against him. As the poem opens, Christ, having fled (i.e. repulsed by sin), now returns to make his entreaty, echoing two poignant Biblical texts: Rev. 3, 20: *Ecce sto ad ostium et pulso* [Behold, I stand at the door and knock], and S. of S. 5, 2: *Aperi mihi, soror mea, amica mea* [Open to me, my sister, my love]. The drops of blood on Christ's head, lines 10–11, further echo the dew on the lover's head in S. of S. 5, 2: *caput meum plenum est rore, et cincinni mei guttis noctium* [my head is filled with dew, and my locks with the drops of the night]. See Woolf, pp. 51–2.

3.   *levely* As Gray notes [*Selection,* p.125], the manuscript form *lyvely* 'probably represents *lefly / levely*'; thus the sense is 'dear' rather than 'lively, life-giving'.

10–11.   The A rhyme *heued / beweued* is better than *lockys / dropys* in L. The emendations adopted in these lines were proposed by Rosemary Woolf. [Woolf, p. 51, fn. 2]

## 72. I am Jhesú, that com to fight [Index 1274]

MS. Edinburgh, N.L.S., Advocates 18.7.21

2.    Christ, the champion of Man's soul against the Devil, fights not with 'shield and spear', but rather, as in *Piers Plowman*, wearing Piers' armour, human nature:

> This Jesus of his gentries wol juste in Piers armes     *for his nobility*
> In his helm and in his haubergeon – *humana natura*.

> [*Piers Plowman*, B, xviii, 22–3]

## 73. In the vaile of restles mynd [Index 1463]

MSS: Cambridge, Univ. Lib., Hh.4.12 (C); London, Lambeth Palace Library, 853 (L). Text based on C.

Text: 21 a paleis] L, a place full C; 31 ever] euere L, ouer C; 40 *Quia*] L, but *Quia* C; 58 in] L, in me C; 75 come] L, cummyth C; 89 make thee] þee make L, make C; 91 thee mene] þee meene L, be-mene C; 92 wilt] wolt L, will C; 101 is (2)] L, is in C; 105–20: *these two stanzas ordered as in* L, *order reversed in* C; 119 I preve thy] I wole preue þi L, I pray the C; 128 *Quia*] L, in blysse *Quia* C.

The wooer of this lyric is the crucified Christ presented as king, knight, lover, mother and husband; a considerable play of wit is evident in the handling of the metaphors employed. The phrase *Quia amore langueo* derives from S. of S. 2, 5 and 5, 8. It recurs in Middle English devotional literature and, again as a refrain, in another lyric. Evocative echoes of the Song of Solomon, as in lines 81–4, give rise to 'an unusual sensuousness of descriptive detail in this poem' [Woolf, p. 188]. The metre is loose; extra weak syllables are common and in many cases (especially with final '-es' and '-ed') it is difficult to tell if the syllable is to be pronounced in full or reduced. However, the many divergent readings of the two surviving manuscripts show that the text is often unreliable.

3.    *trewe love* In the pastoral setting of the opening lines – characteristic of the *chanson d'aventure* – *trewe love* is ambiguous: the poet could be seeking the flower 'true love' or, as it turns out, a true lover – Christ (line 17).

9–12.    The quasi-pastoral description of a wounded man sitting under a tree on a hilltop evokes the image of the medieval 'iconographic theme of "Christ in distress" (*Christus im Elend*), in which the wounded Christ is seated beneath the Cross'. [Woolf, p. 188]

18 & 25.    Cf. S. of S. 4, 9: *Vulnerasti cor meum, soror mea sponsa* [Thou hast ravished my heart, my sister, my spouse]; and also S. of S. 4, 10.

25ff.    The series of bitter contrasts in these lines alluding to the events of the Passion (the scourging of Christ, the crown of thorns, etc.) echo the Reproaches, sung on Good Friday, in which Christ addresses mankind with the words *Popule meus, quid feci tibi?* [O my people, what have I done to thee?]. He reproaches His people for their ingratitude, and contrasts occasions of His compassion (as God) to Israel in the Old Testament with the outrages now inflicted on Him, Christ. Thus, an early fourteenth-century rendering of the Reproaches in Middle English verse by Friar William Herbert opens with:

> For from Egypte Ich ladde thee,
> Thou me ledest to rode tre.
>> My folk, what have I do the, *etc.*

See also the rendering in John of Grimestone's Commonplace Book, **100**, below.

28. *surcote* An outer garment worn over armour, here 'bloody', representing Christ's scourged back and wounded side.

45. *I leve them nought:* lit. 'I leave them not' – i.e. (ironically) the lover never discards the blood-embroidered gloves (his hands!) bought for him by his spouse.

57. The wound in Christ's side is commonly referred to as a nest or place of refuge in medieval devotional writings.

66. The notion here is that of the exchange of messages between lovers. Cf. **1**, 14–16.

68. Both *dangerous* here and *gentilnisse* at line 98 are words of special resonance in the courtly tradition of medieval love literature; they signify the opposite extremes of 'disdainful rejection' and 'gracious acceptance' in a lady's attitude to her lover.

75–6. The sense is: 'Whether she runs away or comes closer, yet . . .'.

77–8. The word *pray* may mean 'a catch, quarry' as in hunting or 'a victim, a captive' as in warfare (or, indeed, in the 'warfare' of love) – see *MED* **prei(e** n.(2), 2. & 3. The basic contrast is between those enemies who lie in wait for their victim and then give chase to 'her' (in this case, Man's soul), presumably to slay her, and the speaker (Christ) who in some sense runs on ahead to protect her by subduing her enemy.

81–4. Cf. S. of S. 5, 1 (AV, S. of S. 4, 16, & 5, 1): *Veniat dilectus meus in hortum suum. et comedat fructum pomorum suorum. Veni in hortum meum, soror mea sponsa; messui myrrham meam cum aromatibus meis, comedi favum cum melle meo, bibi vinum meum cum lacte meo* [Let my beloved come into his garden, and eat his pleasant fruits. I am come into my garden, my sister, my spouse: I have gathered my myrrh with my spice; I have eaten my honey-comb with my honey; I have drunk my wine with my milk]. Also Rev. 19, 8: *et datum est illi ut cooperiat se byssino splendenti et candido* [And to her was granted that she should be arrayed in fine linen, clean and white].

99–104. In medieval allegory the body could be represented as a house containing vices and virtues – in this case carnal vices from which the soul could turn by looking out from the windows of *kyndenisse*, 'natural affection'. The 'choice chamber' of line 102, like the *paleis precious* of line 21, is heaven. Line 103 may echo S. of S. 2, 9, where the beloved stands *respiciens per fenestras, prospiciens per cancellos* [looking forth at the windows, showing himself through the lattice].

107–9. Christ as husband changes abruptly to Christ as mother. Devotion to 'Jesus our mother' was a late medieval form of piety, and the image itself was elaborated by Julian of Norwich. See Woolf, pp. 189–90.

## 74. Levëdie, Ich thonkë thee [*Index* 1836]

MS. Cambridge, Trinity Coll., 323

Text: 11 erendie] herdie MS.; 12 milde] milce MS.; 13 thou] *added*; 15 yif] ges MS.

11. *erendië* Commonly emended to *erndie*, but the metre requires the full form with four syllables.

12. For *milde* (as required by rhyme) as a noun, see *MED* **milde** n. 'Pity, compassion'.

## 75. Of on that is so fayr and bright [*Index* 2645]

MSS: London, B.L., Egerton 613 (E); Cambridge, Trinity Coll. 323 (T). Text based on E, in which the stanza order is 1, 3, 4, 2, 5, but with correction, indicated by the letters 'a' and 'b' beside stanzas 2 and 4, to the order as printed here and as found in T.

Text: 17 ek] ec T, es E; 23 thou] T, *om.* E; 28 it] T, *om.* E; 33 com] T, com3 E.

1ff. Anacoluthon. The poem begins 'Of one . . .' as if it were to continue with a verb like '. . . I sing'. T reads *For ou*. Gray suggests that an earlier version may have begun *O pou*. [*Selection*, p. 102]

2. *maris stella* Beside such obvious references to the Virgin as *Parens et puella* (line 4), this poem uses images traditional in Christian literature such as Mary as 'star of the sea' here (cf. the ninth-century hymm *Ave Maris Stella*) and as *Rosa sine spina* ('rose without thorn') in line 11.

14. The readings *berest* (here), *thou* (line 23), *it* (line 28) and *into* (line 42) are from T; E has *berst* and *to*, and omits *thou* and *it* – all clear illustrations of 'mismetring' due to scribal error or linguistic revision.

32. *Ave:* 'hail'. In the Latin form of Gabriel's greeting was commonly seen the Latin name *Eva* ('Eve') in reverse. This accidental link appealed to the medieval habit of making associations between elements in the Old and New Testaments. Thus, as Christ was seen as the 'second Adam', so the Virgin was the 'second Eve' who undid the harm caused by the first Eve. Cf. *Ave Maris Stella*:

| | |
|---|---|
| *Sumens illud Ave* | [Receiving that '*Ave*' |
| *Gabrielis ore* | from Gabriel's lips |
| *Funda nos in pace* | establish us in peace |
| *Mutans Evae nomen.* | changing Eve's name.] |

## 76. Edi be thou, hevenë quenë [*Index* 708]

MS. Oxford, Corpus Christi Coll., 59, with music.

Text: 6 the] þet MS.

Of the eight stanzas of this poem, only the first five are given in the text. The fifth stanza makes a natural conclusion to a self-contained poem; the final three stanzas may be a later addition. For the evidence of the music with regard to the metre in this lyric, see Appendix A.

6–7. *havest / Levedy* These forms (MS. *hauest / leuedi*) may represent *hast* and *levdi / lady* here. Cf. 75, 14 n above, and see Appendix A.

7–8. Here, as frequently in medieval devotional poetry, the conventions and language of secular love literature are used. The poet addresses the Virgin as a knight would his lady. He begs her for her pity and mercy as her 'knight' (lines 15–16) and as her 'man' in the bondage of love (lines 21–4 and 35).

17. The reference is to Isaiah 11, 1: 'And there shall come forth a rod out of the stem of Jesse, and a Branch shall grow out of his roots'. The descent of Jesus from King David was often represented (e.g. in stained-glass 'Jesse' windows) as a tree springing from Jesse, the father of David, with his descendants represented by its branches and ending with Jesus or with the Virgin and Holy Child. Mary was thus a 'blossom sprung from a single root'.

28. *hire* The use of the feminine pronoun to refer back to *bledë* in the previous line is an instance of the sporadic survival of grammatical gender in earlier ME.

## 77. Gabriel, from hevenë king [*Index* 888]

MS. London, B.L., Arundel 248, with music.

Text: 3 hire] þire MS.; *the scribe frequently confuses* 'þ' *and* 'h'.

43. *fles* A Middle English variant of *flesh* with a final 's' sound to rhyme with *wes*, itself a dialect variant of *was*.

54 & 55. The syncopated pronunciation required for *evry* (line 54) and *hevne* (line 55) is here represented in the manuscript spellings *euri* and *heune*.

58. *yive* The syntax here is elliptical. The verb *yive* 'give', following from *bid* 'pray' of line 51, has two objects, *hevnë blis* (line 55) and the noun clause of lines 59–60; it must therefore be understood again before that final clause.

## 78. Now this foulës singëth [*Index* 2366]

MS. Cambridge, Trinity Coll., 323

Text: 7 king] kind MS.; 12 and] *om.* MS.; 38 non] non wimon MS.; 41 child] suete chid MS.

1. The '-eth' plural of *singëth* is retained for the sake of rhyme with *thringëth* of line 3. Though not sustained beyond the second stanza, these rhymes seem to be a characteristic of the opening of this poem. In line 7 *kingës* may originally have been *kingen* (with an 'en' plural) to rhyme with *singen* of line 5.

25. *tharë* This early ME inflected form (feminine, genitive) of the article is retained

for its disyllabic form here. Other archaic forms, *thire* (21) and *þen* (29), have been replaced by the later fourteenth-century London forms *thine* and *the*.

28. *meindë hirë thought*: lit. 'mingled, mixed her thought'.

## 79. I syng of a mayden [*Index* 1367]

MS. London, B.L., Sloane 2593

Text: 1 I syng of] I syng A of MS.

From a surprising opening, with a matchless maiden choosing the king of kings, through the simple language and incantational repetitions of the middle three stanzas, with the gentle but sensuous suggestivity of the imagery (that of dew falling on grass, flower and leaf and the stealthy coming of a king to his mother's bower), to the joyous exclamation of the final lines, this brief lyric gives an immediate and unique expression of the mystery of Christ's incarnation. However, beyond the simplicity and immediacy lie deeper and more subtle resonances to be understood in the light of the responses of a reader familiar with the Bible and the liturgy, and with medieval love poetry in which the spring season and the courtly conventions of *fin amor* lent rich overtones to the month of April and the setting of the bower. See Gray (1972), pp. 101–6.

7. *dew* The Biblical story of the dew which fell on Gideon's fleece (see Judges 6) was allegorically interpreted as representing the descent of the Holy Ghost upon Mary at the Incarnation. Cf. Luke 1, 35: 'The Holy Ghost shall come upon her.'

12. *flour* The Virgin was commonly represented as a flower.

16. *spray* Mary's bearing of Jesus was represented by the image of a branch bearing a flower, and specifically as a branch of the tree of Jesse – see **76**, 17 n.

## 80. I saw a fair maiden [*Index* 1351]

MS. London, B.L., Sloane 2593

The repetition of the burden is twice indicated, at line 9 by *lull myn*, and at line 14 by *lullay*.

Greene describes this as the 'masterpiece of lullaby carols'. He likens its metre to that of *I syng of a mayden* (**79**), claiming that both poems make 'the same effective use of the "rest"' (i.e. the mid-point division of the long line). [Greene, p. 385]. However, unlike **79**, this lyric is markedly irregular in its metre.

## 81. As I lay upon a night [*Index* 352]

MSS: Edinburgh, N.L.S., Advocates 18.7.21 (A); Cambridge, University Library, Additional 5943, with music (C); Cambridge, St John's Coll., S.54 (J); London,

B.L., Harley 2330 (H). Text based on A. C has stanza 1, H has stanzas 1–5, J stanzas 1–9, and A has 37 stanzas. Stanzas 1–15 and 37 from A are printed here.

Text: 1 lay lay] la A; 2 sing lullay] lullay A; 49 King] kinges A; 55 knave child] child A; 68 herdes] sepperdis A; 70 ther] þt A; 76 al at] at al A.

Dobson also omits stanzas 16–36 of A, though his reasons for doing so [see *MES*, p. 201] depend partly on unacceptably rigid metrical assumptions. For the repetition of the burden after each stanza (it is indicated, by *Lullay*, only after the final stanza in the MS.), see Greene, pp. 94, 95 & 387.

1–2.  For this expansion of the A version of the burden in the light of the readings of J and H and of the musical notation of C, see *MES*, p. 202.

15.  For the likelihood of the rhyme being on a short 'i' sound here, see *MES*, p. 203, note to line 11.

55.  *knavë child* Dobson's emendation [*MES*, p. 204, note to line 45].

## 82. Lullay, lullay, litel child [*Index* 2023]

MS. Edinburgh, N.L.S., Advocates 18.7.21

Text: 22 ful wel]wel MS. In lines 9, 13, 21, 33, 37, 45, 49 and 57, the second *lullay* is abbreviated as *l.*

In this adaptation of an earlier secular lullaby (50, above), the speaker is the Virgin who reflects on the Christ Child's heavenly origin, on His present miseries as a cold, hungry, crying baby, and on the anguish of the crucifixion which it will be this child's lot to endure. Unlike the earlier poem which, as written in the MS., has long lines of six stresses (3 plus 3) as well as lines of seven (4 and 3), this lyric has seven-stress lines throughout (again, as copied in the MS.).

8.  *thing that was thin owe* – i.e. man, created by God.

16.  *list* The common ME reduced form is metrically preferable to MS. *listet.*

22.  The manuscript reading of this line is a syllable short. An original *ful* may have been lost by haplography since confusable and even identical forms of 'full' and 'well' occurred in Middle English.

24.  *drie:* lit. 'dry', here 'shrivelled' – i.e. 'dead'.

40.  Cf. Luke 22, 44: 'And being in an agony [in the Garden of Gethsemane] he [Jesus] prayed more earnestly: and his sweat was as it were great drops of blood falling down to the ground.'

47–8.  An expansion and explanation of *it* (line 46), i.e. the cruel duty of love that Christ had to undergo for man. The vocabulary and associations of the secular poetry of *fin amor* are found in *bond of love-longing* here and in *thin ore* in line 50.

### 83. Ler to love as I love thee [*Index* 1847]

MSS: Edinburgh, N.L.S., Advocates 18.7.21 (A); London, B.L., Harley 7322 (H), stanzas 1–3 only. Text based on A.

Text: 16 lappe] a lappe A, H *differs and has an extra line;* 26 mankin] man A.

Woolf [pp.156–7] argues that stanza 1 is a separate poem, 'an appeal from the Christ-Child to man'. Gray [*Selection*, p.106] views stanzas 2–3 as 'a self-contained and impressive lullaby'.


### 84. Now goth sonnë under wode [*Index* 2320]

MS. Oxford, Bodl., Arch. Selden, supra 74. Versions in other MSS.

These lines are found in the *Merure de Seinte Eglise* by St Edmund of Canterbury (d. 1240), a popular work surviving in over sixty manuscripts in French, Latin and English. In one Middle English translation (in Cambridge University Library, MS. Ii.6.40) the quatrain is introduced as follows:

> Also bihold his moder, what sorow sche had whan sche saw here swete son suffer al þat peyne; & for þis sorow & wo sche becam blake & blo as sche seiþ of hersilf, 'Ne clepe ȝe me no more faire, lesse ne more, but clepiþ me fro hens forþ ward "woman ful of sorow & wo & colure boþ blake & blo."' As Seynt Barnard seiþ in a songe of love 'Ne merveile ȝe þat þouȝe I be broune & pale, for þe sunne haþ mis coloured me.' And þerfore men sey in Englische in þis maner ...                    [Robbins (1925), pp.249–50]

Here are found both the traditional notion that the Virgin's 'fair countenance' (i.e. the *fairë rode* of line 2) was darkened by grief at the sight of Christ's suffering and the association of this with the effect of the sun in the reference to S. of S. (the *songe of love* above) 1, 5: *Nolite me considerare quod fusca sim, quia decoloravit me sol* [AV, S. of S. 1, 6: Look not upon me, because I am black, because the sun hath looked upon me] – ideas fused in this poem.

1. *wode* 'wood' – here both 'wood' and a single 'tree', i.e. the cross, as in *tre* (line 3). The setting sun was a common image for Christ's dying. Cf.

> ... the sonne to reste goinge
> Was the deth of Hevene kinge.                    [B.L., MS. Additional 22283, f.1a]

The setting of the sun and imminent darkness also evoke Luke 23, 44–6: 'And it was about the sixth hour, and there was a darkness over all the earth until the ninth hour. And the sun was darkened, and the veil of the temple was rent in the midst. And when Jesus had cried with a loud voice, he said, Father, into thy hands I commend my spirit; and having said thus, he gave up the ghost.'

### 85. Whyt was hys naked brest [*Index* 4088]

MS. Durham Cathedral, A.III.12. Versions in other MSS, see Woolf, p.28, fn.4.

This lyric, dated *c.* 1240 on palaeographical grounds [see Thomson (1935), pp.101–5], is the earliest of various renderings into Middle English verse of the following passage from the *Liber Meditationum* of John of Fécamp:

> Candet nudatum pectus. Rubet cruentum latus. Tensa arent viscera. Decora languent lumina. Regia pallent ora. Procera rigent brachia. Crura dependent marmorea. Et rigat terebratos pedes beati sanguinis unda.

Woolf [pp.28–30] gives a full account of all versions, including this poem and **86**.

### 86. Whyt is thi naked brest [*Index* 4087]

MS. Oxford, Bodl., Digby 55

Text: 3–4 are ... are] weren ... weren MS.; 6 dimmyeth] dummes MS.

3–4. For the emendation, see Woolf, p.29, fn. 3: 'In the copying of Middle English lyrics tenses were often confused: *weren* in l.2 should surely be emended to *aren*'. However, either *are* or *arn* is required for the metre.

6. An original *dimmieþ* (OE *dimmian*) may have been misread as *dummes* by a northerly scribe unfamiliar with the '-i-' element of weak verbs of Class II which gives the extra syllable needed here.

### 87. Whan Ich se on rode [*Index* 3964]

MS. London, B.L., Royal 12 E.I. Similar versions in various MSS.

Woolf [pp.33–4] gives an illuminating account of this poem and suggests that the source of the 'outline description of the Crucifixion ... could well be one of the paintings of the Passion, which by the second half of the thirteenth century were becoming quite common in churches'. Lines 5–6, 'by contrast, have the precision of the *Respice* imitations', i.e. lyrics listing details of the crucifixion based on the commonplace Latin text beginning *Respice in faciem Christi tui.*

### 88. Worldës blissë, have god day! [*Index* 4221]

MS. Cambridge, Corpus Christi Coll., 8, with music (C); Edinburgh, N.L.S., Advocates 18.7.21, lines 9–16 only, (A). Text based on C.

Text: 5 shadde He] ssade C.

The music of this poem is 'through composed', i.e. each stanza has its own music. It constitutes the first English motet – see Bukofzer (1936), pp.225–33.

1.   *have* In the music two notes appear above *have*; they could be sung to one syllable or (with *have* as *havë*) to two.

3.   *loven* The manuscript form *louen* has a treble *f* repeated above *en*. This repeated note may be merely scribal; the original form may have been *loue* with a single long note in keeping with the prevailing rhythm of the tune.

8.   The stanzas of this lyric vary in their number of lines and their rhyme schemes. In this first stanza, the rhyme scheme may be a a b b c c b c (with *y-tent* for MS. *y-tend* in line 7). Dobson's emendation [see *MES*, p.195] for the sake of rhythm as well as rhyme is unnecessary.

17.  The form *minë* (instead of MS. *my*) requires the breaking of a ligature in the music. However, at this point in the manuscript the verbal underlay appears to be haphazard and the metre requires an extra syllable. For the singular forms *þinë* and *minë* as required by metre, cf. *The Owl and the Nightingale*, lines 35–6.

21.  The repeated notes over *Tech min* are suspect. The music scribe may mistakenly have taken *Tech min herte* as four syllables and, to accommodate the extra syllable, may have repeated the first note over the second syllable, *min*, with resultant dislocation of music and text for the rest of the line.

## 89. The mildë Lamb, y-sprad o rodë [*Index* 3432]

MS. London, B.L., Arundel 248, with music.

Text: 9 His] þis MS. – *the Arundel scribe frequently writes* þ *for* h; 10 abide] vnbiden MS.

19.  *wunden* The manuscript form *wunden* (*woundes* in late fourteenth-century London English) is retained here for the rhyme. The usual short vowels of *y-swungen* and *y-stungen* must be assumed to have been long or, the less likely alternative, the vowel of *wunden* short. For rhymes of the consonants 'nd' with 'ng', see 106, 8ff. and note.

40.  *allë* The pl. form with '-e' was commonly found in later ME before a sg. noun.

43.  *atten* – from OE *æt þæm* 'at the'.

## 90. Jesu Cristës mildë moder [*Index* 1697]

MS. London, B.L., Arundel 248, with music..

Text: 29 saw] soie MS.

This is a version of the Latin Sequence, *Stabat iuxta Christi crucem.*

1–2.  The rhyme *moder / rodë* is not exact.

18.  See **91**, 11–12 n for an explanation of the reference to Simeon.

29.   *saw* The MS. form *soie* is an error for *seie*, a variant form of the past tense of this verb.

34.   *goulingë:* 'anguished cries' – see *MED* **gouling(e** ger.(a) Howling, lamenting, etc. However, Dobson takes this word to mean 'usury, interest' [MES, p.164, note to line 34, and p.162] which would echo *cum usura* of the Latin Sequence: *Nunc extorquet cum usura.* The sense is that the Virgin endured the pain at the crucifixion which she had, against the law of nature, been spared at Christ's birth.

40.   *thee's* MS. *þes* represents the elision of *thee is.*

50.   *H'aros* – MS. *þaros*, with 'þ' for 'h', a common spelling confusion in this MS. The MS. spelling represents the elision of *he aros.*

54.   *bilof* – an early Middle English past tense form of the verb *biliven.*

### 91. Stond wel, moder, under rodë [*Index* 3211]

MSS: London, B.L., Royal 12E.I, complete text with music for stanzas 1–6 (R); London, B.L., Harley 2253, complete text without music (H); Oxford, Bodl., Digby 86, lacks last 2 stanzas, without music (D); Cambridge, St John's Coll., 111, text of *Stabat juxta Christi crucem* with music for Latin text, English words added beneath not properly aligned, both texts to line 27 only (J); Dublin, Trinity Coll., 301, complete text without music (T); London, B.L., Royal 8 F.ii, first stanza, without music (F). Variants listed in full in *MES*, pp.155–6. Text from R with *lacunae* (because of a torn page) supplied from H.

Text: 4 I] T, y H, hi F, ich D, *om.* RJ; 24 no selly nis] no selli RJ, no sellik T, no wonder H, hit is no wonder D; 29 ne wit me nought] ne wyt me naht H, with me nout R, wite ye me noth T, Icomen hit is D; 30 this sorwe] þis sorewe H, sorghe T, serewe D, sorye R; 37 now tarst] nutarst R, nou H, *readings differ in* T *and* D; 46 at alle] H, at alne T, alle at R, alle D; 56 Thy] thi T, þe R, hire H; 57 Wel] wen R, *om.* HT; 58 Moder] [M]oder T, mod. . R, leuedy H.

According to Carleton Brown, 'The ultimate source of this dialogue between the Blessed Virgin and her Son is without doubt a Latin prose narrative of the Passion represented as spoken by the Virgin to St Anselm ... or to St Bernard' [Brown XIII, p.204].

3.   *might* Here this form is 2 sg. pres. indic.

11–12.   These lines refer to Simeon's words to Mary, Luke 2, 35: *et tuam ipsius animam pertransivit gladius* [Yea, a sword shall pierce through thy own soul also]. Cf. the popular Franciscan poem *Stabat Mater Dolorosa:*

|  |  |
|---|---|
| *Cujus animam gementem* | [Through her lamenting soul, |
| *Contristantem et dolentem* | anguished and sorrowful, |
| *Pertransivit gladius.* | penetrated the sword.] |

37.   *now tarst:* 'now for the first time'. For the rare word *tarst*, see *MES*, pp.158–9, note to line 37.

## 92. Why have ye no routhe on my child? [*Index* 4159]

MS. Edinburgh, N.L.S., Advocates 18.7.21

Text: 3 o] on MS.

3.    The metre is easily restored by adopting the alternative forms *tak* (the endingless imperative plural) and *derworth* instead of the manuscript forms *taket* and *derworþi*. The prepositions *on* and *of* both have the weakly stressed form *o*; it seems likely that *o rode* (for *of rode*, 'from the cross') has been miscopied as *on rode*.

## 93. Lovely ter of lovely eye [*Index* 3691]

MS. Edinburgh, N.L.S., Advocates 18.7.21

Text: 15 I] & i MS.; 19 yerte] 3epte MS.

This lyric is in the form of a carol. The burden is addressed to a tear in Christ's eye; the stanzas are addressed to Christ. The poem may well have been inspired by meditation before a crucifix or a painting of Christ on the cross. The final stanza has been incorporated as lines 15–20 of **97**.

8.    *singest* The metre requires the reduced form *singst* here – cf. *brekst* (the MS. spelling), line 4.

13.    *wo:* 'evil', from OE *wōh*, as distinct from *wo*, 'woe', from OE *wā*.

14.    *Th'art* – the elision of MS. *þu art* is metrically preferable.

## 94. I sike al when I singe [*Index* 1365]

MSS: Oxford, Bodl., Digby 2 (D); London, B.L., Harley 2253 (H). Text based on D.

Text: 9 swete] sute D, *line differs in* H; 18 stondeth] stonit D, stond H; 20 waylaway] wayla. . ., *final letters illegible* D, weylaway H; 22 bo] H, boþe D; 25 He hongeth] he honge D, þou hengest H; 32 makie] H, make D; 41 stronge] H, longe D; 52 thurgh-sought] þourhsoht H, þoit soit D; 53 wepe] wende D, wyke (*rhyming with* syke) H; 60 were] was D, H *differs*.

In this lyric, where the poet sighs for sorrow as he sings of Jesus his *lemmon* (line 37), the language and conventions of the courtly love lyric are 'deftly blended with the tone of elegiac love-longing that colours the whole'. [Woolf, pp. 65–6]

17–18.    A telling contrast of images – of clay shrivelling and crumbling (as it dries out) for the shrinking, dispirited friends of Jesus, and of the impassive, unyielding solidity of the rock in which the cross was implanted. See *MED* for **clingen** in this sense of 'shrivel'.

## 95. My trewest tresowre [*Index* 2273]

MS. Cambridge, University Library, Dd.5.64, III

Text: 26 The] þi MS.

This manuscript contains works by the fourteenth-century English mystic, Richard Rolle, and also a number of lyrics possibly to be ascribed to him.

The language of this lyric as found in the manuscript, fairly consistently that of a north-east midland dialect, is preserved in the text, except for the changes of the letters 'þ' to 'th', 'u' (consonant) to 'v', 'v' (vowel) to 'u', 'ʒ' to 'y', and of *þe* ('thee') to *thee*. A reduced spelling *hurld* occurs in line 4, but, though not specifically marked for pronunciation, '-es' and '-ed' were probably for the most part full endings.

14–16. Christ was nailed to the cross as it lay on the ground. It was then raised to the upright position and, with an agonizing jolt, the base dropped into a hole in the rock whereby the cross was held upright. The process is vividly described in the Middle English translation of the *Merure de Seinte Eglise* (see notes to **84**) as follows:

> ... & whanne þe false Iewis hadyn þus fastyned Cristis body on þe crosse as men doun cloþe on a tenconier, þan þei lift up þe crosse for malice of hemsilfe as hiʒe as þei miʒten & lete it squat sodenly into a morteis; & wiþ þat squatynge al þe synows, veyns, & ioyntes of his blissid body to-brosten.
>
> [Robbins (1925), p. 250]

22–3. Christ the Champion descends from the cross having done battle; his mother and her companions unfasten his shield. A comparable heroic presentation of Christ is the famous description of him mounting the cross as a young warrior in the Old English poem *The Dream of the Rood*.

## 96. Gold and al this worldës wyn [*Index* 1002]

MS. Edinburgh, N.L.S., Advocates 18.7.21

5. For the notion of the wound in Christ's side as a place of refuge, cf. **73**, note to line 57.

### 97. Crist maketh to man a fair present [*Index* 611]

MSS: Glasgow, Hunterian Museum, V.8.15 (G); Cambridge, Trinity Coll., B.15.17 (T); Pasadena, California, Huntington Lib., (Powis MS.) HM 127 (P). Text based on G.

Text: 42 hath maad] haþ made P, is maad GT.

For the literary and devotional background to this moving expression of the paradox of love, both compassionate and harsh, in the doctrine of the Atonement, see Woolf, pp. 166–8.

15–20.  These lines, dramatically used here, are from the final stanza of 93.
28.  *thou art* – possibly to be elided as *th'art* here. Cf. 93, 14.
33 & 34.  Clearly *doest* and *brekest* represent the reduced forms *dost* and *brekst* here.

### 98. A sory beverage it is [*Index* 94]

MS. Edinburgh, N.L.S., Advocates 18.7.21

This lyric is a moving expression of Christ's anguished prayer in the Garden of Gethsemane – cf. Mark 14, 36: 'And he said, Abba, Father, all things are possible unto thee; take away this cup from me: nevertheless not what I will, but what thou wilt'; and also Matt. 26, 42.

### 99. Ye that pasen be the wey [*Index* 4263]

MSS: Edinburgh, N.L.S., Advocates 18.7.21 (A); Cambridge, University Library, Ii.3.8 (C). Text based on A. C offers no help with the metrical irregularities in A because the two versions differ so greatly.

This is one of several ME paraphrases of the text from Lam. 1, 12: *O vos omnes qui transitis per viam, attendite et videte si est dolor sicut meus* [[O] all ye that pass by, behold, and see if there be any sorrow like unto my sorrow]. These words were originally a lament for the city of Jerusalem; in Good Friday services, they were transferred to Christ on the cross. See Woolf, pp. 42–4.

### 100. My folk, now answerë me [*Index* 2240]

MSS: Edinburgh, N.L.S., Advocates 18.7.21 (A); Cambridge, Jesus Coll., 13 (C). Text based on A. C adds stanzas, but lacks the two final stanzas of A.

Text: 9 al] C, al aboute A; 29 bitook thee] þe be-tok, þe *marked for transposition* A; 32 thorn] a þorn A.

This complaint of Christ, prefaced and concluded in the MS. with the words *Popule meus* etc., is a paraphrase of the Reproaches sung as part of the Good Friday services. See 73, note to lines 25ff. The Old Testament events referred to here took place in the desert as the Israelites journeyed from captivity in Egypt to the Promised Land. See Exodus, chapters 12–17. For an earlier fourteenth-century versification of the Reproaches by the Franciscan, William Herbert, see Brown XIV, No. 15.

9. The C reading is metrically regular. Unfortunately, C offers no help with irregularities in the two final stanzas.

14. *Angeles mete* – i.e. manna, see Exodus 16, 15.

23. *the herte* – perhaps to be elided as *th'erte*.

36. The line is a syllable too long. Perhaps *Al* at the beginning has been added.

## 101. Jhesus doth him bymene [*Index* 1699]

MS. Oxford, Bodl., Bodley 416

'This poem, which ironically relates the appearance of Christ in the Passion to the fashionable dress and habits of a dandy, shows a quite striking ability to control paradoxical antitheses.' [Woolf, p. 41, and pp. 41–2 for further discussion] The series of contrasts are in the form of Christ's Reproaches; see 100, above. The source of this lyric is a popular passage attributed to St Bernard, quoted by Gray from the version in Caxton's translation of the *Golden Legend* [in Ellis (1900), i, pp. 72–3] as follows:

> ... whereof saith S. Bernard: *Tu es homo*, etc. – He saith thus: Thou art a man and hast a chaplet of flowers, and I am God and have a chaplet of thorns. Thou hast gloves on thine hands, and I have nails fixed in my hands. Thou dancest in white vestures, and I God am mocked and vilipended, and in the house of Herod had received a white vesture. Thou dancest and playest with thy feet, and I with my feet have laboured in great pain. Thou liftest up thine arms in joy, and I have stretched them in great reproof. Thou stretchest out thine arms across in caroling and gladness, and I stretch mine in the cross in great opprobrium and villainy. Thou hast thy side and thy breast open in sign of vain glory, and I have mine opened with a spear ... [Gray, *Selection*, p. 116]

As it survives in MS. Bodley 416, this lyric is quite irregular in stanza form, rhyme scheme and metre.

11. *acros ... armes* Perhaps the sense is 'arms crossed' in dancing close together in the manner of the crossing of arms in the second part of the dance, *Auld lang syne*. If so, a more pointed contrast would be made with Christ's arms outstretched on the cross.

18–19. Man's side is 'open' because fashionable garments had long, wide slits (*spaiers*). Christ's side is 'open' from the spear wound (line 23).

## 102. Lo! lemman swete, now may thou se [*Index* 1930]

MS. Cambridge, University Library, Dd.5.64, III

As with **95**, from the same manuscript, the largely consistent northerly forms of this poem are retained; they are not difficult to understand and include *mare*, *woundes*, *sare*, *dwelles* (rhymes with *elles*), *sa* and *lufe*, for which Chaucer's forms would have been *more*, *woundeth*, *sore*, *dwellest*, *so* and *love*.

7. A reference to the armour of Christ the lover-knight. For the common and important theme of Christ as lover-knight, see Woolf, pp. 44–56.

## 103. Stedfast crosse, among alle other [*Index* 3212]

MS. Oxford, Merton Coll., 248

Text: 5 swete (2x)] swete be (2x) MS.; 6 swetter] sweter be MS.

These verses are a translation of a stanza from the famous hymn *Pange lingua gloriosi* by Venantius Fortunatus (*c.* 530–*c.* 600):

> Crux fidelis, inter omnes arbor una nobilis,
> Nulla silva talem profert fronde, flore, germine
> Dulce lignum, dulces clavos, dulce pondus sustinet.

This hymn was sung at the Adoration of the Cross during Good Friday services, and this particular stanza sometimes sung on its own and sometimes repeated between other stanzas.

5–6. The metre of lines 1–4 is smooth. In view of this, the final couplet (as marked by the rhymes *tre* / *thee*) is suspiciously loose. In the light of the line

> Dulce lignum, dulce clavos, dulce pondus sustinet

in the Latin source, it is evident that the additional verbs in the final couplet of the surviving copy of the Middle English translation – namely, *be*, twice in line 5 and once in line 6 – are suspect. What sense does the English text make as it stands? Clearly *Swete be the nailes* could be taken as 'Sweet are the nails', but the logical continuation, 'and sweet is the tree, / And sweeter is the burden', would only be possible if it is assumed that the second *be* of line 5 and *be* in line 6 are errors, perhaps for *beþ*, since in each case the verb must be singular. Alternatively, it might perhaps be imagined that the scribe who wrote these lines in this form may have been thinking in terms of 'Blessed be the nails etc.', a natural exclamation in the tradition of thought represented in this poem, which viewed the instruments of torture (the nails and the cross) as also the blessed instruments of salvation. However, 'Sweet be, etc.' cannot readily be said to make sense in such a way here. If *be* and its repetition in line 5, and in line 6, are removed as scribal corruptions, the resultant text offers both a closer rendering of the Latin source and also perfectly good sense. Furthermore, the metre of the final couplet is thereby restored to a regularity consistent with, if, in the case of the last line, not identical to, that of the rest of the poem.

## 104. What is he, this lordling [*Index* 3906]

MS. London, B.L., Additional 46919 (formerly Phillipps 8336)

This lyric by the fourteenth-century friar, William Herbert, is a paraphrase of Isaiah 63, 1–7. The heroic Messianic champion returning in triumph from Edom, where he had subdued the enemies of the Hebrews, was understood as an Old Testament prefiguring of, and in this poem becomes, Christ the vanquisher of Death. As adapted to the Passion, certain irrelevant details of the Old Testament passage are here omitted – e.g. the names of Bosra and Edom. In this new context, other details acquire fuller, and sometimes ironic, significance. Thus, the clothing of the Messianic hero, *tinctis vestibus ... formosus in stola,* 'with dyed garments ... beautiful in his robe', becomes *With blod-rede wede ... So faire y-cointised* (lines 2–3), still, indeed, the battle dress of Christ the conqueror but also, now, the blood-stained garments of Christ crucified. Moreover, as in **103**, above, the beauty of the hero Christ thus clothed is also the ironic beauty of the nails and the cross as instruments of salvation.

8. The Old Testament image of the wine-press for crushing defeat ('I have trodden the wine-press alone ... for I will tread them in mine anger, and trample them in my fury', Isaiah 63, 3) acquires here the additional sense of the agony of the cross where Christ trod and also was trodden.

15. Here *The yer of medës yelding* is more than the *Dies ... ultionis ... annus redemptionis meae* ('day of vengeance, year of my redemption') of the Old Testament passage; it is also the Day of Judgement.

16–17. Here the words of Isaiah 63, 5: 'And I looked, and there was none to help; and I wondered that there was none to uphold' become not just the statement of an indignant, single-handed hero, but also the pathos of the solitary and rejected Christ. The tone is that of Psalm 69, 20: 'I looked for some to take pity, but there was none; and for comforters, but I found none', a passage associated with the loneliness of Christ on the cross.

20–23. These lines appear in the manuscript in the order 22–3, 20–21. The order in the text, adopted by some editors, follows that of Isaiah 63, 7. Thus the poem opens with the speaker's question, 'Who is he, this young lord?' and ends with his affirmation of faith, following upon the dramatic revelation of the identity of the blood-stained champion.

## 105. As I me rod this ender day [*Index* 359]

MS. London, B.L., Harley 2253

Text: 17 bet] betere MS.; 23 that me lest] y wole MS.; 41 encens hy] encenȝ MS.; 47 men have ne mawen] ne mai me hauen MS.

A song of the five joys of the Blessed Virgin.

23.   In the manuscript reading this line is short and lacks a rhyme. Both difficulties are overcome by reading *that me lest* on the assumption that a scribe has replaced an impersonal construction with the equivalent personal one, *y wole*. However, perhaps an earlier reading may have been *þat ou lest* – that is, 'if you wish', which would give better sense.

41.   The manuscript reading for this line is short and lacks a rhyme. For *hy* (adopted here as a conjecture to restore metre and rhyme) as 'holy', or possibly 'strong', see *MED*.

47.   The manuscript reading of this line lacks a rhyme. The emendation assumes error arising from scribal transposition of *have* and *mawen*, the latter subsequently altered to *mai*. Cf. lines 4 and 6 for identical rhyme words.

52.   *wont* A one-syllable variant of MS. *woned* is required. Cf. 51, 10 n.

## 106. Somer is come and winter gon [*Index* 3221]

MS. London, B.L., Egerton 613

Text: 7 me fint] is funde MS.; 23 bold] wlong MS.; 32 shamen him] scumi him, *with* scumi *added at end of line for insertion, as marked, before* him MS.; 46 that lif is] þe lif MS.; 47 Ne mighte hit] *erasure, part of second word illegible*, ne mytte hit *in margin in 14c. hand*; 48 falle] walle MS.; 53 socour] saui MS.; 58 She let the teres al of blod] MS. *illegible except for final* d, Hii let þe teres al of blod *in margin in 14c. hand*; 62 changed here] changedere MS.; rode] blod MS.; 82 Grone] grone he may MS.; 88 gon]gene MS.

For an excellent analysis of this lyric, see Dronke (1974), from whom the stanza form adopted in the text and the emendation at line 53 are derived. In the manuscript the poem is written out in four long lines per stanza ending with the 'b' rhymes. As read aloud (or originally sung?) the other rhymes, as the syllable-count shows, are equivalent to internal rhymes and therefore in some cases lose final '-e' by elision or apocope.

7.    *me fint* – as emended by the Sisams [*MEV*, p.17].

8ff.  For rhymes involving words ending with the consonants 'ng' and 'nd' as *longe*, *songe*, *londe* and *honde* in this stanza, and *bond* and *strong* at lines 20 and 21, compare the opening rhymes *bond* and *long* in **108**.

9.    *child* In the context of the nature opening here and the theme of love-longing

characteristic of the love lyric, the word *child* evokes not only the notion of the Christ child but also that of Christ the lover knight. The word *child* was 'a favourite word in ballads and romances for a knight' [Woolf, p.65].

28. *he* – an earlier ME form of the plural pronoun 'they' kept here for the sake of the rhyme.

31–2. Here, and at 42–3, the rhyme fails. The text may be corrupt, but no convincing emendations suggest themselves.

40. *woundës two and thre* – the five wounds of Christ.

48. *falle* – as emended by the Sisams [*MEV*, p.18].

62. *rode* The repetition of *blod* in the manuscript makes poor sense and gives a third rhyme on the same word. The emendation *rode* makes good sense in conjunction with *face* of the following line but, for the rhyme on long 'o', presupposes that the short vowel from OE *rudu* has undergone lengthening and lowering.

65. *deer* Dronke notes that the image of Christ as *cervus* ('deer') is as old as Christian symbolism, but can offer no parallel 'for the concreteness and succinct savageness of its use here (a use that clearly has no literal counterpart in the passion)' [Dronke (1974), p.402].

71. *Mid flode* Dronke suggests that the poet was developing Fortunatus' notion of the 'cosmic dimension' of the power of Christ's blood – *terra pontus astra mundus quo lavantur flumine* ['a stream in which earth, sea, stars, universe are washed']; here it forms a torrent which swept open the gates of hell. [Dronke (1974), p.403]

82. Emendation is required here since the line as found in the manuscript is too long.

## 107. Lullay, lullay, litel child [*Index* 2024]

MSS: Edinburgh, N.L.S., Advocates 18.7.21 (A); London, B.L., Harley 7358 (H). Text based on A.

In this carol the Christ child is addressed not by the Virgin but by the poet who imaginatively becomes Eve and then a spokesman for mankind. As such, it is 'unique among lullabies ... addressed to the infant Christ' [Greene, p.390].

1–2. This burden is a quotation from the opening of an earlier lullaby (50). Its repetition is twice indicated in H.

24. *barun* The reading *barun* (in both manuscripts) gives this line an extra syllable. However, this poem is careful in its versification; all other lines are regular, and concern with form is seen in the repetition of the same rhyme at the end of each stanza. The original reading may have been *bern* or *barn*. The sense of *bern* could be 'lord' or 'infant'. For the former, see *MED* **bern** n.(1) 2.(b) 'a nobleman, a lord; ... often equated with **baroun** baron'. For the latter, see *MED* **barn** n. where *bern* is quoted as an alternative form along with *baren* and *barun*. A pun, with both senses present, may have been intended; but certainly the sense 'child' is appropriate and, in association with *king* in the same line, evokes the common contrastive topos of *humilitas* versus *sublimitas*.

### 108. Adam lay y-bownden [*Index* 117]

MS. London, B.L., Sloane 2593

Text: 8 Writen] *om.* MS.; 9 take] take ben MS.

For these emendations, see Duncan (1987).

9–16. Adam's lapse was known paradoxically as the *felix culpa*, the 'happy fault', since it precipitated all the joy of Christ's redemption of mankind and the necessity, here, of having Mary as Queen of Heaven. The words *felix culpa* occur in the *Exultet* sung in the liturgy for the Eve of Easter:

> O certe necessarium Adæ peccatum:
> quod Christi morte deletum est!
> O felix culpa:
> quae talem ac tantum meruit habere redemptorem!

[O necessary sin of Adam, which was expunged by Christ's death! O happy fault, which merited such and so great a redeemer!]

### 109. Er ne couthe Ich sorwë non [*Index* 322]

MS. London, Guildhall, Records Office, *Liber de antiquis Legibus*, with music.

Text: 4 thole] sholye MS. 27 this] his MS.

Although penitential in character, this is more specifically an occasional poem, 'A prisoner's prayer', as it is sometimes entitled.

In the manuscript, a French text, and, below it, an English text, accompany the musical notation. The French poem was probably written first [see *MES*, p. III]. If so, the English poem is a *contrafactum* of the French, that is, a version in a different language reproducing, line by line, the syllable-count of the first poem so as to be singable to the tune of that poem.

The structure of this lyric reflects that of the early sequence. This was a type of medieval church music which differed from the hymn in having stanzas varying in metrical pattern and melody, each of which, however, consisted of two halves corresponding exactly in number and length of lines. The French and English poems follow these metrical principles closely but not always exactly.

15–26. The manuscript text of this stanza is retained here: its strained syntax may have arisen from the difficulty of matching the French in line length and rhyme scheme.

19. *woning* Comparison with the *peine* and *dolur e peine* of the French text shows that

here and at line 38 the sense is 'misery' (from OE *wănung*) and not 'dwelling' (from OE *wunung*).

27.   *this live* The emendation of MS. *his* to *this* here is supported by *ceste morteu uie* of the French text.

## 110. Somer is y-comen in [*Index* 3223]

MS. London, B.L., Harley 978, with music.

The words of this famous song are sung in canon, that is, in the manner of a round like 'London's Burning'. According to the instructions given in the manuscript, this canon may be sung by four, three, or even two companions. The second singer starts when the first has sung the first line, then the third when the second has sung the first line, and so on. There is also a bass part marked *pes* (i.e. 'foot') for two additional voices; both sing together, the one singing *Sing cuckóu nou! Sing cuckóu*, and the other *Sing cuckóu! Sing cuckóu nou!* Although in the manuscript these lines are copied at the end, after the other words and music, they are in fact meant to be sung accompanying the upper voices from the start and to be repeated as two-bar phrases throughout the song as long as it lasts. For this reason they are given in the text here at the beginning of the song.

As a type of part-song, the rhythm of the music here is, of necessity, strict and measured, unlike the freer rhythms of plainsong-like tunes. In the text some of the syllables have been marked as accented; this is in accordance with the requirements of the *ictus* (the accented beat) of the music. Thus, in lines 4, 7 and 11, and in the lines of the *pes*, the word *cuckóu* has final stress as in French *coucóu*, but in lines 12 and 13 the stress is on the initial syllable as in English. Again, lines 9 and 13 are sung as *Lowth áfter cálve cóu* and *Wél singést thou cúckou*; they need not, of course, be spoken in this way. These instances clearly illustrate the fact that even in measured, accentual music a singer readily altered the natural stress and rhythm of speech to conform with the accentual requirements of music.

10.   *vertëth* Most editors have taken MS. *uerteþ* here as a form of *ferteth*, politely glossed as 'breaks wind'. Silverstein questions whether bucks farting is a very apt expression of summer joy; and who would hear it anyway?! He suggests instead that this may be an early instance of the verb *vert* (see *OED* **vert**, *v.* 1) from the Latin *vertere*, and here glosses 'cavorts'. [Silverstein (1971), p.37] While this verb is first recorded in *OED* from the late sixteenth century, it is to be noted that the verb *ferten* itself (other than this doubtful instance here) is first found only at the end of the fourteenth century (see *MED* **ferten** v.).

### 111. Say me, wight in the brom [*Index* 3078]

MS. Cambridge, Trinity Coll., 323

Another version of this piece of popular traditional wisdom is found in a narrative setting in a Latin exemplum in MS. London, B.L., Additional 11579, where a woman is told by a fortune-teller to go to a wood and repeat her complaint about her husband. There follows this version of the dialogue:

> 'Say, wight y the brom,
> What is me for to don?
> Ich have the worstë bonde
> That is in any londe.'

> *Responsio sortilege anglice:*

> 'Yif thy bonde is ille
> Hold thy tongë stille.'

### 112. Hit was upon a Shere Thorsday [*Index* 1649]

MS. Cambridge, Trinity Coll., 323

Text: 13 He mette] I mette MS.; 49 Lord] crist *erased after* lord MS.; 58 frec] *added*; 64 & 66 knighte] cnistes MS. In the right-hand margin the sign '.ii.' indicates the repeat of 15–16, 51–2 and 63–4 (written as single long lines in the MS.).

No source has been discovered for this story of Judas and his sister. It may have derived from accounts of Judas in which he is exploited by his wife. See Brown XIII, p. 183.

16.  *me stonde thee:* lit. 'that one should stone thee'. The form *me* is a weakened form of the indefinite pronoun *man*, 'one'. Cf. line 60.

48.  This line has elsewhere been taken as part of Judas's reply, with *he* referring to Christ. However, it is Judas who wished to have the stolen thirty coins of silver back, not Christ, who had given them to Judas to buy food with. Thus, line 47 is Judas's direct speech; line 48 is a comment thereon, and *he* refers to Judas.

64 & 66.  *knighte* – MS. *cnistes*. The rhyme requires the plural form ending in '-e' from the OE genitive plural *cnihta*.

## 113. Ich herde men upon mold [*Index* 696; *Suppl.* 1320.5]

MS. London, B.L., Harley 2253

Text: 7 bit] bid MS.; 26 men] me MS.; 28 bidding] bddyng MS.; 29 Men] meni MS.; 43 no] ne MS.; 59 her fille] ar fulle MS.

2.    *he:* 'they'. This earlier dialect form of the plural pronoun is retained here for the alliteration with *herë* ('their') in the second half of the line.

7.    *bit* See *MED* **bite** n.3.(a) where *bid* (the manuscript form) in this line is quoted with the sense 'bite', though *bid* is not listed initially among the variant forms.

15.    The hayward's duties included responsibility for maintaining the fences which separated the common land from enclosed lands.

16.    The bailiff was in charge of administering the lord's land and upholding his rights in law.

17.    The peasant would forage for fire-wood or perhaps, like the Man in the Moon in 114 (below), who is also caught in the act, for briar cuttings for mending fences. The woodward was the official in charge of forests and forest timber.

19.    Lit. 'thus one robs the poor' – *me* is a form of the Middle English indefinite pronoun 'one'.

23.    Here and in lines 31 and 32 the forces of corruption, unbridled power (*Will*) and dishonesty (*Falsshipe*), are personified.

24.    *prikërës:* 'horseman's, rider's'. A contrast is commonly made in Middle English verse between the rich and powerful mounted on horseback with all their finery and the poor and destitute often walking bare-foot and ragged.

33.    *in the stede:* lit. 'in the place'.

34.    The beggars here are those who have been cheated and driven out of land and property and forced to take to the road like pilgrims, i.e. with staff and bag.

37.    The beadle was an official working under the authority of the bailiff, here acting as a tax-collector.

38.    *grenë wax* A seal of green wax was affixed to Exchequer documents containing the names of those to be taxed. Thus 'silver for the green wax' meant money for the payment of taxes. See *OED* **Green wax**.

42.    *fish-day* A religious fast day on which fish was eaten.

43.    Though the spelling *chost* is questioned under *MED* **chest** n., it is clearly required for the rhyme scheme here.

55.    *under gore:* lit. 'under clothes'. This was a common phrase in Middle English love lyrics with a variety of meanings according to context.

70.    Flooding caused by the overflowing of streams and the breaching of banks.

## 114. Man in the moonë stont and strit [*Index* 2066]

MS. London, B.L., Harley 2253

Text: 9 troweth] trowe MS.; 35 nil he] nulle MS.; 40 cherl] cherld MS.

The Man in the Moon was popularly supposed to have been a peasant who was banished to the moon for stealing thorns which he still carries in a bundle on his fork.

6.  *hattren* Plurals ending in '-en', as here and in *doren* (needed for the rhyme) in line 14, were occasionally used in late fourteenth-century London English; so also were the '-(e)th' plural forms of the verb, as in *beth* and *to-tereth* (again required for the rhyme).

8.  The apparent personification of the hedge here may simply be taken as a touch of wry humour – i.e. so elusive is the Man in the Moon that only the hedge he works on knows anything about him – what he wears, for example.

9.  Lit. 'Where does this man believe (himself) to have taken (his) way?'

13–16. What is described here is the contemporary method of mending hedges, which involved two stages. First, cuttings (commonly of whitethorn) were planted in the hope that they would grow to fill the gaps. Secondly, to prevent the new shoots from being eaten or trampled by animals, these cuttings were protected by a further layer of branches, again preferably of thorns. Thus, if the Man in the Moon did not cut a second bundle (the *other trous*, line 15) of thorns for this purpose, his cuttings would be left unprotected and his day's work thereby wasted. [See Menner (1949), pp. 6–11.]

17.  *when er he were:* lit. 'whenever he may have been (sc. born)'.

22–32. The Man in the Moon is imagined as having been off on an errand, namely that of cutting briars; he has not succeeded simply because he has been caught by the hayward. The hayward had the duty of protecting his lord's property from thieves; he has therefore exacted from the Man in the Moon a promise of payment in the form of a *wed*, i.e. a pledge, which could have been any item such as a hat, a pair of gloves, or the like (see *Piers Plowman* C XIV, 44–5, and Skeat's note [Skeat (1886), vol. ii, p. 174]) which could later be redeemed by the payment of money.

32.  *baily:* 'bailiff, steward'. In the general sense of 'an agent of a Lord, responsible ... for the management of a manor' (*MED*, **baillif** n.3.) this term may overlap with *hayward*, an official whose duties included, but were by no means confined to, maintaining hedges (see *MED* **hei-ward** n.). Thus the *baily* here – the word perhaps chosen because it alliterates with *borwe* in the first half of the line – may be the same person as the *hayward* of line 24. This would make for the simplest and most satisfactory reading of the situation here. The trick proposed (doubtless one common enough in the poet's day) was to fill the hayward / bailiff full of liquor and, presumably, to steal the pledge back from him when he was too drunk to notice. Alternatively, if the *hayward* and the *baily* here are to be taken as referring to different officials, one has to suppose with Menner that when the *hayward* is drunk they will steal some money from him with which they will then redeem the pledge from the bailiff. [Menner (1949), p. 12]

36.  *can nought o lawe* For *o lawe* with a verb of motion (understood here with *can*) meaning 'get down', cf. *MED* **loue** n.(3)(b).

37.  The Man in the Moon may be called a magpie here because of his activities in stealing thorn cuttings. The magpie is described as *hosede* because its black legs

beneath its white belly look as if they were clad in leggings or stockings. See Menner (1949), p. 13.

38.   *amarsclëd:* 'bemused' – i.e. by 'the sinister power of the moon which has made the man a prisoner' [*EMEVP*, p. 332, n 36, and see also n 38].

38.   *mawe* means 'stomach'. For *into the mawe* as 'to your very vitals', see *EMEVP*, glossary, under **mawe** n.

## 115. Of rybaudz I ryme [*Index* 2649]

MS. London, B.L., Harley 2253

Text: 21 rybaud] rybaudz MS.

3.   *by pate and by polle:* lit. 'head by head'.

4.   For *take* as 'give' and *tolle* as 'payment' see *MED* **taken** v. 31a. and *OED* **Toll** sb.1.

5.   *Gonnylde gnoste* According to *OED* (under **Gun**, *sb.*) *Gonnylde* here (ultimately derived from ON *Gunnhild-r*) was a name used for a cannon.

14.   *er hit dawe:* lit. 'before it dawns'.

16.   *Gobelyn:* 'a mischievous and ugly demon'. In the twelfth century, Odericus Vitalis mentions *Gobelinus* as the popular name of a spirit. *Gobelyn* here is the first occurrence of the word in English. See *OED* **Goblin**.

16.   *gromene* The ending '-ene' was originally genitive plural (from OE '-ena') but came also to have adjectival force in Middle English.

22.   *dewe:* 'dew', or simply 'moisture' – see *MED* **deu** n.1; the choice of word here is dictated by the alliteration.

24.   *shooëth a shrewe* Possibly a proverbial saying: see Robbins, *Hist.*, p. 260, n 24. The sense is that this is the kind of rascal from whose very looks it is obvious that he is given to every kind of mischief and futile activity.

26.   *as hit were a bride:* lit. 'as if it were a girl'. In Middle English *bride* had the general sense of 'young woman, maiden' as well as the modern sense 'bride'. See *MED* **brid(e** n.(1), 2.

27.   *lowe-lacëde shoon* – i.e. fashionable, effeminate footwear, rather than boots or leggings laced up the leg.

28.   This line is quoted in *MED* under **piken** v.(1) 8.(a), under **provendre** n.(a), and under **pride** n.2 1b.(d) with meanings given respectively as 'steal, rob, plunder', 'food for domesticated animals, fodder', and 'worldly wealth or possessions; extravagant finery'. However, it is not altogether clear how 'they steal from their fodder all their finery' makes sense unless 'fodder' is taken to refer not only to food but (derisively) to any sustenance *knaves* can come by from their superiors, including items of clothing. This would then amount to a final dismissive comment to the effect that all their vaunted finery is merely scavenged from anything such lackeys can get.

31–2.  *companage* – items of food other than the basics, bread or meat – see *MED* **companage** n.(1). Robbins translates 'relish' [*Hist.*, p. 260, n 31]. The coarsely ironic sense of these lines is: no matter what he gave them ('even if he gave them cat's shit'!) yet they would complain about the balance due to them. The translation of line 32 as 'yet he shall grieve about the expense' given by Robbins

[*Hist.*, p.260, n.32] ignores the fact that *arrerage* essentially involves the sense of what is owing. See *MED* **arrerage** n.

## 116. Skottes out of Berwik [*Index* 3080]

MS. London, B.L., Cotton Galba E.ix

Text: 25 Skotte] skottes MS.

The eleven political / historical poems of Laurence Minot (probably a Yorkshireman writing between 1333 and 1352, the period of the events he deals with) appear in the early 15c. MS. Cotton Galba E.ix, along with a miscellany of romances and religious and didactic poems. This poem celebrates the victory of the English over the Scots at Halidon Hill in 1333 as revenge for the earlier Scottish victory at Bannockburn. Minot's chauvinistic, anti-Scottish rhetoric is characteristically personal in tone and gains force from his use of alliterative formulae and colloquial vocabulary.

The northern dialect of this poem has not been normalized to that of late fourteenth-century London. As is evident from *The Reeve's Tale*, Chaucer was not unfamiliar with this form of English. Nor does it present much difficulty to the modern reader since some of its characteristics were to establish themselves in Standard English in the course of the ensuing two centuries – e.g. the pronoun 'their' (here *thaire*) and the '-es' ending of the third person singular present indicative of the verb. The manuscript forms are altered here only in the substitution of the letters 'th', 'y', 'J', 'u' (for the vowel) and 'ee' (in *thee*) for 'þ', 'ȝ', 'I', 'v' and 'e'.

1. *Skottes out of Berwik and of Abirdene* – i.e. Scots from all parts, south and north.
2. The battle in 1314 at Bannockburn outside Stirling, in which the Scots defeated the English, ushered in a period of success for the Scots in their struggles against the English.
4. The revenge was the English victory in 1333, at Halidon Hill near Berwick.
7. *Saint Johnes toune* – a name for Perth, then capital of Scotland, taken from the medieval town church of St John the Baptist.
9. *hosting* Possibly a reference to songs sung by the Scots abusing the English, some to the effect that the Scots would drag the English to the gallows by their tails.
15. *the pelers* Border raids by the Scots were used by Edward III as a pretext for his renewal of war against the Scots which led to the battle of Halidon Hill.
16. *rifild thaire rout:* lit. 'stripped their band' – i.e. the band of raiders.
20. *Berebag* The Scots were noted for the fact that when on campaign, instead of hampering their progress by having a baggage-train with provisions, each man simply carried a bag of oatmeal for food.
22. *Brig:* 'Bruges'. The Scots had close trading links with Flanders.
36. After the battle of Halidon Hill, Berwick, which had been besieged by Edward III, surrendered to the English.

### 117. *Ich am of Irlande* [*Index* 1008]

MS. Oxford, Bodl., Rawlinson D.913

1–3. This lyric is probably a dance song in the form of a carol. As such, these lines are the burden (sung by all the dancers), and lines 4–7, a stanza to be sung by a soloist.

5. Old French *par seinte charite* was rendered as *for seint charite* and as *of seint charite* in Middle English. Both prepositions have been combined here in *For of.*

### 118. Maiden in the morë lay [*Index* 3891; *Suppl.* 2037.5]

MS. Oxford, Bodl., Rawlinson D.913

Text: 10 was] wat MS.; 21, 22, 25, 26 *and* 27 the] *supplied* – MS. *has a four-letter space at the beginning of which the blurred form of the letter* 'þ' *is perhaps to be made out.*

This dance song is recorded in a highly abbreviated form in the Rawlinson manuscript. For the MS. forms *mor* (lines 1, 2, 5 and 6), *seuenyst* (line 3), *seuenist* (line 4) and *seuenistes* (lines 7 and 8) as scribal revisions of *more* and *seueniȝte*, and the rationale of the expansion given here of the Rawlinson text, see Duncan (forthcoming).

3. *Sevenightë fullë* After numerals, some nouns in Middle English (of which 'night' was one) had plural forms with final '-e' or without an ending (cf. Chaucer's *she was seven nyght old*, *CT*, VIII, 2873) as well as forms with the '-es' plural ending. See Mustanoja (1960), pp. 57–8.

27. *wellë-spring* The source of a stream where the water rises (i.e. 'wells up') to the surface.

28. *bour* In Middle English, *bour* had both the general sense of 'dwelling' and the more specific sense of 'lady's chamber'.

### 119. D . . . dronken [*Index* *24; *Suppl.* 4256.8]

MS. Oxford, Bodl., Rawlinson D.913

In the manuscript this lyric is so faded and illegible in many places that the readings and the arrangement of the text arrived at by various editors differ widely. What is given here is substantially the version printed by Robbins [Robbins, *Sec.*, p. 106] who interpreted this piece as the work of a poet 'trying to represent the emotions of a drunken man, who wants everything to stand still; then when he trips, is able to relax his body' [Robbins, *Sec.*, p. 265]. However, to judge from other Rawlinson poems (e.g. 117 and 118), this may, as John Burrow has persuasively argued, be a dance song rather than simply a drinking song [Burrow (1984), pp. 11–12]. The following is Burrow's version of the text with two additions: (1) *Robin*, as suggested by the Sisams [*MEV*, p.169], for the space in the manuscript between *Hay* and *Malkin* which may well have contained a name; and (2) the repetition of the line 8 as line 9, a repetition which could easily have been omitted in error or as an abbreviation of the text (cf. 118). These alterations give three stanzas of 5 lines with 3, 2, 3, 3 and 3 strong accents, a rhythmic regularity required of a dance song. The six lines Burrow left 'formally unaccounted for' [Burrow (1984), p.11] thus form another complete stanza and a final couplet. However, this reconstruction is admittedly speculative.

> Tábart ís y-drónken,
>     Drónken, drónken,
> Y-drónken ís Tabárt,
> Y-drónken ís Tabárt,
> 5 Y-drónken áttë wínë.
>
> Hay Róbin, Málkin, súster,
>     Wálter, Péter!
> Ye drónken állë dépë,
> Ye drónken állë dépë,
> 10 Ánd Ichúllë ékë.
>
> Stóndeth állë stíllë,
>     Stíllë, stíllë,
> Stíllë stóndeth állë,
> Stíllë stóndeth állë,
> 15 Stílle as ány stón.
>
> Tríppe a líttel wíth thy fót
> And lét thy bódy gón.

## 120. *The Complaint of Chaucer to his Purse*

See Benson (1988), p.1191, for the textual authorities, 11 MSS, a transcript of a Cotton MS., and the editions of Caxton (1477–8) and of Thynne (1532). Text based on MS. Oxford, Bodl., Fairfax 16.

Text: 4 but] *some* MSS, but yf MS.; 25 oure harmes] *some* MSS, myn harme MS.

The envoy appears in only 5 of the 11 manuscripts; it differs in form, tone and diction from the preceding stanzas and may have been a later addition. With the envoy, the poem is specifically a begging poem; poems of this kind were written by Chaucer's contemporaries Deschamps and Machaut. Without the envoy, it stands in a tradition of popular poems about money which is well represented by 121, below. However, 'Chaucer's poem is unique in its humorous application of the language of a lover's appeal to his mistress to this well-worn theme' [Benson, p.1088].

4.  *make me hevy chere:* 'look gravely / seriously upon me'. Again, as with *lyght* in line

3, a pun is involved with *hevy chere* as 'serious in manner' but also with *hevy* as 'heavy in weight'. Lady Purse should be both!

13.  *Quene of comfort* – a phrase used referring to the Blessed Virgin in Chaucer's poem 'An ABC', line 77. Cf. his reference to his purse here as 'saviour', in line 16.

15.  *that ben:* '(you) who are' – cf. *Been* in line 24. Throughout this poem the plural of polite address is used.

17.  *Out of this tounë* Various interpretations have been offered. Skeat took this to be an expression of Chaucer's wish to quit the expense of London for some cheaper place.

19.  *shave as nye as is a frere* – i.e. 'stripped clean of money'. Chaucer playfully combines the sense of the friar's tonsure and the notion of the friar's vow of poverty.

22.  A common tradition in medieval literature deriving from the pseudo-historical early twelfth-century *Historia Regum Britanniae* of Geoffrey of Monmouth had it that Albion, another name for Britain, had been founded by a certain Brutus, a descendant of Aeneas. The 'conqueror' here is Henry IV, who came to the throne by deposing King Richard II.

25.  *harmes:* 'troubles' – pronounced here, as in modern English, as one syllable, as the metre shows.


## 121. When I have in myn purs y-now [*Index* 3959]

MS. London, B.L., Sloane 2593

Text: 12 is] *added*.

1–2. Cf. 65, 1–2 n.

9.  Jack was a name commonly used for an ordinary fellow of low social status. See Greene, p. 448.

13.  Greene takes the references to *horn* here and *bow* in line 17 as indicating rather 'that Jack has taken to hunting the deer than that he has become a "vagabond musician", as suggested in the note in the first edition of this work' [Greene, p. 448]. Yet it seems no less likely that Jack has taken to amusing himself with horn and fiddle, and even, with whatever little success (see line 18), to busking to supply his needs.


## 122. I have a gentil cok [*Index* 1299]

MS. London, B.L., Sloane 2593

Text: 2 the day] day MS.; 11 corel] scorel MS.

Compare Chaucer's description of Chauntecleer in *The Nun's Priest's Tale*.

His coomb was redder than the fyn coral,
And batailled as it were a castel wal;
His byle was black, and as the jeet it shoon;

> Lyk asure were his legges and his toon;
> His nayles whitter than the lylye flour,
> And lyk the burned gold was his colour. [*CT*, VII. 2859–64]

8.   The manuscript spelling *tayil* might be taken to indicate a disyllabic pronuncia-
      tion as required here and in line 12. However, *yi* simply represents 'i' in MS.
      *matyins* (line 4).

15 & 19.   In the Sloane lyrics the variation of 3- and 4-stress lines is not uncommon.

19–20.   For the sexual innuendo here, compare the nursery rhyme:

> Goosey, goosey, gander,
> Whither shall I wander?
> Upstairs and downstairs
> And in my lady's chamber.

### 123. *Omnes gentes plaudite!* [*Index* 2675]

MS. London, B.L., Sloane 2593

Text: 9 it] is MS.

This may well have been a song, notwithstanding the seemingly irregular metre,
since extra syllables could easily have been accommodated in measured music
in triple time with three quavers varying with crotchet and quaver.

1.   With these words from the beginning of Psalm 47 (AV: 'O clap your hands, all
      ye people'), the singer of this nonsense-cum-drinking song may wryly have been
      inviting the encouragement of a bit of applause.

4.   If the words *Ego dixi* are meant to echo the beginning of the canticle of Hezekiah
      [Isaiah 38, 10–22], this reference (with the following *have good day*) is blatantly
      ironic since King Hezekiah's observations are far from cheerful, as, for instance,
      in verse 14, where there is mention of birds: 'Like a crane or a swallow, so did I
      chatter: I did mourn as a dove: mine eyes fail with looking upward: O Lord, I am
      oppressed; undertake for me'.

5.   The pronunciation of *federes* here and in line 7 may have been disyllabic as in
      modern English 'feathers'; *lippes* (line 6) and *stikkes* (line 9) may likewise have
      been pronounced as 'lips' and 'sticks'.

10.   *Yeve us onẹs drinken:* lit. 'Give us once more [something] to drink'.

### 124. I have a yong suster [*Index* 1303]

MS. London, B.L., Sloane 2593

Text: 2 beyond the] beȝondyn þe MS.; 7 the] *added*; 19 I] ony MS., *with* ony
*struck through – a deletion then revised, with only the letters* on *subpuncted for deletion.*

20 & 28.   *longíng* The rhyme (with *rinde*) is on the second syllable. Other Sloane
      lyrics have words with 'ng' rhyming with words with 'nd', e.g. *bond* and *long* in
      108, 2 and 4.

21–28.   The change in the last two stanzas from the riddle-like questions previously asked to the answers now given is marked by a change in metre; the first and third lines of the last two stanzas now have 7 or 8 syllables and 4 stresses instead of the 5 or 6 syllables and 3 stresses of equivalent lines in earlier stanzas.

## 125. I have a newe garden [*Index* 1302]

MS. London, B.L., Sloane 2593

Text: 18 right] *two small letters* ag (?) *added above*; home] honde MS.; 24 Jonet] jon- (*ending obscured by mending tape*) MS.

The metre of this lyric, especially with lines 9–10, 15–16 and 21–2 (each pair written as a single line in the MS.) shorter than the other lines, is irregular. The text may be unreliable, as is frequently the case with Sloane lyrics.

1–8.   In this, another Sloane lyric of sexual innuendo (cf. **122** and **128**), the poet's unique new garden and its pear-tree are suggestive of various signs of puberty.

8.   *pere-jonet* An early-ripening pear, ripe by St John's day, 24 June. The association of this fruit with the name 'John', presumably the speaker's name here, is wittily exploited in lines 23–4, where the fair maiden claims that the child is a *pere Robert*, 'a Robert pear', rather than a *pere Jonet*, 'a John pear', i.e. a 'pear' from 'grafting' with one Robert rather than with John.

16.   *in fille:* 'pour out'. For this sense with wine etc., see *MED* **fillen** v.1.(b).

18.   *home* – MS. *honde*, Robbins' emendation, to rhyme with *womb*.

## 126. Seynt Stevene was a clerk [*Index* 3058]

MS. London, B.L., Sloane 2593

The variation of 3- and 4-stress lines is not uncommon in Sloane lyrics. However, in three of the four possible 3-stress variants here the name *Stevene* appears. Perhaps the pronunciation varied between *Stevénë* (cf. Latin 'Stephánus') and *Stéven* (cf. *Heró̈wdës* and *Hérod*). The former accentuation would be suitable in lines 17 and 33, and would allow (if the text is sound) for three stresses in line 45. Likewise, line 1 could be read as *Séynt Stevénë wás a clérk*.

1.   *clerk* Among other senses, this word could mean a household official of various kinds, and here, an attendant at table.

3.   *of bred and cloth* This could mean 'with food and clothes', but it seems better here to take the sense as (literally) 'with regard to food and table-cloth' – see *MED* **cloth** n. 1b. (a) – and so as 'with food at table'.

26.   *brede:* 'rave' – see *MED* **breiden** v.(1) 11.(a).

43.   *Steven out* – pronounced as two syllables here ('Stev'n out') with the medial syllable lost by syncopation.

47.   The feast of St Stephen is on 26 December; Christmas Day is, therefore, the eve of the feast.

## 127. Yong men, I warne you everychon [*Index* 4279]

MS. London, B.L., Sloane 2593

Text: 5 at hom have on] haue on at hom MS. The repeated final line is abbreviated as *I dar not etc* for stanzas 2 and 3, and *I dar etc.* in stanza 4.

Early widowhood and the importance of marriage in respect of property rights in the Middle Ages commonly gave rise to the marriage of young men to older women. For other carols on the perils of marriage, see Greene, Nos. 403–11.

1–2.   Cf. 65, 1–2 n.
17.   *rish:* 'rush' – a thing of little value, cf. *pese* (line 21), and Whiting, *Proverbs*, R 250.

## 128. We bern aboute no cattës skinnes [*Index* 3864]

MS. London, B.L., Sloane 2593

1–2.   Cf. 65, 1–2 n.
2.   *foulë weyës* Medieval roads were not only frequently 'foul' in their physical condition but also dangerous on account of robbers. It was therefore especially advantageous to travel light. However, the 'foul ways' the rogue of this poem had to flee doubtless included predicaments over and above the perils of travelling.
3–5.   The wares of ordinary pedlars or friars are listed by Wycliffe as including 'knyues, pursis, pynnys and girdlis and spices and sylk and precious pellure and forrouris for wymmen' [Matthew (1880), p.12]. This 'pedlar' offers something quite different!
5.   A wimple was a head-dress covering chin and neck.
11.   *jelyf:* 'jelly' – slang for penis.

## 129. As I went on Yol Day [*Index* 377]

MS. London, B.L., Sloane 2593

Text: 35 childe] schylde MS. The repetition of the refrain is indicated by *Kyrieleyson* in the right-hand margin opposite stanza 2, and by *K* opposite stanzas 5 and 7.

In a witty and irreverent manner, the course of Jankin's seduction of Alison is paralleled in this poem with the structure of the mass, beginning with the procession, and then the divisions of the Office – the Kyrie, the Epistle, the Sanctus, the Agnus Dei, the words 'Benedicamus Domino' with which the mass ends on solemn feasts such as Christmas, and the people's response 'Deo gratias'. The burden (lines 1–4, to be repeated after each stanza) is a parody of the words 'Kyrie eleison' ('Lord have mercy') which are six times repeated early in the mass. The metre again varies with lines of three and of four stresses in the first and third lines of the stanzas.

3. *aleyson* This spelling, instead of *eleyson*, suggests a pun on the girl's name, Alison.

11. *dos* The northern ending '-(e)s' of the third person singular present indicative of the verb was already to be found in the language of London by the late fourteenth century and is used occasionally by Chaucer, mostly in rhymes.

20. *crakëth a merie note* This refers to the elaborate style of singing in which long notes were divided into numerous short ('small') notes for ornamentation. Thus, the shepherds in 'The First Shepherds' Play' admire the *small noytys* of the angels which produce *foure & twenty to a long*. See Greene, p. 494.

22. *cote* The type of coat in question would have been a close-fitting tunic or a surcoat. See *MED* **cote** n.(2) 1.(a).

30. *pax-brede* – a 'disc of silver or gilt with a handle and a sacred symbol used in giving the "kiss of peace" to the congregation' [Greene, p. 494].

## 130. Thou that sellest the worde of God [*Index* 3697]

MS. Cambridge, St John's Coll. 195

Text: 3 Com thou] cum MS.

2. Some held that the friars, like their founder, St Francis, should go bare-foot; others allowed that, in view of the difference in the climate of England from that of Italy, the wearing of sandals was permissible.

4. *In principio erat verbum* (John 1, 1) was the conventional greeting of the friars.

7. *symonie:* 'simony' – trading in sacred things.

14–15. See Paul's second epistle to Timothy, 2 Tim. 3, 6: *Ex his enim sunt qui penetrant domos, et captivas ducunt mulierculas oneratas peccatis, quae ducuntur variis desideriis* [For of this sort are they which creep into houses, and lead captive silly women laden with sins, led away with divers lusts].

16. *midday develes* This echoes *daemonio meridiano* of Psalm 90, 6, translated as 'noon-day devil' in the Douay version.

## 131. Allas! what shul we frerës do [*Index* 161]

MS. Cambridge, St John's Coll. 195

Text: 12 They] þat þei MS.; 25 bidde] *added*.

6. *allë* – plural, lit. 'all [sc. things]'; here, everything to do with scripture.

14. Cf. 130, 4 n.

15. *poppe:* 'fop' – see *MED* **poppe** n.(2).

21. *myn habite* – to be pronounced *my nabíte* – cf. MS. *my nabete*.

34. *gile* As Robbins notes, the sense 'harm' required here is not otherwise recorded for this word [Robbins, *Hist.*, p. 339].

## 132. Swarte smekëd smithes [*Index* 3227]

MS. London, B.L., Arundel 292

4. *knavёnё cry* The ending '-ene' of *knavёnё* derives historically from the Old English ending '-ena' of the genitive plural; where it occasionally survives in later Middle English it is often virtually adjectival in effect – cf. *knavene werkes:* 'menial tasks', historically, 'tasks of menials'.

8. *spellen many spelles:* lit. 'tell many tales'. Above these words in the MS., *ech of hem at othyr* ('each of them against the other') has been added in fainter ink.

21. *clothemeres:* lit. 'those who clothe mares' – see *MED* **clothe-mere** n.

# APPENDIX A

*Music and Metre*

The evidence of the musical notation which survives with Middle
English lyrics supports a measure of flexibility in the scansion of these
lyrics. In Middle English verse, lines beginning with an unstressed
syllable frequently varied with lines beginning with a stressed syllable.
Was this variation acceptable in stanzaic lyrics? Because in the case of
stanzaic lyrics music is given with the first stanza only, it is normally
impossible to appeal to music for evidence as to whether or not lines
could vary in this regard from stanza to stanza. However, the music of
the carol *As I lay upon a night* (**81**) shows exactly how this variation was
accommodated. The first line of the first stanza begins with a stressed
syllable. However, the first line of the burden begins with a weak
syllable. The music for the first full bar of the burden is identical with
that of the music for the first line of the stanza except that an extra note
has been supplied before that bar as a leading-in note to allow for the
extra syllable. In *Man mai longe him livës wenë* (**39**) lines 3 and 4 are sung
to the tune of the first two lines. The music is not given twice, but one
note (a repeat of the final note of the phrase) is added, being the extra
leading-in note needed for the initial weak syllable of line 3. Thus, extra
syllables were accommodated by adding a note at the beginning or by
splitting a note at the end of the musical phrase. It is obvious that
without this kind of flexibility it would not have been possible to allow
for the variation of masculine with feminine rhymes.

Another important issue concerns the extent to which musical
rhythm and word accent should coincide. The question of rhythm in
medieval music is notoriously problematic. With unmeasured music
(that is, music of a plainsong kind) the flow of the melody appears to
have a flexibility which is very little if at all constrained by verbal
accent. Measured music, on the other hand, familiar in the 3/4 and 6/8
rhythms of modern performances of medieval songs, clearly has a
regular beat. But even here, the implications of the musical rhythm for
the stress-patterns of a verbal text are not self-evident; one must be
wary, as Harrison warns, of 'presuppositions about stress connected with

present-day use of bar-lines'.[1] The fact that strict coincidence of musical beat and word-accent was not required may readily be demonstrated from *Somer is y-comen in* (110). The rhythm of this two-part song is of necessity strict and measured, and requires that line 9 should be sung in the rhythm *Lowth áfter cálvë cóu* rather than (with natural word-stress) *Lówth after cálvë cóu*. Likewise, a reader would naturally render line 13 as *Wel síngëst thóu cuckóu*, matching the rhythm of line 14; the rhythm of the music, however, requires *Wél singést thou cúckou*. Again, in *Stond wel, moder, under rodë* (91), the natural accentual pattern of the first four syllables of line 39 – *What sórwë háve* – is the opposite of the first four syllables of line 42 – *Mórë sórwë*. Both lines, nevertheless, as corresponding lines within the matching halves of a stanza in sequence form, are sung to the same musical phrase. It therefore appears that this difference in the pattern of word-accent in the two lines does not matter from the point of view of singing; what counts is that the lines are identical in their syllable count. These instances clearly illustrate what, indeed, any musician knows, namely, that even in measured, accentual music a singer can readily alter the natural stress and rhythm of speech to conform with the accentual requirements of music.

The evidence of the musical notation is not, however, unequivocal. Musical notes are frequently found above syllables which should be subject to elision or syncope. For instance, in *Man mai longe him livës wenë* (39), the note '*g*' above the first written syllable of *longe* and *ofte* (lines 1 and 3) is repeated over the second syllable of both words, although in each case the final '-e' would be expected to elide with the following word *him*. The words of a song were usually written first under blank staves and the music added thereafter. It seems that in adding musical notes above the words, scribes tended, without regard to the metre of a song, to write a note above every written syllable, repeating notes as necessary. An extreme instance of this habit is found in the lyric *Miri it is while sumer i-last* (36). The first line *as written* has eleven syllables: *Mirie it is while sumer i-last*. In adding the music, the scribe simply placed a note above every written syllable by repeating notes – giving, by repetition, four notes over *Mirie it*, and two over *while* and over *sumer*. At first sight the music thus appears to confirm an egregiously long eleven-syllable line; fortunately, the repeat of the musical phrase (now without the repeated notes) in line 3 confirms a

[1] *MES*, p. 69.

count of seven syllables for the first line.[2] In the face of this scribal habit of repeating notes over syllables *as written* without regard to metrical requirements, it is sometimes difficult to know how far to trust the evidence of the musical notation in the question of the acceptability of an occasional extra unstressed syllable. Thus, in the first stanza of *Edi be thou, hevenë quenë* (76), the words *hevene* (line 1), *havest the* (line 6) and *Levedy* (line 7) are all accompanied by three musical notes; but metrically all could be taken as syncopated or reduced forms of two syllables. However, only in *heuene* is a repeated note involved; all three notes in *havest þe* and in *levedi* are different, and so, arguably, integral to the melody.[3] Moreover, in measured music in triple time, the singing of three quavers instead of a crotchet and quaver presents no difficulty as the parallel melody of this two-part song demonstrates. It is therefore difficult to resist the view that, at least in music of this kind, an extra weak syllable within the line was an acceptable if occasional variation.

[2] See Duncan (1994), pp. 59–62.

[3] Again, whereas the repeated note over *-er* of *Moder* (line 3) may be discounted by assuming reduction by syncope before the initial vowel of the following word *unwemmed*, the extra syllable represented by *and* in the same line, again accompanied by a note which is not merely a repetition, can only be discounted, as in Dobson' s text [*MES*, p.166], by emendation.

# APPENDIX B

*The Syllabic Analysis of Middle English Verse*

Any appraisal of metre must take account of several important factors affecting the pronunciation of unstressed syllables in Middle English. One is the status of the endings '-e', '-est' and '-eth', and '-es' and '-ed'.

By the early fifteenth century, 'e' at the end of words had ceased to be pronounced. It has commonly been held that this was the end result of a gradual and steady loss of final '-e' which began in more northerly dialects in the thirteenth century and advanced through midland and then southern dialects in the course of the fourteenth century. However, the linguistic processes which led to the loss of final '-e' were complex. Probably from early Middle English the possibility of elision within the spoken chain of language would have given rise to the existence of forms of the same word with and without sounded final '-e' in any dialect. Furthermore, the process of the loss or reduction of unstressed syllables in Middle English doubtless first took place at a colloquial level of speech, from which endingless or reduced forms would begin to appear, however gradually, in more formal registers. In effect, in midland and southern dialects until the end of the fourteenth century, historical final '-e' (that is, the grammatically or etymologically authentic inflexion as distinct from mere random spellings) would have remained available for the more conservative register of poetry, while poets would also have at their disposal optional forms of words without final '-e'.[1]

Reduced forms of the second and third person singular present indicative had been current in southern dialects since the Old English period. They may have been available to poets in other dialects either from their awareness of the southern forms, or from the operation of syncope (see below), or by analogy with such contracted forms as *saist* and *saith* beside *sayëst* and *sayëth*. As the evidence of Chaucer's metre conclusively demonstrates, even when the endings '-est' and '-eth' were

---

[1] See Smithers (1983) for a detailed discussion of this issue in the light of the evidence of *Havelok the Dane*.

spelt as full forms they would sometimes be pronounced as reduced forms. The evidence of metre would suggest that this was also true for many of the lyrics in this volume. Where lyrics survive in more than one manuscript, variation from copy to copy between full and reduced spellings of the same words is not uncommon.

Again, it has usually been supposed that after monosyllabic stems the endings '-ed' and '-es' retained their full forms until the fifteenth century. However, as with the loss of final '-e', it is likely that reduced forms first arose in colloquial usage before establishing themselves in more formal speech. The reduction of these endings has been attributed to the effect of syncope (see below),[2] a process which was not new in Middle English and which was operative long before the fifteenth century. Even in lyrics from the mid-thirteenth and early fourteenth centuries, it seems metrically plausible to view '-ed' and '-es' in sequences like *Y-lóved Ich hávë* (**40**, 23) and *táles untóun* (**27**, 37) as early instances of reduction by syncope. Occasional thirteenth-century reduced spellings also occur as, for instance, *frents* ('friends')[3] and *þar wils* ('there whiles').[4] It is true that such spelling evidence is scarce, but if the loss of final '-e' is more often signalled by a tendency on the part of scribes to add '-e' to words at random rather than to omit silent '-e' from spelling, there is no reason why the conventional spellings '-es' and '-ed' should not sometimes mask reduced forms. Indeed, even in the late fourteenth century, when spellings like *tornd* ('turned') and *tempt* ('tempted') are found in the Vernon manuscript,[5] such evidence of reduction disappears under the cloak of spelling convention in the spellings *turned* and *tempted* of the companion manuscript, B.L. Additional 22283.

Other linguistic processes vital for the appreciation of metre, but also obscured by Middle English spelling, must also be taken into account. These include processes of phonetic reduction, characteristic, doubtless, of ordinary speech, and operative within the spoken chain of verse as it was read aloud – as it commonly would have been in the Middle Ages.

[2] Cf. Luick (1914– ), § 456.2.

[3] See Brown XIII, p. 44, line 34, for this form in MS. Trinity Coll. Cambridge 323.

[4] See Brown XIII, p. 80, line 49, for this form in MS. B.L., Arundel 248.

[5] See 60, 24 and 134.

(1) *Elision* By this process, a vowel at the end of a word was absorbed by an initial vowel (or 'h' plus vowel) of a following word. This affects the many words ending in '-e' in Middle English. Thus the final '-e's of *grede* and *grone* are elided in *I grede, I grone, unglad* (1, 4). The words *the* and *ne* are often subject to elision – e.g. *Th'aghte* (38, 16),[6] *n'answerde* (49, 2), and *nis* for *ne is, passim*. Among many other common words ending in a vowel which may be reduced by this phonetic process are *he, me, thee, to, into* and *so*, and the reductions are sometimes represented in the manuscript spellings – e.g. *H'aros* 'He arose', **90**, 50 (MS. *þaros* for *haros*), *thee's* 'thee is', **90**, 40 (MS. *þes*), *s'ofte* 'so oft', **38**, 33 (MS. *softe*), *s'it* 'so it', **109**, 42 (MS. *sit*).

(2) *Hiatus* Hiatus is the opposite of elision: it is the term for cases where, for the sake of metre, a vowel at the end of a word is retained and not elided with the initial vowel (or 'h' plus vowel) of a following word: e.g. *cherë as* (3, 33), *cussë of* (17, 23), *yowrë hie* (30, 3), *derë He* (38, 43), *wildë as* (51, 27), etc., *passim*.

(3) *Synizesis* This is a form of elision in which the vowel 'i' (spelt 'i' or 'y'), immediately followed by another vowel either within a word or in the following word, becomes the corresponding semi-vowel /j/ (the sound of 'y' in 'yet') and so the first element of a diphthong with the following vowel, and, thereby, a single syllable. Thus *mirieth* (19, 1), *miriest* (27, 64), *many a* (32, 2), *Miri it* (36, 1), *body and* (54, 38), *buried* (60, 84), etc., are pronounced as two syllables as 'mir-yeth', 'mir-yest', 'man-ya', 'mir-yit', and so on.

(4) *Syncope* This involves a reduction of syllables by the loss of an unstressed syllable either within a word or in a sequence of words. Thus, *comely, lovely* and *every* may be pronounced as three syllables, but may also (as in present-day English) be pronounced as two, with the loss of the medial syllable, and are sometimes spelt as two syllables. Likewise, *stevenyng* (19, 33), *soveraigne* (30, 29), *recoverer* (33, 3), *wakenëth* (52, 1), *thrivenë* (54, 21), *gamenës* (54, 41 and 51), *merveilëth* (60, 97), are pronounced 'stev'nyng', 'sov'raigne', 'recov'rer', 'wak'neth', 'thriv'ne', 'gam'nes', 'merv'leth', etc. Syncope occurs frequently where words ending in '-el', '-en' or '-er' are followed by a word beginning with a vowel (or

---

[6] Spelt *þeite* in MS. B.L., Arundel 248, but *þe eykte* in MS. Bodl., Rawlinson G.18.

'h' plus vowel). Thus, in the following examples, the first word is reduced by the loss of the 'e' of the final syllable in each case: *girdel of* (25, 61), *athel is* (27, 67), *litel a* (49, 6), *evel and* (51, 46 and 47), *sutel as* (54, 12); *thriven and* (2, 34), *chosen and* (25, 34), *driven away* (28, 3), *y-loren is* (26, 2), *gamen and* (40, 23), *gamen y-lad* (47, 8), *thriven and* (54, 24), *biforen I* (54, 48); *other a* (2, 56), *power of* (3, 66), *ever and* (4, 7), *water in* (18, 32), *Beter is* (18, 35), *fader and* (24, 36), *never a* (24, 53), *moder and* (24, 69), *ever in* (27, 54) *ever at* (27, 55), *sumer i-last* (36, 1), *water of* (37, 43), *Siker hit* (51, 72), *another is* (60, 64), *over hymself* (62, 14), etc. Likewise, the '-ed' of *y-loved* and the '-es' of *sterres* are probably reduced by syncope in *y-loved and* (13, 3) and *sterres in* (4, 43). What looks like a combination of elision and syncope is seen in *Hevene I* (1, 39), *hevene hath* (62, 69) and *folowe his* (64, 3), which have two syllables each.

(5) *Apocope* This is usually defined as the suppression of a final unaccented vowel before a following consonant. Frequently, where necessary to preserve the rhythmic pattern of a single weak syllable between two accented syllables, a final '-e' is silent before a following consonant. Thus, in 53, line 2, the final '-e' of *swete* is silent in *that swete savóur* before the initial unstressed syllable of *savóur* to preserve the rhythm as /x/, whereas the same final '-e' is retained in *that swetë tide* in the following line, as required by the same rhythm. In such cases, however, what is involved is not the suppression of a vowel but the selection of a variant pronunciation without final '-e'.[7]

(6) *Alternative forms* It is clear from Chaucer's verse that words with alternative forms (e.g. *never* and *ner, ever* and *er*) were sometimes, even though spelt as full forms, pronounced as reduced forms as required by the metre.

---

[7] See Smithers (1983), p. 213.

# SELECT BIBLIOGRAPHY
# OF EDITIONS, BOOKS AND
# ARTICLES

Anderson, J. J., 'Two Difficulties in *The Meeting in The Wood*', *Medium Ævum* 49 (1980), 258–9

Bartsch, K., ed., *Altfranzösische Romanzen und Pastourellen* (Leipzig, 1870)

Benson, L. D., *The Riverside Chaucer*, 3rd edn (Oxford, 1988)

Brandl, A., and Zippel, O., *Mittelenglische Sprach- und Literaturproben* (Berlin, 1917)

Brewer, D. S., 'The Ideal of Feminine Beauty in Medieval Literature, especially "Harley Lyrics", Chaucer, and Some Elizabethans', *Modern Language Review*, 50 (1955), 257–69

Brooke, G. L., ed., *The Harley Lyrics*, 4th edn (Manchester, 1968)

Brown, C., ed., *English Lyrics of the XIIIth Century* (Oxford, 1932)

——, *English Lyrics of the XIVth Century*, 2nd edn revised by G. V. Smithers (Oxford, 1952)

Bukofzer, M., 'The first motet with English words', *Music and Letters*, 17 (1936), 225–33

Burrow, J. A., and Turville-Petre, T., eds, *A Book of Middle English* (Oxford, 1992)

Burrow, J. A., *Essays on Medieval Literature* (Oxford, 1984)

——, ed., *English Verse 1300–1500* (London, 1977)

Dobson, E. J., and Harrison, F. Ll., eds, *Medieval English Songs* (London, 1979)

Dronke, P., 'The Rawlinson Lyrics', *Notes & Queries*, New Series 8 (1961), 245–6

——, *The Medieval Lyric* (London, 1968)

——, 'Two Thirteenth-Century Religious Lyrics', in *Chaucer and Middle English Studies in honour of Rossel Hope Robbins*, ed. Beryl Rowland (Kent State University Press, 1974)

Duncan, T. G., review of Dobson and Harrison, *Medieval English Songs*, in *Medium Ævum*, 50 (1981), 338–41

——, 'The Text and Verse-Form of "Adam lay i-bowndyn"', *The Review of English Studies*, 38 (1987), 215–21

——, 'Textual Notes on Two Early Middle English Lyrics', *Neuphilologische Mitteilungen*, 93 (1992), 109–20

——, 'Two Middle English Penitential Lyrics: Sound and Scansion', in A. J. Minnis, ed., *Late-Medieval Religious Texts and Their Transmission* (Cambridge, 1994), pp. 55–65

——, 'The Maid in the Moor and the Rawlinson Text', *The Review of English Studies* (forthcoming)

Ellis, F. S., ed., *The Golden Legend or Lives of the Saints as Englished by William Caxton*, 7 vols. (London, 1900)

Faral, E., ed., *Les Arts Poétiques du XIIe et du XIIIe Siècle* (Paris, 1962)

Furnivall, F. J., ed., *Political, Religious, and Love Poems*, Early English Text Society, Original Series 15, re-edited (London, 1903)

Gardner, H., *Religion and Literature* (London, 1971)

Goldin, F., ed., *Lyrics of the Troubadours and Trouvères*, with translations and introductions (New York, 1973)

Gordon, E.V., ed., *Pearl* (Oxford, 1953)

Gray, D., *Themes and Images in the Medieval English Religious Lyric* (London, 1972)

——, 'Songs and Lyrics', in P. Boitani and A. Torti, eds., *Literature in Fourteenth-Century England* (Cambridge, 1983), pp. 83–98

——, 'Lyrics', chapter 8 in J. A. W. Bennett, *Middle English Literature*, edited and completed by Douglas Gray (Oxford, 1986)

——, ed., *A Selection of Religious Lyrics* (Oxford, 1975)

Greene, R. L., *The Lyrics of The Red Book of Ossory*, Medium Ævum Monographs, New Series V (Oxford, 1974)

——, ed., *The Early English Carols*, 2nd edn (Oxford, 1977)

Jeffrey, D. L., *The Early English Lyric and Franciscan Spirituality* (Lincoln, Nebraska, 1975)

Kane, G., *Middle English Literature* (London, 1951)

Kean, P. M., *Chaucer and the Making of English Poetry*, 2 vols (London, 1972)

Ker, N. R., ed., *Facsimile of B.M. MS. Harley 2253*, Early English Text Society, 255 (1965)

Kinsley, J., ed., *The Oxford Book of Ballads* (Oxford, 1969)

Luick, K., *Historische Grammatik der englischen Sprache* (Leipzig, 1914– )

Manning, S., *Wisdom and Number* (Lincoln, Nebraska, 1962)

Matthew, F. D., ed., *The English Works of Wyclif hitherto Unprinted*, Early English Text Society, Original Series, 74 (1880)

Menner, R. J., 'The Man in the Moon and Hedging', *Journal of English and Germanic Philology*, 48 (1949), 1–14

Murphy, J. J., ed., *Three Medieval Rhetorical Arts* (Berkeley, California, 1971)

Mustanoja, T. F., *A Middle English Syntax* (Helsinki, 1960)

Oliver, R., *Poems Without Names* (Berkeley, California, 1970)

Osberg, R. H., 'The Alliterative Lyric and 13th-century Devotional Prose', *Journal of English and Germanic Philology*, 76 (1977), 40–54

Panum, H., *The Stringed Instruments of the Middle Ages*, revised by J. Pulver (London, 1941)

Patterson, F. A., *The Middle English Penitential Lyric* (New York, 1911)

Person, H. A., ed., *Cambridge Middle English Lyrics*, revised edn (Seattle, 1962)

Ransom, D. J., *Poets at Play: Irony and Parody in the Harley Lyrics* (Oklahoma, 1985)

Reese, G., *Music in the Middle Ages* (London, 1941)

Reiss, E., *The Art of the Middle English Lyric* (Athens, Georgia, 1972)

Robbins, H. W., 'An English Version of St Edmond's *Speculum*, ascribed to Richard Rolle', *Publications of the Modern Language Association*, 40 (1925), 240–51

——, *The Romance of the Rose*, a translation (New York, 1962)

Robbins, R. H., 'The Earliest Carols and the Franciscans', *Modern Language Notes*, 53 (1938), 239–45

——, 'The Authors of the ME Religious Lyrics', *Journal of English and Germanic Philology*, 34 (1940), 230–38

——, 'Middle English Lyrics: Handlist of New Texts', *Anglia*, 83 (1965), 35–47

——, ed., *Secular Lyrics of the XIVth and XVth Centuries*, revised edn (Oxford, 1955)

——, ed., *Historical Poems of the XIVth and XVth Centuries* (Oxford, 1959)

Robinson, F. N., ed., *The Works of Geoffrey Chaucer*, 2nd edn (London, 1957)

Saintsbury, G., 'The Prosody of Old and Middle English', chapter 18, in A. W. Ward and A. R. Waller, eds, *The Cambridge History of English Literature*, vol. 1 (Cambridge, 1907)

Saltmarsh, J., 'Two Medieval Love-Songs set to Music', *The Antiquaries Journal*, 15 (1935), 1–21, including 'The Music of *Bryd one Brere*' by F. McD. C. Turner, M.A., pp. 19–21

Silverstein, T., ed., *Medieval English Lyrics* (London, 1971)

Sisam, C., 'Ne Saltou Neuer Leuedi', *Notes and Queries*, New Series 12 (1965), 245–6

Sisam, C. and Sisam, K., eds, *The Oxford Book of Medieval English Verse* (Oxford, 1970)

Sitwell, G., 'A Fourteenth-Century English Poem on Ecclesiastes', *Dominican Studies* 3 (1950), 285–90

Skeat, W. W., *Twelve Facsimiles of Old English Manuscripts* (Oxford, 1892)

——, ed., *The Vision of William concerning Piers The Plowman, etc.* (Oxford, 1886)

——, ed., *The Complete Works of Geoffrey Chaucer*, 7 vols (Oxford, 1894 and 1897)

Smithers, G. V., 'The Scansion of *Havelok* and the Use of ME *-en* and *-e* in *Havelok* and by Chaucer', in D. Gray and E. G. Stanley, eds, *Middle English Studies Presented to Norman Davis in Honour of his Seventieth Birthday* (Oxford, 1983)

Southern, R. W., *The Making of the Middle Ages* (London, 1953; Grey Arrow edn, 1959)

Stemmler, T., *Die englischen Liebesgedichte des MS. Harley 2253* (Bonn, 1962)

Stevens, J., *The Old Sound and the New: An inaugural lecture* (Cambridge, 1982)

——, *Words and Music in the Middle Ages: Song, Narrative, Dance and Drama, 1050–1350* (Cambridge, 1986)

Stevick, R. D., 'The Criticism of ME Lyrics', *Modern Philology*, 64 (1966), 103–17

Thomson, S. H., 'The Date of the Early English Translation of the *Candet Nudatum Pectus*', *Medium Ævum*, 6 (1935), 100–105

Waddell, H., *Medieval Latin Lyrics*, 4th edn (London, 1933)

Weber, S. A., *Theology and Poetry in the Middle English Lyric* (Columbus, Ohio, 1969)

Wenzel, S., 'The "Gay" Carol and Exemplum', *Neuphilologische Mitteilungen*, 77 (1976), 85–91

——, *Preachers, Poets, and the Early English Lyric* (Princeton, 1986)

——, ed., *Fasciculus Morum*, with translation (Pennsylvania, 1989)

Whiting, B. J., *Proverbs, Sentences and Proverbial Phrases from English Writings mainly before 1500* (Cambridge, Massachusetts, 1968)

Wilson, R. M., *The Lost Literature of Medieval England*, 2nd edn (London, 1970)

Wolpers, T., 'Geschichte der englischen Marienlyric im Mittelalter', *Anglia*, 69 (1950), 3–88

——, 'Zum Andachtsbild in der mittelenglischen religiösen Lyric', in A. Esch, ed., *Chaucer und seine Zeit: Symposion für Walter Schirmer* (Tübingen, 1968), pp. 293–336

Wooldridge, H. E., *Early English Harmony*, vol. 1 (London, 1897)

Woolf, R., *The English Religious Lyric in the Middle Ages* (Oxford, 1968)

——, 'The Construction of *In a fryht as y con fare fremede*', *Medium Ævum*, 38 (1969), 55–9

——, 'Later Poetry: The Popular Tradition', chapter 6 in W. F. Bolton, ed., *Sphere History of Literature in the English Language*, vol. 1 (London, 1970)

# INDEX

The lyrics are listed by first line (or title, in the case of some Chaucer lyrics) and number. The first lines of burdens are also listed; like the titles, they are printed in italics.

# READ MORE IN PENGUIN

In every corner of the world, on every subject under the sun, Penguin represents quality and variety – the very best in publishing today.

For complete information about books available from Penguin – including Puffins, Penguin Classics and Arkana – and how to order them, write to us at the appropriate address below. Please note that for copyright reasons the selection of books varies from country to country.

**In the United Kingdom**: Please write to *Dept. JC, Penguin Books Ltd, FREEPOST, West Drayton, Middlesex UB7 OBR.*

If you have any difficulty in obtaining a title, please send your order with the correct money, plus ten per cent for postage and packaging, to *PO Box No. 11, West Drayton, Middlesex UB7 OBR*

**In the United States**: Please write to *Consumer Sales, Penguin USA, P.O. Box 999, Dept. 17109, Bergenfield, New Jersey 07621-0120.* VISA and MasterCard holders call 1-800-253-6476 to order all Penguin titles

**In Canada**: Please write to *Penguin Books Canada Ltd, 10 Alcorn Avenue, Suite 300, Toronto, Ontario M4V 3B2*

**In Australia**: Please write to *Penguin Books Australia Ltd, P.O. Box 257, Ringwood, Victoria 3134*

**In New Zealand**: Please write to *Penguin Books (NZ) Ltd, Private Bag 102902, North Shore Mail Centre, Auckland 10*

**In India**: Please write to *Penguin Books India Pvt Ltd, 706 Eros Apartments, 56 Nehru Place, New Delhi 110 019*

**In the Netherlands**: Please write to *Penguin Books Netherlands bv, Postbus 3507, NL-1001 AH Amsterdam*

**In Germany**: Please write to *Penguin Books Deutschland GmbH, Metzlerstrasse 26, 60594 Frankfurt am Main*

**In Spain**: Please write to *Penguin Books S. A., Bravo Murillo 19, 1° B, 28015 Madrid*

**In Italy**: Please write to *Penguin Italia s.r.l., Via Felice Casati 20, I–20124 Milano*

**In France**: Please write to *Penguin France S. A., 17 rue Lejeune, F–31000 Toulouse*

**In Japan**: Please write to *Penguin Books Japan, Ishikiribashi Building, 2–5–4, Suido, Bunkyo-ku, Tokyo 112*

**In Greece**: Please write to *Penguin Hellas Ltd, Dimocritou 3, GR–106 71 Athens*

**In South Africa**: Please write to *Longman Penguin Southern Africa (Pty) Ltd, Private Bag X08, Bertsham 2013*

# READ MORE IN PENGUIN

## A CHOICE OF CLASSICS

ANTHOLOGIES AND ANONYMOUS WORKS

**The Age of Bede**
**Alfred the Great**
**Beowulf**
**A Celtic Miscellany**
**The Cloud of Unknowing and Other Works**
**The Death of King Arthur**
**The Earliest English Poems**
**Early Irish Myths and Sagas**
**Egil's Saga**
**English Mystery Plays**
**Eyrbyggja Saga**
**Hrafnkel's Saga**
**The Letters of Abelard and Heloise**
**Medieval English Verse**
**Njal's Saga**
**Roman Poets of the Early Empire**
**Seven Viking Romances**
**Sir Gawain and the Green Knight**